I0659271

Cristal II.
Dueling Confessions

Ian M. Ferguson

©

Copyright 2018
All rights reserved

ISBN:

978-0-9917589-8-2 eBook

978-0-9917589-9-9 paperback

Other works by
Ian M. Ferguson

Find Ian M. Ferguson on Amazon at

http://www.amazon.com/-/e/B00A8XSOGQ

Fiction Novels

Unintended - eBook

Elephant Theory - eBook

Operation Counterpunch - eBook

Cristal's Revenge – eBook & paperback

The Culpeper Deception - eBook & paperback

Short stories

Culpeper - eBook

Acknowledgments

Thanks again to Bob Glass who has been invaluable in editing and proofreading. Your many hours of tedious work are much appreciated, and you've taught me many lessons.

Thanks to Humphrey Pickering for help on the German information needed for this most recent yarn.

As always, many thanks to Dan Ferguson for the book artwork and covers.

Thanks for the names. I have always had an issue making up names for characters as they don't seem real when I read them.

I suppose I could look up random names online or in a phone directory but some time ago I decided from time to time to resort to using names of people I know or have known. When I can find them, I ask their permission. To be clear, when I've used this shortcut, the characters bear no resemblance to any facet of the real people whose name I have borrowed.

The additional advantage is that they're easier for me to remember when I'm writing and when there are many characters to deal with. So, if I've used your name in this novel then Thank You again, and be assured there was never any thought of matching you with these fictitious actors.

Now, because I have so many characters in this CRISTAL series (at least 35), I've added an appendix to this novel listing most recurring characters and occasionally a few things about them for easy identification in case at some point you get lost in all the names. I wish other authors used this quick reference technique when there are too many names to remember.

Enjoy

Dedication

To my wonderful grandchildren Colton, Kylie, and Cooper in New Hampshire and Colby,

the newest arrival in Quebec with one more on the way.

I hope I'm a more attentive granddad than I ever was a father.

Keep your family close!

Prologue
From "Cristal's Revenge" (spoiler alert)

This book is a sequel to CRISTAL'S REVENGE. So, while this novel stands on its own, the best experience would be to read its predecessor first. If that is your path stop now and avoid the spoilers that follow.

Spoiler/Reminder

Cristal Serpe/Wiggins, by outer appearances a harmless but stunning cheerleader type, is in reality, a former Ninja-style field operative for the CIA. When called upon she has been deadly on more than one occasion.

After a harrowing kidnapping and escape from Al Qaeda, she was recently reinstated as an undercover CIA field agent. She's in a potentially mortal battle with Khalil al-Adel, the Yemeni-born American and more importantly, the most recent leader of Al Qaeda, now based in Somalia.

Apart from her professional mission, Cristal has a personal beef with Khalil who stoned her best friend, Tiffany Winslow, to death in front of her a few years ago in The Sudan.

She has graduated to be Al Qaeda's number one global assassination target after killing all her Al Qaeda kidnappers and intercepting another terrorist attack by the same group.

Having reunited with her love, Commander David Crowe of MI6 who helped her escape her kidnappers, she now knows David was never the terrorist leader in Burundi she helped capture but actually a hero who had been framed by an MI6 mole working for the Bean Stock Boys, a shady organization of mercenaries.

She cannot forgive herself for her mistake, spearheading David's capture and his multi-year stay in Guantanamo where he decided to wait it out instead of instant assassination by either the BSB or MI6.

After chasing Khalil and his diabolical plans all over the world for months, Cristal and David finally caught up with him, and less than an hour ago they disrupted his monstrous attack on New York City, killing two terrorists thinking one of them was Khalil and that she'd finally rid the world of his menace.

But she missed.

The quintessential American bitch in Khalil's eyes, he recognized her from a previous encounter when she was CIA but posing as a CNN producer in The Sudan and where she narrowly escaped his wrath. He's now sure she was behind several failed operations of late here in the US. More importantly, she has just thwarted his huge masterpiece attack on New York City's water supply using lethal radioactive material.

Still, that's of no consequence as he has followed her from the reservoir and now has her in his crosshairs. Revenge and Jihad will be his.

Christmas in the Great Satan

Face crimson, temples throbbing, master of disguises, and brutal head of Al Qaeda, Khalil al-Adel carefully followed the CIA bitch and her infidel partner onto the ramp for the Montvale service center in upstate New Jersey. He was now sure that he recognized her from his Sudan ambush years ago, but still, he was shocked, 'How the hell did she end up here, screwing up everything?'

It was a total mystery how the two of them had just foiled his massive and potentially crippling assault on New York City that would have made 9/11 look like amateur hour; but that would have to wait.

Clearly, someone had leaked information on the attack or there were forces at work he didn't understand. He was seething that his well-laid plan involving a vast global effort in planning, time, money, and even lives had been snuffed out right in front of his eyes just minutes ago ... by her.

The hit to his prestige would be the greatest loss in that he'd told virtually the whole Jihadi world to watch for his Christmas Day tour de force. The more he thought of it the worse it got and the more furious he became. There was no doubt she needed to be made to pay.

The parking lot of the giant service center in the middle of the Garden State Parkway servicing both north and southbound traffic was close to half full on this cool and sunny Christmas morning.

Khalil's driver was instructed to park well beyond the target vehicle, out of sight behind an SUV towing a large camper loaded down with bicycles, likely on its way to Florida for the winter. Khalil, in one of his infamous disguises, and his accomplice Samir, followed the two agents at a distance as they entered the central building to the large food court.

Even from a distance back at the Kensico Dam, he was pretty sure this was the same evil witch, with a new blonde hairdo, that he'd seen recently on CNN; the one who'd been kidnapped in Cincinnati, and the very same CIA agent he'd let slip through his fingers years before in The Sudan. How she'd escaped her kidnappers and what had become of the cell of Jihadis who had infiltrated the US to capture her to use in an exchange was yet another mystery.

Nevertheless, here she was, destroying his masterpiece. The decoy of the cobalt contamination of all JFK passenger terminals had worked like a charm but somehow the CIA had still uncovered the main assault.

JFK was good but it had been the much bigger attack on Christmas Day his supporters were expecting. He had kept his actual target secret, but it was a certainty that word would leak that the main attack had failed.

Her interception of his plan made him physically sick to his stomach and something he really couldn't fathom, but now he had an idea on how to salvage the mission.

Minutes ago, his team had been on the precipice of permanently closing New York City with a dirty bomb at their primary water inlet, the Kensico Reservoir, when out of nowhere military choppers had shown up, apparently with her in the lead. Even if his team had been only moderately successful and radiation levels weren't that high, no one would want to live or work in a city with a radioactive water system that was essentially unrepairable. The terror, disruption, and cost to America would have been incalculable.

In her military-style attack, they had killed two of his team, and given the celebrating he had witnessed from a distance, he had a hunch they thought they'd gotten him in the explosion when his disciple's courageous suicide crash had taken out one of their downed helicopters. It was well known that he often made an appearance at major attacks and this would have been his biggest.

Now the tables had turned in his favor and he was confident he had her just where he wanted her. Cracking more of a sneer than a smile, he figured she was moments away from paying the ultimate price, and then the world would know the reach and brutality of Al Qaeda against its sworn enemies; western infidels occupying Muslim lands.

Christmas morning in the land of the Great Satan and still the food court was moderately busy with travelers, families, and the odd worker, which made it easier for him and Samir to find a table at the far end, mixed in with the others.

The witch and her partner who Khalil reasoned might, in fact, be the infamous Abu Nistal, or whatever his western name was, were at the McDonald's counter and not in a position to notice their stalkers. The fact that they were together confirmed his suspicion that he was her partner and the Jihadi poser who had infiltrated their Burundi cell a few years ago. There was no question now that he was CIA.

If only Jabir Habib, the leader of Al Qaeda's Burundi team and brother of Khalil's second in command, had acted on his warnings, these two might not still be walking around. Jabir's crazy scheme to kidnap her to use in exchange for their former leader Nistal, trapped in that American hellhole Guantanamo, was doomed from the start. Although he had to salute their guts and initiative, there was no question now that this Abu Nistal was actually a western agent and had somehow fooled the Burundi team. Some of it still didn't make sense, like why had a CIA agent been helping an Al Qaeda cell in Burundi and what was he doing as a prisoner for a couple of years in Guantanamo? That didn't matter now. His recent activities had proven his allegiance to the western menace.

As soon as Khalil found out Abu Nistal had supposedly 'escaped' from Guantanamo as part of the secret kidnapping swap, but the US wasn't sending out alarms, he smelled a rat. But Jabir had apparently ignored his warnings. Somehow this pair had outwitted the Burundi cell who had infiltrated the US to kidnap the CIA whore and spring Nistal.

With these two walking free, things didn't look good for Al Qaeda's witless Mid-African cell that hadn't been heard from in more than a month. They were likely all dead or in CIA custody.

Still, that was the past. Sadly, Khalil felt he had his own mission to rescue now. He turned to his fervent follower Samir who was still red-faced and furious. Samir was starting to look a little unreliable in his frantic state. "Samir, for the love and praise of Allah you must listen carefully to me now." It took a moment to get his full attention as he too had been following their enemies and couldn't take his eyes off them.

Khalil continued to whisper with his head bent down, "You need to bury any emotions you have at this moment. I too lost people just now at the dam. I know you were close to Hakim but we must focus now on avenging our fallen warriors. Remember, they are glorious martyrs now and enjoying everlasting life with Allah. Those two have cost us dearly but be assured, we'll exact our revenge in a moment because there's a much bigger opportunity here; an opportunity that will make you famous in our ranks."

Seeing he finally had Samir's attention, he continued whispering, "I know both of these infidels and I'm sure they've caused many deaths of our brethren including I suspect, members of our cell in Pittsburgh and our Burundi team they were helping. I think they're also responsible for intercepting that propane truck bomb attack on the Pittsburgh mall and killing brother Aaban so there's no question they must die, but I want to make the most of this with your help."

Looking around he continued, "I see no security here or anyone who looks like a threat. In a moment I'll personally visit Jihad on these infidels and behead her in front of this entire room and you'll videotape it for the internet showing the world what happens to demonic non-believers like her. Before that, I'll kill her partner, who I believe is also CIA, and infiltrated our Burundi cell years ago calling himself Abu Nistal."

Khalil put his hand inside his leather jacket to unclip the nine-millimeter he wore in a shoulder harness. He had always liked American cop movies and loved the feel of the gun.

Samir looked a bit confused and panic-stricken, but nodded vigorously. Some of what Khalil was telling him was news, but apparently, he had the full picture of the entire situation, and these targets were responsible for much more than the attack an hour ago at the dam. Khalil had a plan, and it was imperative he follow the leader's directions. Al Qaeda had never had a more masterful and accomplished leader than Khalil. Samir thought he was definitely on a par with the hero Osama Bin Laden. Khalil's bold tactics and achievements were legendary and celebrated throughout the Jihadi world. Clearly, a gruesome video of the slaying of this witch would do wonders for the organization. Samir was suddenly filled with pride to be sitting next to their global leader and about to strike in the heart of America, a country that was now his new home but a disgusting place to live for so many reasons with scandalous customs that were repugnant to observant Muslims like himself. Virtually everything on the TV was blasphemous.

Khalil continued while stalking his prey, "I'll attack them alone, but the most important part of this plan is for you to get good video on your phone to show the world. You need to capture the whole attack including the beheading and the reaction of those around her. When the act is done you should be screaming Allahu Akbar on the video and showing the reaction of all the other infidels here. Then we'll make our escape in the confusion.

"The best part of the video is going to be the horror and screaming of all these infidels when I hold up her severed head so don't stop recording too soon."

Samir continued to nod as he stared again across the room at the targets.

Khalil was getting angry, "Stop staring! We must remain concealed until I'm ready!"

Cristal and David, completely unaware of the threat, were now headed for seats twenty yards away as their stalkers discreetly followed their movements.

Khalil averted his gaze and whispered, "Good, she's facing our way. That will be perfect for the video. I'll get something from the counter and position myself behind him. You start recording as I sit down. Rest the phone on the table so it doesn't shake. I want perfect video. I'll kill him with a shot to the head and quickly overcome her, slitting her throat, and beheading her for the world to see."

Samir already had his phone out but hadn't stopped shaking since they'd witnessed the calamity at the dam. He whispered, "I wish there was more I could do but if you think recording this is my role then Insha'Allah, you'll be successful, and I'll do my part. Our entire movement is behind you and I'll never question your instructions. You're the greatest leader Al Qaeda has ever had."

Khalil, with total faith in his masterful disguise as a non-descript truck driver, made his move. His scuffed biker boots, weathered black leather jacket, chained wallet in the back pocket of his worn jeans, and a mid-length black wig with a baseball cap were totally unremarkable.

He quickly got a small meal from the same McDonald's counter. Not showing any attention to his targets, he slowly slouched his way to the table directly behind the man he assumed was the traitor Abu Nistal, or whatever other name he went by, because he clearly wasn't an Arab or a Muslim.

Savoring the moment and knowing he was being filmed, he wanted to give Samir time to frame and focus his video. Paying no attention to his targets he casually opened his breakfast sandwich and per his old habit when he lived in the US, proceeded to sprinkle three packets of pepper on the bland breakfast sandwich.

As he lifted his eyes, he realized the CIA bitch had been watching his habit intently. Suddenly he realized his CIA profile might have listed his penchant for pepper. They made eye contact just as he saw unexpected recognition sweep across her face and they both went for their guns.

Samir almost joined the cacophony of screams as he saw his master surely slain by a quick shot to the head, taking off his cap, the wig, and a good part of his scalp. Blood and brain matter sprayed well behind him and it was all caught on the video.

Realizing they had no way of knowing he was part of the team and in the confusion that ensued, he slipped out a side door almost dropping his phone on the way, and shakily rushed for their car, crying with rage, and never looking back.

***

Cristal could see Khalil was no longer a threat. She quickly rose from her seat putting away her weapon and addressed the screaming crowd holding her badge high, "It's over," she yelled authoritatively. "I'm FBI," she lied. "The danger is over. Anyone who witnessed this, we'll need statements from you so don't leave."

She bent down quickly and delivered a personal message to Khalil as he breathed his last.

Standing again, she could see cell phones out and recording her, not good for an undercover agent. "This is a National Security matter and I'm impounding all recording of this so put your phones down immediately or you'll be charged with impeding a federal investigation. You're all on security video," she hoped, "so leaving here with any photos or video is a federal offense and you'll be prosecuted under the aiding and abetting terrorism laws. You must see me before you leave."

Suddenly she remembered Khalil often videoed his attacks and he might have had an accomplice but a scan of those with phones raised turned up no likely candidates. She finally turned her attention to David who was just now getting back onto his feet and putting away his weapon after hitting the floor in the excitement. He was aggressively rubbing one of his ears.

He mumbled, "You might have given me something of a heads up that you were going to discharge your weapon, virtually in my face," he frowned.

She mustered a nervous laugh, "Lucky you were looking down because you have powder burns on your forehead."

David offered a weak smile, "So I'm guessing that was Mr. Khalil al-Adel," motioning to the body just behind him. "Apparently we didn't get him at the dam after all. What did you whisper to him?"

"Basically, that this was for my BBC friend Tiffany in The Sudan who he and some other animals stoned to death in front of me. You might have noticed I've been wearing a wooden cross around my neck. It was hers. Khalil might have recognized it because he ripped it off her bloody neck as she died and forced it into my hand with a threatening little speech to me and the other press to get out of Muslim lands and take all our infidel scum with us."

David was careful not to react. Unbeknownst to Cristal, he knew much more than he had admitted about the Tiffany affair, but some things were better left unsaid.

She reached up smearing the soot on his forehead making an even bigger mess, "It was the eyes. He was in full disguise, but I'll never forget those dead and evil eyes. The last time I saw him I swore I'd never forget them. But it was the pepper that drew my attention. He opened a bunch of packets for his meal, and I remembered what we had on that habit of his. I was shaking when I went for my gun and nothing was going to stop me blowing that bastard's brains out. I can't tell you how relieved I am that I was the one who got to avenge Tiffany's tortured stoning."

After a few calls police were everywhere, mostly NJ Staties followed later by the NYC FBI team who had been at the dam. They collected the cell phone videos and photos of the scene captured by the few in the audience which were meticulously copied and deleted. Identification was taken from everyone in the food court before they were thanked for their cooperation and released. There was no way Cristal wanted photos of her on the internet killing Al Qaeda's revered leader.

Director of the CIA, Bill Carter, who only an hour before had thought this was all over, was astounded to be told they had missed Khalil at the dam and the world's most wanted monster had actually followed them to settle accounts.

After her report, he said, "Well for the second time in less than an hour you killed Khalil but at least this time we have him ID'd. Congratulations again and Merry Christmas. The New York team just reported in that they've arrived to take over the investigation and we'll need full written reports from both of you but for now go get some well-earned rest before more mayhem breaks out. I'm guessing you didn't get much sleep on that B-1 bomber all the way from Africa. We'll talk soon."

Cristal put away her phone and turned to David, "Well he's happy again. As happy as he can be, given he still has that crazy radioactive attack on JFK airport to deal with, but I think he's going to be able to spin the Khalil thing to make the politicians happy and deflect the press. After all, we saved New York City's water system and killed Al Qaeda's leader, so that has to be good for something."

David smiled, nodded, and yawned.

Cristal smiled back as the adrenalin was finally waning, "Anyway, I don't know about you, but my breakfast is cold and smells like a gun range. It's still Christmas morning with everything closed, and I'm still starving. My last meal, that didn't come out of a vending machine, was I don't know when and anyway it was on the other side of the planet. So, I'm going to get something else from that counter over there, and then we need to find a place to sleep."

David grabbed his ear again and said, "I didn't hear a word," as she started to laugh and finally stopped shaking.

London

(Two months later)

They had just arrived and gotten settled into their new London flat provided by MI6. Having been so focused on finding Khalil and intercepting his assault, then all the investigations, reviews, legalities, cleaning up details, as well as planning their move to London and their new jobs, they'd had no time to relax and recover. So, tonight was their first official 'date night' since their reunification months ago. To say it had been hectic was an understatement, so this was the night to let their hair down, catch their breath and finally have a normal conversation.

Cristal, with the help of the local CIA team, had organized a babysitter for tiny Tiffany and David had insisted they try a quaint London Bistro he had loved in years gone by.

The ambiance was perfectly cozy and everything including the menu was just as he remembered it. It was still early in the evening for London, but the bistro had apparently remained popular and was more than half full.

It had been years, but the maître d' hadn't changed and immediately recognized David to his delight, "Good evening sir. So good to see you back visiting us again."

As they settled in, ordered drinks, and the meal suggestions of their waiter, David opened with what Cristal considered his lovely British accent. "I didn't say anything at home nor in the taxi but when did you make time to find that fabulous dress?"

She smiled, "We women have our ways. I'm not only an accomplished international assassin you know."

"Well, if I met you for the first time tonight, it would be love at first sight this time."

He immediately knew he had stepped in it and blushed.

Petulant, Cristal quipped, "What do you mean this time? You said it was love at first sight in Burundi."

"Yes, yes. It was. I don't know what I was thinking. I must have had something different on my mind."

She frowned, "When? Then or now?"

He stumbled to find his footing. He started to laugh, "I don't know, both I guess. My mind was just wondering. It's the dress … it takes my breath away, maybe my brains too. I mean I'm ready to whisk you back to our flat now, but I promised you a nice night out for a change. And yes, of course, it was love at first sight in Burundi. As I remember you wore a tight-fitting dark grey business suit over a white silk blouse that showed all the right curves, and I was snookered right there and then. I can't decide if it was your dark hair back then or this stunning blonde do that I like the best, but frankly, this dress is almost too much. Have you noticed the heads turning in the room? I'm feeling pretty special right now."

Cristal blushed just enough to make him think he might have ducked a very awkward conversation. He'd have to be much more careful with things that needed to stay in the past.

The drinks, appetizer, and main course were just as he expected; entirely spectacular, delicious, and memorable.

The conversation had naturally turned to their wonderful little daughter Tiffany. Suddenly a question came to David's mind, "So what did you put down for her father on Tiffany's birth certificate?"

"What could I put? I had already told my parents that my imaginary Marine husband had died in a climbing accident right after we were married so of course. I had to put 'Deceased' on the birth certificate.

"Actually, everything surrounding you and my job with the CIA was classified so there was no way I could tell them Tiffany's father was the terrorist Daniel Boone imprisoned in Guantanamo, even if I had wanted to, which of course I didn't. Nice that they now know the truth and finally got to meet the real Commander David Crowe and not the persona I had captured."

David was a little put out and pouted, "Well we'll have to get that birth certificate changed. Maybe your best buddy Director William Carter can help us there. I think he still owes you. I mean I want to be her REAL father on paper too. Which brings up another great question; when are we getting married, Ms. Serpe?"

Cristal laughed, "Where's the ring? Is that what this night is all about? Let's have it. On your knees, Crowe!"

Now it was David's turn to blush beet red. "No, that wasn't my plan tonight, but I just assumed we'd get married. If you want the whole proposal thing I'd be pleased to accommodate as soon as I get a chance to buy a ring but thoughtlessly, I just assumed we were on the same page and completely committed to each other."

Cristal laughed, "Got ya! I guess for Tiffany's sake it would be nice if her parents were married but I haven't seen the paperwork dissolving my marriage to that jerk back home, in fact, you're dining with Mrs. Cristal Wiggins not Ms. Serpe at the moment.

"Let's not sweat it but I'll start looking into how I can get the birth certificate changed and we can start planning nuptials when I finally see those divorce papers AND A RING. But that will mean a trip to the US so my family and any friends I still have from the TV station can be at the wedding.

"On second thought, no friends. Some of them are investigative reporters. What would I tell them about my kidnapping, which they covered intensely last November, you and me, Guantanamo, how we met, what our jobs are, and where we've been for the last couple of months? Yeah, that's not going to work, so that's out."

David just smiled and nodded vigorously as he returned to his dessert. It was like life was starting over for him and he loved his new life with Cristal and Tiffany in his beloved London.

After the danger and pressures of the last few months. Life couldn't be better.

***

After settling into their new 'protected' London flat, it was David's first week back at MI6 after they had both left their temporary assignments at Langley.

Cristal still had a week of online briefings and three-way calls with the CIA's London branch and Langley before she took her new liaison job in MI6.

Their names had been kept out of the news but there was always the chance of a leak. Both MI6 and the CIA had fears of a mole in their midst.

Things had moved rather quickly in the big scheme of things. David had been welcomed back to his old organization with a promotion to the senior team to make up for lost years, a nasty MI6 target that had been on his back, and a few recent Top Secret achievements across the pond.

He wondered if it was intentional that he'd been given Jack Hammond's old office, where only a few months ago the MI6 mole, and member of the BSB, had met his death at David's hands, saving at the same time the life of the Chief of SIS, or Britain's MI6 to most.

Sir Richard Brighton was now in fact his direct boss and probably had nothing to do with the office assignment, but it made him wonder what and whose thinking had gone into it.

The new desk and furniture arrangement had helped to change the setting, but still, he received furtive looks from staff who never dreamed there could be such violence at the normally restrained MI6 HQ. The shootout on the executive floor a few short months ago was still top of mind for many. He wasn't blind to the cautious and curious glances.

Action like a gun battle never happened at headquarters and it could hardly have been anticipated or forgotten. No one had said anything to him directly, but it was a good bet that the majority wanted no part in gunplay in their place of work. After all, most British police still didn't carry firearms and unlike the US, even news reports of criminal activity involving guns were rare.

There was also the reminder that David had been seen as a traitor at one point. Hammond had set him up as the fall guy and charged him as being the mole himself. One more reason for the curious glances in his first few days.

Crowe had been one of MI6's Most Wanted for some time and now he was evidently the hero of the day. Some of the looks he saw were probably from people who still couldn't sort it all out in their heads. After all, much of the actual detail of how he'd come to be fingered as a traitor, had apparently been thought of as assassinated, disappeared for a few years, and then reappears in a gunfight at headquarters was still eyes-only. There was even a growing rumor that he'd been imprisoned in Guantanamo for a time. All of this added to a very cool reception from some who were lower on the Intel ladder and suspected some kind of conspiracy in it all.

He was just settling in for his second morning on the job when suddenly there was an incredibly beautiful and familiar face in his doorway, "How ironic to find you in his office," she said.

"You haven't changed much, I must say, still as handsome as ever. What's it been, four years or so? You know, it took me more than a year, but I finally did stop crying for you after your 'death'."

David smiled, "Nice to see you, Kathy. Let me say, you're even more stunning than I remember!" and that was definitely an understatement in his mind.

They had dated off and on before his reported assassination in The Sudan. At one time they had been the 'it' couple and the gossipy talk of the branch; both extremely attractive and both apparently deadly in the field.

It wasn't common for a female to be given field work in today's MI6, but Kathy had taken to it early and intensely. They had never been teamed up together but her accomplishments in international espionage, spying and deadly confrontations with various threats to the empire were well rumored.

They had been going through one of their 'off again' periods the last time he'd seen her. Apparently not completely 'off again' for her if indeed she'd cried at his supposed demise.

She certainly hadn't changed much but this morning she seemed even more beautiful than he remembered. He reasoned she'd probably dressed up even more than usual for this encounter as she knew he was back and the fact that he had a new woman in his life. It suddenly struck him that she reminded him of a slightly younger Cristal which made him wonder if he had an unconscious profile in mind; gorgeous and lethal.

On further thought, he realized she was the perfectly stunning English rose and for the life of him he couldn't remember why they broke up, beyond the thought that they'd both been rather self-centered at the time.

She smiled that perfect smile as she stepped inside his doorway wearing a revealing suit that was borderline too alluring for an office environment. David grinned as he realized the message was clear, 'I don't know what the new woman looks like but look what you're not getting right here!'

She posed just a little as she said, "So, welcome back. Not sure if anyone has told you yet but just in case you didn't know, Jack Hammond and I saw each other for a while sometime after your reported 'death'. As I said, I cried for quite some time, but life moves on, what?

"So, in a strange way, one old boyfriend is back from the dead just in time to send the other one off in that direction. No hard feelings though, we had been completely finished for over a year and I suppose I shouldn't be surprised that he was the actual mole and not you."

From a slight shift in her posture, he got the impression that she wasn't being completely honest in the matter.

"As I say, Jack was a bit of a mystery and always had the potential to be the bad boy. You always struck me more like the boy scout of the two with him being the sneaky one. Still, that was a helluva way for you to announce your resurrection. I mean for the old man to allow you in here with a gun. He must have had a premonition of what was to come."

David tried a smile, "Yeah, you know what they say; he left me no choice in the matter."

Her smile now seemed unconvincing.

After a pause as she stared him down, she said, "So I hear there's a new lady on your arm; an American, and she's working here. Wow, I didn't see you in the arms of an American; nothing in particular against them you understand."

David was happy to change the subject and put the slight down to poorly veiled and petty jealousy. Something told him his reincarnation couldn't be easy for her, especially if she'd actually cried for him. Or was it possible that Hammond and she had still been a 'thing' before David killed him?

"Yeah, Cristal is American, but we actually met up in Africa. Much of that and the last few years is eyes-only I'm afraid. We have a young daughter, Tiffany, and that's not classified. Cristal hasn't started here yet but soon. She's acting in a capacity of liaison for our partners across the pond."

She frowned, "Wasn't there a Tiffany on your team in The Sudan? Not the most common name."

David was on the alert. At the time Kathy wouldn't have had access to undercover informants on his team.

"Yeah, there was a Tiffany and she was a BBC correspondent who helped us out a bit which is apparently how she and Cristal met. Again, much of that is still eyes-only, you understand, … but Cristal was a CNN producer at the time. Tiffany was killed in a terrorist ambush in The Sudan and Cristal named our daughter after her. They were apparently close friends. Our Tiffany is a really cute little squirt. I'm sure you'll meet her soon."

David was uncomfortable covering material that at the time would have been restricted but any avoidance of her curiosity might pique her interest in looking into matters further. Matters that needed to be left in the past.

There was a long pause as they sized each other up and remembered their 'hot' off-and-on past. The silence was finally broken by Kathy, "So you're a daddy now, well welcome back again to the land of the living.

"Like you, I was promoted while you were gone. No more field work for me and I'm now on senior staff too, so we'll see you around," and she was gone.

He sat there puzzled and shaking his head. Kathy was a bit of a wild card and apparently a peer now. Beautiful, deadly, possibly pissed at him for killing the old boyfriend, and likely jealous that he had committed himself to another. He'd have to come clean with Cristal and warn her. For more than one reason, Kathy could definitely become an unwelcome wrinkle in his relationship with Cristal.

He smiled thinking some parts of his life in Guantanamo had been more simple than dealing with current and former girlfriends.

***

A few days later and after a series of re-familiarization briefings and meetings with the MI6 senior staff, some of whom he knew from his earlier days, he was finally able to sit in his office and his attention was drawn to a young analyst he could see from his open door.

Over the first few days, David had picked up on the lack of direct eye contact followed by the odd sneaky glance when he wasn't looking. Hammond had to have had help running his clandestine ops. So, on a hunch, even though this kid was an unlikely candidate, he called the seemingly petrified young man into his office and closed the door.

David took his seat behind the desk and waited, sizing the kid up and waiting for the pressure to build, "It's James, right?"

"That's correct sir, James Owens. How can I help you Commander Crowe?" he stuttered.

"Well James we have reason to believe that you had, let's say, a rather special relationship with Jack Hammond."

Young James flushed and obviously panicked, blurted out, "Well, I wouldn't say that. I do work for all the directors and some of the managers in here ... I specialize in video surveillance, research, and interpretation. Mr. Hammond was only one of the people I worked with and while it's apparently above my pay grade, it's clear he was into something very bad given he pulled a gun on you and Sir Richard. I was sitting right there when it all happened and frankly that was more than shocking. Change that to terrifying. I never thought I'd see bullets flying around in this office or for heaven's sake, a man being killed right in front of me. I wasn't prepared for that! I'm not naive enough to think that doesn't happen with some of our agents in hostile countries but this isn't a hostile country, so to say it was unexpected would be an understatement.

"With the Chief not ten feet away I must admit I couldn't take my eyes off the three of you and when he went for that gun, I mean, he almost got the drop on you as they say in the movies. You and or the Chief were ever so close to losing that battle.

"As you must be aware, the whole thing is classified Secret, but you were there so I'm not giving anything away.

"But to reiterate, Mr. Hammond was no friend of mine. I've no idea what he was up to, but I'm sure you had your reasons for suspecting him as a threat and had every justification for confronting him and killing him right in front of us all. Honestly, I don't know anything more about his activities and I don't care to. Lots of rumors around here but as I said, the truth of it all is above my job level. But again, no, I had no special relationship with Mr. Hammond."

The kid was obviously a nervous wreck and rambling on. David smiled for a long time and on a hunch, he decided to push further. "The investigation of what Jack was up to is ongoing but that's just it James, Jack left some puzzling clues behind that we're just now coming to grips with, and frankly they're going to require some serious explanations; particularly from you," he lied.

Owens looked like he was about to explode or pass out from the stress. Blushing, swallowing awkwardly as if he couldn't find enough saliva, and suddenly sitting far forward in his chair he said, "Listen Commander Crowe, I knew nothing about what he was up to."

After a long pause as he rethought his position and the trouble facing him, he blurted out, "When he came to me, he told me you were a known national security threat, wanted in the worst way by the Branch and a link to the criminal network known as the BSB. I think you know there was even an MI6 kill order out on you. That part of his story of course turned out to be true."

After another pause, while he seemed to be evaluating his predicament, he said, "That's when he gave me a photo of you and a woman and asked me last fall to find you on any video coming out of Frankfurt. As far as I know, that was a legitimate request for the work I do.

"You had been reported dead but apparently for some reason, he thought you were still alive and a threat. I don't know why he thought you were in Frankfurt, but I did the regular scan of airport footage and any surveillance records we have of known foreign Intel types and that's when I ID'd you entering Franz Becker's flat. Being ex-BND and apparently a freelancer, he was an official foreign surveillance target we had eyes on.

"I had no way of knowing Mr. Becker would be killed based on me telling Mr. Hammond you had visited him.

"When it came out that Becker had been killed, Mr. Hammond threatened me. He told me you had killed Becker, that I had somehow contributed to an assassination and I was at least an accomplice. He insinuated that I had somehow tipped you off to Becker's whereabouts. He said he had ways to put all the blame on me. I don't know what clues he left that you're referring to but believe me, I had to keep quiet. I now see how he was using me. I also think he might have had something to do with Becker's murder but really, I know nothing beyond what I just told you."

Just as he suspected, the young analyst had been involved and was easily spooked. He had clearly and easily been duped by Hammond and was prepared to dump everything. David just stared him down forcing him to continue, "Now that it turns out that Mr. Hammond was the actual threat, I'd be happy to cooperate in any way, but I swear I knew nothing of what he was doing. You have to believe me. I'd never have willingly participated in whatever was going on and I still have no idea what that was. I couldn't say anything because he was threatening me and after his death, I simply thought it better to stay silent."

David could see where this kid would likely help him, including finding Franz Becker's real killer but he wanted more right now while he still had him in the hot seat, "I have a strong feeling that Jack Hammond had significant help, and not just with video searches. I'm willing to bet that you weren't his real accomplice, but I need to find out who if anyone was helping him inside MI6. Who was he close to?"

James looked somewhat relieved, "Sir, I'm highly motivated to help you but actually, Mr. Hammond seemed to be a very private man. Except for Kathy Sloane, who I saw you talking to, and even then, they apparently had a nasty breakup some time ago, I never saw him spend any length of time with anyone else in this office. Looking back that now seems odd, but the man was the most private of types. He may have had close friends outside the Branch, but I think you're looking for someone inside MI6.

"The only other odd thing I noticed was that he frequently left the office to go get a coffee somewhere even though our lunchroom has an excellent selection. It's a fair walk and a security hassle downstairs to get to and back from any coffee stand. So that always struck me as odd. Everyone else in here thinks our coffee and tea are almost a workplace benefit."

David thought this over. His limited memory of Hammond was in fact that he was pretty much a loner and as Kathy had said, a bit sneaky.

The coffee breaks tied with how the CIA had ID'd Hammond in the first place with the CCTV video records from the tube station across the street. He'd been caught because they had the phone records of the known BSB agent from Germany which lined up exactly with Hammond's untraceable phone calls caught on camera from the tube station. His instinct was that this kid was truthful and likely had nothing intentional to do with anything nefarious, having simply gotten caught up due to his naivety.

His sixth sense told him Hammond must have had at least one high-level partner inside the Section to have pulled off years of support for the invisible Bean Stalk Boys, the nickname the Intelligence Community had given to a shady group of mercenaries who it was thought was the muscle behind a few big US Agri companies manipulating fledgling third world nations with an iron fist and lots of dirty money.

Running teams of mercenaries out of this building and setting traps for anyone who became a threat like David himself, required lots of capabilities that Hammond couldn't have handled alone. This kid was probably not the accomplice, but David was even more sure now that one existed. If Kathy had had a messy breakup with Jack some time ago then she wasn't likely to be the one either, though he'd have to watch her.

From what he remembered of 'sneaky' Jack Hammond, it was just like him to move in on David's old girlfriend after he thought he had him assassinated in The Sudan. 'Twisted' came to mind.

It was time to let the kid off the hook, "Listen James, I believe what you've told me, and for the time being we need to keep this just between us, but I must find the man who killed Franz Becker. I think you now know Becker was a friend of mine and I had nothing to do with his death. You're right, Jack Hammond was the one who ordered that assassination. The triggerman we're looking for will lead us to the BSB and any accomplices or moles in MI6, so this has to be eyes-only between you and me."

David knew the CIA had tracked down a key BSB operative in Germany as he had unwittingly hired a CIA agent in Nairobi to kill David and Cristal, but David wanted the actual guy that killed his friend, and he wasn't sure who was who in Germany.

He had the kid's attention, "Sometime in the thirty-six hours after you found me entering Becker's building, someone else paid him a visit. That person must have gotten the jump on him when he returned from somewhere because I know that Becker had an exceptional security setup on his flat and he'd have seen any bad guys approaching. Whoever that was, interrogated him and killed him all because Hammond knew I had been there. They were looking for me thinking Becker knew where I was and he just got caught in the middle.

"He was indeed a friend from years gone by and it infuriates me that my visit led to his death. You unwittingly enabled all of that by telling Hammond who

I had met. Now, I need you to search those surveillance tapes again and find someone entering that building when Becker was out, looking suspicious and who doesn't belong there. Then we need to try and get a name to that face. I have a hunch that the man we're looking for is short, stocky, and sandy-haired," remembering the obvious lookout he'd spotted at the airport when they departed Frankfurt.

Owens could see it starting all over again. Hammond had manipulated him, and this new guy could be doing the same, "Sir, is this sanctioned by the Branch; the top brass I mean? Frankly, I'm not comfortable getting deeper into this affair after I was apparently conned the last time. No offense to you, but you're new here, at least to me and if this isn't sanctioned from above and we're to keep this secret, I've no way of confirming any motivation you may have and any mechanism to protect myself from another setup. I only have your word you didn't kill Becker yourself. I'm not saying you did but I think you see my position."

David smiled, looked like the kid had learned a lesson, "Understandable James. The Director has given me carte blanche on this, so yes it's sanctioned," he lied. "But just to address your concerns, here's what I'll do. In a couple of days after I clear up this German thing, you and I will go see the Director. I'll brief him on the complete file and convince him you had no part in Hammond's schemes. I'll put that in writing for you right now, but you have to sit on it until we deal with that guy in Frankfurt before someone here tips him off. I need that name and because there could be someone on Hammond's team on the loose inside MI6, this has to remain between you and me for a few days."

The kid was hesitant, but the story all seemed plausible and the letter he was awaiting would give him some cover. Still, this new guy Crowe had killed someone right in this office who he figured was on the wrong side. This was serious but what choice did he have but to do as he was told.

It didn't take long. Just before lunch, James was back all smiles. David handed him the promised letter absolving him of any wrongdoing as James anxiously whispered, "His name is Kurt Willems. I have him on video at Franz Becker's building the day after you left. Becker was out at the time just as you speculated.

"We have him entering and leaving so we have a positive ID on him. He's in our database and he's ex-German Intelligence. He fits the assassin profile and your description to a tee, and I even have an address. If he was actually working for Hammond, it looks like he didn't trust him completely because he had him under video surveillance. I never thought to scan the videos to see if someone else visited Becker. Hammond already knew about the assassination and he told me it was you that killed Becker on your earlier visit, but I have Franz Becker coming and going after your visit so if you ever need it, you're in the clear."

David checked the video at the kid's desk and was easily convinced it was the stalker he'd seen at the airport. The name also matched the one the CIA agent in Nairobi was in communication with. So, he was probably the top guy in the German BSB after he and Cristal had killed some, or maybe all his henchmen. He had apparently resorted to doing the dirty work himself and killed David's friend.

He thanked young Owens and dismissed him, then he sat thinking out his next move and how to get away with it. Better to ask forgiveness than permission and given the theory that there was an active mole in the

Section, his excuse could be that this was better handled promptly and alone.

But what about Cristal? He decided he'd have to work around her given there was no point in risking both of Tiffany's parents on a clandestine operation. It would have been nice to include her as backup but revenge for Becker's assassination was really only on him. Neither of them was safe in Germany with various law enforcement types on the lookout for them given they had at least a couple of passports from the Westin and a few dead locals. They likely had a picture from that passport at the airport check points so he decided a modest disguise might be in order at the border. It was also possible that Germany had implemented facial recognition systems. Another good reason for a few changes to his appearance.

Suddenly he realized this was their new life which had issues he hadn't thought of last fall when they were both in danger. Now that he'd met his tiny 'squirt', his attitude about protecting her had changed. They'd have to be a lot more careful in the risks they were taking with a daughter to think of. Teaming up as a pair on missions was probably an awfully bad idea. Besides, they now worked for two different Intel organizations with different mandates.

He realized suddenly that this might mean keeping MI6 ops details from Cristal, and it wouldn't be the first time. He seriously hoped he wouldn't have to outright lie to her … again.

First Day

The following morning Cristal rolled over just around five-thirty in their new London flat only to realize the place beside her in bed was empty. Tiffany usually slept until sunrise which was still a ways off.

Previously used to the burbs, Cristal was coming to enjoy their downtown flat which was actually an MI6 safe house given their recent notoriety and the possibility that some nasty people might be trying to find both of them.

Blinking open her eyes she saw David in their tiny bathroom already half-dressed.

Realizing she was awake he said, "I'm up and in a hurry. I have a busy day and an early meeting. You still have some time to snooze. The new nanny won't be here for another couple of hours and today's your big day, you get to meet the whole gang at MI6 and find a new office to park your pretty butt.

"Oh, by the way, I ran into an old flame at the Section the other day, Kathy Sloane, but that was dead long ago. She knows about you so just so you know she'll likely search you out to check out the new girlfriend," he said with a wry smile.

Cristal frowned, "Thanks for the heads up. No pressure on making a good impression, right? Anything I should know about her?"

He simply smiled. No point in getting ahead of any imaginary issues, he thought.

She laid back down as her thoughts turned to how fortunate she'd been that Bill Carter hadn't only taken her back but had given her the job of her dreams;

Special Liaison between the CIA and MI6 for joint intel on terrorism and working in London with her new fiancé. No dirty or dangerous field work, a no-hassle commute, and home every night for supper with her precious Tiffany.

Her days of cloak and dagger and dangerous wet work for the CIA were behind her. While she'd handled Khalil with aplomb, she hadn't impressed herself with her reaction time that seemed to have suffered from a few years of neglect. He'd almost succeeded in blowing her away and the shootout had been way too close for comfort.

Director Bill Carter probably figured the CIA owed her for that little thing that went down at McDonald's especially given it pretty much saved his career after the JFK embarrassment of the previous day.

Some details of the Al Qaeda leader's death had been kept classified to protect her from reprisals. The world only knew that a law enforcement action had taken out the world's most dangerous terrorist, but no details had been offered and their cover story seemed to be holding.

That wasn't good enough for the world press and interviews with a few civilians who came forward claimed an FBI woman was the shooter, but the press had had no luck in identifying her. Of course, the FBI was happy to let stand the thought that one of theirs had done the job, so they had maintained their 'no comment' stance. To date, Cristal and David's identities had remained a secret, outside of some staff, and most details of the encounter including whether there were any accomplices were deemed Top Secret.

Cristal realized with the expectations of the day ahead, she wouldn't be able to fall back to sleep. She sat up in bed watching David continue his morning routine.

Life was wonderful. He was handsome and as much in love with her as she was with him and then there was their perfect little Tiffany, the ultimate joy to both of them.

She stared intently at him as he dressed; Commander David Crowe of MI6 or Daniel Boone to the Americans or Abu Nistal as he'd been known in Africa. He'd used even more aliases in the last few months in Germany and Somalia as had she.

This was the man she had fallen head over heels for in Burundi and who had fathered her baby. The same man she had turned in to the CIA when she thought he was a terrorist leader for the FLN, a branch of Al Qaeda. The man who had spent more than two years hiding from multiple professional assassins as a prisoner in Guantanamo. All because of her, the BSB, and because MI6 had mistakenly marked him as a BSB mole and traitor. The man who had been sprung loose from that US base, initially through a hostage exchange scheme by a gang of Jihadis. The man who she thought had returned with her kidnappers to kill her before he revealed the amazing truth of it all and had helped her escape and kill all her Jihadi captors.

What a rocky road their love affair had chosen to take. It was only a few months ago that she'd hated him to the point of preemptively planning his execution for what she thought was his terrorist background only to discover he was an actual hero. There and then their love affair was found anew. Her divorce, or legal release, from that poser Gregg Wiggins, or whatever his real name was, still hadn't been finalized but David and she had already started thinking about wedding plans once that was all behind them.

Given Greg Wiggins had still been married when he wed her and had abandoned a young family, their union was clearly illegal, but she still wanted the paperwork to make it all official.

She yawned and her thoughts turned to the Danish twenty-something postgrad student she had hired as a nanny for little Tiffany, or 'squirt' as David had come to call her. Freja would indeed be here later this morning and she was a wonderful find. She had hit it off magically with Tiffany from the start. They clearly loved each other. Freja was registered in an evening Level Seven Master's program at Ulster University in London so her days were free to act as a nanny. Thankfully, Tiffany took a long nap in the afternoons allowing Freja to get on with her studies. A test run the week before had turned out splendidly for everyone.

Suddenly uneasy, she thought back to Christmas. If Khalil had an accomplice who had escaped and the CIA's thinking was that he did, then there was a chance Al Qaeda knew full details of the McDonald's incident. So, due to their possible notoriety MI6 had provided a rotating security team and there was always a car cruising by even when Cristal and David were gone. The major drawback was they had to plan. They had to forecast all their moves so the security team could have them covered for any form of potential attack.

She seriously hoped this would only be for a few months until the Khalil thing blew over or someone in international law enforcement took care of the BSB who were likely still after David. Between the two of them, they had possibly wiped out most of the BSB team in Germany and probably the head of their British operations making David in particular, a full-fledged target himself.

Well, this was their life for now, but it had its advantages and as a small 'family' they were certainly enjoying their new situation. Finally, a nine to five job, minutes from the office in downtown London, comfortable flat, mom and dad home every night, and someone watching their back.

Life was wonderful.

After welcoming Freja and ensuring all was in order it was Cristal's turn. Taking a taxi, she arrived at the iconic MI6 headquarters at Vauxhall Cross a few minutes early and met her contact as arranged at the main entry with her new credentials for access to the building and all non-classified areas. After all, she was a foreigner in one of Britain's highest-security buildings.

The woman was sweet and very business-like, but Cristal detected a little frostiness as she seemed to ooze her best 'I'm British and you're not' attitude.

In America, they'd have walked together in small talk, but this woman seemingly wanted to take the dominant position ensuring she was a step ahead, leading Cristal all the way. Cristal smiled and realized there might be UK norms like this that would be important to understand; maybe not like but tolerate the older cousin's customs.

Over the next few hours, she met one after another of the people she'd work with on a regular basis, and to a man, they were polite but standoffish. And as expected they were almost all men.

In some ways, the CIA and MI6 were competing security organizations and it was clear these people saw her as both a colleague and a potential spy for the US. There were limits apparently to the cooperation between the Five Eyes. She realized it could be tricky and she would need to do her best to build trust in her unusual posting as liaison between two of the most well-known spy organizations in the western world. Canada, New Zealand, and Australia made up the other intelligence organizations in the Five Eyes, but the UK and the USA had the biggest and deepest teams watching and gathering intelligence across the globe.

While it wasn't public, her notoriety in security circles had somehow preceded her and after a few pleasantries, some of her new colleagues whispered their appreciation for 'getting' Khalil and wanted one little piece of news on the engagement they could call their own. Given the CIA hadn't publicly identified her as the agent involved in the takedown, she was a little surprised at how many knew of her role. So, in an effort to build trust she complied and offered some personal color but no material information on the encounter.

'At least,' she thought, 'there was no Kathy Sloane in the introductions.'

That was short-lived however. Just as Cristal was finally seated in her new office right around eleven, a GORGEOUS English bombshell popped her head around Cristal's door and said, "Well you must be Cristal, David's new woman. I'm Kathy Sloane. Our David may have mentioned me."

Cristal tried hard to avoid laughing at the awkward introduction and any seeming surprise at meeting her, "Yes, good to meet you, Kathy. David has told me all about you," she lied. "I look forward to working with the team here in London. We should do lunch sometime or is that just an American thing?"

Kathy blushed, "No we do that here too. We'll have to set that up. Maybe next week when you're settled in. But I'm really eager to know, how did you two meet?"

Somehow Cristal detected that this might be a loaded query but with no time to duck the question she said, "We actually just bumped into each other in really the only ex-pat hotel in the capital of Burundi."

Kathy's face reddened slightly, "Well that's curious. I was sure he mentioned your name in one of his field reports before he was supposedly killed in The Sudan. Oh well, I must have mixed up the names.

"Anyway, it's great to have David back from the dead. I'm sure you'll love it here too. Leave the lunch thing to me. I know a couple of cute restaurants you must try. As I said, maybe in a week or so. Can't wait to compare notes on that hunk of a secret agent we both know," she smiled. "Cheerio for now," and she was gone.

'Okay, that was weird. What's going on here?' Was she just trying to stir up trouble between her and David? Had she actually mixed up names or had their paths actually crossed in The Sudan and David had never mentioned it? Immediately she put Kathy Sloane down as someone to watch. Not necessarily as any kind of a threat to their relationship but still someone who might have a penchant for stirring things up. The other thing David had forgotten to mention was that she was a 'Fucking Goddess!'

Later, as it was nearing noon and with a few pressing questions for David, she thought she'd pop by his office upstairs on mahogany row to see if he was available for a quick lunch.

His office was dark and locked, and she was about to leave when a young nerdy-looking analyst just outside David's office offered, "Sorry he's not in today ... phoned in sick but he should be back tomorrow I'm told."

The expression on her face gave her away as the young man gushed, "Oh my God. I haven't seen you around here before so you must be … his American fiancée?" Suddenly he realized he was looking at the very woman in the photo with David Crowe that Hammond had given him back in November.

She nodded slightly as he blubbered on blushing, "Oh my, and you expected him to be here which means he's not home ill after all." After a long pause as they stared each other down, he blushed even more, bowed his head, and mumbled, "Oh my God, not again."

Cristal was on to him. The name on his cubical was James Owens so she grabbed his wrist and said, "James, you're with me," leading him hastily off to a more private setting. He was shocked at her physical strength.

She hustled him into a tiny coffee room which was empty for the moment. Still grasping his wrist tightly, she said, "Now listen carefully. You know something. You know where David is. I'm his fiancée and we're working together on breaking up terrorist organizations. I need to know where he is. I can tell by your face that you know something."

Owens was frantic, "You're not even MI6. I can't give you any information," he pleaded.

"Listen James, I'm American. I have Top Secret clearance and I carry a gun," she lied. "A big gun. And if you don't want me to shoot off your kneecaps and scream rape, you better start talking."

He wasn't sure about the gun because even as a gun-toting American CIA agent, they'd never let her in the building with one … he hoped … and a quick scan of her pretty physique suggested she was bluffing as he couldn't imagine where she was concealing a 'big gun'. Yet there was an outside chance the rape threat could be real, and she looked furious and serious. No matter, with everything going on with Hammond and Crowe, he didn't need any undue attention.

She was the Commander's fiancée after all and apparently had high-security clearance in her job and obviously, Commander Crowe trusted her. Besides, he was deep enough into this already and didn't want to sound the alarm on any rogue ops which it was beginning to look like were definitely afoot. He wanted to kick himself as he found himself in the middle of it again. How could he be so naive, he wondered?

All things considered and running out of time stalling, he decided it was most prudent to tell her, "Okay, I don't know for sure, but I think he went after Kurt Willems, an ex-German Intel guy in Frankfurt who he thinks killed Franz Becker last November."

Cristal grabbed his wrist tighter, "How do you know this?"

Owens winced at the twisted wrist, "Mr. Crowe forced me to find out who visited Becker after he did last November. We have video records; both Becker and Willems were under video surveillance at the time."

Cristal let go of his wrist. "So, you found and ID'd the guy who offed Becker. Did David have a location for this Willems guy?"

"Oh no! I shouldn't be doing this. I don't even know what your clearance is."

Glaring at the timid analyst, and grabbing his arm again, giving it a meaningful martial arts twist, she said, "My clearance is a lot higher than yours so start talking or else!"

"Okay, okay," he winced, "I told him Kurt Willems is living in a flat on Holzgrabben Strasse.

Number ten is the address, but I don't know the flat number."

Cristal started to release his arm again. This sounded like David all right. She was fairly sure a few weeks ago he'd paid a visit to a prison guard from Guantanamo who had tortured him with glee while he was held on that military base by her own CIA. The CIA Director had hit David with a waterboarding accusation, but the recovering victim had stopped talking, fearful of further reprisals.

It was just like David to settle scores. He seemed pretty pigheaded about not letting any injustice stand. Given David's careless cover story of being home ill, she was convinced his plan was to be back tonight. Clearly, he had gone after the killer of his old friend Franz Becker and she'd have a few questions for him when he returned.

She speculated that this kid, who sat right outside Hammond's old office, was probably the one who provided the original info on who David was talking to in Frankfurt when Hammond was trying to find them last November. So as suspected, Hammond and the German BSB were in it together and one of them had somehow obtained the photo from the Lufthansa gate at JFK.

James looked just naive enough to have been conned into whatever Hammond wanted and was almost certainly unaware of what he'd found himself mixed up in.

Still, it was a mystery as to who had photographed them coming out of New York so that they were met by a BSB assassin at the Frankfurt airport. Then the professional hit team at their first hotel was just sloppiness on their part. Once targeted they should never have gone to a major hotel chain like the Westin.

'Special hotels' had clerks who didn't check or keep passport IDs if you paid a bit more than the asking price.

Hammond had to have been behind all of that, but it was unlikely they were using this kid for surveillance in New York. That was more likely someone in the BSB network who either followed them or just got lucky and recognized David in New York. This kid was just too fumbling and timid to be part of any BSB team.

It was coming into focus for her now. With this analyst's surveillance video of David visiting Becker last November in Frankfurt, Jack Hammond, on the hunt for them, must have sent Kurt Willems to interrogate Becker which ended in his death. She remembered David's face when he heard that morning on the German news that his friend had been murdered. That led to a quick departure from Frankfurt for both of them in crazy disguises. She remembered now that David had spotted surveillance at the airport as they made their escape and he deduced it might be Becker's killer.

Now David was almost certainly back in Frankfurt, likely to find out what Willems knew about the BSB network and any accomplices in MI6. Knowing David's penchant for justice, this interrogation might not end with a living subject. Even loving him as she did, she thought David might be capable of cold-blooded murder in revenge. Willems would know David's type and given he was an ex-German Intel pro, the type the BSB usually recruited, and with nothing to lose, that made the situation decidedly dangerous.

David was going in without backup. It wasn't like he could turn Willems over to the German authorities without getting tangled up in the four dead bodies they'd left behind last fall. Willems probably knew that too, making him all the more dangerous.

David had at least a six-hour head start so there was no way she was going to catch up with him.

She grabbed the kid's arm again, "I'm sure David swore you to secrecy so now you have me to deal with too," and she released him.

She waited all day for news but when David didn't return that night and failed to check in, she knew something was wrong. She bought a cheap ticket online on Ryanair out of London's Stansted airport for the first morning flight to Frankfurt.

Frankfurt

After having left Cristal at home to get ready for her first day in the office, David was in Frankfurt by midmorning. He picked up the weapon where he and Cristal had stashed it months earlier and headed straight to his target.

Holzgrabben Strasse was a tiny one-way street in central Frankfurt. It was near noon by the time he got to the address. On a lunch, he found a secluded alleyway nearby the target's address to observe. Before leaving MI6 HQ, he'd checked out a better photo of Kurt Willems than what young James had on his video.

Kurt was indeed the man he'd spotted at Flughafen Frankfurt in November and who he now saw leaving his flat, walking down the street and entering a small 'Imbissstube', where typically Germans would grab the 'Tagesangebot' or special of the day for a quick lunch.

Sunglasses on, pulling his collar up and pulling down his ball cap, he avoided being ID'd on the MI6 surveillance camera he knew to be across the street watching the door. The building's main entrance wasn't locked so he was quickly inside.

Germans are often extreme conservationists and the main hallways in the building were unlit and completely dark. He didn't bother looking for the light switch as he could see a suitable hiding spot near a side exit to a courtyard with a clear view of the main entrance. About forty-five minutes later Willems appeared, and David got a clean jump on him disarming him before forcing the man to take him up to his flat on the top floor.

As per his MI6 training, he once again frisked the target for any weapons, or devices that could be used as a weapon, such as a pen, and then forced him to sit on a hard-backed chair in the middle of the room away from any potential hiding places for weapons. Looking around, he got the impression that the BSB paid well because Kurt had an amazingly comfortable, fashionable, modern, and undoubtedly expensive penthouse right in the center of town.

David found his own chair and sitting, smiled at the man, "I last saw you at the Frankfurt airport a few months back. I think you know who I am."

Willems didn't respond but the recognition was there.

"You could've done a better job concealing yourself but we were in pretty convincing disguises so I guess I can see where you failed to pick up on Cristal or me. On top of that, it turns out that your friend in Nairobi, Jason Fletcher, is actually my friend in Nairobi."

Out of practice, David didn't pick up on Willems' visible paling at this revelation. So, Fletcher HAD seen them in Nairobi and had lied. The man had hoped this was an interrogation and arrest, but Crowe had just given away too much info. There was no way he could be allowed to live after a double agent had just been unveiled where he could get word to the BSB. He made up his mind he was going to have to go for the very gun that was just six feet away and pointed at his chest. All his other hidden weapons were out of reach and there was no telling how long this guy would wait before killing him. Hammond had emphasized last fall just how skilled and dangerous Crowe was.

David was still talking, "You may know by now that it was me who took out Jack Hammond. Our investigation so far seems to indicate that you two have had a profitable relationship for at least the last few years. Care to elaborate on that?"

There was no sense holding back that piece of info. Hammond was dead and this guy clearly knew something about the Syndicate. Anything that prolonged the inevitable confrontation was to be welcomed and if he was successful, this Crowe guy wouldn't be leaving this flat with any information anyway.

In broken English with a heavy German accent, Kurt responded, "Vee know each other for long time. Ven I vas in Bundesnachrichtendienst vee meet. I retired … medical reason. Jack contact me hinterher … after …for investigations for him. Spater … later I know, his vork vas not done for MI6, but the money vas goot. Mostly I am just middleman for things Hammond needs in Africa. But I think vat you vant to know is … Herr Becker, no?"

David nodded for him to continue.

"Herr Becker didn't know vere you ver but he know you ver traveling next day Somalia. He vood not … give information but I know he has Tochter … daughter? … in Paris. I keep my promise. She is safe."

So, Becker had held out until this animal had threatened his daughter. David considered Becker a friend but even he didn't know there was a daughter to protect. He wondered how he'd react in a similar situation if someone had him over a barrel and was threatening Tiffany or even Cristal for that matter.

As David looked down to gather his thoughts Kurt made his move. David was slow to notice the lunge and had no choice but to discharge his weapon catching Willems center chest. The momentum of the attack carried Willems forward and he took David with him over the back of the chair. Falling to the floor, David rolled him over quickly to get the top position, but it was too late, Willems was gasping his last breath as blood sprayed out of a small entry wound just over his heart. The man lost consciousness and died before David could get anything out of him like who was calling the shots above him, or if he had another contact in MI6.

He was furious with himself for losing control of the situation. This operation was a total bust as he'd uncovered nothing useful on the BSB and now he had a fucking dead guy to deal with.

MI6 had Willems under surveillance and with German law enforcement, they'd both launch investigations into this assassination. David's association, known to at least MI6 and his alibi of being home sick would not stand up for long. He'd have to come up with a plausible story or face serious sanctions back home. That story would have to be a doozy and no obvious ideas came to mind.

There was even the possibility that the political climate might demand that he be turned over to the Germans for trial assuming he could get out of Frankfurt in blood-stained clothes. After all, most would see this as a totally unsanctioned, rogue operation resulting in the death of a former intelligence officer of an ally.

How had this gone so terribly wrong? He was furious with all the amateur mistakes he was making. His only thought was that a couple of years in Guantanamo had taken their toll on his skills. Wow! No new info on the BSB and a dead guy in a foreign country. 'Shit,' what was he going to do now?

He stood over the dead body and realized just how much he himself was covered in blood. Apparently, his interrogation skills needed some brushing up as he hadn't expected the German to take such a risk. Something had to have suggested to Kurt his number was up and there was no way out for him to have taken such a desperate chance.

After a few moments, he reluctantly realized it had to be the Nairobi remark. His hubris in flaunting their escape from Germany had caused him to unveil a double agent. One that would surely be targeted as soon as Willems could get a message out to the BSB. He hadn't interrogated anyone for a few years and now realized just how out of practice he was. It was such a simple and stupid mistake. He wondered if all that time in Guantanamo had completely scrambled his brains.

He washed his hands and gun and buttoned his jacket up completely which covered most of the blood. Willems was short and stocky so wearing any of his clothes would simply attract unwanted attention. Clearly, he was going to have to visit their last cache in Frankfurt to change clothes before he tried flying back to the UK.

Working quickly as someone may have reported a gunshot, he wiped down anything he'd touched, listened for any movement in the hallway outside the flat, and made his exit. The last thing he saw was the bright flash of a weapon being discharged from somewhere down the dark hallway. Then everything went black.

Hell to Pay

The Director of the Frankfurt branch of the BND, Germany's equivalent of the CIA sat behind his desk reading the report of activities on Holzgrabben Strasse as his investigator entered closing the door behind him.

"You shot this guy with no warning? We don't even have jurisdiction in domestic matters."

The BND investigator blushed, "Well I didn't shoot the guy. It was the new kid. We had just heard a muffled gunshot from inside the room and the kid saw blood on this guy and thought he saw a gun in his hand. It was quite dark in that hallway. He's definitely upset about it and worried, but that's not the big story.

"After that tip from the Americans, we've had concerns about Willems, who by the way used to be one of ours out of Munich. Concerns that he might have moved over to the dark side in international crime, so we've had him under legal surveillance for potential international illicit activities with that BSB group.

"They called me when they spotted someone on video looking suspicious and entering Willems' building while he was out, so we hustled over there, and we were on site when Willems returned and this all happened. He was declared dead at the site. Looks like a gunshot right to the heart. The guy we have in custody says it was self-defense.

"But here's the big news. The guy we shot is one of the pair we were looking for a few months ago for those four murders, the one at the airport, the two at the Westin, and maybe even that Becker guy right around the same time. He's the main suspect now in five murders in Frankfurt.

"It only gets better. He's carrying a British passport and the passport we retrieved from the Westin had him as Canadian. It's the same photo in both passports but different names. Something smells very weird here. The passports are very professional fakes. I think this guy is some kind of assassin and we've no idea what his connection was to Willems who we've been watching since before Christmas. We're putting his fingerprints through Interpol right now but even they look tampered with and may not be useful."

Just then a young lady knocked and opened the door addressing the BND investigator, "He was carrying an e-ticket. He entered by air this morning from London and had a return for this afternoon."

As she closed the door, the Director sighed, "Well at least it's international and not some domestic thing we shouldn't even be involved in."

The BND investigator continued, "Listen, if he was sharing a room at the Westin with an accomplice back in the fall, she may be around or on her way here when he doesn't show up. Let's keep it quiet that we have him and get some live surveillance back at Willems' place and at the Flughafen, with the photo we have from her old passport. She could be here with him now or coming in from London when he misses his plane. This is the best lead we've had in months and I want to get her and get to the bottom of all these murders. Her passport also had her as Canadian as I remember."

The Director nodded approval, "What the hell do we have here, a foreign team of assassins shooting up the city?

"Get their photos up on Interpol's Most Wanted if they're not there already."

***

Cristal didn't sleep well and awoke early really worried as there was still no news from David, so he had to be in trouble. There wasn't much she could do except follow his footsteps because sitting at home waiting for answers wasn't in her DNA and the old rule, 'don't phone when in doubt' came to mind.

She made a quick call to Freja to tell her about a short trip out of town. Freja was able to extend her time looking after Tiffany even if it turned into an overnight stay. Cristal told her David was on a trip too and if he returned, he was to call her immediately.

She had to use one of her CIA cover identities for this hopefully short trip to Germany. Being CIA, she was expected to announce any travel to her German security partners in the BND, but this trip was last minute and certainly not sanctioned. Beyond that she couldn't even guess what her explanation for travel would be; safer to sneak in and out quickly she thought.

She left a voicemail at the office indicating both she and David had a stomach bug and wouldn't be in, realizing that was risky if David had been in contact with them.

She really had no idea what she'd find in Frankfurt. All she had was the address of the man David was after. David had to be in some trouble or worse if she hadn't heard from him. On top of that, the cover story was weak and might not last very long. So even the best scenario had him in some significant trouble at home.

She ducked her security detail by heading to the office first and then grabbing a taxi to the airport.

Brexit was making travel between the UK and Europe more difficult, and she had to pass through customs and immigration in Frankfurt. The Germans had passports of both her and David from the Westin last year so if David had run into a particularly astute immigration officer, he may have been ID'd for all the mayhem; but he knew that and had probably figured a way around it. She knew she was running the same risk. She was using a different name in this passport but if they had a photo sheet at immigration she might be in trouble. However, her fears were unfounded as she passed quickly through the checkpoints in Frankfurt.

Just as she was leaving the secure arrivals area three nervous men in suits approached her and identified themselves as BND, 'inviting' her to join them for a discussion at HQ. She was stuck. With three BND officers staking her out at the airport her fears for David went over the top.

Clearly, BND was on to them for some reason, and she suspected too late that whatever David was into, had caused them to be on the lookout for her too because they were linked together at the Westin last fall.

But what was she to do? She wouldn't have been satisfied sitting at home waiting for a phone call and there was no way to put up a fight with these 'allies' who were surely armed. Any resistance would probably just make things much worse, and she had a child at home to worry about who'd be missing both parents if anything went wrong. Still, she couldn't help imagining how she'd take out the three of them with a few quick disabling kicks before they could react. Given her security concerns about Al Qaeda and the BSB, being picked up by legit law enforcement was better than some of the alternatives.

An hour later she sat alone in an interrogation room at BND headquarters in downtown Frankfurt trying to master an Irish accent to match her passport; at least enough of one to fool the Germans.

No one had answered her questions around why she was being detained. They had only explained that as a Northern Irish national, according to her passport, she had the right to request assistance from the British embassy but had declined to do so. She wondered how long it would take her interrogators to figure out the passport was bogus. Germany was a strong ally but with potential BSB moles, you never could be sure who you were dealing with. For the moment she wasn't about to declare her CIA credentials, answer any questions or ask for assistance. When the time came, she'd need some kind of incredible story for the Germans, the Brits, and her own boss back in the US. At the moment, not knowing David's predicament, that storyline totally escaped her.

Her present worry about David was accompanied by concern for Tiffany. If this thing wasn't wrapped up soon Freja would be in a jam. Thankfully, the nanny had numbers to call and Walt Gargarus, CIA's head man in London, was top of the list and would ensure Tiffany was well looked after until they figured out what had happened to her parents. Still, that was definitely not ideal, and her heart broke for the jeopardy she'd put her tiny daughter in. If the Germans had tied her to the mayhem last fall, then this could be a protracted stay.

The door opened and a tall handsome German officer entered and sat across from her. It was a certainty that others, possibly including some senior people were on the other side of the one-way mirror that virtually filled one wall of the small room.

"So, I guess we can dispense with the misdirection," he said in perfect English with just a hint of a German accent. "We know that you are not really Elizabeth O'Brien from Belfast in Northern Ireland, are you?"

This was not good. Cristal simply stared at the man who looked like he was going to wait until she said something.

"Okay, maybe this will get you talking. I also think you are not Belinda Foster, a Canadian who last year participated in a number of murders here in Frankfurt."

Now she knew she was really in trouble. Her worst fears were coming true.

Still no response from her so after waiting he continued impatiently, "You need to understand that this is a VERY serious matter. We have lots of evidence that you've been involved in some capacity in at least five murders here in Frankfurt so you're not about to be released. You are going to be in our custody for quite some time. You may want to contact your embassy of whatever country you're really from because you're going to jail for a long time."

Cristal was shocked at 'five' and it showed just a little on her face.

"That's right, quite a crime spree and I'd suggest you're in a lot of trouble, Jane Doe. We have a Herr Hendrickson at the airport last fall where we have security footage of your pursuit of him, two in your registered room at the Westin, where we have one of your phony passports, and a Herr Becker the next day where we suspect your involvement. All of that last November and yesterday a Herr Willems which we know you're tied to in some way."

Cristal's heart jumped. So, David had killed Willems which meant he'd probably survived the encounter. They weren't asking her about David so what did that mean?

"Are you still going to keep up this charade that you are an Irish …" he looked down at his notes, "an Irish tourist here to take in the sights, or would you want us to believe you're a Canadian from Montreal? I hear the winter activities there are superior to our city. So, what will it be? Would you like to tell us your real name and nationality?"

This was bad … really bad! What would happen to Tiffany, because she wasn't getting out of here any time soon and where the hell was David? The best scenario was that he'd escaped and headed home or was he in some trouble here in Germany?

Langley

Director of the CIA Bill Carter had just arrived at his office in Langley Virginia when one of his aides rushed in, "Sir we have a situation. Our liaison in Germany tells us there was a police action in Frankfurt yesterday. There are two photos on Interpol's Most Wanted this morning looking for ID. One man is dead, one shot and they picked up a woman arriving at the airport today that has something to do with it. Our liaison thinks it's Cristal Serpe-Wiggins, although the Germans haven't ID'd her yet."

"Let me guess, either the dead guy or the shot guy from yesterday is David Crowe?"

"Yeah, he matches the other photo they posted. The BND shot one of them leaving the scene and they're keeping quiet on the one that died but he was a Frankfurt resident, so Crowe must be the injured one and they haven't ID'd him yet either."

"Yup, if they've picked up Cristal then they've probably connected her to that mess last November that we never owned up to with the Germans and the injured guy is likely Crowe. My guess is he was going after whoever killed that buddy that he'd contacted. I remember now that our guy Fletcher in Nairobi ID'd a suspected BSB guy in Frankfurt, so Crowe seems to have figured out who that was and gone after him. We still have no intel that the German Fletcher ID'd was the actual shooter of Crowe's friend so he may have killed the wrong guy.

"I'm still pretty certain Crowe was responsible for that aggravated waterboarding incident down in Virginia. That guy was a guard from Guantanamo who may have deserved it as Crowe told me one of them was a real sadist. He can be a hothead and he's got a thing about serious retribution … at any cost.

"I can easily see this going from bad to worse. I'm pretty sure a whole pile of shit that starts with a bunch of dead guys in Frankfurt is about to hit the fan. What a way to start the morning. I'm about to eat a pile of humble pie. We need to get on top of this immediately.

"Get the plane ready. Inform Herr Merkel of the BND that we need an emergency meeting, it has to do with those two photos, and I'll be at his office in Berlin in the morning. Also, get me Sir Richard Brighton of MI6, on the phone. He'll want to phone into this meeting too."

After a few phone calls where CIA operations admitted the meeting had to do with the Interpol posting, the locale for the meeting of the heads of the BND, MI6, and the CIA was changed from Berlin to BND's Frankfurt branch where they had the two in custody. Sir Richard Brighton had insisted on attending the meeting in person given he had a missing senior agent who Interpol was looking for.

***

It was a frosty morning in more ways than one in Frankfurt as Carter and his EA made their way into the BND's building in downtown Frankfurt. Herr Merkel had been informed of their landing at the airport and had given his approval to immigration. He also had a man waiting to clear them at security downstairs.

They made an impressive picture, the three of them; Sir Richard Brighton looking very British and regal as if he'd just come from tea with the Queen. It seemed he almost always wore an exceptionally well-tailored, bespoke navy blazer, grey slacks, and Oxford Law School tie for almost every occasion.

Herr Merkel, the tall muscular German who could have been mistaken for an Olympic pole vaulter, was also well dressed in a conservative bowtie and nicely tailored light-grey suit if not a touch small, accenting his excellent physique, and Bill Carter the quintessential image of a well-groomed CEO in a dark blue suit, fashionable silk tie, and US flag lapel pin.

Slightly jet-lagged given it was three AM in DC and having caught only a short nap on the CIA plane, Carter opened the meeting by handing out high-resolution copies of the Interpol warrant for the two characters in question, "First of all gentlemen, thank you for adjusting your schedules on such short notice and may I ask that we clear the room of staff, except of course for the recorder."

Herr Merkel hesitated but then nodded and soon they were alone except for a young woman operating a recording system.

"Gentlemen I needed to meet with you personally because I have some confessing to do and in addition to that, I need your cooperation on an extremely sensitive campaign which I believe we've all been going at separately for some time. It's extremely sensitive because we have serious concerns that some, or all of our organizations, have been infiltrated by a very dangerous organization."

Over the next twenty minutes, Bill Carter reviewed the entire fall and winter Al Qaeda operation and filled in any unannounced details of what had led to the death of Khalil al-Adel at the hands of Cristal and David. Both the German and UK Intel Chiefs already knew most of the details from their intelligence-sharing connections, but Merkel was shocked to find out they may be talking about the two people in BND custody. He also picked up on the fact that Sir Richard was NOT shocked by the revelations.

Carter went on to divulge the true nature of the firefights that had taken place in November leaving four dead men in Frankfurt. The CIA's public cover story for the activities on Christmas Day at McDonald's was laid to rest and Carter's suspicions about David seeking revenge on the most recent dead German were revealed.

"So, the woman you're holding is almost certainly Cristal Serpe-Wiggins, the recently re-instated CIA operative who is the one who rid the world of the monster Khalil al-Adel.

"According to this picture, the man you're holding is Commander David Crowe of MI6 and her fiancé. He, I offer, will have some explaining to do. I suspect he thinks the German he killed was the one who assassinated his Frankfurt contact, Herr Becker.

"No doubt David knew that Willems was a member of this infamous BSB, and I believe he must have uncovered information that Willems was the one who killed Becker. I suspect he didn't want to kill him but nevertheless, a potential source of intel on that organization is now dead.

"Kurt Willems is, of course, the one we alerted you both to when he hired one of our African agents last fall to assassinate this couple in Nairobi. Your team here may have had Willems under some form of surveillance but it's almost a certainty that he was BSB in Frankfurt and maybe even their lead man. If David is right, he killed Becker and hired the other three that tried to assassinate both David and Cristal. Surely any evidence you've collected supports these scenarios."

There was a long pause as Merkel offered no confirmation of any of this so Carter reluctantly continued by changing the subject, "So, I understand David may have been shot by your team. How is Commander Crowe may I ask?"

Merkel sneered and simply said, "He'll recover."

Carter was a little disturbed by his German counterpart's reluctance to engage as he looked over at the MI6 Chief who indicated he had a few things to say, "We've all agreed that the BSB is a global threat. The latest intel is that they may be expanding their mercenary services beyond some big agricultural players to be a generalized global muscle for hire, so the threat is escalating. As you now know, it was in fact the same David Crowe we think you're holding who recently saved my life by killing the BSB's mole in MI6 as he tried to assassinate the two of us. The mole was almost certainly one of the BSB's key operatives and I think we all know what a priority that invisible network continues to be. They are responsible for many of our problems in Africa and expanding beyond that. Their trail of murder, mayhem, and political manipulation is long and sordid. I suspect that both of your countries are just as demanding that you do something about them as well.

"I too believe our investigations will show that the German who was killed by David was also a BSB mercenary and we have evidence he was connected to the MI6 mole. It's not clear to me if one was directing the other but that doesn't excuse Commander Crowe from an unsanctioned engagement with Herr Willems two days ago."

Again, there was no engagement from the German, so Sir Richard Brighton continued, "As a matter of interest, David Crowe was on the run for several years when the BSB saw him as an existential threat and he'd been framed as the MI6 traitor by the real mole, Jack Hammond. Believe it or not, David actually hid out as a prisoner in Guantanamo fearing instant death from the BSB or MI6 and yes, I'm told he has been absent from work and his whereabouts unknown. So, it appears he was here interrogating and settling scores with another enemy of us all."

It was finally their German host's turn, "Gentlemen, much of this is news to me and not good news. You two clearly have known much more than us about what has been going on in this city for some time and that is very disconcerting. I cannot tolerate such obfuscation. I truly wish you had been more forthcoming in the past and if we're to remain partners, I think it's only fair to demand MUCH more openness in the future. You've been sitting on critical information to do with major criminal activities which our local police are wasting their time pursuing.

"According to what you've just told me, it seems counter-terrorism operations have been launched in my country with no proper jurisdiction or notice. This is of course completely unacceptable, and you can see where German agents running amok in your countries would also be unacceptable. I don't see how this doesn't escalate into an international incident when the truth leaks out. Yet you arrive here asking for cooperation. We now have five dead Germans I must account for. There are domestic investigations going on in all these cases. I'm under enormous pressure to turn these two agents over to the Frankfurt City police. We have plenty of police eyewitness reports from the recent shooting plus video surveillance and passport photos in open and active cases linking them to all these attacks last November. Some of that has leaked and the rest cannot stay secret for long. The only thing we have going in our favor is that we took these two into our custody and we haven't officially shared anything outside of the Intel community at this point. So, I bought myself a little time to handle this mess. But make no mistake; this at its very best is a major catastrophe for us. I mean really, five dead nationals and you want it all covered up as an international terrorism action? Opposition politicians in each of our countries will have a field day with this, even if these victims were criminal characters as you propose. Again, I see front-page news stories and a major international incident in our immediate future. I see no other outcome to this, even if your motives were honorable which I have yet to see evidence of."

Bill Carter could see this spiraling out of control and tried to redirect the conversation, "Again, we're sorry to have put you in this terrible situation. If I may ask, what have your investigators learned from David and Cristal? Have they offered explanations for these encounters?"

The German hesitated, "I'm told they've offered pretty much nothing. This Mr. Crowe will only say he shot Willems in self-defense but neither of them has even provided their true identities never mind how they participated in the other killings."

Carter interrupted once more, "Again I must apologize for not including German Intelligence in the operations last fall, but all of this conflict was a complete surprise to us and couldn't have been predicted. For some time we had been hunting down international terrorists as well as this infamous BSB gang. Germany only became involved last November because David thought he had contacts here who could provide key intel on operations in Somalia. Nothing to do with Germany.

"There were no operations initiated or anticipated for your country. The fireworks seem to have started when the BSB somehow were given a photo of the two of them boarding a Lufthansa flight at JFK and then intercepted them as they landed in Frankfurt on a totally unrelated pursuit of Al Qaeda in Africa.

"So, all of the mayhem was frankly unanticipated, their actions were all in self-defense and they were out of here within three days. Looking back there's still no assurance that alerting German Intelligence could have changed or even predicted any of the outcomes. Given we knew nothing of the BSB's existence in Germany or their intel on our two agents, what is there that we could have alerted you to? There was no notification because there were no operations anticipated in Germany. The plan was to meet an old contact and leave immediately. Frankly, the outcome, after all, is that you have four fewer BSB agents in Frankfurt. Again, nothing that we intended or either of us could have predicted.

"I know we left you holding the bag on dead 'bad guys' but I think you can appreciate that this was in the middle of multiple nuclear threats to our country, one of which at JFK airport was at least partially successful as you know. I think if these were nuclear threats to Germany you'd have been focused on the threat and possibly a bit distracted on the subject of keeping allies informed of impending meetings that were to be totally inconsequential.

"Still, we should've done better after the fact and you have my commitment to seeing things from your perspective and being much more forthcoming in the future. I hope we can move forward and come to some better arrangements for cooperation. But I think you know by now that David and Cristal were the targets in these encounters and carry no legal culpability for the deaths involved. Still, I offer my heartfelt apologies for the mess this has created for you. We'll do anything we can, short of initiating another international incident, to help clean up this mess."

Carter felt he'd done enough groveling and waited for a response.

Herr Merkel seemed furious and sat at the head of the table arms crossed and wanting to give his counterpart from the US a piece of his mind. He wanted to ask him how he'd feel if German Intelligence was responsible for five deaths in the US but thought the better of it.

The fact that the Brits knew more than he did about happenings in Germany was infuriating too and he put it down to the Five Eyes alliance where Germany was locked out historically. He was in favor of making it the Six Eyes but that was an ongoing, internal German political battle yet to be won. As an Intelligence Chief, he couldn't handle being left out of such matters.

As he was staring down the CIA's Director, a knock came to the door and Frankfurt's Head of Station entered. "Gentlemen I have information here that is pertinent to your meeting."

Merkel nodded for the agent to proceed.

He entered and closed the door, "About a fortnight ago we intercepted internet communications to a Munich server that originated from an internet café in the Pittsburgh area. A video was uploaded to a shadowy video relay server we've been monitoring and at first, we thought it was some propaganda piece that may have been staged. We had yet to translate the message accompanying the video.

"Yesterday one of our analysts saw this unidentified woman we picked up at the airport being led into the office and thought he recognized her. We now believe the video is of the killing of Khalil al-Adel by this very woman. Khalil isn't facing the camera but as of this morning translation of the narration of the video claims it's him and this is, in fact, the infamous McDonald's takedown. I must say it now seems clear but initially we didn't make that connection."

At that, he approached a video setup at the end of the room and inserted a USB drive.

There was no question in Bill Carter's mind that it was in fact the execution of Khalil al-Adel by Cristal. He was shocked at how close David and Cristal had come to being the victims themselves. "Gentlemen, that is in fact Cristal Serpe, the CIA agent being held here, and the video confirms her report of how it all went down. We've suspected for some time that Khalil had at least one accomplice and now we know he did, and he took a video."

Turning to the Frankfurt station manager he said, "Were you able to intercept this and stop it from being forwarded or posted on that site?"

The man blushed and looked at Herr Merkel for permission to proceed, "As I said we didn't understand what we were looking at until now and we didn't want to signal that we had infiltrated this video depository used by Al Qaeda. So no, it's been on that site for about two weeks and available for download by anyone in the Al Qaeda network who knows how to get to it on the dark web. The fact that the event was months ago could mean this video was available elsewhere before we intercepted it on this site.

"It would do no good to take it down now as copies are surely on many Jihadi websites and we'd only lose this intel source if we showed our hand. We knew Khalil had been eliminated but with the scant information we had, we didn't connect this video to that action at first. In our defense, he was wearing an elaborate disguise and we had no current photos of him.

"But to answer your question, I suspect all of Al Qaeda knows by now how their leader met his end, and this woman's face if not her full identity is well known to them by now. I tend to agree with you, she seems to be the woman we're holding."

Herr Merkel dismissed the German station chief who took his USB key and quickly left the room as Bill Carter resumed the discussion, "Herr Merkel, I think you'll agree that this information, coming out of Pittsburgh should've been shared with us some time ago. This is highly critical and time-sensitive intel. We'd have ID'd the event immediately, protected our agent, and hunted down this accomplice. Clearly, we both need to work to ensure better cooperation between our services."

Merkel sat back with the slightest of blushes on his face. All his leverage over the US for their actions in his country had just evaporated. Now he too was on the hook to bury everything short of admitting to the incompetence of his own team.

Carter continued, "Gentlemen we have now witnessed what went down at that McDonald's in upstate New Jersey on Christmas Day. To bring you up to date, our investigation is still open. Khalil must have had at least one subordinate with him who took this video. We discovered almost immediately that there were no unclaimed cars in the parking lot. It was unlikely that he'd been dropped off, and he couldn't have walked to that site, so we've been looking for one or more accomplices, but no luck so far. Now we know they took a video and shared it with the world. There may be something we can glean from the video to assist us in tracking the videographer; some metadata, a reflection, the angle to detect where he was positioned. Obviously, we will redouble our efforts to find any accomplices now that the stakes have been raised on reprisals.

"We also now have intel that we missed Khalil's number two Mustafa Habib in a drone attack in Mogadishu on the same day. We're still determined to wipe out that master cell. I think at one time or another we've had about a third of the taxi drivers in Mogadishu on the payroll but of course, they don't know they're working for us. Still no results on that front but clearly Cristal has a target on her back. There's no question they're going to want to strike back."

There was silence in the room as they all let this settle in.

Bill Carter continued, "Gentlemen we have more reason than ever to cooperate on the search and prosecution of both the Al Qaeda leadership and the BSB. We believe the BSB is likely based in the US and we have suspicions that these mercenaries aren't only running criminal operations in lawless countries but in fact have expanded their reach to be a generalized muscle for hire in Africa, the US, and likely other countries. Possibly even a recent, mysterious, yet abandoned attempt on our President.

"Unfortunately, the key operatives in the UK, Jack Hammond, and Germany, Kurt Willems, have been taken out by David Crowe before we could interrogate them. I believe the BSB will be looking for retribution, so the couple you're holding most certainly have death warrants on them both, and frankly may be the bait we need to bring the bad guys out into the open.

"I posit that these two are the most wanted law enforcement operatives in the world right now and there's just a chance they will provide an additional reason for BSB and Al Qaeda to at least attempt to join forces.

"This is only a theory at this point, but we know they move in the same circles with mercenaries from time to time and may already have crossed paths. When you think about it, they often have complimentary goals. We have no evidence they've been in communication, but our strategic team claims it's a very serious threat that we must consider. Remember, BSB's Intel network is nearly as strong as ours especially if they continue to have high-level moles in our organizations. Some of our strategic analysts believe it's only a matter of time before these two terrorist organizations find some reason to cooperate on something. They have at least one common target in Crowe and Serpe. Now I'm not saying that's a sufficient reason for them to form any kind of alliance, but it does offer one more reason for them to meet and cooperate on something. These two agents are not an insignificant nemesis for them, having taken out either their leadership or very senior members of their organizations."

Carter turned to address Merkel directly, "With your permission, I think we need to get both of your detainees in here, and let's hear their story. They're both incredibly talented intelligence officers who might be the solution to their own problem, as well as ours. I assure you they are very professional and have no animus toward Germany and with Sir Richard and me here we're quite safe in their presence."

As they sat in small talk waiting for the staff to retrieve the prisoners suddenly an alarm sounded and Frankfurt's Head of Station stuck his head back in the door and said, "The building is in lockdown and I have an armed guard at this door. It seems the male prisoner in question has overpowered a guard who took him to the Klosett … sorry, the bathroom. We have no reason to think you're in any danger. He may have escaped already or is attempting to escape wearing the guard's uniform. The guard is alive but seriously injured. If you would, please stay in this room until the All Clear."

Sir Richard Brighton simply bowed a shaking head. Merkel didn't seem happy at all. Carter simply stifled a smile. While Crowe was a handful, he had to admire the guy's gumption. Something in him wished there were more David Crowes in their combined intelligence services.

Carter finally broke the awkward silence. "While clearly, we cannot condone any of this behavior from David Crowe or even Cristal, it's clear that these two are an exceptional team. Remember they've fought off several attempts here in Germany to assassinate them.

"Cristal was kidnapped by Jihadis in the US and with David's help, killed them all to orchestrate her escape. David himself was kidnapped and held in Somalia, only to incapacitate three angry Al-Shabaab terrorists to escape and you've just seen the video of how close they came to becoming Khalil's most recent victims. All that to say that no matter what they've done, I wish I had a dozen of them in the field tracking down both the BSB and Al Qaeda."

Suddenly an announcement, translated for his guests by Herr Merkel indicated the building was cleared of any threats. Frankfurt's Head of Station reappeared and blushingly admitted that a full search of the building hadn't uncovered the prisoner who they now had declared as escaped and wanted.

Before any further discussion, recriminations or apologies were forthcoming Cristal Serpe-Wiggins, handcuffed, was ushered into the room.

She was visibly shocked at the gathering of her boss Bill Carter, Sir Richard Brighton, whom she'd yet to meet formally, and Herr Merkel who she recognized from news photos.

The gig was up and all she could think to say was, "Whoops!" which shockingly came out with a distinctive Irish lilt.

Somalia

Mustafa Habib was borderline frantic as he awaited his visitor in his basement bunker. This had to be the worst of ideas and he had no experience at being the front man of the organization.

Only a few weeks ago he'd been Al Qaeda's number two, fairly invisible and rarely under direct threat, but after Khalil's assassination, he'd been reluctantly forced into the big chair. Still, succession planning had never been a thing for Khalil or any Al Qaeda leader for that matter.

The US had announced Khalil's demise leaving out key details and now there was no doubt he was dead with the video of his assassination out there for everyone in Al Qaeda to see. On the very same day as Khalil's slaughter, the Americans had tried to take him out with a precision missile strike demolishing one of Al Qaeda's Mogadishu safe houses. It had been too close for comfort and his hearing in one ear was still impaired. Clearly, they'd attempted to wipe out the whole Al Qaeda leadership simultaneously.

His nerves were frazzled, and he found himself jumping at any sound. The impaired hearing only made that worse. This personal terror was entirely new to him and he wondered how Khalil had dealt with it. The boss never seemed to flinch or openly worry about attempts to kill him. He had either been numb to it all or had been a terrific actor. Mustafa found it hard to believe that Khalil was religious enough to think death was welcomed and he'd live on with Allah, so it had to be a different mindset. As much as Mustafa believed in everlasting life, he could not shake this fear and loathing in his new role.

While his name wasn't universally known in the world press, Jihadis, mercenaries and the like surely knew who he was. Until a few weeks ago the western world's intelligence agencies hadn't come looking for him. Now he was a marked man and all the paranoia that comes with that was new and very uncomfortable. He wasn't sleeping well at all and struggled to find a way to cope with all the new pressures. He prayed to Allah constantly to help him find a way to deal with it. Still, he was committed to the cause and wanted badly to do whatever he could to advance their agenda. So he had reluctantly agreed to this more-than-crazy meeting.

Khalil had had a fine-tuned sixth sense of threatening situations his whole life but for Mustafa personal security strategies, now that he was target number one, were a completely new responsibility. Having been known primarily as a strategist, he wracked his brains for some kind of strategy to minimize his exposure. Apparently, he was failing, as he'd agreed to this meeting with someone who raised all kinds of red flags.

There was no end to the international security forces and even mercenaries who wanted him dead, never mind his so-called impatient 'comrades' and competing factions in the worldwide Jihad. Even the local Al-Shabaab were fair-weather allies and there was always the chance that some minor grievance would shatter their uneasy alliance turning them into yet another threat.

Then there was the ever-present risk of a bold young pup in his own organization too impatient to wait for the plans of his elders and wanting to make a quick jump to the top by a ruthless coup d'état with daring plans to put the organization's aggressiveness on steroids.

Now he wished he'd paid much more attention to how Khalil had handled these challenges.

How the Americans had found him for that missile strike on their Christmas Day was a VERY uncomfortable mystery, as there was always the fear they could do it again. They must have known by now that they missed him and there was no doubt they'd try again. Still, no amount of grabbing potential traitors and 'leaning' on them had turned up any leads on how the Americans had decided to bomb that particular building just after he entered.

The missile had taken out the entire building he had entered only minutes before, but apparently, they were unaware of the tunnel used to transit to another building for the very purpose of avoiding such attacks. Ever since Abu Musab al-Zarqawi was killed in Iraq by a precision missile attack, tunnels to a nearby structure were more than a good idea for Jihadi leadership.

Until now, all of Al Qaeda Somalia's security precautions had been Khalil's doing, not his, because Khalil wanted it that way. Understandably he wanted to handle his own security, not trusting anyone.

Mustafa was now keenly aware of the lengths he had to go to in order to avoid exposing himself to assassination attempts. Even his own inner circle wasn't above suspicion as he assumed some of them would relish taking over his role if there was even the slightest suggestion that the boss wasn't up to the task or showed even the slightest weakness. Unlike Khalil, Mustafa didn't have the brutal reputation of dealing with even the hint of any internal subterfuge. That he put down to Khalil's short foray with ISIS when they were at their peak. Mustafa had never been baptized in that kind of brutality where barbarism was the order of the day, even for internal issues.

On investigating the Christmas missile, his own methods of leaning on people had taken him to the edge of what most would think of as torture, and even then, he was uncomfortable treating fellow Muslims in such a manner. Besides, he had a deeply held feeling that information gathered from torture was unreliable at best. Anyway, his efforts had been fruitless, and he was left as nervous as before. The Americans apparently had some way of tracking him and he had no idea what it was.

Today would be his biggest nerve-wracking test yet as a new leader, and he seriously questioned how he'd been talked into it.

He was about to meet with someone he only had friendly assurances was an important potential collaborator. Several 'trustworthy' contacts had suggested the meeting but now, as head of Al Qaeda, he was all too aware that deep subterfuge from apparent 'friends' was the best way of getting to him.

The little information he had on the visitor was that he was either American or closely tied to a shady American organization who'd have 'an offer he couldn't refuse'. Given what he perceived as the sky-high expectations of his new position, he was eager to get something going and was willing to take the risk if there was any chance a solution for new attacks might be gleaned from such a meeting. His closest aide, Nasir had at first used the English expression 'Nothing ventured, nothing gained,' but had later flip-flopped and warned against it.

Yet even though all the appropriate assurances had been given, there was always the chance this emissary was a deep undercover agent of Western Intelligence who desperately wanted to eliminate Al Qaeda's new leader. There was never a way to have enough intel on strangers, especially in the secretive domain these mercenaries worked in.

Possibly out of overcompensation for his fear or maybe sheer nervousness he decided to take a bold, unexpected, and dangerous path. Wearing a bulletproof vest and against his team's advice, Mustafa decided to show some bravado and face the danger straight up by meeting the man at the door of the house he'd personally picked for this meeting only an hour ago.

As he stood in the entrance, two men exited a local taxi. One of them, Mustafa's security man, nodded, indicating all security precautions had been taken.

Mustafa unconsciously glanced skyward. It was unlikely western enemies would send in a missile from a drone if they had one of their agents in the blast zone, but he couldn't help the furtive glance. Beyond that, he'd been told that the drones flew silently and so high that he was unlikely to see or hear them.

As the visitor approached, he bowed slightly in a sign of respect and said, "As-salaam 'Alaykum," seeming to know the local customs, Mustafa took the man's hand to shake it believing him to be western and said, "Marhaba."

Mustafa's bodyguard, who had accompanied the man and seeing Mustafa's nervousness, bent forward and whispered, reassuring Mustafa again that all security steps had been taken and that the man had no weapons or electronic devices on him.

As part of their protocol, the man had even been forced to strip his outer garments and wash his hands, in case he harbored some chemical weapon. Still, another guard standing with Mustafa kept his AK-47 at the ready. Everyone was on edge as they all recognized the danger in such a first meeting.

Inside, again in their below-ground bunker, they settled on a ceremonial rug with tea and flatbread as was customary. The guest opened the dialogue, "Brother Mustafa, I hope I can call you brother as I believe we're in this fight together and most certainly on the same side. Thank you for your hospitality, and your meeting with me. I bring sincere greetings and admiration from the organization I represent. I also bring condolences on the loss of your previous leader and praise for the recent successes your people have achieved."

Moustafa was surprised to hear the man spoke good Arabic even though there was the hint of some yet-to-be-discovered foreign accent. Surprisingly, he suspected the man wore some subtle form of makeup darkening his skin to blend in with the locals. In dress and appearance, he truly looked like a local peasant and could have passed unmolested through the city market. Mustafa was thoroughly impressed with the disguise and suddenly wondered how many other foreign agents were roaming the streets looking as authentically local as this man.

The man continued, "You can refer to me as Mr. Tom. I thank you and I honestly appreciate the risk you're taking in meeting with me. I think you know I am also taking a big risk, so I won't waste our time and come right to the point. My organization has a proposal for joint cooperation in a single project that I think you'll find very attractive and rewarding. We think this comes at an opportune moment and may be just the thing you may need to launch your new command of your organization."

Moustafa thought this was a bit disrespectful and more than impertinent. This opening defined the man as a westerner and likely an American; jump right in, establish control, bypass the niceties of relationship building. He hadn't even touched the refreshments or commented on them as someone from the region would've done.

Sizing the man up further he finally nodded as if to say 'continue.' His pre-briefing had indicated this emissary was well connected with a shady organization that Western Intel had labeled BSB and that they seemed to share some of the same enemies. Rumors had circulated about such a shadowy mercenary group, but the Al Qaeda network didn't yet know what BSB meant or what their real purpose and goals were. The one thing he was assured of was that there had been no conflicts or even interactions, positive or negative, with this group to date so he was eager to find out as much as he could about them.

Mr. Tom hesitated to ensure he had his host's full attention as he seemed distracted, and then continued, "We represent powerful political and commercial people with interests across the world but predominantly here in Africa where we've helped new governments secure their positions and develop their economies. Many of them, as you know, are Muslim governments who are naturally suspicious of the West and who are very appreciative of our assistance.

"If you've never heard of us then we've been successful. While we've been very active in Africa, we have also been very quiet about our successes. We like to keep a low profile so many of our accomplishments go unheralded, but I can assure you they are numerous and significant.

"For understandable reasons, Western Governments seem to dislike our objectives and methods and as a result, we've found ourselves frequently in conflict with them. They like to think they are exclusively in charge of international foreign and commercial policy and only they can pick the winners and losers in the politics of Africa. This limits the prospects of legitimate Muslim governments, who are our clients. We like to think that we're here to level the playing field. Our supporters, mostly large commercial entities, are very pleased with our accomplishments."

Even though his Arabic was excellent, Mustafa was more convinced by the minute that this man was American by his choice of words and idioms, like 'level the playing field.'

Mustafa squirmed a little as the man continued, "As you know, Western Governments' international policies often exclude or are a detriment to legitimate Muslim-based political parties and national aspirations. You know more than I that there's a fair amount of Islamophobia in the West and that has been growing in recent years. So, what we see is an uneven playing field and a great reluctance on the part of the West to give Muslim governments the credit they're due for all the advances they've made. To be very frank, they just don't want Muslim governments to be successful. Again, that's Islamophobia in action.

"We believe these western bullies shouldn't have complete reign over the progress of African Governments who have the best interests of their own citizens in mind as opposed to Western Governments who only care about their native commercial interests. This is the situation globally and includes the policies of many Western Governments but it's particularly true of the American government and their imperialistic maneuvering.

"Now to be sure, our sponsors have their own agenda which simply stated is reasonable and honest profit from their commercial operations, but absent all of the political influence of the Western Governments. Often our funders are in a position to make major investments in growing economies if commercial arrangements that are good for them and the new young governments can be reached. We're really not interested in politics.

"Our organization brings much more than money to the table. We bring international expertise on building successful industries as well as exceptional access to international markets that are often closed to African countries. This has been shown to be an incredible opportunity for new Muslim governments to establish themselves with a robust economic component to their success. You cannot maintain control if your people remain poor and cannot eat.

"So, to be precise, you and I have some of the same friends and enemies as I'm sure you've been told by our mutual friends. Our interests are strictly commercial and have nothing to do with the moral or religious leanings of any client states or their particular brand of politics or governance. We only want countries and governments in Africa to be able to deal with who they choose; on terms and conditions they feel are fair. Our commercial activities are mostly agricultural, so we apply our skills to rapid agricultural development, land use, productivity, and opening markets, none of which seem to conflict with your completely independent efforts to secure and protect Muslim lands. So, in many ways, we support your aspirations for vibrant and successful Muslim societies.

"As just one example, but an especially important one, Genetically Modified Organisms or GMOs are the greatest advance in agriculture since pesticides. African countries MUST have this advancement in agriculture. GMOs provide much greater yields on crops due to plant growth rates and ultimate size, insect and disease protection, and drought resilience. So as African countries enter the world markets and expand their farming land, GMOs are critical to their competitiveness, rapid growth, and success. African crops frequently fail due to infestations or drought and to compete you need maximum yields even in sub-prime soils.

"For various reasons, Western Governments have targeted this economic growth. As a result, they've outlawed GMOs and in other cases forced restrictive labeling regimes for GMOs, closing markets and cutting off the rapid development envisaged by these new and expanding African economies. In Africa, Western Governments have put tremendous financial and political pressure on nascent governments to yield to their selfish demands and demanding they too outlaw GMOs. That is clearly not in the best interests of the people and the growing economies of these countries. In fact, these tactics are designed to cripple new development and protect the West's domestic agricultural businesses at the cost of our sponsors who are global players. In the US domestic market, farmers have a very loud and powerful political lobby which of course affects international trade policies that are very detrimental to emerging economies as we find here in Africa. Add the Islamophobia and you have a disaster for new African countries.

"In this one example, we are the solution to this by helping governments throughout Africa and supporting them so GMOs can thrive, and labeling isn't an issue for international sales. Then agricultural products can be marketed directly to the right buyers with our help or to Western Markets through intermediaries in Europe and the East where labeling restrictions can, with our assistance, be bypassed for flow-through sales; a win-win all round. We make our money through agricultural commodities you need like farm equipment, GMO seeds, fertilizers, and the like.

So, both we and our clients benefit enormously when we cooperate.

"This is just one example which across Africa is worth billions. I think you can see our value to Africa and the fact that we have no conflict with your own goals.

"I'm sure you don't care at all about our expertise in agriculture but that's just it, we're not in conflict but we often run into the same obstacles and share the same enemies; bullies from the West trying to project their own morals, laws, politics and business practices on to Muslim countries."

Mustafa thought, 'This guy is a real salesman and he's selling hard. There's no assurance that they even care about Muslims but much of what he says is true.' He nodded for the man to continue.

"My organization has lots of money, people in high places with power, intel, and influence in several major Western Governments. We have strong political connections and more importantly, military-style global intelligence and the will and muscle to make things difficult for Western Governments to achieve their greedy goals.

"You, on the other hand, have complementary objectives and lots of capability to initiate and carry out heroic direct action. We see no reason we shouldn't start working together, at least in areas where we have common goals and on one project we have in mind at the moment. Our feeling is that we'd make an ideal, deadly and effective force if we united on some limited and well-defined projects.

"In general terms, our organizations are too different and have different ultimate objectives to consider anything more all-encompassing or permanent if you understand my meaning. Each of us is concerned for our own objectives and security. So, we're not proposing any kind of a long-term merger, just an alliance of convenience from time to time on mutual targets.

"We would propose working on this one project we have in mind and then assess where we individually want to go from there. We'd only be interested in situations where it was a win-win for both of us."

Moustafa finally spoke, "What or who is this organization you speak of?"

Mustafa had a general understanding of the BSB, but he wanted to hear the perspective from an 'insider'.

Tom smiled and relaxed just a bit, "As you can appreciate, we don't have a Public Relations department. It wouldn't serve our interests to be very visible. In fact, the opposite is true. We want certain things to happen without the world knowing who we are and why we're doing what we're doing.

"Let's just call us the Syndicate for now. Some Western Intel organizations have labeled us the BSB, a derogatory name meaning Bean Stalk Boys because they assume we started by working for big US agricultural entities to drive their commercial objectives. As I said, some of that is close to the truth as our founding members are specialists in agricultural commodities as well as farming policies, procedures, and food marketing.

"Actually, we're now an independent group of people delivering on the agenda for large and rich entities with specific goals in mind. Yes, that would include the agricultural sector but other initiatives as well. I gave you one real-life example but I'm sorry, I can't be more specific than that at this time."

Moustafa paused and stared him down, "How do I know you're not CIA trying to trap me?"

"I can see where that's an obvious issue for you. All I can offer are my references and actions we can prove were initiated by us, some of which your friends have already confirmed, or I wouldn't have been able to get this meeting. I think you'll find we have several common friends who can vouch for my organization.

"But of course, there's always a significant risk we must deal with in this war we're engaged in. One thing you need to be assured of is that we're just as committed to our goals as you are to yours. You have major capabilities and so do we. And of course, there are times that our objectives won't align but at the moment they do, and our complementary capabilities could be very useful."

Mustafa thought about this for a long moment staring down his visitor. The man had just admitted they wouldn't always be on the same side yet here he was, now with the knowledge of what Al Qaeda's leadership looked like, one of their safe houses but more importantly they had demonstrated they knew how to find him; something Khalil would never have allowed. How much more did he know that he wasn't disclosing. The 'playing field' as he had called it, was definitely not level in this regard. Al Qaeda had no comparable intel on this BSB or Syndicate as they called themselves.

He continued, "Say more about these common enemies and complementary capabilities."

"Well, for one, there are the two people that killed your brother Jabir … I understand you may not know what happened to him but yes, I'm afraid to tell you that we have solid evidence that he was indeed assassinated by the woman he had kidnapped and the man they were trying to free from Guantanamo. The entire Burundi team was killed and two others from a Pittsburgh cell were captured the very night Abu Nistal was released from that illegal prison in Cuba. I'm sure you also know that a bold attack on an American mall was also thwarted the next day; again by these two.

"By the way, the person your Burundi team knew as Abu Nistal used the name Daniel Boone with the Americans after he was captured. His real name is Commander David Crowe of MI6. At the time he was a discredited MI6 agent with a kill order on him and for some reason, he chose to 'hide' in Burundi and later in Guantanamo. He's a target of our Syndicate as well because he has killed several of our members in Europe."

Mustafa didn't know but he'd always assumed his younger brother was dead or in the hands of the CIA, yet he sat stoically. Even with his religious fervor and belief in life everlasting, his thoughts turned to his little brother. His fondest memories were teaching him football when they were young. But these reflections would have to wait until later.

This guy might indeed have good high-level intelligence but so far, he seemed not to know of the video showing the woman killing Khalil or he'd have led with that one. The man with her in the video was probably this David Crowe although they only had the back of his head in the video and according to 'Mr. Tom', the Burundi team, most of the Jihadis who could identify him, were all dead.

Mustafa, being more religious than Khalil at least felt the contentment that his brother was now rejoicing with Allah as he had died in Jihad.

Mr. Tom continued, "We've chased these two assassins and a few months ago we lost them on their way here to Mogadishu."

Mustafa was stunned but tried hard not to show it. So sometime between his younger brother being killed and Khalil's encounter with this team, they'd been here in Mogadishu. That made them the key suspects in the missile attack on the safe house he'd barely escaped.

Tom continued, "We assume you were behind the cobalt attack on JFK airport and possibly another foiled nuclear attack on New York City. It would seem reasonable that they must have picked up some intelligence when they were here in Mogadishu that led to the intercept in New York."

The American picked up on Mustafa's increasing unease and decided to offer more in terms of establishing his credentials. "The CIA has two deep covert agents in Mogadishu who would have hosted this pair. We don't know their local names or whereabouts in terms of identifying them for you, but they've been here at least a year and somehow tracked your counterfeit police car. That's how they brought in that strike on you."

Mustafa was stunned. This guy either had cooked up a great story or more likely his intelligence was truly amazing and had to be coming directly from sources high up at CIA Headquarters.

So, it had been the police car that had betrayed them. He wasn't sure how that could have worked but given it was destroyed in the missile attack, it meant they'd lost the means to track him.

GPS came to mind. There might have been some way for them to track him using the GPS built into modern vehicles. That made sense and the fact that their tracking tool had been destroyed in the failed missile attack was a great comfort.

At least he was getting some important intel out of this meeting and now he was glad he had agreed to it. He was more than curious to find out how they'd discovered Khalil had created a dummy police vehicle but felt it better not to divulge his paucity of information on what was going on in his own backyard. Still, there was a mystery around what intel the CIA had discovered that led them to the dam attack north of NYC.

Tom continued, "We suspect this couple may have had some role in the assassination of your previous leader which the US is, of course, boasting of."

Mustafa decided not to enlighten the interloper. Clearly, there were limits to this man's intel inside US Intelligence if he couldn't confirm that the same woman who had been kidnapped had killed Khalil. Or possibly he knew and had decided to hold back that information for some reason.

"As I said, the man's real name is Commander David Crowe and he's an MI6 agent and the woman you know as Cristal Serpe or Wiggins, is a re-engaged CIA agent and they're personally responsible for wiping out your team in the US and much of my organization's German and UK operations. As you might appreciate, rebuilding a professional and well-connected organization in these Western Democracies is a monumental and risky task and so these two have cost us both dearly. We'd like to see them dead but even they aren't worthy to be our primary targets.

"We propose that the CIA, MI6, and the FBI would appear to be our primary common enemies. They, along with German Intelligence, the French, and others, are hunting both of our organizations. The Americans are the lead, and we want to cut off the head of the snake as they'd put it."

Mustafa was still suspicious of this man and his shady organization. An organization he'd never even heard of before this meeting was requested only two days ago.

One part of the story that made no sense was that this David Crowe was MI6. According to younger brother Jabir, this Crowe, using the nom de guerre of Abu Nistal, had actually led an Al Qaeda-affiliated cell of the FLN in Burundi and had been captured by the woman and held in Guantanamo. What was a western agent doing in Burundi helping out and was it even possible that someone could hide as a prisoner in that American torture site in Cuba? Who would do such a thing? The Americans were thought to be diabolical in their interrogation techniques. Had he actually been a prisoner or were the Americans simply hiding him there for some reason?

Yet Khalil himself, before his fatal trip to the US had also been certain Crowe was a western agent. He too must have wondered why an agent of an ally would be held in that Cuban hellhole. Some of this man's explanation was a bit too crazy to make sense. Either he wasn't relating the full story, or he was misdirecting for some reason.

Still, why not get as much intel from this mercenary while he had him, "Let me start Mr. Tom, or whatever your real name is, with asking how you came to find me and set up this meeting? You understand I'm sure, that I must be careful and frankly we know very little about this organization you speak of. So how did you find me?"

Tom smiled, "Unlike the CIA who need to deal with a large unwieldy institution, double-check all their informants, and stay within the confines of their American constitution, we have no such constraints. We work on a much freer and stripped-down 'tradecraft' basis. With no rules, the right contacts, lots of money, as well as occasionally trading favors, many obstacles can be overcome. Often, we need to acquire materials, other resources such as forgeries, exert or hire muscle and as a result, we share some of the same friends. It's not important how we found you, just that we have now met and that we have common interests and complementary capabilities.

"Our mutual friends have only good intentions for each of us as we're both important partners to them and they wouldn't want to disrupt their good working relationship with either of us. So, I wouldn't want to put any of them in jeopardy or interfere with your ties to them.

"Frankly, we want to limit how much you know of us and how to track us. Just as I'm sure you don't want to divulge more of your network and operations than is necessary for us to cooperate on this initial mission."

Mustafa was unsatisfied. This was way too one-sided. The Syndicate already knew how to get to him, Al Qaeda's top man, and they could probably do it again whenever they wished. He had no such information on them. In fact, he didn't even know where this Mr. Tom hailed from or his position in the Syndicate, who ran the Syndicate, how many were at the center of the organization, or even where they were based. Still, they were in it now and he wanted to hear what the plan was, so he decided to move on, "Why do you think we need each other?"

The Syndicate's emissary continued, "Our two organizations have occasional overlapping objectives, but very different capabilities. As I've said we have access to important resources including money and we have well-placed contacts in very high government and intelligence arenas in the West and in countries where we do business.

"We've had great success in moving political opinion in several countries but we're only successful in that we're invisible. As a result, our network is extremely fragile and susceptible to collapse if discovered. If one of our well-compensated and well-connected government members were caught, they'd likely save their own skin by making a deal with law enforcement and our network would surely be severely damaged. There are limits to our compartmentalization.

"We go to great lengths to ensure these key, high-level people don't know much about our network but still we're vulnerable in some places. Unfortunately, they're mostly motivated simply by money so if any of them are discovered we'd be forced to abandon them, or something more permanent and we try to ensure they know that.

"Therefore, we never take credit for anything we do. It wouldn't serve our purposes to attract the attention of any law enforcement types. We need to keep our fingerprints off any actions we take and make it exceedingly hard for Western Intelligence to learn anything about us.

"Trying to stay invisible, we do outsource as much as possible. For direct action and to stay unconnected to that action, we use subcontractors who frequently don't know who they're working for. Even our subcontractors don't want to be visible, findable, or pursued by law enforcement. When we contract with such partners, we're focused on their unique ability to complete the mission in a way that neither they nor we are pursued. That's the proven formula for us and it has worked very well. Even better if there's misdirection involved, and law enforcement is sent off in a different direction.

"Your organization, on the other hand, is more than happy to take credit for your attacks and you even use it as a recruiting tool. Your members are ultra-loyal for religious reasons and would gladly die before giving up your network. Death as a Jihadi is honorable and rewarding as I understand. Their loyalty to the cause has paid big dividends for Al Qaeda. Just look at the torture some of your people have endured in rendition sites, as well as Abu Ghraib and Guantanamo, without giving up enough information to hurt your network.

"Osama Bin Laden hid for years but there were members of Al Qaeda who knew where he was, and some were even captured alive. The same must have been true of Khalil. Our intel is that the Americans didn't find him even though they were working very hard at it and had some of your team in custody. Our information is that it was Khalil who found them and not the other way around. Until the last, they couldn't find him and by that time they must have interrogated many.

"So, as you see, we both have powerful networks, but they differ in important ways that you and the Syndicate can exploit."

There was a long pause and then the guest continued, "On a related and important subject, our understanding is that Khalil was essentially your fundraiser-in-chief, so in his absence that must be more of a challenge for your new organization. As a peace offering and a welcoming gift of a sort, the Syndicate will deposit one hundred thousand American dollars in an account of your choosing, completely at your disposal, to cover any initial expenses, no questions asked, should we agree to join in this current effort.

"It may not be much but it's a start. With my money, intelligence sources, political contacts and logistics, and your manpower and bravado, there are certain objectives we can best pursue together."

Mustafa stared the guy down and thought, 'What would Khalil do in a situation such as this?' Likely he'd have killed this guy given he was surely an American and Khalil's hatred of Americans and the bigotry that had cost the lives of his father and older brother back in Detroit were well known. Yet this could turn out to be a great opportunity. With Al Qaeda losing their highly respected leader, they needed something to show they were still active and effective. At the moment Mustafa was a bit at his wit's end not knowing where to go next and this could be the opportunity he needed.

"Please get to the meat of the matter as they say. What exactly are you proposing?"

Mr. Tom smiled, shuffled in his sitting position, and relaxed a little more. His boldness in setting up this meeting dissipated the moment he stepped out of that taxi and came face to face with the leader of an organization who killed … no martyred at the drop of a hat. There had always been a chance these Neanderthals would kill him before he even got his message out, but it looked like he had piqued their interest.

Mr. Tom continued, "For reasons that should be obvious to you, we'd like to eliminate several members of the US law enforcement and political establishment. Ideally the heads of the CIA, FBI, NSA, and the Democratic Senate and House leaders as well as key members of the Intelligence Oversight Committees in the US who as a group have much of the classified institutional knowledge of our existence and the drive to pursue us. To make it appear like a terrorist attack these assassinations will all be simultaneous and on a major US holiday. Our goal is to disrupt some of their investigations but more importantly, we want to deliver a message to them and others pursuing us that we can take them out at will.

"We won't take credit, but I think the message will be clear. 'Get too close to us, or you for that matter, and pay the price.' The public message will be that Al Qaeda can strike when and where they want in the US mainland.

"Our organization thinks there are limits to how much they know about us, but we want to eliminate as much as possible while sending a strong message.

"In one area, there's some concern that they're closing in on identifying some of our leadership. We feel if this attack is successful, we can change the balance of power and possibly get some people into key jobs who will be a benefit to us. Certain investigations can be killed or redirected. We're really not a threat to their National Security, only to their commercial aspirations overseas. So, with the right people in the right jobs, their focus can be shifted and that is key to the Syndicate's continued security.

"As a follow-up to the attack, we have high-level political allies who have domestic plans to influence the replacement of these leaders with people who are more amenable to our cause. It's clear we won't get all of our targets in one attack, but likely enough to achieve our purposes. As I've demonstrated, that will make life for new Muslim governments in Africa much better too.

"In exchange for your cooperation we'll allow you to take full credit for the operation and deliver to you, access for assassination, the two people who killed your brother, your entire Burundi team who infiltrated the US, and possibly your former leader."

This man's intel was good given he seemed to know some of the details about the Burundi insertion and their attempted operations.

Mr. Tom was still pitching his deal, "We will provide all intel, planning, materials, logistics, and funding for the attacks and you will provide the manpower for an attack that will be magnificent and very public, demonstrating once again that you can retaliate by taking the fight to the top of the US power structure on their own home territory, on an important American holiday.

"As you might imagine, the Syndicate has major backers in the US, and they'd normally not support an attack in their home country but in this case, we have mutual enemies and it's important for the survival of the Syndicate that some or all of these obstacles be removed. As I said, our goals won't always align but they do in this case we believe.

"Of course, we must remain invisible, so we want none of the credit for our participation. It must be seen as a terrorist attack. As to your two personal targets, we'll leave it to you to decide how to deal with them, but we'll provide your team with a precise location on them after the main target has been prosecuted. If our planning works out, they will both be within easy reach of your team involved in the attack. All you need to do is agree to the detailed plan we'll provide and furnish a team that can carry out your orders exactly. We'll take care of everything else including manufacturing, delivery, and placement of the specialized and powerful IED-type weapons that we need. Your people simply have to pull the trigger."

He smiled waiting for Mustafa Habib's response.

Mustafa smiled, "Why should we accept the notion that you want to be complicit in an attack on your own country?"

Tom smiled back, "Because we're transnational. We're an international force and certain US nationals are standing in our way to achieving our goals. It's as simple as that. We could do it ourselves but again we need to remain invisible, so a terrorist attack is the best solution.

"You want Western Governments out of Muslim lands, and we have no objection to your goals or your methods. As I've said, we've helped Muslim Governments get a foothold in several African countries where you too are involved in the fight. Burundi is a good example where the opposition there is supported by us and where Abu Nistal and your cell were engaged in fighting the West's evil and corrupt puppet administration, although we have to admit, it's still a mystery to us as to why Commander David Crowe was involved.

"To answer your question directly though, on this project our goal is not to kill a lot of Americans, but it is to cut the head off various snakes in the government which supports your goals too. So, what do you say?"

After a long pause and showing no emotion, Moustafa said, "You understand I don't know you and therefore I don't trust you. For all I know, you could still be CIA.

"You'll have to leave this with me so I can do some checking. You should provide our mutual friend with enough detail on any operations you've run so we can check you out, but if you're who you say you are, and everything turns out to be true then I'd want to hear more about this planned operation. I can say that if conditions are right, and we believe in the quality of your proposed plan, we'd be interested in working together on this first mission as you call it."

In his head Mustafa could see the reprisal for Khalil his comrades expected. Killing a few top American officials was attractive but the image he had in mind was a decapitated female CIA agent, right on US soil, on their media sites to avenge both his brother and Khalil. It would firmly establish his leadership and his ability to attack the West as well. He needed something like this to motivate the thousands around the world who were looking to see if Al Qaeda still had what it took in Khalil's absence. If this guy was as good as he claimed then much of the risk in setting up a major attack would be taken care of and if anything went wrong in the run-up, it couldn't be traced back to a failed Al Qaeda attack. His team only had to come in at the last moment to pull the trigger as it were. So, there was little exposure of Mustafa himself or his assets in such a plan. Except for the fact that this man had been able to track him to the point of a meeting.

Mr. Tom smiled, "I thought you might be interested but we have to move quickly, there's a lot of logistics to put in place and our goal is an attack on America's Independence Day, July fourth. That only gives us a couple of months to pull it all together."

As Tom left, Mustafa smiled. There was even more reason now to work with this man if he turned out to be real. Shortly before he left, Khalil had let it be known that he'd started a program to find a way to hit the US on their Independence Day, but many details had gone with him to his unmarked US grave, rumored by the press to be on a US military base somewhere in the deserts of Nevada.

Khalil had loved the idea of getting the attention and notoriety of attacking the Great Satan on well-publicized holidays like Christmas just to show he could stick his finger in their eye any time he wanted, and they could do nothing to stop him. This was well known within Al Qaeda and the Christmas failure was still reverberating throughout the network. Now, an Independence Day attack was an expectation throughout Al Qaeda but until now Mustafa had few ideas on how to make something like that a reality. There was even a chance he could complete Khalil's earlier plan for Independence Day and use the Syndicate's attack as a cover.

His smile faded as he returned to the present. The fact that this man had found him was more than disturbing. Khalil had been a master of security among other things. 'This would never have happened under Khalil's watch', he thought. Now there was a man and an organization that knew who he was, what he looked like, and how to find him. 'What would Khalil do?'

Nasir Abboud, Mustafa's top lieutenant entered to get an update on what had just happened, "So who was your mystery guest? I was surprised you agreed to meet him given we had so little intel on him."

Mustafa frowned, "He already knew where I was and how to find me, and I thought it best to know what was going on. We need to find out how he got here. He claims mutual friends put us together.

"Anyway, it turns out he's some kind of mercenary with what he claims to be an organization simply called the Syndicate that has high-level connections in various country's politicians and intelligence, and he claims to have lots of money and resources. He also claims they've had more than a few successes here in Africa which we need to check out.

"Some of his intel is truly amazing if it's all true.

"He wants to team up with us for an attack in the US on their Independence Day which is July fourth. He claims we have similar goals and targets. If we agree they will fund and organize a major attack if we supply the manpower and take the credit. Apparently, they need to remain invisible."

Nasir was shocked, "And you're going to go along with it?"

"So far I see little risk to us and a major opportunity. Beyond what they're planning, we could use the cover of their operation to launch an attack of our own. I've had some early thoughts on what that might be. I think that is what Khalil wanted and would do. Use them and leverage off them.

"His one mistake is assuming we have similar goals. They have enemies in the US and want to assassinate them. Our goal is to use terror to change the political behavior of the West. They won't retreat from Arab lands until their population grows tired of being terrorized and or suffer major financial losses as they did after 9/11. Assassinating a few big shots isn't going to terrorize the average westerner or kill their economy. That was what was so appealing about those planned attacks on New York and the shopping mall. Every American could see himself as a target and closing malls and a major city like New York would definitely hurt their economy.

"No, we may play along with this Mr. Tom, but we need to establish something that will terrorize the population and my own plan might just do that.

"But I have some sad news for you. He claims to know for sure what happened to your comrades from Burundi. They're all dead including my brother and your leader Jabir. Killed by the very same witch we saw on the video butchering Khalil.

"This man also claims that Khalil was right, and Abu Nistal is actually an MI6 agent working with this woman. I forget his western name but some of the story about his capture, his imprisonment, and his release makes no sense to me. Apparently, he too is responsible for my brother's death and much more. We need to treat him as an enemy no matter what we thought of him when he was with the FLN."

Nasir dropped his head, "Your younger brother Jabir is now with Allah. He was a true Jihadi, a martyr, and a great leader to all of us in Burundi. As to Abu Nistal, we knew he was a westerner, so we never discussed our full objectives in front of him. His contributions were intelligent and strategic, but he was very timid in operations where people might be killed. I put that down to his lack of knowledge of Allah's mercy but still, it's shocking that he might have been ... he was and still is a western agent. If he killed Jabir, my hatred for these infidels only grows. Insha'Allah we will have our revenge.

"But master this ... Mr. Tom, we know nothing about him or his organization. How is it that they found you? I don't like it that we have 'mutual friends.' Mutual friends don't betray your location or set up meetings with strange characters like this man. I've no doubt he's an American and they cannot be trusted.

"You must be careful. You know that not only are the Western Intelligence agencies after you but our whole network is watching to see how you handle the organization in these early months after Khalil's death. You cannot be seen as weak or subservient to some other organization. I think for the moment at least you must keep any alliance with this Syndicate very quiet and in our small circle.

"As you say, assassinating a few big shots may not achieve our goals or impress our network. This other plan you speak of would have to be our central focus and deliver on our goals. A double attack on the same day would be desirable, yes, but we must be seen as in control of it all and not a puppet of some other organization.

"What can you tell me about the second plan?"

"I'm afraid Nasir, it's a bit too early for that. Khalil had an idea but if he had detailed plans then he took them with him. I need some time to complete the planning and assess whether we can do it but I agree with all of your points. Working with this Syndicate comes with several problems. We cannot be seen to be delivering on THEIR agenda so information on how they're involved should be kept between us only.

"Again, as you say, our immediate issue is how they found us and what they know about us."

London

Still wearing an oversized guard's uniform after his mandatory stay with the BND, David made the short walk to retrieve everything he desperately needed, stashed in a drop box in downtown Frankfurt. The BND had his phone with all his messages and notes, so he was thankful he still remembered the combination to the cache they'd hidden in town last fall. He thanked his lucky stars that they'd had the foresight to stash a couple of very helpful care packages around town and this was the last one. There was no telling in their business when you might need fresh clothes, ID, a first aid kit, weapons, a credit card, and cash even when your stay in a foreign country was intended to be short and benign. Cristal had insisted on this preparedness when they were leaving the US and he'd never skip this step again.

The shoulder hurt even more since he'd had to overcome the BND guard to get free. There were likely a few torn stitches that might need some fixing, but he felt for the unfortunate guard who was certainly being treated for a concussion.

The evidence against him at the BND had to have been mounting and he didn't feel like going into long complex explanations on how so many dead locals were attached to his visits. There was also no telling how cooperative the German Intel Community would be in these matters and he didn't want to spend weeks or months in their custody to find out.

It was a sure thing they'd figure out in the end who he was, and international protests would be filed but it was better to try to negotiate from home at MI6 than from a German jail cell.

That was only half of the problem. This would certainly get back to the boss but more immediate than that was Cristal. 'God knows what she thinks has happened to me or worse … what she's done about it?'

He decided that a call to her with his newly acquired burner phone, while he was still trapped in Germany avoiding the hunt, was out of the question. There was nothing she could do to help, He needed to get back home by his own means and handle her face to face with some plausible excuse.

Given his fugitive state from the very capable BND and using his limited German, he quickly hitched a ride to the Frankfurt Hauptbahnhof. Avoiding the police he saw at the station, he took an InterCity Express train to Strasbourg, France arriving back in London on an EasyJet shuttle from Entzheim in the afternoon.

He headed straight to the office. On the plane, he'd been working on a creative story for Cristal given he hadn't been home for two nights.

The shoulder was very painful where he'd been shot but the stash in Frankfurt had included some powerful pain killers and they were doing the job of giving him some mobility. The German hospital the police had taken him to had done a professional job in patching him up, but he knew his left side would be tender for a while. That was another problem he had, explaining an obvious bullet wound to Cristal. He still didn't have a reasonable story for that one.

As he got to his office, young James Owens looked shocked and blurted out, "The big boss was just down here. He said he wants to see you in his office immediately. He didn't look too happy. Please don't involve me in any of this; you promised. What happened anyway, did you go to Germany?"

David just said. "Later," and headed towards the elevator. The story he had cooked up for his absence about a family emergency was thin and had holes, so he was hoping he didn't get the full interrogation.

He was ushered into Sir Richard Brighton's office immediately and found him with his afternoon cup of tea and a plate with some small biscuits arranged in a tiny pyramid, staring out the window at the Thames. Some customs like afternoon tea had apparently survived modern-day norms.

"You made it back in good time," he said as he turned. "I must say you look rather fit. How's the shoulder?"

David just stared. How could he know about the injury? As far as he knew the Germans had never ID'd him.

Suddenly Dick Brighton didn't look so welcoming as he sat up straight in his chair, "Come now agent Crowe, start speaking or I'll yield to the Germans' request and extradite you back to Frankfurt on the next plane. I was there this morning when you escaped their custody. I could have offered you a flight back on the company jet if you hadn't been in such a hurry to get away. All things considered; I found the BND visit a tad embarrassing but quite hospitable. How was your experience? I dare say they weren't as kind to you. And apparently, you returned the favor to an unfortunate Frankfurt Polizist who by the way has a likely skull fracture."

'Wow!' thought David, 'He must know everything.' He instantly felt sorry for the cop who was only doing his job.

He spent the next hour owning up to his botched plan to get BSB info out of Kurt Willems and being shot by what had to have been a stakeout team on Kurt's flat in Germany. He wondered why he hadn't noticed the stakeout when he was waiting to spot Willems. Either the Germans were really good at it or he was REALLY out of practice. Suddenly he thought of the city layout where Kurt's flat was only a few blocks from the BND headquarters, so they likely had a camera on the building and scrambled a team when they saw him, ball cap and collar up, entering right after Kurt left for lunch.

About halfway through his interrogation with the boss, he realized there may have been a way to go about Willems officially, informing the boss first and asking for BND assistance. Still, he couldn't know who inside BND or even MI6 might be on the BSB payroll to give Willems a warning.

After every mea culpa David could muster, he made the mistake of finishing with "So in a way I was just doing my job, tracking down the BSB."

Brighton nearly exploded. "By killing a man in an ally's territory? We knew Willems was BSB already. The Americans tipped us off when their guy Jason Fletcher fingered him. Willems was under BND surveillance and you'd have known that if you had used the proper channels like telling me what you were up to."

Crowe made the further mistake by pushing back, "Yeah but they were doing nothing about him, and he murdered an innocent man Franz Becker, for no good reason."

Brighton was furious, "And how were they supposed to know he killed Becker? The Americans couldn't tell them what they knew, or that whole mess you were involved in last November would've come out. Besides, we have no intel that Willems was the triggerman. You may actually have killed the wrong BSB agent."

Suddenly David realized he couldn't come clean without repercussions that he knew for sure Willems had been the one at Becker's flat. He decided he had to continue to protect the video analyst downstairs.

Brighton was still on a roll, "The Germans were only told that there was credible intel from a confidential source that he was BSB and needed to be watched. AND now we've lost him as an intel source with your antics. He was our ONLY hope to find out who is at the center of that criminal organization. You've set back the hunt for the BSB immeasurably. Seriously, this lone wolf nonsense must stop NOW or you're no longer going to be working for us. We cannot have a rogue agent roaming the world creating havoc and frankly that is what you're starting to look like. Carter thinks he has a case on you for a waterboarding incident. I know you've been done badly for the last few years, but you have a decision to make. Are you part of the solution here, or part of the problem? You know it would be easy for us to cut you loose and make you accountable for all this lone wolf nonsense."

David saw his jeopardy, realized he'd pushed too far, so he sat quietly until Sir Richard Brighton finally gave him the terms of his German release and some additional restrictions on his movements in MI6. Brighton left out the whole Cristal angle. That would be a new surprise waiting for him at home and he didn't want to soothe the sting of that confrontation yet to come. One hard condition was definitely no more travel to Germany unless he wanted to unleash an international incident and spend years in a German Gefängnis.

He was desperate to get out of the room before he made matters worse. After swearing he was back in the fold and wouldn't be doing any unsanctioned solo missions, Brighton put him on probation; a short leash where he had to notify top brass of any movements and he was released.

***

Earlier in Frankfurt and after a heart-to-heart with Cristal, Bill Carter headed home to DC leaving the Germans with a hell of a mess to clean up.

The Germans reluctantly agreed with Carter's rendition of each of the deadly encounters as it matched the evidence they had accumulated. Additionally, Cristal's subsequent interrogation had supported everything Carter had laid out. So, she was released with conditions similar to David's and on her own, made it back to London late afternoon, and headed home to an anxious Freja and an excited little Tiffany.

On finishing his dressing down by the boss, David swung by where he expected to find Cristal, but her tiny office was empty. A young analyst, that David didn't know, sitting across the aisle smiled, "If you're looking for Cristal Serpe so am I, but apparently she called in sick again."

David nodded. This wasn't good. She had probably woken to find him still not home and decided to stay home again waiting for his return. According to the boss, the whole German thing was going to be classified so he could make up whatever story he wanted but it would have to be a good one. He decided to head to the flat as it was getting late and he made it home in a taxi in under ten minutes. Cristal, having just dismissed Freja, heard the taxi and was at the door when he entered.

He put on his best charming smile, "Hey Honey. Wow, you must have been worried. I got called away on an urgent matter and God damn it, my damn phone died, and I had no charger. I was undercover in France and couldn't get one of their crazy payphones to work so I wasn't able to call or text you, so I sincerely apologize. You know how these things go. Even had to sleep in a rental car for two nights on a classified stakeout. I'm truly sorry but these types of rushed classified missions have to be expected. I wish I could fill you in on all the details but as I said, 'classified'. I hope this doesn't happen often. Maybe they're just making me make up for lost time.

"Hey, I was just at the office and they said you phoned in sick. I hope you're okay. Just keeping the home fires burning waiting for my return?"

Cristal just stood there smiling at him, "New clothes I see, but somehow familiar," and in slow motion put her fist on his left shoulder and pushed hard.

As he fell to his knees in excruciating pain he mumbled, "Oh shit."

Reconciliation

As David gathered himself and followed her wincingly into their tiny kitchen, Cristal was making herself a coffee. Not knowing what she knew, he had no way to know where to start. She was the first to speak. "So, are you ready to come clean on your little blitz of Frankfurt?"

This was worse. Clearly, she knew something, but it couldn't be the whole story, "Who told you I was in Germany?"

She stared at him for a long time, partly torturing him and partly giving him an opportunity to come clean or possibly dig his hole deeper. Exasperated, and not wanting to force him into another pack of lies she finally said, "Let's just get this all out on the table. I know you went after Kurt Willems, killed him in self-defense, and got shot by the BND stakeout team in the process."

He was stunned. She wasn't in the office and it was unlikely Sir Richard had phoned her at home to give her all the details, "How do you know all of this?"

More exasperated she just stared at him for a while before she spoke, "I went to grab you for lunch a couple of days ago ... my first day at the Section. After interrogating the kid outside your office, I put all the pieces together, waited until yesterday morning for your return, and when you didn't call or show up, I went after you and got picked up at the Frankfurt airport. They were waiting for me. I was interrogated and spent last night in their high-security cell at BND HQ on a very hard cot, probably just down the hall from you unless you were still in the hospital. They need better beds in that lockup, but the Germans feed you well."

The shock, he felt, must have been obvious on his face.

"Thankfully Freja was here with a backup plan or I would have had to do something crazy like yield to all of their questions just to ensure I could call home.

"Anyway, I didn't give them anything until this morning when I spent an hour with a very angry and jet-lagged Bill Carter, a very silent Sir Richard Brighton and the head of German Intelligence, also not a happy man.

"Oh, by the way, that wasn't how I had planned on being introduced to your boss. I've no idea what Sir Richard Brighton thinks of me now after such an awkward introduction. He didn't say a word to me, but I got the impression I won't be getting any Christmas cards from him.

"So, I'm pretty certain they all loved the fact that you positioned yourself as the top international security issue of the whole world today, forcing them to drop all their other pressing issues and fly across the globe over your unsanctioned escapades and retribution. As it turned out they ALL ended up with egg on their faces for various reasons and had to prostrate themselves, begging forgiveness in front of their allies. Now they must find a way out of this without creating multiple international incidents.

"Add to that, they were more than a little perturbed when they discovered you had escaped their custody by overpowering one of their guards, evading capture, and exiting the building. Pretty embarrassing for the three of them you must admit.

"The German BND has the biggest task, finding a way to bury five murders that they can't allow the local cops to get into.

"Oh, by the way, as I left their custody today the guard was still in the hospital. Probable skull fracture they said. Director Carter was forced to eat lots of 'crow', no pun intended, and he apparently had to spill the beans on all our exploits last fall which you can imagine was shocking to the Germans. You might know that he doesn't appreciate his hand being forced like that, especially with an important ally.

"Brighton had some apologies to offer too although he didn't know all the details of our brief visit to Frankfurt. You know, running clandestine ops in an ally's backyard is more than frowned upon. Killing their locals is really beyond the pale, but that didn't seem to dissuade you from going after Willems.

"It also turns out the Germans have their own embarrassment to deal with having sat on an important piece of intel for weeks.

"So, in retaliation what do you think they did? For the rest of the morning they decided to beat up on me as part of what they called the 'wrecking crew' who were responsible for so many German deaths. Your boss and mine apparently pleaded our self-defense case and soothed the tempers over there and made some sort of a deal so that I could be released. You, on the other hand, being involved in even more deaths and seriously injuring that guard, are truly persona non grata. When we left, they still had a manhunt out on you and things would've been very different if they'd found you.

"I of course didn't offer the fact that we had a drop in Frankfurt, so I knew you had a good chance of escaping. One of us had to get back here for Tiffany. All charges against us are held in abeyance for now but we're not to think of visiting Germany again. I guess that puts any plans for Oktoberfest on hold."

David stayed leaning against the refrigerator, nursing his throbbing shoulder and staring at the floor.

"But there's more and it ain't good. That intel the Germans sat on; apparently Khalil did, in fact, have a sidekick who filmed my starring role at McDonald's and it's been on a Jihadi website, the Germans are monitoring, for a few weeks. The BND didn't realize what they had until this morning.

"The CIA and the FBI figured Khalil likely had an accomplice at that service center in New Jersey, but they've made no progress in finding him. Now we know he filmed it and recently someone distributed it worldwide on the Jihadi network. The three of them saw the video this morning and were all surprised that we're both still alive. Apparently, they were unimpressed with my reflexes.

"So where does that leave us? Our combined intel suggests that the bad guys know who you and I are, and we're targets number one and two for the religious fanatics. Given all the German deaths and Hammond here in London, the BSB are probably after us as well. On top of that, no doubt a new fatwa has been issued for our deaths, so every Jihadi wannabe and the BSB want our heads.

"Our bosses are taking this very seriously. You may have noticed our new security shadow sitting in a black car across the street. They've upgraded the whole security detail so we're now virtually prisoners. According to Carter, Sir Richard Brighton wanted me to know that it's not normal for MI6 to be protecting their own or a 'visitor' in London, using up a safe house and in particular he wanted me to be aware of the cost of it all. If we hadn't been as successful in New York and here with Hammond, I think they'd be of a mind to dump us as just too much trouble."

David was now focused on the car across the street. Hell, he was rusty as he hadn't noticed what out the window right now was the obvious stakeout vehicle. The idea of temporarily living in an MI6 safe house suddenly made even more sense; now with 24/7 surveillance.

Cristal continued, "While they're still clearly appreciative of our accomplishments you're aware we've left a terrible mess behind in Germany AND we're now eating up scarce resources to keep ourselves alive.

"We've become a little too 'central' to the overall campaign to rid the world of these villains. I think they want us to acknowledge that this isn't a normal set of circumstances for undercover assets. We're not so much 'under cover' anymore.

"I don't know all the terms of the deals the three of them came up with, but you and I are free for the moment to come up with a plan to go after both Al Qaeda and the BSB before one or the other gets us. They had no suggestions to offer on how we might do that. The term 'BAIT' comes to mind.

"If you're right, and Jack Hammond had an accomplice in MI6, then you had better watch your back, even at work. We know Al Qaeda is after me and it's a pretty good guess BSB really wants your head, especially after you just killed yet another of their guys in Frankfurt who, if you're right, was their top guy there. After all, you've likely decapitated both their UK and German operations."

She took a sip of her coffee as she stood waiting for some response from him.

Suddenly he realized the pain killers were starting to wear off and his stomach was churning too. Sheepishly he said, "I'm truly sorry I got you mixed up in this. My plan wasn't to kill Willems but just to force some info out of him and then make a call to a guy I know in Germany to hand him over to the BND, but he lunged at me and I had no option but to defend myself. The plan was to be back at the office by afternoon but then some trigger-happy cop who must have had the place staked out, shot me as I left his flat. Honestly, I'm not sure if he was a bad shot and was trying to kill me or if I just got lucky.

"Anyway, things looked like they were going to go from bad to worse and it was only a matter of time before they ID'd me. They'd already connected me with an old passport from the Westin last fall, along with those two dead Germans. With all that and phony passports they rightly concluded I was a professional assassin or Intel of some sort using multiple identities, so I decided to break out and disappear before things got serious. There was no telling how the Germans would take it if I tried to explain self-defense in each case. I was looking at months of investigations, likely an international incident, and maybe years in jail. My thinking was that if they didn't have me in a cell, where even the local Frankfurt police would want a piece of me, then some of this might get handled diplomatically behind the scenes.

"I didn't think I hurt the cop in the washroom that badly, a fractured skull? I thought it would just be an embarrassment.

"Thankfully, we had that one drop left in Frankfurt because they had my ID, phone, and money and all I had on was that guard's uniform and he was taller than me. My German isn't great so wandering around Frankfurt in an oversized guard's uniform wasn't going to work. That drop was a godsend, especially the painkillers.

"I stopped by the office when I got back. Just enough time for Sir Richard to read me the riot act. He failed to mention your involvement and I suspect that was intentional.

"So, while I was busy escaping, the DD and old man Brighton were in Frankfurt this morning? That was a hastily arranged meeting and I concur that they wouldn't have been a happy bunch. Brighton and Carter must have had some egg on their faces if all that stuff from last November came out. I know they're allies and share lots of intel but airing that kind of dirty laundry is hard on the ego."

Cristal put down her coffee, "You got that right because they were all in a foul mood when they dragged me in there in handcuffs. Apparently, the Germans were embarrassed as well because they had that video for a while, it was from Pittsburgh, they hadn't informed the CIA and they hadn't ID'd me even though they had those old passports. So, none of the three of them were feeling very good about the entire mess and that may have helped us out. They all owe each other for failures in one form or another."

David took her by the shoulders, "So again, I apologize for this mess and I'm glad they released you even if we're facing potential assassination teams."

After a pause Cristal sounded serious, "Listen David, you're a father now. What would have happened to your daughter if Willems had killed you? I had to leave her here with Freja and I got stuck there too. You have to think about these things now."

There was a long pause as Cristal stood at the counter staring at a sheepish David Crowe. She had one last beef and surprise to dump on him.

"So, all of that aside, when were you going to tell me the whole story about Kathy Sloane, beauty queen of central London?"

Now David really turned red. By his calculation, Cristal had only been in the office a few hours two days earlier and still she had met his old flame. That had to have been planned and he was sure Kathy had been all dolled up and rehearsed for the Cristal ambush.

He was speechless as she went on, "The fucking goddess dropped by my cubicle to say hi and check me out. After she left a helpful neighbor filled me in. Tell me she wasn't voted most attractive woman in MI6 ... or all of London for that matter."

David stumbled a bit to find his voice, "That was a long time ago and we had broken up before I went to Africa. We were never a good fit, but you didn't expect me to date anything less than the best, did you? Besides, she doesn't hold a candle to you. Did she also admit that she'd dated Jack Hammond after me?"

Now it was Cristal's turn to blush, "So her old boyfriend killed the newer boyfriend? I'd watch my back."

As Cristal threw the last of her coffee down the drain, David thought, 'could this day get any worse?'

The Big Eye

Saturday morning was bright and sunny, and they rose late with Tiffany jumping on the bed. "You said it's my birfday mommy. Can we go to the big wheel in the sky, you promised?"

Indeed, it was her third birthday. She, a precocious toddler, seemed older every day and was a singular joy to both Cristal and now David who adored her. In fact, Cristal had promised her a trip to the London Eye after they passed it one day in a taxi.

Breakfast was a quick affair because Tiffany just couldn't sit still with excitement. David struggled to dress with his injured shoulder which had stiffened up some. He checked quickly that the MI6 car was still across the street and sent him a text that they'd be heading to the London Eye so there were no surprises.

Cristal checked online for the logistics and tickets for the Eye and ordered a taxi.

It was cooler than normal for March, so they dressed warmly and wore scarves.

David closed the flat's outer door as Cristal opened the taxi door and Tiffany rushed in. She loved that she could stand up in the London taxis and always tried to get into one of the pull-down seats before her mother protested.

As Cristal went to enter, she noticed a black gym bag on the floor at the far side behind the driver and stepped back. She was leaning forward to tell the driver that his last passenger had forgotten something as the bomb went off.

David was a few steps behind them, and the blast threw him onto his back at the foot of the three steps to their flat's front door. His hearing was gone, and his eyes were singed but he could see Cristal lying on the ground, bare skin, torn clothes, and blood coming out of … everywhere. The motion to his right was a car door opening halfway down their short city block. A Middle Eastern man was now running toward them with gun drawn. He got off one shot that hit the sidewalk near Cristal's head before David was able to get his gun out and put three slugs in the man's chest who was now only about fifteen feet away. His forward momentum dropped him at David's feet, but it was clear he was dead or close to it before he reached the ground. Picking up rapid motion again, David swung to his left but raised his gun to the sky as the startled MI6 agent who had been across the small street arrived around the front of what was left of the burning taxi.

Tiffany and the taxi driver were nowhere in sight, so his attention was drawn to Cristal who at the last second, trying to get the driver's attention, had been protected to a large degree by the frame and front door of the heavy London taxi.

David just stared at the burning vehicle, 'She was only three … today,' he thought … and he'd only known his daughter for a few weeks. Long enough for him to think of her as a perfect little angel. His mind couldn't focus on Cristal or his own injuries as he simply kept staring in shock at where his tiny daughter had been only moments ago but there was absolutely no sign of her now.

In a weird state of shock, he kept wondering where she'd gone. He needed to find her to make sure she was okay, but that side of the taxi was now just a gaping, smoldering hole.

He was only vaguely aware of the MI6 agent making calls for help and attending to Cristal. It seemed every emotion swept through him. Fear of these monsters, rage at what they'd done, love for a tiny little girl he couldn't find, but mostly it was the shock and a growing feeling of bottomless sadness and helplessness.

As unconsciousness started to wash over him, he looked down at the man's body at his feet and put one more slug directly into its head just as he passed out.

Mogadishu

Word reached Mustafa Habib in Mogadishu that a suicide assassination attempt in London had essentially failed. According to CNN International, a presumed Jihadi suicide team had somehow panicked, and the resultant explosion had killed the child and the suicide bomber but only injured the woman and her partner. While the reports hadn't identified the targets, the headshots provided were familiar to Mustafa; the two from McDonald's. The man wasn't seriously injured, and the female was in critical but stable condition. He was surprised to find that the two had somehow settled in London and shared a child, but that was immaterial.

He immediately suspected that if the woman recovered, they'd come looking for the man who they had to assume had murdered their daughter. According to Mr. Tom, they had secretly entered Mogadishu before, and he'd have to expect they'd do it again after this.

This had to have been an Al Qaeda-inspired team that had gone after her because of the Khalil video and possibly the fatwa Mustafa had ordered.

Wanting revenge for Khalil had prompted the fatwa well before the Syndicate had made their offer. In reality, he had always wanted to deal with them himself, especially now that he knew they had killed his little brother. Knowing that particular aspiration was highly unlikely, the fatwa had gone out. There was no protocol to retract a fatwa. What was he going to say, that the religious order had been withdrawn because someone else wanted to kill them personally?

The argument had persisted with some of the Islamic clergy that Al Qaeda leaders were not religious leaders and couldn't issue fatwas but that seemed moot as an Al Qaeda fatwa had essentially the same effect on any Jihadi; they'd execute the order as if it came from a recognized religious leader.

It wasn't a long shot to think that some sympathetic, wannabe Jihadi had spotted her and matched her to the video online. He wondered if it was the BSB going after the man but then again, they were holding that out as the prize for their new potential partner's cooperation. Besides, the British press had already identified the attackers as at least Jihadi sympathizers and they likely wouldn't have needed any persuasion from the BSB to attack the two who killed Khalil.

If it hadn't been a priority before, the Brits and the Americans would have their two agents protected like no one else, so it wasn't going to be easy. If this shady new Syndicate could deliver them, then why not take them up on their offer. The news reports suggested the male might be the father of the child, so they'd likely be found together. He desperately wanted the two that had killed his younger brother and Khalil even if it took until America's Independence Day, unfortunately still a couple of months away. So, he'd just have to be patient.

He still wanted proof that this BSB group could do what they claimed. He wasn't excited about putting his people out front unless this Syndicate could deliver all the intel, security, and assets that would be needed for such a bold attack on the US government and law enforcement right in the center of Washington DC on a national holiday.

'What would Khalil do?'

He lifted one of his many cell phones and called Nasir "What have you learned about this Mr. Tom?"

"Our mutual friends are quite certain he's real and so is his organization. They have indeed been very busy in African countries. While they're definitely not Muslim or even care about our plight or our goals, much of what they've done has been helpful to us and he was right to tell you that sometimes our goals are in alignment. So far, we haven't found ourselves in any conflict with them but it's hard to see how that might not be the case at some point in the future.

"Our friends also tell us to be very careful with them. Their network is very stealthy and can be ruthless. They use almost exclusively expensive and high-end mercenaries to do their dirty work as they seem to keep tight security on their management who never get their hands dirty. Their typical hired agent is an ex-special forces person with a proven track record of clandestine missions and remaining invisible themselves. He was truthful when he said they go to extreme lengths to remain invisible. They're doing a great job of that. Our friends only know what they're allowed to know.

"Again, people we trust urge us to be cautious with them. They could just as easily turn on us and send in very capable people to eliminate us, some of whom might seem like friends. Remember, if in fact, they're ruthless then they don't have to buy allegiance, they just have to threaten mayhem, to say a family member, to get one of our 'friends' to turn on us.

"They also think it might have been a bad idea for you to meet this Mr. Tom. At least in their minds, it might seem to give them the upper hand.

"As to Mr. Tom himself, I've tracked him down using some of our most reliable friends. He'd have to be one of their senior people to be sent on such a mission to meet with you, but no one knows anything about their organization's structure, how many they are, or where Mr. Tom fits in.

"As you suspected, he's an American but he lives in London. He'd definitely be representing the top tier in the BSB if he had the intel to find you, but he wouldn't be on their executive team which is unknown to anyone we know and most likely based in the US.

"Remember, it's widely believed that they do have top contacts in the US Government and elsewhere. That means that if they found you once, they could potentially do it again and on a whim, they could tell the CIA or MI6 or even the French, how to get to you. We must be careful in dealing with them.

"That's all we have so far."

Mustafa thought this over for a while. 'What would Khalil do?'

Finally, he spoke, "Use that secure email they gave us and tell Mr. Tom we're in. After that, I have a separate but related operation I need you to take care of."

Hospital

It had been several hours since the explosion as David was released from emergency with a concussion, a blown eardrum, a few cracked ribs, and only a few outward signs of stitches to attest to the shrapnel, mostly glass, he'd taken from the car bomb. While he was being stitched up local police and MI6 had interrogated him on the assassination attempt. The taxi driver's remains, and there wasn't much to examine, had yet to be identified but the gunman had been known to police as a Jihadi sympathizer although not under surveillance. It remained a mystery as to how they'd intercepted the call for a taxi. The taxi company had dispatched a unit, but the attack was executed before their car arrived on the scene.

David had been getting updates on Cristal who was in intensive care with serious head trauma, various lacerations, and other injuries to be determined. Her upper body, only partially covered by the heavy taxi door and frame, had taken most of the punishment. A major injury to her left arm had come close to requiring amputation but for the quick assistance of the MI6 security agent on the scene. For the moment, the doctors thought they'd saved her arm.

He made his way back to the ICU as her seemingly worried doctor approached, "The next seventy-two hours are critical for Cristal. We have her in an induced coma to try to minimize the swelling of the brain. She took a hell of a hit being so close to the bomb.

"We're working on her other injuries right now. The guard outside the ICU says they'll be here 24/7.

"So far, we know she has a collapsed lung, broken ribs, dislocated shoulder, and both minor and major lacerations. You already know of the threat to her left arm. She was actually quite lucky. We build those damned taxis like tanks or she'd have had lots of organ damage. I just saw a photo of the scene on TV. Being that close to an explosion of this type is pretty much always fatal. Whoever gave her first aid on site and stopped the major bleeds probably saved her life. For sure they saved her left arm."

David was teary-eyed as he spoke, "I suppose there's no point in asking but has there been any news about my daughter?"

There was a long pause before the doctor responded, "I'll give it to you straight. Word from one of your colleagues at the site is that she was right on top of the bomb. She would have felt nothing. We must confirm the DNA of course but as I said, we have a law enforcement officer who confirmed seeing her enter the taxi and she was just behind the driver where we believe the bomb was planted. All the markings of a suicide bomber. Again, all I can tell you is that it would've been a merciful and instant death."

David could hold it in no longer and sobbed in fury as he sat down in a seat in the hallway outside the ICU. All the doctor could do was stand there beside him with his hand on his shoulder.

Sobbing, David said, "She just wanted a ride on the big wheel in the sky. That's all she wanted for her birthday. Now she'll never get it."

***

It was almost four days before Cristal was allowed to regain consciousness. Some people lose all track of time and short-term memory with a traumatic head injury, but not Cristal. From the moment she opened her eyes she simply stared at David with tears streaming down her face. There was no point in asking. She just mouthed 'Tiffany' and started sobbing.

Apart from minimal conversing with the nurses and the doctor she said nothing to anyone for the next few days. She even refused to speak with the investigators.

David had tried with "Are you in pain? Can I get you anything?" but she just stared off into the distance.

There was no engagement, and this persisted to the point that David wondered if she'd ever speak again; at least to him.

Days later as she started to build back some strength, lying on her side staring at David, there was finally a break in the tears as she wiped her eyes and simply said, "I'm going to kill every last one of them!"

Stoically, David simply nodded.

***

April was an unusually cold and wet month in London as Cristal recovered at home in another safe house as clearly the first one had been known to someone.

After his own short recovery, still nursing broken ribs and a gunshot wound, David was back at his desk doing mostly make-busy work as the investigation into the assassination attempt was proceeding too slowly for his liking. He of course was limited in participating in the actual investigation, but sympathetic agents were keeping him up to date.

His own recovery was moving right along, and he took advantage of all the rehab protocols and the gym in the basement of headquarters to build back his strength.

Homelife was even more of a drag than the office as he couldn't get two words out of Cristal and didn't want to push it. As expected, she was taking Tiffany's loss very badly.

She had a visiting nurse and physical therapist for the first few weeks as she staggered around wincing occasionally from the pain. Simply going through the motions, conversation was near zero, and Tiffany was never spoken of.

David had no idea what to do besides making sure she ate from time to time and helping her with her exercises to get full motion back in her damaged arm. She slept a lot which he reasoned was good for her recovery. She cried constantly but wouldn't hear of any drugs to ease the emotional trauma.

He was grieving too, but nothing like Cristal who had given birth to their little angel and raised her for her first three years. Apparently, she just couldn't get her mind to return to anything normal ... like the present. He was at a loss as to how to snap her out of the funk she was in. He was tortured too and realized that even if he could get her to talk, he had no idea what he'd say to try to help her.

It was left up to him to get a message through the CIA in Langley to Cristal's jailed 'ex' that Cristal was recovering, and sadly little Tiffany was gone. Not that he'd be allowed out of prison for a funeral given the nature of his crimes against Cristal, but he'd been the only father Tiffany had known for most of her short life. She had been such a lovable little toddler that to David, there was no doubt the man probably had real feelings for her, no matter his subterfuge.

Even though David had never met the man and he likely had heard something from news reports, giving him a personal note seemed like the honorable thing to do.

When Cristal was strong enough, a small private service was held in a tiny chapel so filled with flowers it seemed ridiculous. There was all manner of large bouquets from management at MI6, Sir Richard Brighton, the CIA London, CIA Langley, Bill Carter, employee groups in both London and Langley, the funeral home, the hospital nurses, the London police and ambulance service, the local fire service, one of the local TV stations, the local tenants' association, two local Mosques, a local soccer club, various pro and anti-Muslim groups and many others who had heard of the tragedy. David swore there were more flowers than any flower shop he had ever been in.

They had no friends in London and it was viewed as too unsafe for her parents to join so there were very few people at the service.

As David stood weeping at the back of the room that was difficult to move around in for all the flowers he thought, 'Little girls should have lots of flowers in their lives, but not like this. Not a room full of them at their funeral.'

What they'd been able to recover by way of remains was buried in a nearby cemetery on a typical London dreary and drizzly day, David weeping and Cristal sobbing through the whole thing.

A Confession

The next few weeks were all the same. David making busy at work and Cristal, recovering at home was spending most of the day crying. Finally, near the end of the month, sitting at the dinner table Cristal teary-eyed and pushing the food around on her plate, in a very rare moment of engagement finally spoke, "We can't go on like this; not talking, sleeping in separate bedrooms. It's unfair to you. This is not a life at all, and I don't see me making anything of a life here in London after this. I'm going back to the States. I need to be with my parents and I'm probably not coming back."

David was stunned and just stared at her. After a long pause, he said, "What does that mean for me ... for us?"

"I don't know. I'm no part of a couple right now," she said, tears starting to run for the hundredth time in the last few weeks. Sobbing again, she said, "I don't know what you want me to say. I don't know what to do but I can't go on like this. I'll kill myself if life is to go on like this. I can't stand being here. You're on your own as far as I'm concerned. I can't love anyone right now. I don't want to be around this place or around you for that matter. I'm sorry," she sobbed, "do what you want. I can't decide for you. Do what you think is best for you. I just can't be what you need right now and maybe never."

He was speechless, what was she saying, they were done?

She looked him straight in the eye sitting across from her, tears rolling down her cheeks. While still crying and in a voice broken constantly with sobs, she said, "That's my two Tiffanys I've killed. My best friend and my tiny daughter," she sobbed uncontrollably, tears again streaming down her face.

David was stunned.

Sobbing even harder she said, "It's all my fault. I talked Tiffany into joining me on that ambush in The Sudan. They said they were looking for a female spy posing as a journalist … they were looking for me and I didn't have the guts to admit it and she was the one they picked to stone to death. I stood there as they buried her up to her head and I watched them laugh as those animals stoned her mercilessly. It was unbelievable in its brutality … something I can never unsee. You can't even imagine the horror of it. I get physically sick every time those images pop into my head. The more she bled the harder they tried to knock parts of her skull off as they got closer and closer and used bigger and bigger rocks."

The sobbing was now out of control.

"I was a complete coward. She was such a beautiful young woman in every way, with everything to live for and I couldn't bring myself to save her. I loved her. I walked her into that ambush and like the worst coward I froze and just stood there and let them kill her instead of me."

David couldn't believe what he was hearing. How had he missed this? Somehow, he had never picked up on the guilt trip Cristal had been on … probably forever. How had they never discussed this? But then again, at least from his side, he knew the answer to that one. She was riddled with guilt but had never said anything and he'd had plenty of reasons to stay silent.

His mind was racing; this was a catastrophe beyond belief.

Sobbing she continued, "Then that video of McDonald's goes viral, and they came after me here, but again they got the wrong person. They killed my precious baby Tiffany, named after the first angel I killed."

Her sobbing became much heavier as she pushed away her plate and collapsed with her head in her arms on the dining room table.

David was in a total panic. He couldn't have seen this coming. How had he missed this tragic misunderstanding happening right in front of him? How could he not have seen she was torturing herself over this terrible and catastrophic misconception?

He swallowed hard, this was going to be treacherous and there was no telling where this was going to lead once it was out of the bag, but there was no way he could live with this situation. He might lose her but he loved her too much to let her suffer under this pain. He couldn't have known these thoughts were brutalizing her. No matter the cost, she had to know the truth. It had to be done.

In a low confessional voice, he said, "I killed your friend Tiffany and maybe even our baby. It's all on me … not you. You had nothing to do with it."

His heart was racing as she looked up through red watering eyes and after a long pause, confused and looking for an explanation in his face, she said angrily, "What the hell are you talking about? You don't know what you're saying … what the hell is it you're trying to say?"

He took a deep breath. After wondering again where this was going to go, he finally lifted his head to make eye contact and said, "Look there's no easy way to say this and until now there was no reason to drag up old traumatic memories for you or for me. I had no reason to think you blamed yourself for The Sudan or even this bombing. How could I know? We don't speak. I can't get a word out of you. I never know what you're thinking.

"Neither of those murders had anything to do with you. I'm a fool not to have realized you were putting the blame on yourself. But you never said anything. How could I have known?

"It was and still is all classified, but I sent Tiffany on that ambush outside of Khartoum, not you. She worked for me. I recruited her for MI6 from the BBC just after she arrived in Africa months before she met you. As a mainstream journalist, she was invited to that fake interview just like you were. She was a true patriot and determined to help us get Al Qaeda. We discussed it and decided it was too good a get; to get an interview with a lead Al Qaeda spokesperson, not knowing it was Khalil himself who'd show up. It was too good for both the BBC and MI6 to pass up. Apart from the intel opportunity, she saw it as a possible milestone in her journalistic career. I couldn't have stopped her if I wanted to, but we needed the intel badly as well."

Cristal was just staring.

"We thought there was minimal risk but as you say, Khalil was behind it and someone must have tipped him off there was a female journalist who was a spy in the group. We pieced all this together in a dozen debriefs after the fact. There was a contact we were using who disappeared and in the end, we figured that he likely turned and fingered Tiffany to Khalil. You may have thought you convinced her to go but the decision had already been made. She went into it enthusiastically. I was destroyed when we found her body. I wanted to kill myself for getting conned like that. I'm only relieved he didn't get both of you."

She sat staring at him with her mouth agape wondering if she even knew this man. How had he kept this all a secret?

David continued, "They were looking for a female journalist, right? You said it yourself. Everyone knew you were a CNN 'producer' not an on-camera journalist. Tiffany went into that meeting with her eyes open just like Intel operatives do every day; just like you did. She knew there were risks. She had no idea just as you had no idea it was a trap. It's on us for not having better intel. Believe me, I was beside myself when she was killed in such a horrific way, but you were there, and you saw it. You already know why she never told you she was MI6. Like I'm pretty sure you didn't tell her you were CIA.

"She was only a couple of years younger than you, but she was like a daughter to me. I recruited her. I almost left the service right there and then but just after that they tried to kill me. You know the rest.

"So, there's no way you had ANYTHING to do with Tiffany Winslow's death. It was all on me! I had no idea you thought it had anything to do with you; how could I? We never discussed it and I wasn't about to bring up classified information about the worst day of my life and probably yours up to that point, where you were almost a victim too."

David's eyes were wet as he continued, "As to our daughter, I can only tell you that there was an overwhelming sense of delight when you told me you had named her Tiffany. I loved her to death even though I only had a few short weeks to get to know her. She was my only child too.

"I'm connected to the team investigating the bombing. The only evidence we have is that the two Jihadis who attacked with the taxi were very low-level Jihadi sympathizers. Habib would certainly have picked better candidates so there's no evidence they were after you. The BSB are diabolical. They could just as easily have made up a story to entice those two that it was all for Allah to take me out."

Cristal was still just staring at him, slack-jawed. It was all too much to absorb.

David's heart was pounding as he continued, "Add to that the fact that we were in an MI6 safe house for God's sake. How the hell would Habib find us in London, in a well-protected MI6 safe house after all the precautions we took? He has no intel capability like that. What, two random Jihadi sympathizers just happened to recognize you from the video? It's much more likely a BSB mole in MI6 knew where we were and hired a hit team to make it look like Jihadis. That's the way they work! That's their M. O. So, in my books it's much more likely it was an attempted hit on me than on you. The guy in the car just panicked when he saw you backing out."

Cristal was speechless as David continued, "And how do you think they arranged the right taxi? We still haven't figured that out yet. That's tradecraft, not Jihadis. It would have taken someone with pro intel skills to arrange a tap on our phone.

"So, there's zero evidence they were after you and a mounting body of evidence it was an attack on me that went wrong only because you spotted the bomb. The plan was to kill us all. You didn't think it was a bomb when you saw it but your instincts told you something was off.

"It's my choice of a career that's responsible for our two Tiffany's being dead not yours."

Cristal's despair was rapidly changing to rage. "What are you saying to me? How could you have kept all this from me? You knew Tiffany Winslow and you never thought to tell me? Who are you? What kind of a man are you?"

David took it down a notch and said calmly, "One who loves you. The one who is still bound by secrecy documents. And don't ask me why I didn't tell you. I had no reason to. I had no idea you felt you were responsible for Khalil killing Tiffany. When did you ever tell me that? And as for our daughter, I haven't been able to get two words out of you since you left the hospital. How is your not communicating my fault? Was I expected to rub your nose in the attack and bring up those memories while you were clearly devastated by it all and couldn't even talk about it?"

David was now angry too, "You seem to have given no thought to my loss. I only knew our child for weeks. Just enough to fall totally in love with her and now you know that it was me who sent Tiffany Winslow to her death in that ambush. I was probably as close to her as you were. What do you think my life was like after that, knowing I had sent her to her death because I was too stupid to see an ambush?"

She wasn't listening anymore. Something was bugging her that just didn't fit. Something she'd forgotten to ask him. As she wiped her eyes it came into focus. Furiously she turned to him with something that had been building. "Kathy Sloane said something about my name in one of your reports before you were supposedly assassinated. Did you know about me before we met in Burundi?"

David was shocked. He'd been afraid this part would come up but surely not now. How had Kathy seen that report? Back then she hadn't held a position that would've been on the distribution list. Her assignments were elsewhere, and she wouldn't have been read into operations in The Sudan.

After a long hesitation, as he realized it was all going to come out, he said, "How could I NOT have known about you?

"Tiffany worked for us. We often had watchers or backup or security on her and you two being so close, you were often spotted together. We HAD to try to get to know who you were. It would have been malpractice if we didn't check out everyone Tiffany had any contact with. And you two were close and spent a lot of time together. It was an essential part of supporting and protecting her to know who you were."

Cristal had a feeling of what was coming next, "So why was I in one of your reports. As an American CNN employee, it couldn't have been because I was viewed as a threat in Khartoum. No, I was a recruiting target, right?"

David sneered, "Well you were never approached, were you? We thought you might be CIA and frankly yes you might have been approached if I had 'survived' long enough but we never got that far. Is that so alarming? You know the business. We have to use human intel where we can find it. We're recruiting all the time. We can't wait for a journalist to come up to us and say, "Hi! Can I work for MI6?" So yes, you fit the profile and you may have been approached but that never happened. They tried to kill me before it ever got to that point. Tiffany was gone. We needed more eyes on our targets. So YES, you could have been an asset to the Branch.

Again, is that so alarming? Don't tell me you never tried to recruit an asset."

She was furious, "So that night we met in the bar in Bujumbura you knew who I was, you figured I was CIA, therefore you knew I was there looking for a westerner running around with the FLN. Why else would a CIA agent or even a news producer be in that backwater hole of a nothing country?

"It was all a setup. You were in that bar looking for me while I was looking for you except you already knew who I was, and you tricked me into bed. Keep your friends close and your enemies closer, right?"

David straightened up, "Hold on, I don't deserve that. It was nothing like that and you know it. I was taking a big chance and yes, I thought you might be there looking for me but I fell for you hard that first night and you KNOW that! You know how I felt about you right from the start. How could you even doubt that? Think of the risk I was taking getting close to you if in fact you were CIA. A risk, by the way, that turned out to be real and you turned on me. But I think we've already been through all of that, and I've forgiven you."

"FORGIVEN ME?" she yelled. Cristal wiped her eyes again and sat up straight with the loudest voice she could muster, "It was all a lie. Everything! You knew who I was back then, but you kept silent, even when we reconnected last fall. You never explained any of this. You've been lying to me the whole time just like that other jerk I'm divorcing."

"Don't you dare compare me to anyone, especially him. And when was I going to spill all of this classified information? In Burundi when you thought I was a terrorist? In Pittsburgh last fall when Jihadis were about to kill both of us? When you told me we shared a daughter? When we were running around the world trying to stop a terrorist's nuclear attack? When was a good time do you think and what would it have changed? We love each other. That's all that matters. We didn't pick the way we met or any of the things that happened to us. It wasn't like I set out to track you down so I could bed you, and you know that."

She was furious. "You don't get it, do you? You kept this all secret. There has to be trust between two people and you broke that trust. Oh my God, So many lies!

"And Kathy! Hell Kathy Sloane must have had a good laugh when she told me you had me in one of your reports and it was clear I didn't know. So, I was a recruiting target reported by you … not someone else … you. You had seen me and were checking me out. Probably running background checks. For sure you did. You wouldn't have put me in an official report to London without checking me out personally. So, you knew all about me when you turned on the charm that night. I was a target in more ways than one, wasn't I? And Kathy now knows that. She knows you PLAYED me like an ignorant little sucker. She knows you're still playing me! You know how it feels to be the last to know when it's stuff about yourself? So, what is it? You get off on your little secrets and your little conquest at my expense?"

"Cristal STOP! You know none of this is true. You're looking at this all the wrong way. It was nothing like that. I had no personal interest in you in Khartoum. I knew nothing about you really. Remember you too turned on the charm in Burundi and I fell for you hard. It was almost instantaneous, and you know that. You know that!

"What was I supposed to do? I figured you were probably CIA, sent to find me, and then suddenly I was deeply in love with you. I was taking an enormous risk because I was completely lovestruck. It was an impossible situation. There was no conquest, it was an unmitigated disaster. I wasn't playing you. You have to believe me. There was nothing sinister or malicious in this like you seem to think. And who gives a shit about what Kathy Sloane thinks she knows?"

She was buying none of it, "Even if any of that is true, you let me walk into a confrontation with your old girlfriend, 'Miss MI6' and I got totally blindsided."

David was furious, "I had no idea she knew we had crossed paths in Khartoum. Those reports were classified above her security level."

This only made her angrier. He wasn't appreciating the position she was in now, "How can I ever face her again? I'll bet she's whispering to everyone about the stupid little American who got played by the big handsome stalking Brit. With all your lies and everything you've told me now, how could you not have seen that coming? Kathy knows, your boss knows and probably everyone on that floor knows that you set all this up and I'm the only one in the dark. What must they think of me now; naive and completely useless as an intelligence officer if she's duped this easily? I can never go back in there!

"Not only have you been lying to me, you've destroyed my career!

"That's it! I was starting to feel sorry and guilty about leaving you here but not anymore. I'm out of here," and she stormed out of the room.

There was no stopping her. Within two days, still injured, moving slowly, and refusing to engage with him, she was gone; resigned her post in London in a long email to Bill Carter, packed a large suitcase, and jumped on a flight to be back with her parents, half thinking she might get her old news producer's job back at the local Cincinnati TV station.

David was devastated. He had lost both of the women in his life just that fast. He wondered if it had been entirely his own fault and what he might have done differently. Some of what he had admitted to her was still classified like Tiffany Winslow's role with MI6 and the security clearance they'd done on Cristal in Khartoum.

Surely his mostly unintentional silence was understandable and something they could get over eventually. Or was it? How could she not see his side of it all? Then again, she wasn't herself; injured and grieving their daughter had her in an incredibly fragile state.

He reluctantly realized how serious was the competition she might feel from Kathy, but getting blindsided by it all … that was definitely his fault, and looking back, it was something he might have anticipated and something he now realized could be devastating to Cristal.

She was right, several key people in MI6 probably knew by now that she'd been unaware that she had been a recruiting target of the man who ultimately bedded her, and if that wasn't set straight somehow, she wouldn't be able to work with them.

Of course, he'd seen her with Tiffany Winslow in The Sudan, but he'd totally forgotten there was a report with Cristal's name on it from back then. It was surprising to learn that Kathy knew of it as at the time she wouldn't have had access to those kinds of field reports. Someone must have hinted to her and she dug it up to confirm it was actually about the new girlfriend.

Suddenly he realized it had to have been Jack Hammond himself who would've had access to the reports. He was apparently hitting on Kathy back then. He could've made up a story that David had a cute new CNN producer in his sights and probably spun it that he was pursuing her romantically. It would be just like him to try to put a nail in the coffin of any residual feelings Kathy had for him while he was pursuing her.

Whether Kathy had believed anything Hammond might have told her she'd have known from the report she now had access to, that Cristal had never known about the background checks done on her; so why not get a leg up on his new love interest by spilling that little secret on their first meeting. Office games and politics were apparently still a contact sport; one that he hadn't had to participate in for a few years.

It was hard to take anything positive away from his confrontation with Cristal but at least one major secret was behind them that he could take credit for. He had relieved her of the misguided guilt that she was responsible for both Tiffanys' deaths. That wasn't enough though. That relief to her psyche was heavily offset by her loss of trust in him and the secret some key MI6 people had on her.

Given Cristal's most recent loss and subsequent weakened emotional state, he could see where she might have a very hard time facing Kathy and others on a regular basis. Maybe if she'd been stronger emotionally, she could have strategized around that. If she really felt threatened, she could've taken the position that 'I have him and you don't' with Kathy. Not an in-character thing for Cristal to do but an effective defense if she felt the need. David was sure there was a way to tackle the Kathy thing. Women had their own defensive strategies in these matters he figured, but nothing he'd understand, he was sure.

For any others who knew the story, there was always the old fallback that certain things were deemed secret, confidential, or eyes-only and it had no bearing on their relationship or her competence as a senior Intelligence Officer.

Looking back, Kathy's ambush had clearly been the thing that put her over the edge. The hurt on her face on that particular revelation was burned into his brain. Maybe those kinds of confrontations were a bigger thing for Americans. Brits usually solve those issues with a razor-sharp comeback; one-upmanship of a different kind. Still, in Cristal's weakened state he could see where it might all be too overwhelming right now.

Whatever the case, she was gone now and he wondered if she'd ever be back. If one thing was clear it was that she was REALLY hurt by his actions.

The task ahead of trying to win her back was enormous. Even if she believed he'd been at least partly responsible for both Tiffanys, there was the secret Khartoum thing, the Burundi episode, and the Kathy ambush to overcome. In retrospect that was a lot for a love affair to deal with.

In his own weakened state, he wasn't sure he'd ever see her again.

Back in the USA

By the time she landed in Cincinnati airport somewhat jet-lagged, Cristal had figured the TV gig wasn't a solution. Even in her fragile physical and emotional state, she knew she wouldn't be satisfied living in the burbs and commuting to a dead-end job after the high of slaying Al Qaeda's leader and knowing they were after her. What had she been thinking when she fired off, of all things, that long and sappy EMAIL to the boss?

So, the call to Director Bill Carter was going to be a tough one given she'd pretty much just up and left with a weak and much too personal explanation. She hadn't even waited for a response and checking her email now, she wasn't surprised to see he still hadn't responded.

This was no way to treat him. He had always been a mentor and even a sponsor for her career in the CIA and she'd probably left him in a very awkward position. Insubordination came to mind and termination for cause might even be on the table if she hadn't already resigned.

Actually, she now really wanted to hang on to her old job. It was all that she knew and, in some ways, had provided a fulfilling career for her, even with all the risks. Even if she'd passed a point of no return with the resignation, at least she needed to apologize.

Still at the airport, she eventually got Bill Carter on the phone and tried to launch into her prepared apology. He was very blunt and clear that he didn't want to address the issue immediately and instead ordered her to take a few days off. He was curt, telling her he was busy and needed a few days to think over her situation, and hung up quickly. She took that as meaning he hadn't yet accepted her resignation, which was good, but he definitely was angry with her and needed to count to ten before he made any decisions.

With people rushing by, some happy, some not so much, she sat down on a nearby airport bench to evaluate her situation. But the more she pondered her situation the more depressed she became. No career, no home, no daughter, no fiancé, no friends, and Jihadis hunting her. She didn't want to sit here in full view in an airport and start crying. Besides that, she had left her security back in London, and probably every Jihadi on the planet had her face burned into their memories, so sitting in the open in a public place wasn't wise.

What to do? The TV gig was out which was the only reason she was here in Cincinnati. So she decided to head out to the only home and people she might still have left; her parents.

Her mom and dad had been advised to lay low while Cristal had been in some danger, so even they weren't at their home in town. They had relocated to a small rental cottage on Chippewa Lake in northeast Ohio about three hundred miles away. Besides Cristal, only their good friend and landlord knew where they were.

There seemed little threat to them but there was always the chance the bad guys would try to track Cristal down through them, kidnap one of them or take revenge in some fashion. Before leaving the States, she had been warned that a couple of Middle Eastern men had been by the TV station looking for information that could lead them to her parents, so the threat had been real at least back then. She was glad they had agreed to an extended vacation.

She rented a car and headed out northeast giving her about six hours to think and work a few things out. Tiffany was never far from mind, so much of the ride was spent in tears for her and occasional thoughts of her life and that jerk David, the love of her life who had stabbed her in the back.

***

After getting over their shock of how serious her injuries had been, her parents were furious that David had apparently downplayed the state of her wounds and convinced them not to fly to London, impressing upon them the need to stay clear, given the unknown nature of the threat. Cristal felt he had read her mind as having her mom around right after losing Tiffany would have been unbearable.

Mary and Frank were more than thrilled to see their grieving only child and lavished love, support, and sumptuous meals on her.

It was good spending some time with her parents who were desperate to comfort her in her anguish over tiny Tiffany. She had been a gem in their eyes, and it was obvious to Cristal that the loss of their only grandchild had hit them so hard it seemed to her that they had both aged significantly over the couple of months since she'd last seen them. Mary couldn't look at her at first without crying.

Over breakfast, on the second morning, Mary finally said in a cracking voice, "I'd easily have given my own life to have saved that little one."

"I know mom. There's just no sense to it. We don't even know who they were trying to get but I'm glad you and dad decided to spend some time here at the cottage just to be extra safe. I couldn't stand it if I thought you were in danger too.

"If there's anyone after me, I'll get them first just like I've done before so don't worry about me. I'm always heavily protected and as you know, I can handle myself. I never told you all that went on in Africa when I was with CNN and undercover for the CIA but believe me, I know how to watch my back and I've taken care of more than my share of bad guys in some of the most dangerous places on the planet so again, don't fear for me, I've learned a very painful lesson.

"The attack in London happened simply because my guard was down. We thought we were secure in an MI6 safe house, there were two of us on the lookout for trouble and we even had an MI6 guy watching us from across the street but maybe all that security made me sloppy, and they got us. That will never happen again."

Later, her mom wiping her most recent tears said, "What are you going to do about David? When we met you two just after Christmas you seemed so much in love. That love story of how you met, fell in love, and then reunited is the material for a blockbuster movie, my God."

Cristal smiled, "Yeah ... I don't know about David yet. As I told you, he kept some very important information from me that I don't want to get into further. As I told you some of it is classified. Still, his secrets were very hurtful to me and damaging too."

"Yes dear, but he seemed like such an upstanding young man, even though he's a Brit," she smiled. "Could it be that he was just trying to protect you and aren't some of the things you people deal with Top Secret, even from you? Could that be part of it?"

"I don't know mom. I'm just so confused right now and any time I think of him, what he said and did, I just get a headache and even more confused. I know he loves me but he kept some things secret that really hurt. There has to be trust between people."

Mary seemed exasperated, "But dear, to me it looks like you're back where you were when you came back from Africa so depressed. Now we know that was the first time you lost him. You weren't only pregnant, you were visibly hurting from that loss. It was clear you missed him dearly and once we knew the whole story it was obvious why you were so distraught ... just like you are now. After what you told us, it seems to me that he has a point. How and when was he going to tell you everything? That didn't make his love for you any less real and I saw you together. He loves you deeply. All I'm saying is, think hard about it before you make any long-term decisions.

"You know your dad and I had serious reservations when you rushed into marrying that imposter Gregg Wiggins; I forget his real name. Don't let that con job of a jerk taint your feelings in this case. I can't stand by and see you throw away a wonderful life with a man you love. I'm just saying."

Cristal simply smiled at her mom as the headache returned.

Frank Serpe wasn't a big talker, but his hugs and tearful glances said it all. The only thing he said during one of his bear hugs was, "You know we'll never get over Tiffany, but I hope you find your way back to David. He seemed like a keeper."

Knowing she couldn't hide out at her parents forever and knowing they couldn't help themselves from pushing her back towards David, after three days of mostly crying she called for an appointment with the Director and headed to Langley.

Bill Carter seemed to have counted to ten and was more understanding of the situation given the recent attack on her family, "Listen Cristal, we don't usually put spouses or significant others together for this very reason. Any family tragedy can have widespread effects. David doesn't work for us but you get my point. A tragedy like you two faced takes two critical assets out of the mix.

"Besides that, professionally, you just can't up and leave an assignment with no notice, even if you were still on medical leave, and then expect us to find a landing spot for you. All that aside, how are you? We really haven't spoken in the weeks since this all happened. You must be devastated."

Holding back more tears and feeling repentant after her hasty actions, she said, "Physically I'm doing a little better every day but in my life, I never thought I'd have to deal with anything like this. My parents dying someday yes, but my daughter being slaughtered? Who could be prepared for such a thing? I think you know it has only strengthened my resolve, to put it mildly, to get back at these barbarians. But thanks for asking."

She went on to fill him in on the highlights of why she'd broken up with David, some of which she had already poured out in her completely unprofessional and verbose resignation email.

"As to the job, I understand the position I've put you in, but given the hit on us, losing my daughter and then finding out David has been lying to me all this time was too much. I couldn't stand it another hour. I had to get out of there.

"If you take me back, I'll do whatever you say but don't send me back there. I can't work with him or the others who knew so much more than I did about how and when David targeted me, and frankly, I'm ready to stay quit if you want me to. I'll even take a formal dismissal without a fight if that's the way it has to be."

Carter was quick, "Don't even think about leaving us. You're one of our top agents. Your loss would be felt in a big way. Not only are you one of our most talented field agents with deadly skills, but you also have a brain on those shoulders that has come up frequently with the one spark that we needed to solve the big puzzles. To be very frank, I believe you think like a terrorist. Besides that, this country owes you a massive debt over the Khalil thing. What you and David did tracking down those attacks and eliminating him deserves a Presidential medal.

"Think about it, after the JFK airport, a second more serious hit on NYC would've ended my career in disgrace never mind closing New York City for a thousand years. So, even though it should not even be a secondary consideration, I personally owe you a great debt.

"No, I'm not accepting a resignation. If you're ready to go back to work, then fine. Let me work on that."

***

He pulled a few strings and found her a position on Carole Glass's terrorist hunting team at headquarters. This didn't make her a direct report to him as she had been in the London job, but given her recent challenges and rumored insubordination, it was probably best for her to take a step back in position for the moment.

She was glad just to be back in the mix.

It took a few weeks to get settled into Virginia and back at work, but Cristal was finally getting some of her mojo back. The physical pain was still a bit annoying, but her wounds were healing very nicely and with her diligent rehab, her left arm was almost good as new. The British plastic surgeon had done a wonderful job and a little makeup hid any remaining evidence of her wounds.

Still, her all-encompassing grief had turned to anger, a sense of vengeance, and a thinly veiled rage against those who had authorized and planned their assassination and taken her precious Tiffany. Whether it was Al Qaeda or the BSB, she wanted revenge, but nothing was moving fast enough for her.

She didn't even want to think about David and refused to answer all of his voicemails and texts. After a while, they even went unread.

She wondered from time to time if she'd ever really loved him in Burundi or even after their weird and magical reunion last fall when she'd discovered he wasn't the heartless terrorist she'd believed but instead a senior and accomplished MI6 agent fighting the same terrorists she was chasing.

Still, deep down she knew David was indeed 'the one', BUT he'd hurt her too deeply to dwell on that for now. The one hard link between them, their daughter, was gone. The headaches persisted; a leftover she'd been warned, from the head trauma, but thinking of David always made it worse.

Life was starting to become familiar for her in Langley. Back temporarily in a CIA safe house known only to a few in the 'company', CIA HQ Security was still looking for a more permanent living space that terrorists couldn't easily locate.

Her routine, or lack thereof, was established to ensure no one followed her as she traveled to and from work, usually in something of a disguise even if it was only large sunglasses and a scarf covering her hair. For the moment, Carter had assigned a security detail on commutes, but they kept well back. There was a pool of cars available at HQ and she rotated the one she signed out daily. This was a temporary accommodation and eventually, she'd have to get a car of her own.

This morning a special briefing had been called by Bill Carter, the CIA Director but more commonly referred to by his nickname 'DD' from his earlier Deputy Director job.

Carter kicked off the session himself, "This is an eyes-only meeting so no notes and no discussion outside this room. There's recent and growing evidence that we may have a mole in CIA headquarters so any information in this briefing has to be eyes-only."

He looked around until he saw nods from the eight people in the room, mostly Carole Glass's direct reports including Cristal and his own Executive Assistant or what the others called his EA or 'bagman'.

Carter started with, "The BSB seem to think of themselves as untouchable. The thinking is they're getting inside information on intel we have or operations we're launching. They often seem one step ahead of us and given the international reach of their crimes, our operation is the most likely source of any intel they'd want. So, on top of everything, we must keep our eyes open for any hint of a mole.

"Word from London is that the investigation has bogged down on the attack on Cristal's family. Both of the assassins were known Jihadi sympathizers but no further connections to Al Qaeda have yet been identified. Lots of Jihadi browsing activity on their computers but no mail or texts to known operatives. That leads us to believe that Cristal may have been the only target due to that video from McDonald's at Christmas making the rounds. Therefore, this could have been a locally initiated hit by simple sympathizers with no direct connection back to Al Qaeda Central.

"Turns out the bomber was a legit taxi driver. There are lots of Arab taxi drivers in London and it's not a stretch to think that a random Jihadi ID'd Cristal from that Khalil video, arriving or departing her MI6 flat, and put a simple plan together; wait near the house until they exited, on the likely chance they'd called a taxi. We just don't know. I know there's another theory out there that it was the BSB hiring Jihadis to go after David Crowe but that's our alternative theory for the moment.

"We have very little current info on Al Qaeda Central's operations in Somalia but that is changing, and not for the good. Our guy Rick Sawyer in Mogadishu, who some of you here are familiar with, has just reported that one of his contacts claims that a westerner, probably American by accent, may have met with Mustafa Habib on at least one occasion. Apparently, our informant, another taxi driver, dropped a shady westerner off with another local and recognized who he thought was Mustafa Habib greeting them. Guys guarding the host with AK-47s were the other tip-off.

"That would confirm the host was either senior Al Qaeda or less likely Al-Shabaab and the taxi driver thinks he was the same guy in the photo Rick showed him of the Toyota Land Cruiser shot we took of Habib at the football match last fall.

"The house wasn't one of the addresses from our surveillance list, but it has of course been added as a potential Al Qaeda safe house now. If Mustafa's team knew he'd been seen by the taxi driver it's unlikely he will return to that hideout, ever.

"Rick staked out the house later in the day but there was no movement, so they were all gone.

"If Habib met him at the door, then they either know each other, have met previously, this guy is a really important contact, or all of the above.

"Al Qaeda leaders are hard to get to and you must go through deep levels of security on an initial visit. It was careless of him to be seen in public but then again, until recently he was the behind-the-scenes guy and possibly not as savvy about being invisible as Khalil was.

"Our profile on Mustafa Habib has him as more religious and a very smart cookie. He was behind most if not all of Al Qaeda's forgery work and apparently, he was exceptionally well connected throughout the terrorism and black-market world. So, even if he isn't as personally brutal or a master of disguise as Khalil, he's still the man at the top, a proven strategist, and our number one target. Our best estimate is that he's known and somewhat respected throughout the Jihadi world, but our analysts think that he's on probation, or let's say he has a honeymoon period in which he has to prove himself, making him extra dangerous.

"Now Mr. Mustafa Habib would only meet with top operatives. So, this isn't some sub-contractor, and assuming this guy was in fact American, financing or gunrunning is unlikely; they're usually from places like Lebanon or Turkey or even Malaysia.

"Obviously our fear, given this guy might have been American, is that this person is BSB-linked. Sawyer reports that the taxi driver thinks this guy is new in town, but our guys haven't been able to track him down. The taxi he and the local took to Habib was picked up in the central market, so no leads there.

"Apparently, he looked very much like a native and spoke excellent Arabic but when he picked him up, the taxi driver heard him talking on the phone in English and he thinks he had an American accent. Westerners speaking English tend to stick out and stay in the regular places but there was no sign of him or anyone he might have been with, so he had likely left town by then.

"I spoke with Sir Richard this morning and they've hit a dead end on their searches for the BSB as well, David Crowe of course having killed our only potential leads in both the UK and Germany."

He turned to Cristal, "When Jason Fletcher saw you two in Nairobi, he let us know that his German connection, Kurt Willems was the one on the hunt for you two. We immediately engaged the Germans to keep an eye on him so that's why he was under surveillance in Frankfurt when they picked up David snooping around. There was hope he'd lead us to other BSB agents and maybe some headquarters guys. When Crowe showed up in Frankfurt and started shooting, they had to assume he was a bad guy too, but admittedly they were a touch trigger-happy. They're a bit embarrassed over that, which is one of the reasons why the Germans are reluctantly cooperating."

Cristal couldn't help herself, "You knew about Kurt? Why didn't you tell us you knew who he was and where he was? He killed a friend of David's."

Carter blurted out, "Are you serious? And when was I supposed to do that? The hunt for the moles these guys are using has to be eyes-only for obvious reasons and besides, you were out of Frankfurt by then and chasing Al Qaeda with a potential nuclear bomb. We didn't want either of you distracted by looking for the BSB. Your hands were full with a MUCH larger issue and David hadn't yet cleared his name with MI6. Could you see me at that point admitting to the Germans and MI6 that we had David on the payroll, never mind having to try to explain dead bodies all over the city?

"Who'd have thought that when you were posted to London, David's first thought was a trip to Frankfurt to avenge a friend's death? Evidently, according to Sir Richard, he still hasn't come clean on who helped him ID Willems as the killer, something we weren't sure of ourselves. We don't know how big that German BSB cell is so Becker's killer could have been someone else."

Cristal realized David had still not implicated James Owens, the kid outside of his office who had ID'd Willems as the stalker of David's friend Becker. The kid had helped them both out and she wasn't about to volunteer anything to get him into trouble.

Carter continued addressing Cristal directly, "As you know, we still haven't discovered how Hammond or Willems knew you two were on that Lufthansa flight from JFK and had the photos you picked up at your encounter in the Frankfurt airport. Whoever took those photos at JFK last fall is still on the loose. He or she is clearly one of the bad guys and likely either another MI6 mole or someone on this side of the Atlantic familiar with David and obviously part of the BSB. So again, we could have a deep mole here in Langley."

The room was suddenly very quiet. Blushing, Cristal made a mental note not to confront the Director in front of the staff again.

One of the other attendees to this exclusive meeting gave a stifled shiver remembering his chance encounter at JFK where he recognized the supposedly dead David Crowe from his short exchange stint in Langley a few years earlier.

Carter turned back to the full audience, "Anyway, with the help of the Brits and the Germans, we've traced the money Hammond and Willems had hidden in numbered accounts. It was substantial and all coming into accounts in Luxemburg as royalties on fictitious books they were supposed to have written but the publishing companies never existed, and the trail has gone cold. With Interpol warrants, they looked for anyone else getting similar payments in the form of royalties from those dummy companies, but no luck there.

"Some of the addresses used by Hammond and Willems in their communications were mail drops, temporary email addresses, or texts to burners in the US so we still surmise BSB is US-based and likely has pretty high-level contacts, including potentially in this building.

"As I said, they seem to be one step ahead of us too often. It's shocking how little we know of them, to the point that some in our less informed sister organizations wonder whether they really exist. The FBI has zero on them and if it wasn't for us, they wouldn't even have a file open or anyone investigating any domestic goings-on. As far as we know the BSB have had no ops here in the US with the possible exception of that weird and abandoned van near the White House that may have been intended for a hit on the President. That investigation by the FBI has gone nowhere but I still have a hunch it was BSB-related if only because big industry had it in for the President at the time.

"If there's a mole in our midst, we must find him or her. I have internal security working on it. They're going through what information the BSB seems to have gleaned, who in the CIA would've had access to that information, and through a process of elimination, they might get to a shortlist of who knew what and when. I'm determined to find any mole in our own organization."

Again, one person in the room was careful not to show any reaction.

Carter turned back to Cristal, "As to that meeting in Mogadishu, we have to assume this is what we've feared. BSB and Al Qaeda may be joining forces on something. With the McDonald's video on the table and David's trail of dead BSB agents, the one predictable common target would be you two. But if they have joined forces then it's likely they have much more than the two of you in their sights. Neither of them needs an alliance to go after you but it might serve as an introduction.

"In Mogadishu, Sawyer and Lulham have miraculously maintained their cover and are watching for any developments. We'll have to pull them out of there at some point because sooner or later all their questioning and curiosity will mark them.

"Mustafa Habib as you know, escaped our attempt to kill him. Subsequent examination of the ruins of the building uncovered a tunnel. We'll have to assume in the future that any potential safe house we haven't already been in has escape routes. Unless we have a drone directly overhead at the very moment he's entering a building, we can't rely on missile strikes that are doomed to create significant collateral damage. Two minutes after he's in the house, he could have moved next door in a tunnel. We'll have to get him up close and personal, mano a mano or hit a vehicle with him in it."

Carter continued, "On a separate but related topic, because of the video we've confirmed, as we always suspected, that Khalil had an accomplice who got away. As you all know, we've had no luck in finding him. Clearly, he's either a Jihadi who infiltrated the US like the Burundi team from that yet-to-be-discovered entry tunnel in Texas, or more likely he's part of a cell here in the US. My guess would be he's from the Pittsburgh area again."

He turned to Cristal again, "Khalil would've wanted local knowledge and we surmise from his resisted orders to kill you both that he wasn't directing your kidnapping."

Not everyone in the room knew the whole story. To fill in the rest of the group he continued, "Some of this is classified. As you may not know David Crowe is fluent in French. When Cristal's kidnappers brought David to meet her, they got into an argument because Khalil had sent word to kill the both of them as he smelled a rat; likely because we hadn't announced an escaped prisoner from Guantanamo.

"Some of the kidnappers didn't know or forgot that David understood as they were speaking French which is a second language in Burundi. David and Cristal moved on them before they could react, killing the whole bunch. One of them was Mustafa's younger brother Jabir and the leader of the kidnappers. One more reason for Habib to want revenge, if he knows what went down. We've never gone public on what happened in that warehouse.

"Therefore, the Burundi team must've been a rogue op not directly under Khalil's control if they were arguing about his orders. That team had help from Pittsburgh as we picked up two of them after the confrontation.

"Khalil may have used the same US cell for local support. The two killed at the Kensico Dam provided no leads except they too were from the Pittsburgh area. So, there was, or more likely is, a terrorist cell in the Pittsburgh area we haven't yet run to ground. They keep popping up and we have to find them. Look at all the attacks that have come out of or were assisted by Jihadis from around that city.

"Either way we want to find the driver slash videographer and see what he knows about how they pulled off the attacks in New York, who else is in this

Pittsburgh cell, and whether they have other plans in the works.

"Cristal, David, and our team in Mogadishu did an incredible job starting from zero in figuring out how to track Khalil and Mustafa with that counterfeit vehicle and then from its GPS history how they were shipping the nuclear material to the US.

"That was amazing investigative work but that still leaves us with many important open questions. Who was involved in the shipping and what the network is that made all that happen? All the way from the nut who ground up the nuclear material and killed himself, to the Jihadis in Somalia that came up with the idea to strap it on the bottom of a ship, to whoever orchestrated the sale and re-registration in Tunisia and on and on? We need to understand every one of these steps if we ever hope to get the upper hand on these thugs.

"Frankly that videographer is the only live thread we can chase right now. We've had those two Pittsburgh guys that showed up at the kidnapping in custody for months, but we've gotten nothing out of them and it's unlikely they have much useful info on anything in the future. Al Qaeda compartmentalizes amazingly well and besides, they've been out of circulation for months now.

"The Germans helped us track that internet café near Pittsburgh where the video was uploaded but the café's security tapes loop weekly, and forensics says an initial test indicates we'll get nothing on who uploaded that video.

"So, I need a full-court press on trying to track down Khalil's accomplice or accomplices. Carole Glass and Bob Boutet will lead that part of the investigation. Do your best but frankly, we have very little to go on and it's critical we get more intel on these barbarians.

We can almost be sure they're plotting more attacks as we sit here.

"Mustafa has limited time in his honeymoon period so there's a good chance he has his eyes on another attack and if it's in the US, it's our job to intercept it. That tells me our internal security level should be Yellow."

As the meeting broke up Carter said, "Cristal, until we have some kind of target maybe you could help with finding that car on the Garden State Parkway and for God's sake keep your head on a swivel. If they found you once, they can do it again. Your security detail can only do so much."

Kathy Sloane

It had been weeks since Cristal had stormed out on him and still, she wouldn't return any of his texts which had diminished to about one per day in his frustration. He was starting to think of his life without Cristal and wondered if they'd ever resolve their differences. At the moment it wasn't looking promising as she apparently didn't want to make any attempt at reconciliation.

The investigation into the attack that had killed their precious little Tiffany appeared to be going nowhere and it seemed to David that the center of the pursuit of Al Qaeda and probably the BSB was now back in the US. So, his role at MI6 was in a bit of a holding pattern waiting for some break in the case. This only served to depress him even further. Nothing to do and no contact with Cristal. He was beginning to think Cristal had been right and it was a couple of random Jihadis after her that had cost them their tiny daughter; a loss he thought he'd never get over.

There were moments where he let his mind wander to the future and whether he'd ever have a life with Cristal. Losing them both was just too much. Life had been so wonderful just a couple of months ago.

As the weeks went by with zero contact, his hopes were fading. Taking a chance, he had dug up a cell phone number for her parents and called them. Her mother offered that Cristal had spent a few days with them but that she was depressed and confused. She told him that both she and Cristal's dad were pulling for him, but they didn't want to offer any false hope that there was any future for them as a couple. For the most part, Cristal had refused to get into it with them.

It was about seven PM on a dreary Thursday evening as he sat, drink in hand, in a miserable mood in his secure flat looking at the invitation for tonight; a black-tie event at the newly renovated Sondheim Theatre hosted by Sir Richard Brighton himself for about twenty of his senior staff and their spouses. He sat staring at Cristal's invitation. Someone had either forgotten to delete her name or out of hope and political correctness they had included her.

The invitation was to see the latest reincarnation of Les Misérables. It had been a long time since he'd been to the old Queen's Theater and even longer since he'd seen a good musical; tempting but why could it not have been on a different night when he didn't feel so low?

Reviews raved about the current cast of Les Mis, but he was definitely not in the mood. Still, how did he say no to the boss, especially if he felt he was still in the doghouse for the German mess? Rumor was the old man, as many referred to him, was paying for it out of his own pocket but if he was celebrating something, it had remained a secret. David realized his absence wouldn't go unnoticed.

He had seen Les Mis probably a decade before and only remembered it was breathtaking. There seemed no way to duck the obligation so running out of time to decide, he dug out the tuxedo that had been rented on his behalf and headed off to the theatre for the eight PM pre-show cocktail in a private room.

He knew most of the Section heads of the Branch, all on the senior staff, except the financial team, but the shocker was the late-arriving Kathy Sloane who made a major entrance wearing a stunning floor-length, sparkling strapless black gown which featured a waist-high side-split showing off every inch of an amazing leg, turning heads and causing more than one wife to reprimand her husband. She was a sensation, and at first, he couldn't take his eyes off her. That changed quickly when he realized she had spotted him gawking.

Brighton was charming, as he could be on occasion, and thankfully kept his remarks short, centering on a warm thank you to the staff who 'seldom got the credit they deserved.'

There was just enough time to gulp down a few glasses of champagne to take the edge off. David attempted to make the courteous rounds while avoiding Kathy. He was afraid that he'd be all googly-eyed when confronted with her spectacular appearance. His heart was racing already with every glance across the floor as she gracefully moved around the room. On top of that, given their earlier romance, rumors would spread immediately if he showed any weakness in her presence.

Nevertheless, and possibly because they were the only two singles on the team, Kathy and David found themselves seated together in excellent end-of-row seats on one wing of the elevated Dress Circle of the magnificent concert hall giving them a superior and almost private view of the stage.

As the lights went down and the curtain warmers started to fade, Kathy leaned over and whispered, "This is my third time. With this cast, I hear we should be in for a real treat. Shockingly, the first time I saw it, as the music started and the curtain rose, the whole row in front of me started crying. Clearly, it wasn't their first time. The second time it was me that was blubbering. Such a beautiful yet tragic and sad story. Life-changing is how I'd put it. Don't be shocked if I can't keep it together."

Suddenly David knew what she was talking about as the familiar music hit him and he started to mist up himself. Memories came flooding back of his first experience with this unbelievably dramatic and tragic musical. Already his heart rate was up with the anticipation and pathos.

The latest cast was indeed exceptional, and it wasn't long before it seemed Kathy was running short of tissues. At the end of the first act as the entire enormous cast was on stage and they went into the medley 'One More Day', quietly sobbing by now she grabbed his hand, "I hope you don't mind. I just find this SO damned moving that it fucking hurts. My heart feels like it's going to burst out of my chest."

David couldn't help himself, 'And what an awe-inspiring chest!'

At the intermission with both gulping down a few more champagnes to calm their raw emotions and compose themselves, she excused herself ostensibly to raid the lady's room for all the tissues she could stuff into her tiny purse. As she moved away David again became aware of what a head-turner she was in that gown as more than half the men around couldn't take their eyes off her retreat. It wasn't only the gown, it was the way she moved in it. A few of them who were caught red-handed by David simply smiled and nodded approval.

No question, she was stunningly sublime, and the dress just put it all over the top.

Seated once more, he had forgotten just how completely emotional this musical was, and given his own wounded psyche, he ended up discreetly using some of her stash of tissues after the intermission.

Now hugging his arm tight through the final songs of the performance her head ended up on his shoulder sobbing as the climax came.

Tears streamed down her face and David was having all kinds of problems as well. After the many well deserved, and long, standing ovations and multiple cast bows, they were in no hurry and took their time like many others, to pull themselves together before they headed for the exit. David was emotionally drained by the performance and was surprised how deeply it had affected him. He was exhausted and feeling incredibly vulnerable. He could see that others seemed to have the same problem, and few were clear-eyed enough to make eye contact with those around them as they queued, heads down, to exit the magnificently restored old theatre. There was more than one face in the crowd smiling and wiping tears at the same time.

As they approached the main staircase down to the exit, she held his arm for balance in her stilettos and whispered, "Why don't we share a taxi. At the intermission I relieved your security detail telling him I'd get you home safely. E5's can do that you know. I surmised you weren't looking forward to meeting your ride red-eyed like the rest of us. Need to keep up your tough guy field operative façade, what?"

David was enjoying his evening so much he decided just to go along with it and anyway he wasn't in a hurry for the evening to end and to leave her to head back to a dull and empty flat. They had taken their time with their exit so there was no other staff he could see that would question their closeness given most were keenly aware of Cristal's sudden disappearance; fodder for the rumor mill for sure.

It certainly was pleasant to be out, wearing a tuxedo and having probably the most beautiful woman in the theatre on his arm. She was spectacular and all the men they passed confirmed it. The champagne hadn't hurt to bury any guilt of still being in mourning or being disloyal to Cristal. He was enjoying himself for the first time in quite a while and it felt good.

The short ride to her flat was silent as both were lost in the incredible enjoyment of the night, the moving performance, and the raw emotion of it all. Mostly they just sat, linked arm in arm in silence in their own warm glow. Thoughts of their earlier days together and what could have been came to them both. As they turned the corner nearest her flat, the parting came into focus and her tears flowed once more as she held on to his arm tightly like she didn't want to let go.

He realized they'd broken up more than once partly because he found her self-centered and a little full of herself but tonight was very different; she was completely vulnerable; a decidedly different Kathy. Maybe the last four years had changed her for the better. She had always been gorgeous and hard to take one's eyes off, but this new vulnerability was intoxicating.

As they came to a stop in front of her flat, she didn't want to let go of his arm, "Come up for a drink. We can't end the night like this with me blubbering all over you. Darling, don't be a downer. I'm not leaving you like this. I insist."

As he followed her up the narrow stairway, he was conscious that every step was one closer to danger and conflict, but he kept moving forward. The high, side-split, gown was truly spectacular showing off a perfect body and a spectacular leg, all the way up to her waist and he couldn't take his eyes off her. After all, Cristal hadn't returned a single text in weeks, had left him high and dry with every expectation that they were through.

He didn't want to believe that but part of him was saying 'deal with it … she's gone … stay in the moment.'

Both wanted it so badly that they didn't even make it to her offer of a nightcap before they kissed and started hastily ripping each other's clothes off. He held her against the wall kissing her furiously, finally tearing off the last of her magnificent gown and exploring her perfect body. There was no thought of backing out now, even if any guilt tried to make an appearance. They slid to the floor and he was on top of her thrusting forward.

Somewhere upstairs another tenant had apparently just returned from the musical and had turned on some of its most emotional movements. This only added to the magic and she whimpered and cried tears of sadness and joy as he ravished her. They came magnificently together with both of them crying out loud in ecstasy.

As they lay there, breathless and naked, he waited until they both had caught their breath and finally said, "Maybe we should close the door, turn on some lights, and have that drink you offered."

She laughed hysterically.

They cuddled later, naked under a blanket near her fireplace with their nightcaps and he spent the night with her wrapped in his arms. In the morning he made tea as best he could in her unfamiliar flat and brought it to her in bed.

She was just waking as he sat on the edge of the bed and handed her the tea. Smiling he said, "Well that was unexpected. I came close to skipping that shindig last night, but my God am I glad I went."

After sipping her tea and frowning then smiling at the weak brew she said, "Was it ever that good … I mean, were we ever that good together … back then? Just saying, that was the best sex, maybe ever."

He smiled, "Honestly I think the musical and the champagne helped but that dress of yours put it over the top for me. I'll get aroused the rest of my life just thinking about it. For God's sake don't lose it. I hope I didn't damage it ripping it off you last night."

She smiled, "Even if you did it was worth it."

They both sipped their tea and smiled at each other like two teenagers after their first magical time.

This went on until he broke what was becoming an awkward silence, "I don't really know what this was or where it might go. I mean it was beyond wonderful and I don't want to leave but frankly, I'm not myself these days. I feel like I've been in a washing machine emotionally for the last while. Hell, I wept so much at that musical last night and that's not like me. I'm definitely not in control of my emotions and I don't know what I think about us and what this might be. I hope you understand."

She said seriously, "You're dumping me?" ... and then she smiled. "I think I understand. You've lost a child and I can tell you're not over your American. I have no idea what this was either. Yes, I suspected you'd be there last night, and maybe I did put a little extra effort into looking presentable, but it would be very wrong to think I could ever have imagined how the night would end. I'm just as shocked and grateful for last night as I think you are.

"We are a little older and wiser now. We know how relationships flourish and die so there's no point in us getting ahead of ourselves. I'd love to spend the rest of the day in bed with you seeing if we could repeat the magic of last night ... that would indeed be magical, but we do have to get to work and hope no one saw us leave together or the rumor mill will be red hot.

"Let's just agree last night was more than amazing and see how we feel down the road."

Suddenly she seemed so mature and … what was the word … 'balanced', he thought. Not the Kathy from years ago but above all he was happy she wasn't trying to press the point and wanted to leave things to take their natural course.

To be extra careful, David left first and rushed home to change out of his wrinkled tuxedo.

From what they could tell there had been some gossip as surely someone had noticed her hanging on to him during the performance, but a stiff upper lip was the best cure for that.

The Car

The small Langley team assigned to the videographer, led by Carole Glass, was gathered around a techie's workstation as she brought them up to date on what had been done to find Khalil's accomplice. Her name tag just said, Anne.

Anne was more than a little nervous with all the heavyweights over her shoulder. Still, she felt confident she'd done everything possible with her assignment, "We've pretty much given up on finding video of an accomplice at the McDonald's engagement, so we have no leads from there. That service center is in the middle of the highway so there was always the possibility that someone dropped him off because he couldn't have walked there; it's situated in the middle of the north and southbound lanes of a very busy highway.

"There was nothing useful on the security cameras in the food court or the cell phone footage confiscated at the site. We're now sure there was an accomplice because of the Al Qaeda video but it looks like they ducked the security cameras around the building as we don't even see Khalil arriving.

"Given the assumption that this guy might be heading south back to Pittsburgh or New York we checked the cameras on the gas pumps which luckily happen to be only on the south end of that service center and cover the northbound off-ramp and the southbound on-ramp. There were some cars getting gas, but we discarded them as we figured it unlikely an accomplice making an escape would stop for gas. Obviously, there were some cars just getting gas as anyone visiting the food court would have been held by law enforcement after the shooting. So, we discarded all cars that stopped to fill up.

"We acquired the video from the pumps for the whole day but there's nothing significant before the shooting just in case they came from the south. The theory is that they followed Ms. Serpe from the dam which is north and there are no external cameras on that end of the service center.

"After the shooting, there's no one seen leaving for some time as they were being interviewed by law enforcement, so there's always the possibility they followed Ms. Serpe from the north and the videographer headed back which would explain why we see nothing. So as you can see, we've covered every angle we can think of. Any ideas?"

A young female analyst sitting across the room had been listening in and said, "Maybe you've got the wrong time."

Anne seemed perturbed, "What do you mean the wrong time? The timestamp is on the video from the pumps, and we know the exact time the shooting happened from all the cell phone videos we confiscated."

The whole team was looking at the young analyst across the room looking for an explanation, "I mean if you're relying on the time on videos from the gas pumps, the time stamp on them is often wrong. I got into a big argument at a local gas station over this when I went back to get a receipt and the young kid couldn't find my transaction. We finally realized they hadn't adjusted the time on the cash register for Daylight Savings Time, or anything else for that matter. In fact, I found out that some countries don't even use DST and if the cash register is running foreign software it could be even worse. Many of these places don't even tell the cashier how to set the time in the system. I'd call the cash at the service center and ask them what time stamp they have right now."

They all looked at Anne who blushed, "I didn't think of that."

Using another screen to look up the phone number of the service center, Carole Glass called herself and had the answer. "The official shooting time was 10:23 right? Well, the guy on the cash right now says his clock is seventeen minutes behind mine."

Anne was already searching the video files, "Pump one has the best angle on the ramp leading back to the southbound GSP. Seventeen minutes earlier, right?"

Carole nodded.

It took Anne less than a minute to find the right segment of video and there it was, less than two minutes after the official shooting time, a midsize silver car, almost out of control, was the single car racing away from the service center, down the ramp to get back on the Garden State Parkway headed south. Ostensibly everyone else was being held in the food court by Cristal and the cops for the better part of the next hour. So, this guy had exited probably seconds after the shooting.

"That's got to be him," Carole almost yelled. "Get this to video analysis and see what we can get."

Anne, shocked that within minutes they had the answer she'd been looking for for weeks, jumped into action.

Within the hour they had their answer as the video tech arrived and explained, "We're almost certain it's a late model silver Nissan Versa. That car can come equipped with a GPS or the driver could be using a mapping app like Waze or Google Maps. All of those systems take you through several toll plazas pretty much whichever way you use to get to Pittsburgh or New York City. So, if our assumptions were right and he was headed south or west, we hope to get a photo of the car and the driver at one of the toll booths."

Carole looked around the group gathered at the video tech's desk, 'Let's get on it!' she almost yelled. Finally, they had something to work with.

It took a day to get the right videos from all applicable toll booths for Christmas Day and the young video tech was back, "We were really lucky, they keep all their videos for court challenges and cheaters. Unfortunately, those cameras aren't cleaned very often and it was winter so some of the videos or still shots were of poor quality.

"Still, we think we have the car on multiple toll booth videos. There was more than one car like his so we had to get sophisticated and use things like the angle of the mirrors, dirt on the car, and the timing between toll booths but we're pretty certain we have him. Problem is we didn't get a good look at his face or a clean read of the plates as they either had some kind of reflective filter on them or they'd been modified in some way, but by the blue, white, and gold they were Pennsylvania plates which increases our confidence we're chasing the right car. It does look like he was driving alone, and he was on the expressways heading Pittsburgh way.

"What we did get however was an 'Enterprise' logo on the back bumper of the car and it had a dent in the left corner of the bumper. Right now, we're working with Enterprise for dates bracketing Christmas where a silver Nissan Versa, rented in the Pittsburgh area was returned with high mileage; we suggested over seven hundred miles. If we find the right car, we'll have whatever credentials he used to rent it assuming he was the one who picked it up. A credit card would be nice or a driver's license which is hopefully not bogus. Otherwise, we have a much wider search in front of us.

"Enterprise thinks they can get through their records in the next couple of days. Unfortunately, there are quite a few locations and they have to call each rental site around Pittsburgh and go through the rental agreements manually until they find it, if it exists. No details but we told them it was an urgent national security request and they seemed willing to put in the extra effort.

"The good news is the guy said he didn't think they had many Nissan Versas in the fleet so if that's true, the search might be easier."

***

Within forty-eight hours the search at Enterprise bore fruit. According to their investigation, Samir Abadi, clearly an amateur at covering his tracks and a recent Somali refugee had registered an old beat-up car which apparently, he didn't trust for the trip to pick up Khalil and drive to the dam. He had used his new credit card to rent the only silver Nissan Versa from one of the Enterprise locations and had returned it with over eight hundred miles on it. According to the franchise manager, the vehicle did have a dent in the left rear bumper. The FBI staked out his home and later raided his place of work and had him in custody without a fight.

Shocking to everyone was that they easily confirmed him as the culprit because he still had the original video of the McDonald's altercation on his unlocked phone's camera roll; date and time-stamped at the exact time of the shooting.

Under Homeland Security protocol for foreign-actor terrorism, the CIA took custody of the accused and soon had him helicoptered into Langley and in an interrogation room with an adjoining room packed with interested onlookers including the FBI and an Arabic translator.

Samir was clearly nervous and unsure of why he was being questioned. Expectations were that he'd offer little help without extended interrogation, if he knew much at all.

The young agent assigned to the interrogation was about the same age as Samir and switched back and forth between English and Arabic. Samir hadn't been told why he'd been detained, and the strategy was to get him to relax and think they weren't on to him about Christmas Day. Instead, they questioned him in a way that made him think it was about his reading material, internet searches, and the fact that they saw him as a potential target for recruitment by Al Qaeda.

Samir was nervous but impressed that the mighty CIA was interested enough in him to helicopter him across the country; but knowing the fear Americans had of Al Qaeda, maybe this was how the crazy CIA spent all their money and handled every potential Al Qaeda recruit. He was sure he could outsmart them in the questioning.

After about two hours the young interrogator let it slip casually that a video of a major Al Qaeda leader being killed by a woman was on the internet.

Samir seemed to come to life, "I saw this video you speak of, and believe me that CIA witch is going to die a painful death as soon as any real Muslim can find her. There's a fatwa on her you know. I hear someone already tried to kill her somewhere."

Remembering where he was, he said, "Hey, is she really CIA?

"Do you know her?

"Does she work here?"

All the men in the adjoining room took a peek at Cristal who stared ahead stoically at the prisoner.

The young agent paused, "No, I don't know who she is, but I saw this video on your phone. Where did you get it?"

Samir hesitated and blushed, "I don't know. Someone must have given it to me."

"Are you Al Qaeda?"

"Of course not, but I can read and follow things on the internet you know. That's not against your law, is it? I know my rights. I'm here as a refugee but I have rights too, don't I?"

The young agent just smiled, "Well if you've been following Al Qaeda news, they recently tried attacks in the US and besides JFK there may have been an attempt to make a big splash on Christmas Day that didn't work. That's where that video came from. So, it looks like Al Qaeda isn't as dangerous as we think. Your friends are failures as terrorists if they can be killed by a woman. They missed their big opportunity and lost a leader as well."

Samir became very irritated, "You know nothing. You tell YOUR friends that Khalil was a great leader. All Muslims know this. I'm not Al Qaeda but you should truly fear them. They have lots of money and strong fighters. They have Allah on their side and his followers are very resolute and capable. You should be very afraid of Al Qaeda! America needs to leave Muslim lands and there will be no rest until you do!"

The young interrogator switched to a very sarcastic tone, "I think your friends are amateurs Samir. I think they aren't a threat to the US. Maybe in Europe or elsewhere but not here in the US. They will never attack us again in the USA. They're too afraid and we're too good at stopping them."

Samir, red-faced almost yelled, "Oh yeah? They're NOT afraid. I hear there will be an even bigger attack on your July fourth. One you won't be able to stop and even without Khalil, they have many strong fighters to make it happen."

The shock behind the one-way glass was palpable. Al Qaeda, presumably under new leadership, was still intent on making a big splash again in what they kept referring to as the 'Great Satan'.

The young interrogator continued, "Where did you hear that? Are they going to try to attack New York again?"

Samir turned beet red and backtracked realizing he may have given up something, "How would I know that? It's just rumors and anyway, I'm not Al Qaeda so they'd never tell me anything even if I knew who to talk to. I just read the gossip on the wires. But you had better watch out. They aren't finished with you yet."

The whole team knew he was downplaying his own role in Al Qaeda and trying to throw them off the scent. Their monitoring of his web history showed no sites that weren't under constant surveillance by Homeland Security and everyone in the room knew there were no 'rumors' of an attack planned for July fourth anywhere. It was clear Samir had gotten this somewhere else; either from some current operational team or possibly from Khalil himself but that raised the question of whether the operation was still in play with

Khalil gone. Unfortunately, it was instantly clear to everyone they had to take this seriously.

There was a very high probability that Al Qaeda did indeed have plans for a big attack on America's Independence Day.

Cristal was first to speak. "Not this again; big attack and all we have is the date. Here we go, and on top of that, they have a blood lust to take me out. This feels like a never-ending circle of terror. Big attacks with no leads. I'll bet this character knows nothing more about it."

Carole took over, "If this guy really was Khalil's driver, and there's no reason to doubt that, then the boss may have let slip there would be other attacks, but I agree, this guy knows nothing beyond that. Khalil was a paranoid professional Jihadi and really drove compartmentalization in his organization. I can see him teasing this guy with the promise of a big attack to come but he'd be unlikely to have shared any details like the target. We're effectively starting from zero and we have to assume a plan for July fourth is still in the works."

Further questioning of Samir simply demonstrated what they'd feared, that he'd simply been a pawn, a useful idiot to drive the boss around and take videos of their attacks. It was clear he knew nothing more about any upcoming attack. Just as bad, they could find nothing that linked him to other US-based Jihadis. If there was still a cell in the Pittsburgh vicinity, Samir was either not a part of it, or the cell had done a masterful job of compartmentalizing their operations and Samir wasn't about to give up even a single person as a suspect. A quick search of his computer and cell phone turned up nothing useful leaving the team puzzled how all pointers seemed to go back to the Pittsburgh area but they had no links to tie anyone together.

At least they had him on terrorism charges based on his phone recording of Khalil's end. They still had some work to do to tie him to the Kensico Dam site.

Within a few days the 'war room' with about thirty experts covering all security functions, was stood up at CIA HQ and would take the lead for Homeland Security given the threat was likely international. Homeland had raised the internal threat level to Yellow. The FBI and other key law enforcement agencies would have their own war rooms and protocols were renewed to share anything they found but not knowing anything about a proposed target, it was too early to alert state and local law enforcement. They knew of course that Homeland was Yellow and looking for something and all law enforcement was asked to be vigilant.

Bill Carter kicked off the first meeting of the CIA's new task force, "I want us to start by dusting off all the analysis that was done after 9/11 and then again last Christmas on potentially vulnerable targets. All we know for sure is that we were completely wrong and surprised by their targets a few months ago in New York. Even though it's an overused construct, we have to think outside the box. The one area they seem to excel at is surprising us.

"We know they've used cobalt and cesium as weapons against infrastructure targets that were likely not aimed at mass casualties but rather massive economic disruption which again, was one of the unexpected lessons from 9/11. That attack caused mass disruption of air travel for more than a year and two very expensive wars that are still costing us.

"Even the attempted attacks on that Pittsburgh mall would've killed dozens but its primary intent was to scare the hell out of American shoppers and families across the nation and shut down retail. They seem to have concluded they can inflict more political pain with economic disruption than by killing Americans.

"We've no way to know if that radioactive stuff they brought into the US was all used up or being stored for a follow-on attack.

"Remember, because only the first New York attack was successful it was bad BUT a follow-on attack the very next day would have been like the second bomb on Nagasaki, catastrophic and more than twice as bad in terms of terrorizing the country and that's the strategy these barbarians seem to employ. So, if the Kensico attack had worked on top of JFK the night before then ... well you get the idea. A stream of attacks is much more terrifying than a one-off.

"The other thing is that Khalil is dead. So, if he was the mastermind behind July fourth, his plan was either fully developed by Christmas or it could be dead too. The intel we have on his successor is that he has no established chops for operationalizing these types of attacks and therefore he has some proving to do. That's both good and bad. He may not yet have the talent for these types of ops ... putting all the pieces together and keeping it quiet, but he must certainly have the desire and we know he's a master strategist. If he can get the operational side worked out, he could be a horrifying threat; one that is even harder to anticipate and defend against, and frankly anticipation hasn't been our strong suit.

"If I were Mustafa Habib, I'd want to follow through on the threat and take credit for an attack on the 'Great Satan' on July fourth. He needs it to show the troops who's in charge. If this low-level soldier in the US knew about July fourth, then Habib certainly knows that and likely a lot more of the plan. So, he'll either change Khalil's plan, if he even knows the details, or plan his own attack to earn his stripes. Hell, as the master strategist he may have written Khalil's plan. Therefore, I'd say there's a very high probability they do have something in the works for Independence Day. Our job is to figure out what that is and intercept it.

"Jim, where do we stand relative to the work after 9/11 on vulnerabilities?"

Jim Saxon was the Homeland Security go-to guy on the subject and had been brought in as the expert to brief each of the agencies involved in heading off the anticipated attack.

Jim stepped to the front of the room, "Obviously we're a lot better off and safer than on 9/11. After lots of preventative measures, we've had very few attempts on air travel, and those have mostly been either intercepted or failures like the underwear or shoe bombers.

"The mall attempt was something new and it will take years of architectural changes to zip up that hole. Kensico was new in the type of attack and JFK will turn out to be more of a nuisance but an expensive one.

"Frankly, our biggest risk is still the internet but the Jihadis have shown little interest or capability in that domain. There it's the Chinese, Russians, and North Koreans. Every piece of our infrastructure uses the internet so that's been our primary focus over the last couple of years. Even some hardened facilities from traffic lights to power plants, dams, banks, Air Traffic Control, and hundreds of other facilities still depend in some way on the internet. Again, we haven't been able to harden every one of those to the degree where we can feel completely safe. All we have are reactionary strategies when we sense intrusions.

"The one thing we have going for us is the size and distribution of the internet itself. You could probably takedown a hundred thousand computers and most people would only see a short delay in their connection as virtually every link in the network has many alternate routes. So the internet itself is an unlikely target but any critical infrastructure using it is fair game and to be honest, it's a glaring weakness. Firewalls and virus scanners do a good job WHEN they're used properly.

"Even though the Jihadis haven't shown any capability in internet attacks, they use it, as you know, extensively, and honestly I'd keep an eye on it because we think they're missing an easy opportunity that will avail itself to them at some point. It's only a matter of time in my opinion until they come up with a scheme to use the internet to terrify us in some way. You can still be brutal, intimidating, deadly, and scare the hell out of people using a keyboard.

"To date, our focus has been on the growing capabilities of the Russians, North Koreans, and the Chinese in hacking but more to the point, Black Hat Hackers; former experts of their hacking teams we feel could be freelancing ... and that could have terrifying consequences.

"We think at least a half dozen trained super-hackers have disappeared and possibly gone rogue or could be cyber mercenaries. So far, they've mostly applied themselves to a bunch of lucrative consumer financial scams and ransomware that you're familiar with, but you don't want one of those hackers stumbling upon some Jihadis with money to spend. I saw one of your reports that claims this Habib character has extensive contacts on the black market. So, our best guess is that the next attack could be cyber given its potential for stealth, success, and major impact.

"Even a fast-moving, hard to identify and track cyber worm could be devastating. That however, doesn't address your concerns about any nuclear material being used. And it doesn't fit the Jihadis model where they've shied away from any sophisticated attacks on the internet.

"Our best intel says they think we're so far ahead of them on deep internet interventions that they'd be caught before they moved on us, even if they could find the expertise. We do have sophisticated capabilities but it's the holes in the fence that are growing faster than our ability to close them.

"I'd say there are still real vulnerabilities across the board, and we just have to keep hardening everything we can get to, as fast as we can.

"A recent GAO study showed many critical infrastructure computers with passwords like 'password' or 'admin'. Computers are still being installed in critical sites at speeds faster than we can lock them down or train their IT people. That even includes government computers, data switches, phones, and peripheral devices in this building. I'll bet within an hour I could find a way into this building's intranet through something that was installed in the last week or two. Believe me, the bad guys have bots trying to find weaknesses 24/7. The main firewall in this building must log thousands of attempts per day and only one of them has to work to give them access.

"Some idiot comes in on the weekend with his own laptop because IT makes it too hard for him to get his job done. He connects to the internal systems without proper protections, clicks on Google to get something, has to open a port on the firewall, some hacker's bot spots the hole with a known vulnerability, and boom, you're infiltrated. It's all automated now so it only takes seconds. They either have their fun or plant some trojan and come back to activate it when they want.

"That's what we're up against. A single new hack is all they need until we detect it and put additional security in place. We can usually do that in a matter of hours AFTER we discover the intrusion which itself isn't guaranteed. They can steal or change internal data or worse, leave something malicious behind that we don't detect. Now if that's banking information or Air Traffic Control or a dam's sluice gates, we're in deep trouble.

"You folks must have heard of Stuxnet where it's thought WE hid trojans in foreign systems for years before they were discovered. The sophisticated bad guys are trying to do the same to us and these ex-employee hackers are almost certainly offering their services to do the same."

Bill Carter interrupted, "Okay this isn't going the way I thought. Jim, you're right of course. I know NIST has done a lot of auditing and sending out warnings as well as doing free training all over the US but I'm told they don't get the attendance they need or even then, both civilian and government departments need funding and the expertise to buy and install solutions so that's indeed a major worry.

"But as you concede, that's not the Jihadis' M. O. Remember the last couple of attacks were much lower-tech like dumping radioactive material in a reservoir or blowing up a propane truck in a shopping mall. Granted JFK did take a bit of chemical science to make it work but that was the exception. In short, ALL options are on the table and we need to redouble our surveillance because we have to assume this next attack is still in play for July fourth. Yes, cyber is a worry but my sense is the

Jihadis will stick to what they know and that means simple and failsafe like a pipe bomb on the side of a propane truck."

Jim felt he needed to salvage his presentation, "I know this all sounds too techie for them but honestly, think about it. You guys have been making up the lists of the obvious targets since 9/11. You've got identification, protection, and mitigation covered for all those identified areas. I think we all know about aircraft, bridges, tunnels, water supplies, electrical networks, nuclear, malls, schools, and the like. Some of which we're in better shape with, like nuclear and aircraft but others are just undefendable like truck bombs into malls and schools.

"I'll leave you with this, domestically every law enforcement organization is just like you. They have their own lists of potentially vulnerable targets along with protection and mitigation strategies. Not one of them is comfortable in the cyber dimension. With Jihadis the planning is international and that's where the CIA comes in. Find the bad guys overseas and find out what they're planning and don't be surprised if it all comes down to a computer terminal in a basement somewhere. Remember we've learned to expect the unexpected."

The meeting broke up with no definitive action plan which had everyone on edge.

BSB

Less than thirty miles northeast of Carter's meeting, a large black SUV pulled up beside two others behind an abandoned factory south of Baltimore and not far from BWI. As Number Two entered the others were waiting. While these men knew something of each other, the use of pseudonyms was an extra level of security in case of any surveillance. Number Two's main contribution to this secret cabal was the money and the connection to their funding sources. Agri had indeed been their original source of funds but a few others with their own international agenda that needed some muscle had recently been joining the 'fund'.

Number One, responsible for the political and intel side of the business kicked off the meeting, "Let's get right to it, I have a private meeting with Senator Fox Trot in ninety minutes. I expect she will NOT be a happy camper. In fact, her whole gang is VERY angry given our recent manpower losses. Remember, they and we are vulnerable to any involvement with law enforcement. Between Germany and the UK, we've had way too many losses and investigations tied to that wrecking crew of a couple. If any of these field people were caught alive, they could turn and dump whatever they know of us, which hopefully isn't much. Now Madame Fox Trot and her gang of QAnon leftovers want to know what we're doing about it."

"Who the hell told these senators about our losses?" exclaimed Number Two, the member in charge of the 'clean' or financing side of the business.

The other two looked at him in disbelief with Number One re-engaging, "Are you serious? How do you think this place works? America's Intel organizations wouldn't know those two have wiped out several of our people and brag about it to certain senators? Of course, they know we're bleeding capability.

"In her eyes, we've become vulnerable to being discovered and apparently we're working in slow motion. According to her, the feds are closing in. You may think you have a friendly relationship going on with your 'very close' funding friends, but those very sponsors, along with her and her wacko gang in DC will waste no time burning us if they think we're about to be exposed. They'd take us out in a New York minute if they thought we were truly vulnerable.

"Until now we've had a relatively unhampered and solid run of promoting their agenda and it's been very lucrative to not only them but for us and the people in our network; a network that was very hard to put together and is now shrinking. We've lost the whole team in Germany and a key player in the UK. Among other things, they were important to our intel capabilities.

"Remember, recruitment is one of our biggest vulnerabilities. If you pick the wrong person as a recruit, or say the wrong thing, they'll report us to the authorities. I'm not looking forward to getting involved in recruiting again. We've been more than lucky to this point.

"So, we're under an existential threat from our own Intel organizations and in particular, this couple from the CIA and MI6 as well as from those on top of us for not doing something about it. Too slow, vulnerable, and losing capability at the same time; not a great picture. So, we're going to have to double down and make some things happen."

At this point, he felt he should give Number Three a chance to respond, "I'm hoping you have an update for us?"

Number Three, in charge of the field agents and operational matters, and who had suffered the said losses to his team, looked around to ensure the bodyguards were all well back and out of range to hear anything. As usual, the three principals were sitting in the middle of a large vacant warehouse floor at a bare card table. Their bodyguards and drivers were much further away in a corner.

These men had to trust each other given they were responsible for untold crimes around the globe through their organization that certain law enforcement entities had humorously labeled as the Bean Stalk Boys because their founders were primarily in the fast-growing GMO seed business.

They thought of themselves as the Syndicate but with their moles, political and law enforcement contacts, they were well aware of what the Intel community thought of them and called them. They all felt that if they weren't the biggest targets of Western Intelligence then they were certainly near the top of the list. The pressure to produce and stay invisible was always mounting and the threat of being discovered and 'neutralized' had some of them permanently paranoid. Number Two had just demonstrated that he was the most naive of the three and a potential weak link.

Three finally spoke, "Number One is right. These two have hurt us deeply over the last several months but that's my problem to solve. We may in fact be able to kill two birds with one stone and keep our hands clean.

"A British agent of ours going by the alias of Mr. Tom recently made contact with you know who in Somalia. All I can report is that there's interest but no commitment at this point. He left them with an encrypted email link for communications. If they join in our project, they will take out the two agents as they want them even more than we do. If you don't know it already, they tried to take them out recently and missed, killing only the baby daughter.

"Al Qaeda now knows these two killed their leader Khalil and also the brother of the current head of their organization and I believe we can direct them to the targets precisely when the time comes for their revenge. It's a significant draw for them to join in this operation and as you know, we absolutely need them to pull it off. So, we get them to hit our primary targets with no links to us and they also wipe out that couple."

Number Two interrupted, "Are we really going to do this? I mean these are terrorists. They're responsible for atrocities I don't even want to think about. Hell, they've beheaded Americans and burned people alive in cages for God's sake. Do we really want to get mixed up with that? Yeah, we've broken some laws and played hardball using some mercenaries but this is an entirely different level. I'm not even sure our funders would be okay with this."

Number One was furious, "We've had this discussion before, and we've decided. I just explained the stakes to you. Our lives are literally on the line here. You agreed last time we had to proceed. Don't go backing out now!

"Our funders don't have to know any of the details. In fact, they DON'T want to know any of the details. If we don't act soon, either the FBI, MI6, or the CIA will bring this to our doorstep, and believe me they'll have a wonderful time parading us and our friends in front of the press and then putting us all away for life. BUT before that happens your sponsors will hire another team to make sure we aren't a liability. Do you understand?

"Listen, Senator Fox Trot claims they're closing in on us and that guy they held at Guantanamo who wiped out most of our European team is dedicated to the case. He's highly motivated. They killed his daughter and severely injured his fiancée, and he thinks it could have been us. So, he's on a personal mission to find us.

"The woman is no less of a threat and she's back stateside now working at CIA Headquarters. If those two can find and take out Khalil then they'll have no problem with us, so we've got it coming from both ends."

Number One wanted to leave it there. He knew even more on these matters but there was no reason to violate more Top Secret restrictions when these two had their own sources who had confirmed some of the classified stuff. It didn't suit his purposes to let them know just how close he had advanced to the center of the Intel community. His full role and current job description had been kept from them.

Number One who often took the lead continued, "I don't know why we're talking about this again, we have no other options. There's no walking away from this. We're in a sorry state at the moment and we have to get back to where we're in control and that means decapitating the organization where all the knowledge rests. William Carter and his FBI counterpart won't rest until they've found us. So, it's a job that has to be done and certainly with no way to connect us to it. Making it all appear to be a terrorist attack is a brilliant solution if I do say so. In fact, I see it as the ONLY solution in the time frame we need to get Fox Trot off our backs. Who else are we going to get to do the job, one of her white nationalist groups or radical militias? QAnon idiots?

They can't be relied on to pull off a 7/11 heist never mind something at this level. Hell, they all invaded the Capitol not even realizing they were guilty of insurrection the moment they went through the doors and windows; and all of it on a hundred cameras. Are these the idiots you'd have us rely on?

"These terrorists are capable and highly motivated especially when we tee it up for them to hit it out of the park.

"Hell, they pray to be martyred in a Jihad for the cause their masters have laid out. They're told nothing about the overall plan or where they fit in, but they follow orders religiously. That way they've nothing to spill if they get caught. Clearly, they're not ideal and highly risky to partner with but remember we found them; they didn't find us. If they accept our proposal for something we both want, then good. If anything goes wrong, we can always dump the plan, get a new plan and dispose of them at will. Three here tells me we have their leader under surveillance as extra insurance. If all goes as planned, after the fourth, we go our separate ways."

Number Three stepped in focusing on Two, "On top of that, Number One here told us that the CIA now has intel that Al Qaeda originally had their own plans for July fourth. Independence Day works for us in several ways. One, they know Al Qaeda had plans already. Two, it's a believable target for Jihadis being a national holiday. And three, our targets will be grouped together in the parade. I've seen to that. We control everything so I'm very confident we can pull off our side of the operation. The blame will all go to the Jihadis as well as any issues with collateral damage. In fact, that's the way Al Qaeda wants it."

One spoke again, "I say we're still a go, and Number Three, let us know as soon as you hear their response."

Just then Number Three's phone beeped. As he read the email message his face paled, "Well, perfect timing. I have good news and bad news. This is from the people in Mogadishu. First, they want to work with us with certain conditions. Mostly that we keep our distance from their leadership and stop tracking them."

Number Two interjected, "And the bad news?"

"To make the point that they didn't appreciate us tracking down their leadership, they blew up our Mr. Tom and a buddy this morning in London. Jim Harden was a personal friend. They found him somehow, figured out how we found them, and left a pointed message. Fuckin' Neanderthals!"

Two jumped in again, "Hell! What about us, can they find us?"

Number One answered, "I doubt it but keep your eyes open.

"So where does that leave us? Are you both still onside that we're all in on this? We'll use these animals to do our dirty work on July fourth? I don't see any other way to fix our problem with those chasing us. We have to decide now. And no waffling on this. Our own lives may depend on pulling this thing off."

Number Three was in immediately and after a long moment, Two nodded acceptance.

On his way back to his office Number Three placed a secure call to one of his senior agents in the UK, "Listen you should know better than to leave the reservation and think you wouldn't get caught. I just left an executive meeting and while it didn't come up, I've had private messages with them that they want you under surveillance now. You know how these things work. You don't want them to think you're a liability that must be handled."

There was a long pause until the voice on the other end said, "Are you telling me that you idiots killed Jim Harden?"

"No, of course not. Jim didn't leave the reservation. Actually, he went above and beyond putting his life in severe jeopardy on a recent assignment. No, we didn't kill him but we know who did. You on the other hand are not acting very responsibly so get your shit together. You know I respect and support you, but I can only cover for you so much," and he quickly hung up.

The Threat

Shortly after CIA Director Bill Carter's meeting broke up with no action plan, Cristal grabbed the key individuals and corralled them into yet another secure room. Cristal led off, "Okay the Director has made the problem clear but it's up to us to come up with an action plan. We need to hit these people before they hit us and we've only weeks before they're likely to pull off another attack in the US. As far as I'm concerned, here is what we know:

"They may or may not have more nuclear material. They may also be in a state of some disruption with Khalil's departure. Then again, they must be even more motivated to hit us after his death. We missed Mustafa Habib in Somalia so he's their presumptive heir to the network and we need to find him, disrupt any plans and take him off the field.

"He likely knows or suspects we killed his little brother some months ago. We know he's a big-time gambler and a soccer nut. Knowing that helped us immeasurably last time. He'll take risks to get to the big games but sadly we took out his counterfeit police vehicle so we can no longer follow him around with that. Yes, that attack was the right call to target him and try to dispose of a few more Jihadis but now we have no way to track him.

"We've been unsuccessful in tracking down the entire network around Pittsburgh but everything we know points to that area as ground zero for Al Qaeda's network involved in these attacks. We can't ignore other potential cells, but Pittsburgh is a sure thing in terms of budding Jihadis. I know the FBI has a focus on that area so let's make sure we know of anything they find.

"We theorized and now Rick Sawyer concurs that the BSB and Al Qaeda may have formed a tactical alliance in that they have complementary goals, move in similar mercenary circles, and might already have formed a joint plan, maybe even the plan for Independence Day. We must assume the worst given our guys in Mogadishu think that a connection and maybe a deal might have recently been made.

"We have no good leads on either the BSB or Al Qaeda outside of Somalia and that videographer we have in custody doesn't seem to know anything beyond a date. We're still searching his devices but assume we get no more from him.

"Why would they join forces? In my mind, that's an easy one. To pull off some big attack and take the focus off the BSB and on to Al Qaeda, who will gladly take credit. But that's a snake making a deal with a mongoose. They'd just as easily turn on each other which might be something we can use down the line.

"Homeland thinks cyberattacks may be next. That could open up an entire universe of potential attacks, but so far we've seen nothing so sophisticated from Al Qaeda. BSB might be different. With their Intel moles, they might have something they can bring to the table in the way of cyber capabilities.

"Just to remind us, Al Qaeda has tended to more manual things like dumping magnetic nuclear material in an airport and trying to dump more nuclear material into a reservoir, as well as trying to blow up propane trucks in shopping malls but there's no telling what the BSB's appetite is for a more sophisticated attack so we need to keep that cyber threat in the back of our minds.

"The thing from that briefing that scared me was the possibility of rogue cyber agents for hire. I think he called them Black Hat Hackers. I could see Mustafa making a deal if that opportunity crossed his path and I suspect the BSB are always on the lookout for weapons for hire. Remember, one thing we know about Mustafa is that he made his money on the black market throughout Africa and Asia, so he has friends who were and still are buyers and sellers. Some of those rogue cyber agents could be available to him.

"By themselves, they're not good with any science or techie-related things. They demonstrated they knew little about the nuclear material as their original mechanic on the subject killed himself with it. The stuff at the reservoir was partly shielded in coolers but again they showed little knowledge for safety precautions, if their Jihadi minds even care about safety.

"Homeland thinks that they could acquire hacking experience, as I said, from one of those rogue cyber agents, but remember they're a very insular organization and would be wary about inviting outsiders in unless they come from a strict Muslim Jihad background or they could be isolated in some way. A Muslim intermediary might be a solution too.

"But if there's a joint plan for July fourth why would BSB have turned their attention to the homeland? My money would be on a specific, high-value BSB target using Al Qaeda tactics and manpower if in fact there's some alliance going on. The target would have to be mutually agreed to but the execution easily blamed on Al Qaeda. Remember, if I'm right they're going to want it to look like a terrorist attack to keep the focus away from the BSB to maintain their invisibility which so far, they've been great at.

"So, if there's such an alliance and this is an attack in the US, what targets would the BSB want in the homeland? As far as we know they've been focused mainly in Africa pursuing their agenda of controlling local governments. What would they want to target here in the US and why?

"Here's a crazy, outside-the-box idea. Our theory is they represent agribusinesses, but I suspect not all agribusinesses are on side so why not go after a competitor who isn't on the team by say, blowing up a chemical or fertilizer plant and taking out that competitor. Remember these guys are all about profit and a focus on controlling market prices for commodities isn't out of the question. Blaming it all on Al Qaeda would be easy. Let's keep our eyes open for such an opportunity where Al Qaeda might also rack up a significant headcount if it was near a populated area. Still, we've seen no desire on BSB's part to kill lots of Americans. If their funders remain mostly American, killing our citizens could be problematic for them.

"Again, this all supposes they HAVE actually teamed up on a hit so we can't lose sight of the fact that this could be an Al Qaeda-only attack for July fourth.

"As always, we seem to have more questions than answers. What and why would BSB want to target in the US? Why would Al Qaeda agree to a deal? Is there a deal for July fourth? We have to assume the worst and that all of this is true as well as looking for an Al Qaeda only event."

After a long pause with no help from the audience she continued, "On a related note, we've no idea of Al Qaeda's current funding as their salesman-in-chief is now gone so they could be strapped for cash. We should watch for strings of big value robberies, holdups, and bank robberies especially in the Horn of Africa or other strongholds like Germany and the UK where ISIS fighters have returned home and may have connected with Khalil's reborn Al Qaeda.

"Intel says BSB might be well funded so that might be another reason for an alliance.

"Given Mustafa's base is still in Somalia we should also watch for a resurgence of some bold high-seas piracy of commercial shipping held for ransom. Sometimes that can bring in some hefty coin like millions for the ship and crew. The downside of that strategy is that it often takes weeks or months to make those hijackings turn into cash and they need the money now if they're going to hit us on July fourth. Looking backward, we should look for leads on any hijackings since Christmas."

Carole jumped in, "As you know, these guys may have boldly tried to take out Cristal and David a few weeks ago."

Cristal wondered if the plastic surgeon's tiny marks on her face were completely gone as Carole continued, "They almost certainly spotted the protection detail on the street, but they didn't care. They remind me of Leiningen and the Ants. They will sacrifice anything for the cause and as you know and must remember, they believe they go straight to Allah and untold rewards if martyred in the Jihad. I mean really, they use suicide bombers. That taxi driver blew himself to bits to try to get Cristal.

"So as the DD said, we have to continue to think outside the box. Don't dismiss any wild idea if you think it's too weird or too far out. Who'd have believed flying planes into buildings with not one but five suicide hijackers on board each plane could be a thing before it happened? And most of those guys had university degrees so they're real religious fanatics ... not stupid kids who've been conned into something. That act horrified the world but inspired them to do the most outrageous things like underwear bombs. So, think broadly when you're looking for vulnerable targets."

Cristal took over again, "Carole is right. Now we need the teams focused immediately on several areas. Firstly, finding these people; here and abroad. And that means both Al Qaeda and the BSB if our agents Sawyer and Lulham in Mogadishu are right, and they've teamed up on something.

"Secondly we need to double or triple our focus on vulnerabilities especially anything with a July fourth theme like replacing fireworks with mortars."

A couple in the group wanted to laugh but caught themselves when they saw Cristal was dead serious.

It was Carole Glass's turn again, "There's one item apparently most of you aren't aware of. It is classified but you need to know, so treat it as such.

"If you remember, when we found the ship in New Jersey that had transported the cobalt and cesium, there were no useful videos of any unloading but once we had the pickup at the dam we went back and reviewed other videos from security cameras in buildings nearby. We found the pickup around three AM on a storefront video, not far from the ship. It wasn't alone. There were two pickup trucks and the other one had something on it that could've been a homemade crane. Makes sense that they'd need a crane to lift the stuff up onto the pier. Nuclear material is always heavy, but we still have no idea how much they had.

"Now, they needed scuba gear, divers to get that heavy stuff off the ship's bow, and maybe other stuff requiring a second pickup, but our analysis is that because of the possibility of a crane, the load could've been big, and they may have split the load either because it was too heavy or just split it for security reasons in case one was caught. We didn't get enough data from the camera to track down the other pickup so there could well be more of that stuff out there.

"We've no way to assess if the stuff was recombined at some point before the attacks but we have to assume they have more cobalt and or cesium available. All of our radiation scans of suspected areas have turned up nothing, but it could be well shielded in storage, and remember, it doesn't take a whole lot of that stuff to screw things up like JFK or the Kensico Dam. They used less than a couple of hundred pounds in each case, but it did or would've done the job of closing everything down and terrifying the population.

"I know some of you know that both cobalt and cesium are not the normal nuclear weapons of choice because there's much more dangerous stuff out there. Remember, at Christmas they weren't trying to kill people with it necessarily, but they were trying to terrorize. Just the idea of having that stuff on your hands from an airport or in your pipes in your home is enough to do the damage. No one wants to take a chance with radioactivity.

"These are scare tactics only, unlike the propane tanker that would also have killed lots of people. The reason they went for cobalt and cesium seems clear. We work very hard across the globe to nail down any access or movement of more lethal nuclear materials, so they simply have no access to them. But they did a hell of a job planning two incredible attacks with a marginal weapon. If they still have some of that stuff they could be going after another attack that by itself won't kill many but scares the hell out of Americans or creates incredible financial havoc. Keep that in mind.

"Nothing ever came of the investigations in Pakistan where the trail started for the nuclear stuff. We have a good idea what their source of the material was but no idea on how long they were accumulating it.

"It's used in medicine and mining applications and unlike the really dangerous stuff, it's not traced properly in that part of the world. So, we have no idea how much they got into Pakistan or how much they shipped out of Somalia to New Jersey. Strapped to the bottom of a ship and possibly lifted out of the water with a small crane means it could have been substantial.

"We tracked down everyone from that ship but no leads. It's quite possible the captain dragged that stuff, attached to his bulbous bow, all over the world not knowing it was there. Remember they changed registration, ownership, and crews in Tunisia so the trail working backward has been lost. The new crew may not have known anything about the stuff. There was some shady paperwork done in Tunisia. Both the before and after owners were untraceable so that rust bucket was confiscated in New Jersey.

Again, another meeting broke up with no clear direction to finding the bad guys or identifying their targets leaving everyone even more tense with the lack of progress.

The Search

Early on the CIA knew that Khalil's driver and videographer had the typical Jihadi websites on his computer. Samir Abadi had apparently used a common encryption tool for email but in addition, his mailbox had been regularly flushed. It also appeared that he had a new hard drive so there would be little that forensics could get out of it.

A few days later, pursuant to a warrant, several aliases were discovered and a trace through the Internet Service Provider's site found a few suspicious encrypted emails from dummy email addresses. One message, in particular, raised some red flags. The CIA's cipher division was able to crack the encryption leading to a query from an unknown source dated well before his arrest.

Carole Glass showed the message to the team when they met later that day, "Samir Abadi received this email in April." She flashed the translation up on the screen.

Your eyes only – do you know how to fly a hobby drone? Can you get one and practice before July? Needs night vision camera and 3 kg payload capability. Respond by regular means. If yes, money to follow soon, Insha'Allah.

This sent shock waves through the team. Chip Attwood was first to speak, "The odds of this guy being an active Jihadi and not just Khalil's day driver just went way up. I'd call this a big solid lead but what the hell does it mean and where do we start?"

Carole continued, "We asked Samir directly about it but he simply blushed and said he knew nothing about drones and had never seen the email. That's a lie of course but for the moment he's uncooperative. So far we haven't found any response from him to this query so they must have had another way of communicating. Also, as far as we can tell, Samir hasn't acted on the email. No drones or related purchases or training we can find but it's only been a few weeks and he could've been planning on following through on this.

"Chip got it right … a big lead, but to where? The FBI has taken over the domestic part of the search and they assure me this guy is on the top of their list. They'll leave no stone unturned trying to find out what involvement he had, if any, in any other Al Qaeda initiatives, who he's connected to, etc. They're combing through all of his finances as we speak."

They had their response within a day. Nothing stood out that someone with a low-level manual labor job wouldn't normally have and no unusual connections to people, places, or events. As a recent refugee, he had little in the way of assets and for the most part, it seemed he'd been a loner, and having entered within a year from Somalia, he might even have been a Jihadi plant.

His few contacts would be looked into, but it was even questionable whether he'd been a part of the Pittsburgh cell as there seemed no connection with his movements and all the other Jihadis that had been identified and killed or captured from the area. It was a mystery how Khalil had picked him as his chauffeur. The working theory was that he must have crossed paths with Khalil in Somalia and was planted in the US to assist Khalil when he arrived at Christmas, meaning it was plausible he knew nothing of the Pittsburgh cell.

There was no evidence he had shopped for or bought a hobby drone but the implications of such a device had the team scratching their heads. Drones carrying a three-kilogram payload could mean just about anything and was Samir the only one being asked to prepare for something?

A three-kilogram bomb dropped on the right head or vehicle could be very impactful and drones were not easy to guard against, at least ones with night vision.

The team came up with several possibilities for drones with a small payload. Even a large firecracker going off in a crowd could start a stampede and scare the hell out of people. A drone hitting Air Force One was unlikely due to the speed differential. A fleet of drones each carrying a grenade might be a different matter. None of them seemed to be something Al Qaeda could turn into a terrorist attack.

The CIA had hundreds of potential Jihadis under surveillance and this was enough to get further warrants on some of them putting key check words on their email and text data directly with ISPs. It also opened up some surveillance on hobby shops around Pittsburgh and any key potential targets for July fourth such as DC itself.

Many of those suspected Jihadis were non-citizens and could be surveilled under the still active FISA court system's warrants. Warrants on US citizens needed much more of a predicate.

Again, the team was left with more questions than answers. It seemed that every clue they uncovered simply made the task more threatening but got them no closer to an understanding of what they were facing. Another meeting came to a close with no clear direction.

Mustafa

Mustafa sat in yet another 'safe' house, as if any of them were truly safe, waiting for his most trusted lieutenant.

Nasir Abboud entered and removed a scarf from his face.

"Is that really necessary?" Mustafa inquired. "Aren't you just drawing attention to yourself?"

"Master, they tried to kill you a few months ago and that Mr. Tom found some way to track you. I don't know if anyone knows my identity but better to be safe. Besides, it's very dusty out there today so I'm not the only one. The humidity must be zero."

Mustafa was growing impatient, "What do you have to report?"

"The 'Syndicate' as they call themselves responded to that secret email. They're very angry that we took out their Mr. Tom in London, but they agree to keep their distance. Not sure we can trust that commitment, but they still want to proceed. Even though we eliminated Tom, we still have no idea how he found you in the first place.

"For the attack, their first instructions are for you to assemble a team of three operatives and any security they need … they suggest security will not be needed but a maximum of one lookout per triggerman as there will be three sites. They want them to be in Washington DC a few days before July fourth and they'll send instructions on how to use the bomb triggers they've specified that we must furnish. They claim it will be a massive and glorious attack on a parade that is scheduled there."

"Why do we have to furnish the triggers?"

"They said they don't want any direct interface with their people and triggers are our responsibility. I think they want to keep their fingerprints off any purchases in the US. They did transfer money you said to pay for them, right? The trigger specs are quite detailed. They even gave us the exact model number of the remote-control device we need and where we could buy it near Pittsburgh."

Mustafa smiled. The fact that they specified Pittsburgh once more demonstrated their US intelligence capability. Mustafa nodded for him to continue.

"The targets are at three different sites all in the DC area on July fourth. It will be critical that our team all have working burner phones so we can pass the numbers on to the Syndicate.

"The Syndicate will take care of planting a total of five enormously powerful bombs, three at the main parade and two single IEDs on specific targets' vehicles not in the parade. Our team will simply have to position themselves within radio range and trigger them with the remote-control devices. In the single cases, they'll be instructed on how to identify the targets so we don't blow up the wrong vehicles. Those specific targets are expected to be in hardened vehicles so the IEDs will be very powerful.

"The bigger attack at the parade will have three different targets with multiple politicians in each car. The trigger instructions for each attack will be relayed by phone to our man directly by a Syndicate spotter at the parade. Ideally, our triggerman should be behind protective cover about three hundred feet from the bombs to ensure success, avoid harm to himself, and make an easy escape.

"All the targets are highly placed politicians or law enforcement chiefs.

"We should also be ready to announce and prove our responsibility at the time. Shortly before the attack, they will give us information that will allow us to definitively take credit for the attack. The main attack will be at the televised Independence Day Parade so we can watch it live-streamed to know if and when it's successful, to trigger our announcement.

"When the announcement is made, they'll give us the location of the two people we seek."

Nasir shuffled his feet uncomfortably staring at the ground as he ventured a question that had been bothering him, "Master, do you not think we're being treated like puppets in this matter? I mean do you trust these men not to cross us in some way either by trapping our team or possibly announcing we had little to do with the attack? Is this our new way of operating; to act as someone else's errand boy?"

Mustafa, recognizing the risks, thought for a moment before he responded, "We have an opportunity here that could be as meaningful as September eleven. No, this isn't how we'll operate but I want to see if we can make it happen. These targets are people we'd like to hit as well and our ability to strike at the heart of America's political elite will be celebrated by our brothers.

"Only our team here needs to know our limited involvement. Even the team in Washington doesn't need to know the whole picture. So, our insignificant role in this doesn't need to become widespread. In the end, if there's anything I don't like, then I won't announce our participation.

"What I haven't shared with you yet is my final plan for the second attack led by a team the Syndicate knows nothing about. We will in fact use their attack as a decoy. Our second attack should be much bigger than what they've planned, and it will be one hundred percent Al Qaeda and that will be obvious to all.

"Even if they set us up or abandon their plan, we'll have a glorious day on America's July fourth and we'll avenge your cousin's righteous martyrdom. If all goes as planned, we will again show the world our ability to strike at multiple sites, when and where we want. That should create real terror in America and hopefully move public opinion on their occupation of Muslim lands. Our main attack will potentially cost them billions if not trillions and should come with a significant death toll as well.

"Unfortunately, it's too early for me to reveal my plan but you'll be the first to know when the time comes.

"Now what about the other thing?"

Nasir shivered and look down. Any time he thought of America, instantly he had an image of his cousin as he drove towards the gigantic mall in the stolen propane truck only to be wiped out by what the press had suggested might have been a missile from a drone.

After a moment he spoke, "Our friends in Pittsburgh have found out that brother Abadi was arrested by FBI at his workplace a few days ago and hasn't been seen since. As you know, he was with Khalil at the New York dam and at McDonald's. He was recruited when he lived here in Mogadishu by Khalil himself. I know you don't remember him, but Khalil did have him at one meal we shared before he left. As you know, he's the one who recorded brother Khalil's assassination and uploaded it to the internet.

"I know Khalil had told him that we had plans for Christmas and July fourth but at that time for Khalil, it was only a target date for 'something' so the Americans can have no idea what is planned. Because of your wise leadership, we now have two targets, and we'll have our revenge. Abadi only knows the date of the attack which won't benefit the Americans much. I think you are the only one who knows the main target."

Mustafa smiled, "Yes ... I have information that the assets we need for my plan are still under our control so there's nothing to stop us. That's why information must be closely held. Even an overheard discussion could kill our chances for a victorious day.

"Again, following Khalil's policy, I think you'll understand that I'm not sharing the plan with anyone not directly involved and even then, the plans I've discussed don't include the actual target. You are my most trusted lieutenant, so you'll know the details just before the attack unless I need your help. For the moment I have it all under control myself."

Nasir nodded, rose, and left. He was pleased to see the new master seemed to be following the same kind of precautions as Khalil.

Mustafa, suddenly worried, looked out of the small window in his darkened room which was covered by almost see-through burlap allowing him to see out but anyone outside couldn't see in. The squalor of these safe houses made him long for the five-star hotels he had frequented in his days when he was free to pursue his love of a game of chance or racing fast cars on newly paved roads with his friends in rich Muslim countries.

He felt he had forfeited much for this life, but it was for a noble and religious cause and Allah would reward him in the end.

He was concerned that Abadi was to have been one of the attackers in his main assault but now he was off the table and being interrogated and tortured by the CIA. There was probably an email or a text out there that mentioned drones. 'Not good', he thought.

He lifted one of three burner phones by his side and dialed a local number.

"I'm told you have received the special delivery, is it true?"

The voice on the other end said, "Yes master, we paid part of the sum to the North Korean agent and downloaded it this morning. As agreed, we'll do a safe test with it in the coming days to make sure it does what he claims. If it works this will be a massive tool but one that will likely be discovered and countered quickly. It's very expensive and the Americans will likely figure out what we did and block this hack for future attempts so your target should be worthy. You likely won't get a second chance to use it."

"Don't worry about that. Just assure me it works and be ready when I give you instructions before July fourth on what to do with it. We're paying a very large amount of money to a very suspect source so it's critical we know this thing works before we use it. Keep me informed of your tests and DO NOT expose it anywhere they could detect it."

'If this one works it should be MUCH bigger than what the Syndicate had planned,' he thought.

It would also clearly establish his new reign of the organization proving that he was a master strategist. The

Jihadi world was waiting for something big, and this would be BIG. Much bigger than even 9/11.

Unexpected

The team at CIA Headquarters were heads down working on far too many possibilities for potential attacks on the fourth of July. The eight core team leaders were just wrapping up a review meeting with little to review when an assistant stuck her head in the door and said, "Ms. Serpe, the Director needs to see you."

As she was ushered into a small conference room near his office, he entered in his usual hurry and opened with, "Before we get started, when did you last speak to David?"

Cristal froze and stared at the floor. Her romantic life was something she hadn't been prepared to discuss with her boss. Blushing just a little she said, "Actually we haven't spoken in quite a few weeks. He keeps texting me, but I can't talk to him right now. The one big thing we have in common is just too hard to think about. And besides that, you know from that rather unprofessional resignation email, that he held back so many very important facts from me. How can I ever trust him again?"

Carter knew he was treading on very personal ground by injecting himself into her private business, "Listen, I understand, and I can read between the lines and before you ask, I haven't spoken to David. You need to ask yourself, on the trust thing, what options did he have? Surely some of that stuff was classified by the Brits. How would you have handled the situation if the shoe was on the other foot? You know how seriously we take classification around here. He likely exposed himself to repercussions by admitting to you how everything went down back there.

"To me, you two looked like a very loving couple and yes you've had to endure what no one should ever have to endure but that would seem to indicate that you need each other more than ever now. I have absolutely no idea how I'd handle the loss of a child even though we've never had children.

"As to David, I understand your disappointment in him keeping things secret but again, what could he have done? He was on the run for his very life with God knows how many professional assassins after him from the BSB and his own MI6. Any one of them could have put a bullet in the back of his head at any time. That really messes with your brain and you become paranoid about what people know about you. You're facing a similar threat now, so you know how anxious you can get.

"And while we're on it, who tries to hide in Guantanamo and tolerates waterboarding? That shows you how much trouble he was in and the pressure he was under to keep his real identity secret from not only you, the one who captured him, but also the entire Intelligence Community. Frankly, he's the one who should have trust problems with you after Burundi. I'm not judging but from his perspective, he must have wondered how you could love him yet turn on him and give him over to us.

"In Africa, at some point, it didn't take a rocket scientist to realize you were an existential threat to him, yet he brushed that aside. You must admit that if he did love you, and the evidence seems to support that he did, he must have been terribly conflicted and then shocked when you turned him in. That had to have made those years in Guantanamo even harder to take and likely burned into his brain that he had to continue to hide anything to do with his past, even from you. Honestly, I don't know how I would have handled similar circumstances. Remember, he's a pro and probably takes mandated secrecy very seriously.

"Listen, while my role isn't to act as a relationship counselor, I have great empathy for you, and I suggest you take some time to think over your decisions before things have gone too far. Not talking to him will solve nothing.

"One question that really brings it home to me is when I ask myself 'How do I know who to trust, who has my back, who would I want on a dangerous mission covering my six?' Essentially, I wonder if I'd trust them with my life and that puts it in stark contrast. For me David, even though I have some issues with him, fits that bill. I know in love things are more emotional and that might not apply … but it works wonders for me."

He paused as her concentration seemed to be waning, "You two were an incredibly effective team on the Khalil chase and now we're facing an unknown threat that could be just as big or even bigger. I'd love to see you two working together again on this. Moreover, I'd like to see you happy.

"To get personal for a moment, if I haven't already crossed that mark, I've always thought I had a special relationship with you. That's a double-edged sword. I fear for you when you're in danger and I relish your achievements but it's painful to see you in distress like this and yes it's obvious to me and I venture everyone on that team in there."

He took a deep breath, "But that's not why we need to talk, and your private life is just that, private.

"We have a significant new wrinkle in the works.

"Infowars, that's this podcaster Alex Jones and his crazy conspiracy website, has just published the picture of you two from the JFK airport last fall. The headlines are that the photo is of a CIA spy team who are responsible for the unsanctioned deaths of five Germans, we're hiding you, and that you're both still on the payroll of the CIA. Luckily, he didn't provide the names of the alleged spies. The photo is grainy, and you were blonde by then so no one has connected the photo with that bikini shot of you that was broadcast widely when you were kidnapped last fall. Otherwise, they'd have a name. Someone will eventually put two and two together.

"Now given Infowars' history, many people will doubt his claims but there will be enough evidence to point to the truth of it all and some legit investigative operation will eventually publish an exposé on such a juicy story, and this time with names. You were a news producer. You know what kind of a story this will be if it gets picked up and investigated. My guess is that someone like the AP, Reuters, The Guardian, or CNN will authenticate parts of the story in the next forty-eight hours. Whether CNN wants to 'out' a previous employee is another thing. They'd have to explain why one of their African producers was a CIA spy back in the day.

"God knows that conspiracy nutjob was destined to actually fall onto a true story one of these days.

"As you know, there are limits on how much we can investigate someone with press credentials, but we'll do what we can to figure out how he got that photo. This was obviously a planted story. His history says he has no legit contacts in the Intelligence Community. None of his previous crap has been anywhere near the truth. He got this info from someone connected to the BSB and their objective is clearly to neutralize you and David, as if we didn't know that already. This confirms they still see you two as an ongoing and significant threat. We've passed everything on to MI6 as well so David can take precautions.

"So the bottom line is your cover is blown and to some degree, the bad guys now know where you are. We, MI6, and the BND now have some scrambling to do. We need to get a viable and consistent narrative out on this that not only protects the two of you but gives the Germans much-needed cover for those ongoing police investigations in Frankfurt. They still have open cases on five dead Germans.

"No question this Alex Jones will refuse to identify his source claiming freedom of the press but only the BSB here, in the UK and Germany, had that photo. The one you recovered in that encounter at the Frankfurt airport is still in my safe, so I believe his source is BSB. We never gave copies of that photo to MI6 or the BND.

"I'm afraid you have to disappear, like now. There will be press at the front gate looking for you if they're not there already.

"Chip Attwood oversees all safe houses. I think there's one in Colorado that may have to work for now. You can stay engaged to some degree on your current assignments but not from here. You're too hot right now. We can't have some reporter tracking you down and forcing you into a whole bunch of 'no comments' with lots of close-ups on how you look today. But this is no vacation. We need you on this Independence Day thing, so I'll leave it up to you and Carole to figure out how to best use your talents.

"I'm told the place in Colorado is comfortable, secure and the scenery is spectacular. It should only be a couple of weeks until this blows over in the media or we find a better way to hide you."

Cristal wasn't sure hiding was the best strategy and certainly didn't comport with her penchant for addressing threats head-on, but they'd surprised her in London. Given her recent insubordinate departure from London, she was in no position to push back on the Director.

It wasn't clear to her how she was going to contribute to the organization from some shack in the Rockies. On a minor note, this was at least the fourth safe house she'd been directed to in the last couple of months and she was getting sick of turning them into livable quarters. She hoped this one at least had a comfortable bed and some food in the cupboard.

The company jet was set up for the following morning so she had very little time to pack clothes that would include cold-weather gear given the Rockies could still be dealing with late spring snow.

***

Exhausted, David had been spending long hours at MI6 headquarters and running down any leads on the two involved in killing his daughter. None of the leads had produced any useful results. Yes, the two of them had belonged to the same mosque and the few members he could get to talk to him had them as two loners, not tied to anyone else in the mosque and actually pretty private about their radical Jihadi beliefs.

Yes, one of them was a legit taxi driver and was often positioned at a stand near their old flat so it was looking more than possible that he had recognized Cristal from that Jihadi website, killing Al Qaeda's top man who had been revered by all Jihadis for his brutal treatment of infidels around the globe. After all, Cristal was a hot blonde, so it wasn't a stretch to think a taxi driver, parked nearby and with nothing to do, would instantly focus on her coming or going from the flat.

It had been a couple of weeks since the Kathy thing and they'd been cordial in the office but apparently, neither of them was ready to mix it up again just yet.

This evening he was on his second scotch when he opened an encrypted email on his laptop from Bill Carter. Mail directly from the head of the CIA was more than unusual and this one was also addressed to the boss, Sir Richard Brighton. The gist of it was that the cat was out of the bag. The Infowars piece would quickly hit the British tabloids if it hadn't already and the big shots at the three Intel organizations were going to need to work up a narrative covering the mess in Germany. The message ended that Cristal had gone into hiding and David might want to do the same.

It was five hours earlier in DC, so breaking protocol on inter-agency communications and taking the chance he'd get through, he dialed the private number for Carter's cell phone and was surprised not to get voicemail.

It was late in the day in the US, but the Director seemed full of energy, "David, I thought I might hear from you. Lucky for you I recognized the number. I guess you saw my email on the Infowars thing. I just heard CNN International has picked up the story but not confirming it yet. So, you and Cristal are in a bit of a pickle as they say over there. I shouldn't be joking. This is serious as I'm sure you're aware.

"By the way, how's the shoulder and even before we go there, we can't prove it but you're not fooling me. I know it was you who went after that Guantanamo guard in Richmond, Virginia.

"If he ever decides to talk, you could be facing extradition to the US to face aggravated assault charges. At least you didn't kill him like the guy in Germany.

Now I bring this up because you need to know that you're skating on thin ice with me these days. That mess you left in Germany is still causing me grief as I'm sure your boss has informed you, and now our hand has been forced with that Infowars piece.

"Still, I'm not losing sight of the incredible work you and Cristal did last fall but man you're making it hard to appreciate you.

"Now just forget all of that for a moment. This is the first we've spoken since the attack. My heart goes out to you and Cristal. That was an unimaginable loss for the two of you and it broke my heart for you both when the news came through. My apologies for not being able to get to the funeral. Things were a tad busy here.

"Unfortunately, I have a couple of late meetings coming up. What do we need to talk about?"

David was just a little surprised at how hyper and confrontational the DD was. Still, that was pretty much his style; get the most out of every twenty-four hours even if it meant jumping back and forth between topics.

"Well sir, we've made virtually no progress on this end of gaining any intel on the Jihadis that attacked us and also no progress on finding any mole in MI6.

"I'm more convinced than ever that somehow the BSB found these guys and hired them to take me out. If the alternative of them targeting Cristal is to be viable, we haven't been able to figure out how they found us or got their hands on explosives, or handled the taxi call intercept. I don't believe in coincidences so a London cabby ID'ing her and just waiting around for an opportunity doesn't work for me.

"We have their hard drives and the one phone that survived the attack. Someone definitely coached them because both had new hard drives with no signs of the old ones. The telecoms have nothing important so they must have used bogus emails on international anonymous mail servers from something other than their own machines like a cyber cafe.

The one phone was a burner and no signs of any personal phones although they both had subscriptions, so the real phones are likely at the bottom of the Thames. Basically, a dead end on our tracing so far.

"I did just read your email on Infowars and that Cristal is safe. Not sure what I'm going to do yet. Yes, I see where the top brass including yourself are handling the narrative on the attack and my misfortune in Frankfurt. Again, sorry about that; my zeal to track down BSB didn't go as planned.

"Listen, it's only a hunch and I haven't brought this upstairs yet but there was a professional hit job on a shady character here the other day. They used a pipe bomb. A James Harden and his friend were the victims. Harden was an American by birth and he was on our list of suspects for connections to the BSB. Local police told me he had a passport stamp from Nairobi, Kenya a little more than a month ago. I think he was ex-American Special Forces. There might be something there. I've no idea what the motive might be for his execution but just one more data point. The attack looked to me like an Al Qaeda op."

Carter jumped in, "Get me the passport picture if you can and the date of that travel. We think BSB may have met with Habib recently and the visitor was likely American. Sawyer in Mogadishu has a taxi contact. I want him to ID Harden from that passport photo. If it's him, we might be on to something. It may support the thinking that the BSB and Al Qaeda have been planning something in tandem."

There was a long pause and David took over, "I know this is not very professional but how's Cristal? She won't answer any of my calls or texts."

"Honestly David I think she's still in shock. I don't know what the chances are for you two but there's no question she's hurting bad. I spoke to her yesterday and she's in pain from all the things you kept from her. My only lame advice is to give her some time.

"We have her in a safe place right now, but you know her, she won't be happy on the sidelines for more than a day or two.

"Get that passport photo to me ASAP and keep in touch with any developments.

"On second thought, you need to be here. You're not making any progress on the hit and we now believe there's a threat to the US homeland out of Somalia. You helped us immeasurably the last time, so without objection, I'm calling Sir Richard to get you assigned to us for a while. There's only one condition and that is no surprises please like Virginia and Frankfurt, okay?"

David agreed and had no objections. He always wanted to be in on the action and being closer to Cristal was the upside.

As he hung up the phone, Carter thought of his last remarks on Cristal. He needed to give her something to do; something to keep her busy. She was a lot like David; leave her alone too long and she'd take matters into her own hands.

A New Friend

It was Cristal's first morning waking up in yet another safe house; a modest yet cute little cabin in the foothills of the Colorado Rockies with a big stone fireplace and man was it safe.

With a new code name of Sapphire, she was nestled in beautifully treed nature, about an hour from the closest decent runway or fast food for that matter. Given she had such a hard time finding the place, she expected threats would be few. Still, the 'company' had installed the latest heat and motion-activated alarms and cameras throughout the property, and she had all the weaponry and ammunition she needed to hold off a small army.

The place was a small, wooden, winterized cabin and really comfortable. A perfect getaway if that was what you were looking for. Whomever they had maintaining the place had been in just before her arrival, so the food was plentiful and an excellent selection to choose from even though the person seemed to lean towards high-calorie meals, whole milk, cream for the coffee, and the rest.

Still, there was no changing her mood. Being alone just gave her too much time to think. A lost daughter, a lying fiancé, terrorists trying to kill her, and a threat to the US that she seemed sidelined on.

So, it was surprising when after a quick breakfast her sat phone rang with an unusual area code. Her first thought was it had to be a wrong number.

The voice said, "Good morning Sapphire ... or should I say Cristal Wiggins-Serpe-Crowe. Not sure which of those you're using now."

She was furious. The first morning in one of the CIA's ultra-safe houses and some mystery man knew all about her. She decided to try to duck this one with what came out as a very lame response, "You must have the wrong number. I know no one with any of those names."

There was a short pause and then the caller said, "Let me guess, they've got you in that cozy little hideaway in Colorado. I spent some time there too. Watch out, the flue on the fireplace doesn't stay open and you can fill the whole cabin with smoke."

Still furious she saw there was no point in continuing the ruse, after all this guy seemed to know everything about her. Her code name, surnames, location ... "Okay, I'll bite. Who is this?"

"We haven't met. My name is Mohamed Latifi. I'm what you would call a Jihadi."

It was like she'd been struck by lightning as she grabbed her gun and ran to the side of the main window looking for the attackers. There had been overnight snow in the foothills and while the area was well forested, there was enough space between the tall trees allowing the sun to shine through. She could see for about a hundred yards in the direction of the only road into the cabin and the snow was undisturbed, at least on the driveway side of the cabin.

All she could think in response was, "Okay, say more."

Again, a long pause as this nutjob seemed to want to play with her. "Okay let's call me an ex-Jihadi. And to get your heart out of your mouth, Bill Carter asked me to give you a call. My western name is Paul Petrillo; one of my grandfathers was Italian and I liked that name. I do some work for Carter from time to time."

"And how do I know this for sure?" she asked.

"Well, how else would I know this number and your code name? I must admit I put some of the other stuff together myself like your real name and where they parked you. I keep up with the news including Infowars, I've participated in a few CIA briefings and I'm pretty good at internet research.

"Seriously this is a friendly call. Bill thinks some of my expertise might come in handy for you at some point. I may know more about Mustafa Habib than anyone else outside of Mogadishu. We were Jihadi buddies a few years ago. That was before his time with Khalil who I never met so that might explain why Carter never saw any advantage in introducing us.

"As for me, my earlier career was never about a religious leaning. After growing up in Yemen to what locally was a wealthy family with their own vices violating Allah's laws, I was educated in the West and had this romantic idea of freeing Muslim lands of the nasty westerners who disrespected the Koran and were occupiers of our lands. You must admit Western Democracies have their own flaws and there are many excesses that some in the world find offensive, even intolerable.

"Reluctantly I came to the conclusion that most Jihadis are uneducated scum and simply mindless followers of a cult. A cult whose cure is many times worse than the disease they were trying to eradicate. They killed more Muslims than the West and justified it all with magical thinking that if they mistakenly killed the wrong Muslims, they'd be happier in everlasting life with Allah. Free raping of captured women didn't sit well with me either.

"You can probably fill in the gaps on how an educated idealist with critical thinking skills soon tired of that. My biggest regret is that it took me a couple of years to see this all so clearly. Cults with magical thinking can be hard to break out of.

"So, at my first opportunity, I made my exit and orchestrated an incredibly careful introduction to Western Intelligence with a broad immunity agreement and eventually got linked up with Bill Carter.

"As to you, if I read between the lines Carter sees you as a major asset, and hiding you in Colorado is unproductive. I also get the feeling he's worried about you going off on your own if you're left there too long.

"Tell me, what is this special relationship he seems to have with you? I've pieced together that you're the one who offed Khalil ... my congratulations. That was a close call. I saw the video. You're quite the looker.

"He almost got the drop on you but given he had obviously planned the videotape, I suspect he really wanted a decapitation which may have screwed up his timing on the gun. Not to take anything away from you. I have to say, you're pretty fast with that gun, and man did you make an impression on the Jihadis. The comments associated with that video are monumental in their hate for you. And for a movie-star-looking American woman to have killed their vaulted leader, well that was just too much. You can imagine, the hatred is off the scales.

"Now with that and the Infowars thing that portrays you as a lethal assassin with many notches on your belt, I can see why Bill wants you out of the way for a while. A fatwa from Jihadi Central just adds to your peril. I'm afraid you're a marked person for a long time to come. Salman Rushdie has nothing on you.

"But back to my question. It seems to me there's something more between you and Bill Carter. Is it romantic in nature?"

Cristal didn't like this guy from the start. He was way too playful, irreverent, and mysterious. She didn't want to propel his curiosity so she simply said, "He recruited me years ago right out of college and we must have worked together on a dozen ops, and no there's nothing romantic nor could there be. Now, why don't we get to the meat of your message? I'm sure this line of inquiry wasn't what Director Carter had in mind."

He didn't like her put down but after a long pause, he said, "Okay, have it your way.

"Bill wants to get Habib. Apparently, there's some upcoming threat to the US mainland that I haven't been read into but like many things, all roads lead back to my old stomping ground, Somalia. I have no love lost for Mustafa who I see as having turned to the dark side even more after I left. I've been trying to help Sawyer and Lulham with their tracking of Mustafa in Mogadishu so I guess the best I can do for you is a dump of what I know.

"I think you know he's an absolute football nut. Soccer in your country."

The 'in your country' reference reminded Cristal of the odd area code. She'd have to look up 905.

Latifi continued, "He'll go as far as to take any personal risk imaginable not to miss his beloved Banaadir when they have a home game. They recently were renamed Mogadishu City and they're on top in Somalia's Premier League so there's no doubt he'd want to be at their games but probably in disguise and surrounded by an invisible security force. As a youngster in Yemen, he was a pretty good footballer, or at least that's what he told me.

"He uses many aliases. Tarik Aziz was one I saw him use more than once.

"He is or at least was, a heavy gambler even though he's more religious than Khalil but like many powerful men in that part of the world, somehow he justifies his infractions of Allah's laws. Last I heard he engages in some local secret games of chance but at least until recently he traveled to open or secretive gaming countries partly just to get in on the action. In his earlier days, he made an annual trip to Monte Carlo just for the Casino Blackjack experience.

"He has his own money. You need it if you have a gambling problem. His family had money and you may know that he's an exceptional forger which was a very lucrative career in that part of the world before he teamed up with Khalil. Apart from potentially skimming some money from Al Qaeda as all the top guys do, he probably has some hefty bank accounts spread around the world. He was a good businessman with fingers in many pies on the black market. That's where he made heaps of dough.

"He loves fast cars which are few and far between in Somalia so when he travels, which I venture is not often these days, he tries to get some time in a hot car or two. Some of his contacts are rich Saudis and I think you know how crazy they are about hot cars. Unfortunately for him, a supercar would stand out too much in Mogadishu. When I knew him he was on track to get a test drive in a Formula One car in Bahrain. So, he gave up a pretty racy life to chase what he sees as the altruistic goal shared by his Jihadi brothers.

"He has a younger brother Jabir, but I think you might know more about that than me.

"But most of all what made him move up the ranks so fast was his interest in forging documents. As I said, he's excellent at it, made lots of money at it but I think his network of forgers and black-market buyers is even more important. That kind of business puts you in contact with a whole universe of shady characters which is probably the genesis of his amazing contact list and as I said, most of his personal wealth. Black market dealing can be lucrative for a well-connected middleman.

"I always thought he was the brains in Khalil's operation. Sure, Khalil took the credit, but I suspect much of the strategy started with Mustafa. The brutality was almost certainly all Khalil's doing.

"Mustafa's a bit of a brilliant nerd and having him now at the top of Al Qaeda isn't a good omen for America, especially if his brother is in jail, Guantanamo, or worse.

"As I said, as Jihadis go, he's not particularly vicious compared to Khalil. Khalil was a really sick bastard which incidentally goes a long way with the troops as long as it's aimed at infidels. Years ago, he personally stoned to death a young BBC reporter in front of her colleagues. She was blonde, very photogenic, and recognizable to BBC viewers so that video is still making the rounds on some of their sites. Still, I can see Mustafa having to stage something brutal, against his better side, just to prove to the team that he has the balls for the job because it's widely suspected that he's a bit of an elitist and doesn't have the stomach for it."

Cristal shivered at the memory of the ambush in The Sudan and was shocked that the video of Tiffany Winslow's brutal slaughter was still being used as a recruiting tool.

Latifi continued, "His network has been built over the years, and even when I knew him directly, he had contacts all over the world including some shady characters in Pakistan, Afghanistan, and possibly even some crooked Asians. Sometimes he was the seller slash provider of falsified documents and sometimes the buyer of weapons or anything the black market can offer. He sacrificed a lot financially when he joined Khalil where he was much less free to roam the world for his own business.

"Now, as I said, I never met Khalil but to confirm, word from old connections claims that he was the brute and Mustafa was the brains. I know some of what went on at Christmas in New York but if it was strategic then my bet would be that Mustafa Habib planned it. Khalil was much more into the terrorizing PR side like on-camera decapitations, more into horrifying messages than strategic accomplishments.

"If there's really an upcoming plan to attack America then it will be diabolical and probably multifaceted if Habib is pulling the strings and I think we all feel he's the man at the top now.

"As far as finding him, sorry but again he's strategic and probably set up the secure safe houses for Khalil so that's made it hard for your guys in Mogadishu to get a read on him. Unlike Khalil, I don't see him taking a direct role in any US attack. He'll manage the puppets from home is my guess.

"And again, there's the issue of his brother. If he was in fact killed instead of captured during a US operation and Mustafa knows it, all bets could be off in terms of him hitting back in brutal fashion. Martyrdom and going to see Allah isn't the whole picture for a smart guy like Mustafa, even if he's more religious. He will definitely want revenge against the infidels and believe me he's committed to the mission of ridding Muslim lands of your type".

The 'your type' comment gave Cristal pause. Was this guy really on the side of the West or did he still harbor animus toward 'infidels' engaged in what the Jihadis thought of as the 'excesses' of western culture?

Latifi or Petrillo continued, "One last thing that isn't commonly known about Habib; while he's intelligent and pragmatic, he's also incredibly superstitious as many from our part of the world are, but he takes it to a higher level. He believes in the Evil Eye, Jinn, spiritual healers, and Witchcraft so you can be sure he has tagged you as a witch with supernatural powers giving him even more impetus to fear you and to be committed to eliminating you."

This was a surprise to Cristal, but she wasn't sure what it meant or how it might help in tracking him, stopping him, or eliminating him. You never knew what detail might be useful. Who could have thought the fact that Khalil used to put loads of pepper on his food would be the tip that saved her life and taken him out?

Again, a long pause as Cristal decided what to do about this guy. Clearly, he had some useful information and she believed Carter had set up the call to be helpful but she was uncomfortable that one more person knew her whereabouts.

She'd had it with this guy, "Listen Mr. whatever your name is, I hope this information will be helpful at some point so give my regards to Director Carter," and she hung up.

***

Mohammed Latifi aka Paul Petrillo sat there staring at his phone. He couldn't believe what had just happened; she'd just hung up on him. It was his place to end the call. Shockingly she was not showing him the requisite respect for his unique knowledge of the Jihadi world. Even Carter, much higher on the ladder than her, showed him some respect and afforded him a certain stature. This behavior was outrageous and intolerable. He'd never get used to the idea of women being equal in so many ways to men in this western world and she'd just disrespected him massively and seriously infuriated him. The more he thought about it the angrier he became. In no way could this be tolerated.

After thinking it over for a few minutes, his new career as an intermittent counselor to Western Intelligence organizations wasn't as lucrative as he'd imagined. Lately, he perceived that his information might be viewed as dated and it appeared they needed him less and less. He didn't like the weather around here either and the vibe was all wrong. His current location had its fair share of xenophobes and Islamophobes.

As his blood came to a boil, he went back to the fact that in this latest case they even had him working 'for' a woman who had just disrespected him and hung up on him. No, she was not acting like a woman in his estimation, more of a bitch he thought. A total bitch and a true infidel who didn't know her place. If they had been face to face he had no idea where his temper would've taken him. At the very least he would have slapped her silly for her impertinence. More likely the punishment would have been much more severe.

With no ties to his new home and thinking of a move, Mohamed Latifi switched on his laptop in his bedroom in Mississauga Canada, and sent an encrypted Arabic message to an address he thought he'd never use again:

يشتري سويسري حساب في يورو م 1 -- للوقت حساس عرض
الحالي الوقت في محمية، غير هي، حيث من GPS لك.

(Time-sensitive offer -- 1 m Euros in a Swiss account buys you the GPS of where she is, unprotected, right now.)

There was no question the other end would know who SHE was, especially with the seven-figure price he'd just put on her head.

***

Cristal was growing angrier by the minute realizing that it had only taken a few hours for her cover to be blown, and by her boss; a man she trusted. They'd found her before and there was something about that guy on the phone that had really rattled her.

Furious and anxious, within an hour she had a plan, but it would take most of the day given she was so remote. Still, she reasoned that being so far off the beaten path and probably at least a flight away for any bad guys, she had the time to set it up properly.

By nightfall, she'd connected the newly acquired hardware and grabbed only a few of her things, and headed out. At the motel paying cash in advance for two nights, she registered as Betty White, mistakenly thinking that 'Rickie' the teenage clerk was too young to know the actress. She was wrong and this raised a few more questions where she gracefully tried to advance her initial ruse.

"Actually, that's my nom de plume. I'm a writer on a deadline with serious writer's block. I just need peace and quiet for a few days to get my work complete so I can't say how long I'll be here. Looks like a quiet enough place though."

"Yeah, it doesn't get much quieter than here. This is our shoulder season, and you may be the only one tonight. Skiing is pretty much dead around here and the summer crowd is still a ways off. You won't get disturbed, I'm sure. What do you write? Would I have read anything of yours?"

She had to think quickly, "Not unless you're into medieval female religious biographies. 'Hildegarde – Mercenary Nun of the Fifteenth Century' was my latest work."

She was proud of the quick thinking but thought she might have pushed it just a bit too far.

The young man smiled, not knowing what to think of her answer, and handed her the key. "Well, if you're trying to avoid your hordes of adoring fans, then Betty White and paying in advance in cash is okay with me and the boss, but sadly Hildegarde sounds a bit off my preferred genre." he quipped.

Her wry smile acknowledged that Rickie was maybe just a little too smart to be fooled.

Settled in she got the surveillance system set up so she had a 360 view of everything at the cabin. Given the comprehensive satellite security setup the CIA had installed, it hadn't been difficult for her to set up an additional uplink using her sat phone so she could monitor it all remotely. If HQ had violated her security already, there was no reason to tell them about her plan.

It was getting late and there was no sign of anything happening on the monitors so she turned in and got the best sleep she'd had in some time, thinking the only person on the planet who knew where she was, was a pock-faced teenager named Rickie and if she was lucky, he really did believe she was a writer.

The following day was off and on sunshine and wet snow showers in the foothills and she periodically did a full sweep of the cabin's monitoring system to no avail. There was every expectation that the safe house was indeed safe given all the trouble the CIA had gone to, but this was a case where she wanted both a belt and suspenders. She had been sloppy before and it had cost her her only daughter.

Getting a little tired of the fried food from the diner across from the budget motel and vowing to never try the Rocky Mountain Oysters, she simply had a BLT and a coke and turned in early.

Being a type-A personality, she was up early and turned on the laptop to get a view of the safe house only to find the signal was down. Her laptop recorded any movements so looking back over the record she could see that the line just dropped dead about four AM and there had been no alarms from the perimeter sensors. After a quick breakfast, she wanted to try again in case the local router or wifi system had gotten out of synch and had rebooted but again there was no signal from the hub at the cabin.

Thinking it could be a loose cable, the sat phone had dropped the line, or some other minor issue that needed a physical reboot of the hub, she decided to go back the ten miles to the cabin cautiously.

With the window partly down in the lightly falling snow and listening for any sounds, she smelled it before she turned the corner and saw the smoldering ruins of the cabin hundreds of yards away.

There were tire tracks in the latest snowfall which made her think that anyone around had left sometime earlier. Still, there was no point in remaining, so she hightailed it out of there.

Back at the motel watching for any tails, she went carefully over the main recording from the front of the house that wasn't on a sensor but recorded continuously, and sure enough, she caught a bright flash out of some trees near the road just before everything went dead. Likely an RPG she thought. Not the easiest thing to find stateside without alerting the ATF. So, the most likely candidates were again either the BSB with all their rumored infrastructure or Al Qaeda who could have smuggled one in.

The discovery gave her mixed feelings. While it was terrifying that they had chased her all the way out here, she was pleased her mojo was back and she had beaten them.

Either a mole in the CIA had tipped off a hit team or that unsolicited call from Latifi just after her arrival was the culprit. More likely the latter she figured. Her hunch to get out of there and on her own terms for security had been right. Bill Carter would need to know that his favorite ex-Jihadi had probably flipped once more, which made her wonder about CIA HQ. They must have seen a break in their own monitoring of the cabin; probably even before she discovered it. Could be they'd initially think she was toast too until they reviewed the tapes and saw her leaving two days before, if their recordings went back that far.

What to do?

The bad guys were likely confident they'd gotten her so no reason to panic. Still, this was the second assassination attempt on her in just the last few months.

For now, she was on her own. No point in welcoming Langley back into her world until she knew that a mole wasn't responsible for setting her up. She decided to stay put, keep her head on a swivel, park the car where passersby, satellites, and drones couldn't see it, and noodle this thing out.

Something in her realized this latest crisis was helping her to get back to her old alert self. Her sixth sense had told her to get out of that cabin. Yeah, her mojo was definitely back.

***

Director William Carter was in early and an aid rushed in with the news that a CIA site known as Sigma II had been wiped out overnight. The hair went up on the back of his neck with alarm and worry for Cristal as well as an immediate thought that his Canadian friend had flipped.

Few people knew where Sigma II was and what it was used for.

Suddenly he wanted to kick himself as he remembered that Latifi was one of them.

He was being called to a meeting in the CIA's situation room with Carole Glass and Chip Attwood who had been alerted overnight and were already there and looking over the tapes.

As he entered, heart racing and expecting bad news, Chip spoke, "Looks like an RPG overnight that took out the cabin which is one of our deepest safe houses. One of our security cameras picked up the flash but no video of the assailants.

"We sent a drone in about an hour ago which has just come on site. The sun isn't up just yet in Colorado, but we have night vision on the drone and so far, we see no trace of a car so either they stole it, unlikely, or for some reason she wasn't at the cabin at four in the morning when they attacked."

'Thank God', Carter thought, 'They may not have gotten her.'

The scene from the drone on the big screen was conclusive. There were only smoldering remnants of a building and nothing was higher than three feet off the ground save part of a fireplace and its chimney. The longer shot showed some tire tracks about one hundred yards down the road and a few footprints heading into the woods alongside the road. It was hard to tell how old the faint tire tracks from the side of the house were. They were all hopeful it had been Cristal abandoning the site versus someone stealing the car.

Carole joined in, "There's no way she survived that attack and drove off so she may have abandoned the cabin earlier for some reason. We knew she had a car, but the attackers may have thought she'd been dropped off or was hiding it somewhere.

"Her phone was last pinged there which is worrisome but as I said, no car. So, she's either dead in that smoldering rubble or she escaped before somehow, leaving her phone behind. If she'd survived the attack by getting out before they fired, there would likely be some signs of her confronting her attackers, but the site is pristine save the wreckage of the cabin. It looks to me like they had serious worries about her ability to defend and they just took a shot from a distance. One RPG could take out that whole clapboard structure in an instant. I mean it's not like it was a solid log cabin. My bet is she wasn't there when they attacked and for some reason, they didn't realize she was gone."

Being in charge of CIA's safe houses Attwood felt a deep responsibility for this, "How could this have happened? Only the three of us knew she was there."

After a short pause as Carol and Chip looked each other over, Carter said, "Not true. There was one other. A big mistake on my part and he'll be hard to find now. I didn't tell him where she was, but I can see now where he might have worked it out. I was afraid she'd get stir-crazy and head out on her own, so I asked someone we have on retainer to call her to bring her up to date on

Habib and everything he knows about him. You know him as agent P-16 and yes Chip, if you remember, we had him in that cabin out west at one point.

"Something told him that's where she was and for some reason, either loyalty to the cause or money, he flipped, left our employment, and sold her out. I don't think he has the capability to do this himself, so he sold her location to someone else, and I'd bet some of them live in the Pittsburgh area.

"The question is, did she survive? My gut tells me she did but how do we reconnect with her?

"It's still early out there. If she got out before the attack, she may not even know yet that they tried to get her. Even then, she may be very reticent to call in as her cover was blown from this end. Knowing her, when she discovers this, she'll lie low trying to figure out who she can trust and what to do next. I suspect she'll be very hard to find. I think we just have to wait and see if she contacts us. She's going to be very angry with me too, so that doesn't help.

"For now, all we can do is pray she wasn't in that cabin when they attacked."

$***$

David arrived from London late in the day and, immediately summoned to the DD's office, was given the news that Cristal had been targeted again. Carter, clearly terrified in private, gave him the full briefing including the open question about her status and whereabouts. "I think you know I have a special relationship with that very complex young woman, and I'm devastated that I inadvertently pointed that turncoat in her direction. Frankly, there are times I think of her almost as the daughter I never had. That may not be professional, but it's the truth.

"Now, we know she had a car, so I'm still hoping beyond hope that for some reason she wasn't at the cabin when they attacked. There are a hundred scenarios and many of them not good but I think you and I have the most skin in the game here and we can only pray she used her instincts to stay safe."

David was trying to remain calm even though he was furious at Carter for his shortsightedness. How could he have engaged an ex-Jihadi when she was the most hunted woman on the planet?

Hopeful but petrified, he thought he knew the answer to why she hadn't checked in with headquarters … if she was alive.

David turned away from the drone video, "Yeah, I'm not ready to leave it to prayer. If she's still alive she hasn't checked in because she's worried that someone here leaked her location."

Carter nodded, "But she has my personal number."

"True but you're in the doghouse, no disrespect intended. She probably figured it was your Jihadi guy that organized the attack and you're the one who gave him the number. I think she's paranoid after London and that's not a bad thing. She likely took off out of that safe house right after that guy called. At least that's my hope.

"With or without your permission, I'm going to go get her and bring her back. I know how she thinks, and I refuse to believe they got her. I just can't allow myself to go to that dark place. After our daughter Tiffany, that would be just too much." David wiped his eyes that had suddenly become misty.

Carter just nodded, "You be careful out there too. Remember they want you dead as well and they may be waiting for you to show up after the attack on her. I'll send another pair of eyes out there with you. I have some good security people."

"No. If I find her, I need to be alone, or she may bolt just out of spite."

***

Cristal sat on the bed of the budget motel, lights off and the Venetian blinds open just a crack so she could see anyone coming. There were no great answers on what to do but laying low in this relatively safe place was good enough for now.

She wondered if the Jihadis had been smart enough to notice the lack of a car at the cabin. They could have thought she'd been dropped off or was hiding a car somewhere. Either way, they might not be sure they'd taken her out which meant they could still be around and searching for her.

Clearly, they were timid as according to the video she'd now seen at least twenty times, they'd shot a rocket from cover instead of storming the building. The camera that picked up the event was the main front-facing scanner which recorded constantly and didn't need motion or heat to activate. Try as she might, all she could make out was some minimal movement in the woods and a shadow leaning against a tree as the flash of the RPG came. She could also just make out the shadow of a car on the road as they had approached with their lights off. And it had been a very dark night.

Apparently, they had been afraid to approach the building but then again, Latifi said he'd been in the cabin and if he was the culprit then he'd undoubtedly told them the building was heavily surrounded by security measures and she had enough weaponry to hold off a platoon. In that scenario, they'd have been fools to approach the building, even at four AM.

That RPG into a wooden building would have created a fire so big they wouldn't have been able to approach, and they likely didn't want to wait around twelve hours or so until the ashes cooled so they could search for a body. They had to know there was always the chance police or fire would show up as the blaze must have been visible for miles. No, they'd taken their shot and beat it out of there … she hoped. The missing car was the only concern if they happened to be smart Jihadis.

As to Langley, they could wait. There was no doubt they'd have sent a drone or an agent to check out the loss of signal. Unlike the Jihadis, they probably figured she had a good chance of being elsewhere especially if they had sat photos or drone tapes that showed no car before the attack.

Pretty much the whole day she spent sitting on the bed watching through the Venetian blinds for the attackers. Gun at the ready, she only took one trip in the dark across to the diner to bring back as much as she could carry.

It was late the following afternoon, and she was getting really antsy now that no bad guys had shown up again to kill her. She was even more conflicted on what to do. The more time she had to think, the more she doubted her own reasoning. Exposing herself while Jihadis were bent on killing her was problematic but she couldn't hide in this dumpy motel forever. Besides, she felt a sense of responsibility to get back in the fight to intercept the Independence Day attackers.

She reasoned her best course of action was to take backroads to a nearby state and fly out of there. Just as she'd finally decided to call Bill Carter's private number an unexpected and threatening knock came to her door; could be the cleaner or the clerk or bad guys.

Nerves on edge, she couldn't see who it was from the window. The person seemed to know to stay out of sight. Foot on the door and gun just out of visual range she cracked open the door. To her shock and relief, David was standing there.

Surprised and yet puzzled, she had never been so happy to see someone in her life and immediately hugged him as she dragged him into the room and slammed the door.

"You're supposed to be in London. What are you doing here?"

All the pain in London of weeks ago was forgotten for the moment. He was absolutely the one and only person on the planet she wanted to see on the other side of that door. Someone to have her back. Someone to trust, just like Bill Carter had said. Someone to bring some peace to her troubled mind. Someone to watch the door so she could finally get some sleep.

Someone, anyone not there to kill her.

Someone to love her again.

She let him go and stepped back. Before he could answer, she blurted out, "Wow! How did you find me? I thought I was where no one could find me."

"I think I know you better than you think." His relief at seeing her in one piece was written all over his beaming smile. Until that moment he wasn't sure if he'd actually tracked her down or if he'd ever see her alive again. Betty White looked pretty good right now.

"Before you go peppering me with a thousand questions, Carter asked me to transfer to Langley a few days ago and when I showed up, they were all overwrought with your disappearance. He told me you were either dead or hiding.

"I arrived here this morning on the company plane with a few investigators and we drove out separately to that cabin. They had forensics types looking for traces of the weapon and a body and I was having none of that.

"That safe house is way out there. On the radio they were talking about possibly the last snowfall of the season being a few days ago and that old dirt road is still covered.

"I noticed there were relatively fresh tire tracks that had stopped and turned in the snow a ways from the cottage. Besides ours driving in, they were the only other set near the cabin so it sure looked like it was from the hit team.

"I was able to follow them until they took a turn about a half-mile down the road to the cabin. On a hunch, I decided to see where they went. About two miles down this old logging road I found a Pontiac in the ditch up against a tree.

"These guys probably know little about winter driving on crowned logging roads in the dark. Anyway, Pennsylvania plates and two frozen Jihadis as well as an empty RPG hidden in the back. Looked like they had both been injured in the crash and there's no cell coverage out there. I'm guessing exposure took care of the rest. So, they won't be a threat to anyone. They had no IDs, so I left them for someone else to find. I was still hopeful that another set of tracks on the main road that made a U-turn might be yours coming partway back to check the scene.

"On the hunch, you'd be laying low I fired up Google Earth and started looking for a non-descript budget motel within a dozen miles, where a car could be parked unseen from the road or drones.

"According to Rickie at the desk, a 'beautiful' young lady by the name of Betty White, author of a weird genre apparently, had checked in three days ago.

"You were in only the second motel I checked but honestly there aren't many that fit the bill in this part of the country and man am I relieved to see you."

There was a long pause as their recent past swept through both of their minds. Suddenly a wave of something came over Cristal and the tears started. All the pain of losing Tiffany and then losing him came flooding back. She lunged at him and hugged him, "David, I'm so sorry how I treated you and I couldn't be happier you're here. Thank God I'm not alone anymore. I haven't been able to sleep since they blew up the cabin, thinking they were still out there, I'd fall asleep, they'd sneak up on me and I'd be alone against these nuts who'll risk anything to get me."

She held him at arms-length and wiped her tears, "This latest threat and being alone here with my thoughts has opened my eyes. I spent some time with my mom, and I think she talked some sense into me. Carter also lectured me on some story about always knowing who to trust to have your six. Some of that must have sunk in.

"I'll never get over the loss of our daughter no matter who they were trying to kill but I know one thing for sure, I love you and need you now more than ever. I don't care anymore about what you had to keep secret. You had your reasons. To hell with Kathy and what she thinks she knows. We can get past anything if we love each other."

It was David's turn, "You know I love you and I could never give up on us. There was no way I was going to sit in Langley and wait for you to call in. We need each other to get over these last months as much as we need each other to face what is now a perilous future after that Infowars nonsense."

He pulled her to him and held her tight as thoughts of his infidelity with Kathy came to mind. How had he been so stupid to get tangled up with her again, knowing this reconciliation with Cristal was just a matter of time? But at the time, he thought, it didn't seem inevitable, and Kathy had been just too familiar and WAY too alluring. That tryst had to go to the grave with him and he'd have to convince Kathy to bury it forever too, but he realized her cooperation wasn't a given.

Cristal hugged him even tighter. "I'm not over losing our baby, but my mind has cleared up some. I still want to kill them all … but before that, I just want to hold you and forget it all for a few hours."

Later as they lay together on the cheap motel bed she said, "I want to make love to you the way we used to."

She surprised herself with that last remark given only recently she'd been avoiding him, maybe even hated him. But that was all about decisions he may have been forced into. It had never been about their love for each other. He had always been the solution, not the problem. She was the one who had disengaged and become lost for a time. Since Burundi, there had never been any doubt that he was the one and her mom had been right.

They checked one more time to ensure David hadn't been followed and then squeezed into the tiny budget motel shower before they fell naked and wet into the floppy bed.

He wanted it just as much as she did but thoughts of his mistake with Kathy threatened to distract him from time to time.

She had no such worries. All the stress of the last few days and weeks was gone, and she devoured him in every way possible. She hadn't felt this warm, and safe, and loved in what seemed like such a long time. Even the cheap motel room had taken on magical properties in the fading light.

They made slow and sensual love for most of the next hour. For him, even though Kathy came crawling back into his mind from time to time, this was the best sex he'd had with Cristal since their reunion last fall. He hesitated to compare it to the wild night with Kathy but had to admit that while it was different in some ways it was at least as exciting. It wasn't just raw sex like it had been with Kathy which because of the lust had seemed all about 'taking'. This was even more satisfying knowing the woman in his arms loved him unconditionally. There was something about 'giving' when he was with Cristal.

For her, it was heavenly, thrilling, exhausting, and comfortable all at the same time.

Before they fell asleep David sent a quick text to Carter that simply said, "All is well."

They both slept together soundly for the first time in months that night. Tiffany was never far from mind, but this seemed like the beginning of something new for the two of them. The pain was still intense, but the blaming was behind them and the deep depression starting to fade.

He was up long before her given he was still on London time. She was exhausted after the stress of the last few days as he checked out their surroundings and checked their two cars for any signs of tampering. The only other vehicle around the motel was a beat-up old pickup with a snowplow in front and a truck bed half full of snow. The lack of tracks in the snow told him it had been there a few days.

Famished and over breakfast at the diner across the highway they brought each other up to date on their separate quests. Cristal tried only once to get him to order the Rocky Mountain Oysters claiming they were great, but he didn't go for it.

David got serious and changed the subject, "So Director Carter realized we were at a dead end in London and wants my help with the threat you've uncovered here in the US. The last bit of news in London was that one of the Jihadis, the driver, had specifically requested to be stationed at a taxi stand just down the road from us. So, the thinking is still that either the BSB with that photo from JFK or Al Qaeda with the video of you taking out Khalil had convinced these two loners to assassinate one of us. Still no telling if they were after you or me and we have no info on any solid connections to either organization. We now know the bomb was a large type of pipe bomb with easy-to-access explosive materials. Something you could put together from internet sources. So, the trail has gone stone cold."

Cristal sat back to finish the last of her coffee, "So what do we do now?"

"Well, there's no question you and I have made a formidable team in the past according to Carter so the best thing we can do is go on the offensive."

Cristal frowned, "But they're all after us. They tried to get one or both of us in a safe house in London and now they almost got me in an ultra-safe house in Colorado. Between the two of us we've been in two safe houses in London, one in DC and now the cabin here.

We've nowhere to hide apparently and as you know, I like a peaceful sleep."

David smiled, "That's just it. We're safe nowhere so let's forget about safe houses. Or more to the point, go for ultimate security if only for the duration of this threat. I say we head back to Langley and set up camp at headquarters. I assume they can handle a temporary living situation while we're working on this threat and if we have to travel, we'll take care of our own arrangements so only we know where and when we're going."

"You want us to LIVE at the George Bush Center in McLean Virginia?"

"Unless you have a better idea where we won't be looking over our shoulders all the time."

Cristal finally smiled, "Wow, camping in a large office building, how romantic. Okay, but whatever we set up for a bedroom, I want it swept for cameras and microphones and it has to be quiet at night. Some parts of that building are noisy 24/7. And I don't want to hear about ordering in pizzas every night."

David laughed, "Agreed."

***

Bill Carter was ecstatic about the news from Colorado. His hope that Cristal had intuitively gotten out of there had been well-founded. He suspected his arrogant ex-Jihadi had said something she interpreted as a threat or a risk to her hiding spot; probably indicating that he had an idea of where she was.

Initially, he thought the idea of setting up a love nest at headquarters was silly. He had to admit though, it was better and a lot cheaper than providing 24/7 security teams for the two of them. Being happy that they seemed to have patched up their differences and were an effective team again, he reluctantly agreed to their odd living arrangements.

CIA HR was tasked with the novel problem of providing a 'minimal' living arrangement for the two at CIA headquarters as well as coming up with a plausible cover story as to why two agents were getting such over-the-top concessions which could be seen by some as preferential treatment.

The first couple of nights were challenging, but eventually, they found an unused executive office with a private washroom and shower. A hot plate and microwave were added, and a great bed was brought in and they had access to the cafeteria around the clock. It was still weird but better than the alternatives and becoming more livable by the day.

As they settled into their new situation the pressure started to build because absolutely no progress was being made on the Independence Day threat and everyone's nerves were frayed.

They all knew that while their progress was stalled, the enemy was likely making great headway towards their latest scheme to terrorize America and no one had any idea what that might look like.

Somalia

Mustafa Habib was on edge but increasingly excited as the date of the attacks neared. In the last twenty-four hours, he'd been assured the prep for the BSB attack on America was on track, but more importantly, his own attack was if anything ahead of schedule, looking doable and his confidence was building.

This one would be his marquee event demonstrating he could outdo Khalil when it came to strategy and effectiveness against the Americans. They'd definitely be cowed after this and would have to take seriously the demands of the Muslim world to keep their disgusting culture, business, politics, and everything else out of Allah's lands.

He had three drone teams to choose from who claimed they'd mastered their newfound skills in piloting drones and were excited about working directly for Al Qaeda's new leader. That was a double-edged sword. He needed this attack to be successful, and not knowing much about how difficult it would be to become proficient with drones and execute the rest of his complicated scheme, he had decided on multiple teams as a backup for his master attack. Unfortunately, that meant three teams out there that could be intercepted or discovered putting the attack in some jeopardy, so through trusted intermediaries, he got the message to them to lay very low until July fourth, and not to be seen with the drones. He was still worried that the CIA had found that one message to Abadi that had mentioned drones.

Each team was informed that they'd be contacted just before Independence Day and given last-minute instructions and additional material to carry out their attack. At that point, he'd pick the team that seemed most suitable and disclose the target which at this point he was still keeping secret.

The teams knew the absolute minimum so that the interception of any one of them would not affect the others. Clearly, if one of them was intercepted the idea of a drone attack would be known and likely the date, if indeed Abadi had spilled the timing of the attack. As an ultimate precaution, Mustafa had planned on keeping the nature and location of the target to himself until the last moment.

Additionally, his team in Mogadishu had found a way to test the needed relay software they'd purchased from a North Korean defector. Mustafa's most techie disciple had claimed that the tool worked, was easy to use and in addition, the rest of the team was in place and knew their roles.

While there was no way to do a full dry run of the attack, they were confident that if they could get past the physical and internet security, they could do something very damaging if not achieve their entire goal. They just needed the Americans to follow their normal procedures. Even a near miss on this attack would send massive fear through America.

The one area where he didn't have a backup strategy was his own role, so he decided it was time to brief Nasir.

This was indeed going to be a very special July fourth in America.

Langley

Spring had quickly turned into summer with no movement in terms of leads on what Al Qaeda's July fourth target might be.

The best guess on the London attack was that a self-radicalized pair had spotted Cristal and given the fatwa or the Khalil video, had cooked up their own plan that could have worked if it hadn't been for Cristal spotting the bomb before it went off. The fact that no one had ever claimed responsibility for the attack added credence to the idea that the two Jihadis who were killed at the scene had worked alone.

In terms of the threat to the US, Homeland had put out a BOLO; a bulletin to law enforcement to 'Be On The Lookout' for any suspicious activity especially where it might concern July fourth, infrastructure, or large public events.

Getting nowhere, meetings at headquarters had started to become even more tense and even testy.

With only a few days to Independence Day, Carole Glass entered the war room they now referred to as 'home base' with a uniformed DC police officer, "Sergeant Murphy here showed up at our front gate of all places to respond to our BOLO. He has quite an interesting story. Sergeant, please repeat what you told me and be as detailed as possible."

The sergeant looked completely out of his element and truly wondered if this showing up in person had been a good idea. Just off duty, and still in uniform, he thought he'd be filling out some paperwork, not waltzed into what looked like a very intense, high-level war room.

The table in front of him was filled with phones, laptops, coffee cups, and food wrappers. The walls were completely covered with maps of the US, DC, New York, and other cities with scribbled lines and circles everywhere. There was some kind of high-tech whiteboard at the far end of the room that looked like it was about to fall over from overuse.

This was obviously some kind of CIA war room and the eight people in the room looked important, tense, and completely focused on him. He could sense that their expectations of him were sky-high. Swallowing hard he had trouble finding his voice at first. "Okay, I don't know if this is what you're looking for in your BOLO but here goes.

"About a week ago I was just finishing my late shift which ends at midnight. I was driving down the National Mall, well really Independence Ave. just west of the Washington Monument ... actually, almost even with the World War II Memorial ... anyway, I come across a road crew feverishly tearing up the center lanes of the road. It looked like a rushed affair with guys running back and forth. I saw no police presence which is required for road construction, especially at night so I stopped, found the supervisor, and before I could get a word out, he says, 'Thank God you're finally here'. He goes on to tell me they couldn't wait any longer and they had to start their work without a cop standing by. Apparently, they had to be finished and out of there by five-thirty.

"Long story short, he assures me their client had arranged for police presence, but no one had shown up, he's on a deadline with big penalties, he's got all the right paperwork and he couldn't wait any longer.

"Anyway I ask him what they're up to and he tells me they're burying this big metal pole, more like a skinny fuel tank or a torpedo. Apparently, it's some new green-energy thing that powers itself by picking up the weight of the traffic passing over it and somehow boosts the cell phone coverage in the immediate vicinity. He goes on to say he has three of these to bury over the next three nights, about a hundred yards apart and it has to be done before the July fourth parade with all the dignitaries. Apparently putting up cell towers on the National Mall is not allowed and they need maximum bandwidth with many people expecting to live stream video of the parade. I already knew that cell coverage right now on the Mall isn't the best; again, too few towers or cells or whatever they call them.

"Don't ask me how these things work without new antennas unless they're in the torpedoes but I'm a novice when it comes to cell phone technology. It's all black magic to me.

"Anyway, I checked his paperwork which all looked legit, so I have to admit I took a 'donation' to the 'police fund' instead of calling it in and I stayed with them each night after my shift until they were finished burying these things and repaving the road which had to be reopened each morning. Some of my team are on duty on the fourth for the parade that goes right over those buried things and then I saw your BOLO which got me thinking. I checked with our admin and they'd never seen any police request. So, on the chance that it might mean something, here I am."

The room was awe-struck. Cristal spoke first, "You just ticked all the boxes for a potential terrorist attack so sit yourself down, we have about a thousand questions."

As the room took turns peppering the cop with questions the following became clear; the objects were about two feet in diameter, twenty-five feet long, and covered most of the center of the three-lane westbound section of the road. A quick check with the Park Police confirmed that this was indeed part of the July fourth parade route, but they knew nothing about augmented cell coverage for the parade.

The planning called for many congressmen and senators as well as a couple of Supreme Court justices to be in cars in the parade representing a selection of states and government bodies. Mostly the lawmakers were from the current administration and a credible target for someone like the BSB or even Al Qaeda.

According to the sergeant the objects had no exterior markings, wires, or attachments other than welded eyes to connect chains for manipulation, anchoring, or transport. They were laid on a gravel bed, covered in gravel, and paved over. A perfect IED setup was everyone's concern. But these things were massive. Much bigger than they had to be to even take out a couple of cars at a time.

A quick check confirmed there was nothing on the internet about technology like the sergeant had outlined and a call to the major cell providers indicated they had no such work planned for the area or knew of any such technology.

The sergeant knew the construction supervisor only as 'Dave' and the company was Michelin Excavation who was doing the work. At least that was the logo on their trucks.

Within hours they'd investigated Michelin who seemed to be a long-standing legit road construction outfit and 'Dave', who had no criminal record, had been convinced after two Secret Service agents picked him up, to join the conversation.

Dave knew little of any use to the team and admitted he wondered how these 'torpedoes' could provide cell phone coverage but other than that, it was just a regular telecom job. All the work orders, engineering drawings, and communications with the customer had been handled online. Calls back to Michelin provided information on the contracting customer who no one had ever met as everything again had been handled online.

Concerns on the team went up another notch when the company contracting the work hadn't been in business for a few years and had nothing to do with any kind of telephone technology. The one promising lead Michelin could provide was a shipping document that showed the materials had been picked up from a forwarding company in Long Beach, California.

It was now late in the day by this time and there were no answers on the phones at the forwarding company, so Cristal and David took a company plane overnight to Long Beach and walked into a tiny forwarding office in the port at first opening, shipping documents in hand.

Sally, from the nameplate on her tiny desk, was the forwarding agent on duty. She was a middle-aged woman, so Cristal took the lead, "We're with the Secret Service," she lied. "We want everything you have on this waybill," and she handed her the shipping bill from Michelin.

The woman looked them over. Something told her not to resist even though she still hadn't had her first coffee and visitors to her tiny office were close to unheard of.

The woman was nervous to the point of not asking to see ID. After asking her visitors to step aside in the tiny space, she did a quick search through a file cabinet against a facing wall and handed them a file with the rest of the documents she had on the shipment. The three items listed matched what arrived in DC and they'd shipped from Surabaya, Indonesia through Singapore. It was a pretty sure bet that the originating company was likely another dead end. Still, it was enough to start some international inquiries. Who knew, the Surabaya port might have security video given the war on drugs and terrorism so there might be a clue to follow up from there.

David and Cristal sat at a small desk in the tiny trailer office going over the paperwork.

The items were listed as three 'antenna'. From the description the cop had given, and the weight and size, these things might have passed as antennae that could be mounted on a very tall building. Given they were sealed with no other markings, any close inspection would have been useless even if they were selected by customs for a closer look. Besides that, they were probably built so even an X-ray might not raise suspicions. A stamp on the documents explained by Sally showed a nuclear scan had been done and passed. At least that was a relief but then again, objects this big and totally sealed could have had heavy shielding.

They thanked the clerk for her help and turned to go when she said, "You're only interested in the stuff that went to DC?"

Both turned quickly and David spoke first, "What do you mean?"

"The total shipment was bigger. It was split up at source and only some of it sent to DC. Here's the other half of the load."

Cristal grabbed the file from her and opened it, "It says here two other items shipped to an address in New

Kensington, Pennsylvania. Same description but they're smaller and weigh a lot less. Did you see these things?"

"Hell no, I only see the paperwork. I must process more than two hundred shipments a day. You'd have to talk to Charlie or one of his guys. Hang on I saw him on the dock when I came in."

She lifted a radio, pressed a code, and said, "Sally to Charlie."

"Yeah, go ahead."

"Charlie, I need you in here at the office. There's a couple of cops asking about a shipment."

Not wanting to get accused of dragging his feet and thinking drugs all the way Charlie was soon in the now overcrowded trailer office.

"What's up?"

Cristal introduced them again as Secret Service and handed him the two files, "What can you tell us about this material and the two shipments that went out of here?"

Looking at the file Charlie's eyes went straight to the date, "Hell this was more than a month ago. Do you know how much shit we forward through here?"

David noticed a military tattoo on Charlie's neck and took over. Leaning forward he whispered to the man, "This is important. We think these are IEDs destined for an attack here in the homeland. That's National Security information so keep it quiet."

The blood drained out of Charlie's face as he took another look at the paperwork laying it out on Sally's desk.

"Actually, I do remember this. Yeah, we had an issue with the feds because all we had was "antenna", the damn things were heavy and nothing on the X-ray or the radiation monitor, but they eventually let it go."

"So, you remember these items?"

"Yeah, three of them were about twenty-five feet long and two feet in diameter. My first thought was, 'if these are antenna, where do you connect the wires?' because there were no access ports or anything. The CBP guy said maybe they were some kind of newfangled wireless things.

"The other two were similar but about ten feet long and eighteen inches in diameter. That's about all I know, everything else is here on the paperwork."

He leaned forward to David and whispered, "I was in Iraq for the first wave. If these are IEDs they're ten times bigger than anything I've ever heard of."

Sally broke in, "I just remembered, I think some guy phoned a couple of times determined to get these very things cleared and shipped. Yeah, I remember because he called them antennas. I'm pretty sure he left a voicemail on one of his calls which I should still have."

Cristal and David recorded the voicemail and the number it came in from. A DC area phone number from what sounded like a middle-aged Caucasian.

After assessing that these two had no more to offer they reported back to Carole Glass to get the team checking out the leads on the second shipment and the phone call.

They knew where the three larger items ended up, but the two others were a new puzzle just when they didn't need any new puzzles. If they were in fact IEDs of some sort, then the parade wasn't the only target given these hadn't been shipped to DC.

***

With the private CIA jet, they were back in Langley by late afternoon. The team was called together in their war room as Carole reviewed what they knew so far, "Okay, looks like there's a high probability we have IEDs planted on the Mall and two smaller ones on the loose. First question is, do we evacuate the Mall and send in bomb disposal teams? Jim Wilson here is Homeland's bomb tech expert and I've added him to this eyes-only team. Jim, what can you tell us about the risk of these bombs going off before the parade or by digging them up? The parade is only a few days away now and we have thousands of cars driving over these things every day."

Jim looked nervous, "You understand I've only had a few hours to look at what we have. The size of these things is enormous which is the first issue. No matter what explosive they may have used and what projectiles they've surrounded them with this could be gargantuan, like with a kill radius of maybe two hundred feet or more; depending on what they've packed it with.

"Knowing they came from Indonesia is no help on that matter, but the logistics indicate a well-organized and funded source. I checked with Documents and they claim all the paperwork is really professional, down to the type of paper Michelin provided that came along with the shipment, so it's a good bet these guys know what they're doing.

"The description of the IEDs leaves no doubt that it has to be a direct radio-activated trigger."

Carole was first in, "How can you be so sure?"

Jim continued, "Well my thoughts are that they want these things to go off exactly when they want at some point in the parade when their target is directly over the bomb and not before. So they've given serious thought to comm delays, and any stray radio signals or interference.

"If they want to target individual cars in the parade then a timer is out and a cell phone is too unreliable for the connection, interference and the timing required.

"What they'd need is a direct radio connection like a radio-controlled hobby system and close up like a few hundred feet so that means the trigger guy or guys will be at the parade. They probably have to be there anyway for precise targeting of cars as broadcast TV signals are usually on a delay.

"With heavy cell usage in a poorly serviced area, they couldn't rely on getting through when they needed to and any kind of a wrong number or robocall could set it off so, again a cell phone trigger is out of the question especially given these things were planted well before the parade. So it has to be a direct radio trigger.

"Now that's a large park area and there's no doubt some kids will have RC toys in the area between now and then but there's one thing we can be sure of, none of those will be RC planes or drones. There are too many restrictions in the area around the White House and other monuments for drones and notices are posted everywhere with hefty fines. They may even have scanners on the Mall to catch violators ... not sure about that but it's definitely verboten. So, the only real solution to their problem is an RC plane or drone controller that will trigger the explosives.

"Assuming these guys know what they're doing, it will be one of the lesser-used, high-channel frequencies and a control channel that is also less popular just to be ultra-safe. Likely they'll use a controller with a lot of channels like twelve or more, at least six more than the most popular devices and they'll use the higher channels, so they reduce the chance of anyone triggering the devices by accident. They'll use a different high-numbered channel for each bomb so they can be triggered independently. As a result, there seems to be little chance of these things being triggered before they want them to. I can't see any other solution where these things are protected against any kind of interference and premature detonation and yet gives them instant response time.

"Those high-end controllers have great differentiating notch filters so that some guy with a really cheap and crappy taxi radio or old walkie-talkie spewing all kinds of RF frequencies won't accidentally set it off. If they spent this much money on the bombs and the logistics, they're using top-of-the-line controllers to trigger them just to be sure they get their targets.

"BUT if I'm right then it should be easy to jam them AND we'll be able to triangulate on the triggerman when he tries to activate the device."

"WHOA!" Chip Attwood was the first to interject. "You want us to leave MASSIVE bombs on a busy parkway for a few more days and during the parade in the hope that jamming them will save the day? Can you imagine the blowback if one of these went off, killed a bunch of people and we knew it was there?"

There was silence in the room until Carole spoke, "Chip has a good point BUT, they've already been there for more than a week. We don't know where the smaller IEDs are and digging up the big ones may rush their plan and execute the part with the smaller IEDs right away.

"Just because they're smaller means nothing. Even the little ones are massive. Probably overkill for whatever they have in mind. What if they were planted under a railway track or on some bridge, or on a dam?

We need to find them. So, I say until we do, digging up the ones on the Mall is off the table as long as we get some really effective and backed-up jamming in there.

"So far the leads we have like that voicemail number and the shipping address for the smaller ones are dead ends. I repeat, an IED ten feet long and eighteen inches in diameter is still a huge bomb bordering on a WMD. No question we have to find them before we let the terrorists know we've uncovered part of their scheme.

"Jim, how sure are you we can jam those signals, and can we do it now?"

"DOD has the gear to jam EVERYTHING at a hundred percent but that would shut down just about anything in the area like taxis, cell phones, police radios, etc. That might be a tip-off to someone so it would be better to know the frequency and jam just the right one. If I'm right it will be in the 72 MHz range which is reserved for RC aircraft. That's the band for both RC planes and drones. As I said, they're forbidden in downtown DC for obvious reasons. The more I think about it the more I'm sure that's what they've done so we only have to jam that band. Jamming only the 72 MHz band would be less likely to raise any alarms. It's not used downtown and it's not like these guys are going to risk getting caught with an RC plane in DC just to test their signal and accidentally set off the bombs. The military can have round-the-clock jamming planes orbiting DC in an hour or two.

"On another thought, you might want to search for someone buying multiple sophisticated RC controllers as it looks to me that there's more than one, probably simultaneous target sites. The easiest thing for them to do was to tell the triggermen to buy the controllers locally and tell them precisely what to buy. A local cash purchase leaves fewer footprints to follow and less import paperwork and chances to get tripped up, etc."

"Great idea." Carole pointed to one of her staff who got the message and headed off.

Cristal was anxious to get back into the mix, "How do we find the other two bombs?"

Chip spoke up, "Maybe they hired another company to bury them or given the size of the IEDs maybe they just rented a small backhoe to do it themselves. Sadly, these bombs are powerful enough but small enough that they could be parked in a van or truck next to something and still do amazing damage. I'll start on that," and he left.

Suddenly Cristal had a thought, "Wait a minute, you said the Capitol area has rules against RC drones and planes."

Jim looked puzzled, "Yeah, what about it?"

"These things came from the other side of the planet. Did they just take a chance they'd never cross paths with the right radio frequency and blow up aboard ship or in transit from the west coast?"

Jim smiled, "Good point but easily addressed. You just include an arming circuit in the bomb that doesn't activate until you're sure it's where you want it. Say the day of or the day before the blast. It can work on any date and time source, so the device is 'safed' until you schedule it to go active. Date and timing sources with long-life batteries are easy to implement. But IEDs this size you'd want the jamming in place now and right through the parade."

Suddenly Carole interjected, "Have we forgotten that email looking for drone pilots?"

She addressed Jim directly, "This is classified but we have a Jihadi communication looking for a person with drone capabilities. The drone needs night vision and a three-kilogram payload. Why would they need those two things? The parade is in the daytime and your theory is that they only need the controller to trigger the explosives."

Jim looked puzzled. "Well, that's news to me and off hand, I see no reason for the actual drone in my scenario. The guy could probably stand five hundred feet away and given the site you've discovered, I see no reason why he'd need a drone to deliver the signal. I guess a three-kilo payload could be the controller itself but that makes no sense either and overly complicates the whole attack with new potential points of failure. I have nothing for you. The way I see it, it will be a guy at the parade holding a controller to trigger the bombs.

This left the room in confusion as Jim made his exit.

Had Al Qaeda's plans changed after the intercepted email or was there some other twist to this that had yet to reveal itself?

The meeting broke up after Carole had assigned tasks to address the threat as Jim Saxon had defined it.

Within a few hours, the military had jamming aircraft orbiting DC jamming all 72 MHz channels which it was hoped would be a temporary safeguard while they planned something more reliable. The cover story was that the military was assisting TV crews who were testing aerial shots of the parade which was now in the final stages of planning.

Amateur radio junkies on the internet picked up the jamming but assumed it was a security precaution, so no crazies tried to fly drones over the upcoming parade as drones were seen as the new go-to threat for public events.

In consultation with the White House, Bill Carter convinced them to leave the IEDs in place and not inform the congressional delegation and specific senators who'd be the likely targets and who had planned to be in the motorcade.

The CIA's pitch was that ALL senior politicians would have to be informed and there was an excellent chance one of them was feeding intel to the BSB; a high-risk decision for the White House to be sure. At least the President had the military on his side taking ownership for the jamming they agreed should be a hundred percent effective 'if and only if' the CIA had figured out the right frequencies.

When the detailed plans were reviewed showing key individuals about ten to fifteen car lengths apart, the immediate worry was that someone had helped the attackers by planting the bombs one hundred yards apart for a simultaneous attack. This confirmed that somehow, they were getting inside help on the planning. A search for the person or persons who could have leaked that information was stopped when they realized that more than a hundred people knew that level of detail on the parade and had played some role in planning it.

Strategists on Carole's team suggested the bombs would likely be detonated one after the other starting closer to the front and trapping the vehicles behind a massive crater and picking off their targets as they tried to escape if they were not in the right position and had to back up on the road which had no other escape routes at the point where the bombs were buried.

Special precautions were taken to make any CIA information on the parade eyes-only to avoid any further leaks to the attackers. Even the military wasn't told why they were jamming radio signals. It was easy for them to figure out that it had something to do with RC aircraft but to what purpose, they didn't know.

The theory they were working on was the higher-placed the individual, the more likely they were to be a key target in the parade. There had been enough publicity about the event that by now any attacker knew enough so that additional intel wouldn't be needed, therefore the desperate search for any moles was put on the back burner for the moment.

A special law enforcement team was assembled and given a minimal briefing that, undercover, they'd be deployed along parts of the parade route to apprehend expected terrorists. Details on their operation would be furnished just before the parade.

At a review meeting, Carole took the DD and the war room 'eight' through everything that was being done to run down any leads on the manufacturers of the IEDs, estimates of the kill and blast radius of the enormous IEDs, the possible targets in the parade, the checking that had been done on the jamming efforts, the efforts to find the missing two IEDs, an order that had gone out for Independence Day on prohibiting vans and trucks parking near government buildings, parade routes and public gathering places, the search for anyone buying drones or RC controllers, the latest intel on any movements of suspected Jihadis under surveillance in the US, as well as a watch for any last-minute cancellations of participants in the DC parade in the off chance that a BSB member or possibly a mole with knowledge of the attack was to back out to save themselves.

Bill Carter took over, "Listen team, this is all well and good but again we find ourselves in a position where even after all of this amazing work, we're still naked in front of this threat. Right now we believe we have a solution for the parade, but someone is going to be successful in setting off two huge IEDs, ten feet long and eighteen inches in diameter. As you now know, that could be almost as big as the Oklahoma City bomb and we've no idea of the target. We need to do better."

Somalia

Mustafa Habib had assigned his top lieutenant Nasir Abboud to be the liaison with the US attack team for Washington. Nasir seemed excited as he entered to bring Mustafa up to date on the plans, "We're ready to go. The teams are in place and have their equipment and the Americans are playing right into our hands. With only a few days to go, they've started building viewing stands close to our IEDs and they're within the kill range. We'll have an even bigger body count on July fourth."

"Could this mean they've discovered the bombs?"

"No, there are five viewing stands but three of them are near but not right at our bombs. The Syndicate said the kill radius is potentially two hundred feet and the blast radius much greater so it should work out well. Our team has already picked out their stations. The one at the parade has identified his cover position about four hundred feet out, protected, and a clear exit path. The RC controller they demanded is quite large, so he has acquired an over-the-shoulder tote bag to hide the controller. He only needs to put one hand in the bag to trigger the device and he has an earpiece for the phone to accept 'fire' commands from someone from the Syndicate who will ID and synchronize firing on the targets. All he has to do is trigger the bombs, drop the tote bag and phone and run away with all the other fleeing parade watchers.

"This Syndicate has proven to be very efficient, and so far they've delivered exactly as they told us. If this works as planned, then I take back my earlier concerns. We may want to do more of this from time to time. They appear to have amazing capabilities and organization.

"Our other two triggermen will hide in their cars nearby their targets, so their task is easier, assuming their targets cooperate and leave their homes on the morning of the main attack. They know which cars and the occupants to look for. They should both be hit before the parade which occurs later in the morning. Individual assassinations shouldn't raise an alarm for the parade. Even if the two targets work from home on that holiday, the blast at the parade will bring them out as their offices will need them.

"At the parade, the Syndicate says they'll likely go for the lead car first and then try to pick off others as they scramble to escape. These bombs are immense so we might even hit two of the targets with one bomb. We should get several of the prime targets for sure, maybe all of them if the cars are separated as planned. The individual targets at the other sites are being left to the last moment but all seems to be ready."

***

Tension was mounting on the CIA's task force with only a few days left before the expected attack. No progress had been made working backward to see who had built the bombs. Indonesian Intelligence services had been cooperative but didn't have the resources and skills to do effective tracing. Initial investigations of the builders of the bombs again lead to a fictitious company. There was significant video available from the shipping port but it overwrote itself weekly so they couldn't go back far enough to see anything of use. A small team of FBI agents had been assigned to assist them, but nothing had turned up so far.

Still, a haunting issue was, 'What happened to the smaller devices? Were they intended for an attack that didn't require a larger device? Were the larger devices too big and obvious as weapons for a different kind of target? Where the hell had they gone after being dropped off at a now-empty warehouse outside of Pittsburgh and why had that earlier email specified night vision and a payload for the drone?'

As to the location of the smaller bombs, they couldn't jam signals if they didn't know where to go.

The team was somewhat confident that DOD could block the signals meant to explode the bombs at the parade if Jim Saxon had been right, but the fear remained that that needed to be seen to be believed.

Carole had to bring Director Bill Carter in to read the riot act to the team as there was a fear someone on the team would get cold feet, would panic envisaging hundreds of innocents being blown to bits, and therefore leak a warning to the press neutralizing one of the only advantages they had in capturing the terrorists.

He gathered everyone who knew the details about the attack in a conference room, "Listen, about the parade, I'm as nervous as you are. Part of me wants to go dig up those bombs or cancel the damned parade altogether but I'm completely convinced our guys can block any signal to trigger those bombs," he lied. Bill Carter didn't consider himself a techie and all the assurances in the world didn't comfort him that the military could GUARANTY their solution. He knew of too many times the military's whiz-bang crap had failed but he couldn't turn back now.

"Okay, this is new. By order of the President, at the last moment, as the parade arrives at the site, they'll jam ALL frequencies just to be sure. Still, we absolutely need to find those other bombs and capture all the terrorists. They could hit their targets early with the smaller ones if they find out we've discovered the parade attack.

"In addition, we need to find these attackers and find out what we can about terrorist cells in the US, especially that one in the Pittsburgh area. You would think by now we'd have figured out how they're all connected and find the core of the cell, but even with our best minds and the FBI having a full-court press on it, that hasn't happened.

"If we blow this opportunity to grab these triggermen then we're setting ourselves up to allow one attack after another. We must root out these barbarians. I don't have to remind you how many threats we've seen coming out of that one cell in the last year.

"Remember, just because those other bombs are smaller, they're still huge and might even do more damage than the big ones depending on their targets. Right now, they're the bigger threat because we don't have jamming on them. We need to find them. So, I'm asking you all to be professional, stick with the plan, keep all of this totally secret, and keep on working as hard as you can to intercept this attack. I swear if it made anyone feel better, I'd go down there and stand beside one of those bombs during the parade, that's how much confidence I have in our jamming ability." He hoped his actual lack of confidence didn't show.

Thinking he'd done all he could, he thanked everyone for their diligence and exited.

The last-minute plan to build viewing stands hiding large jamming hardware was a mixed blessing. While it increased the chances of a proper and reliable block on any RC-triggering radio signals, it also invited hundreds if not thousands of people to crowd around the IEDs. With the enormous size of these weapons, many of those parade viewers would now be in the kill zone. If this went sideways, Carter and possibly others would probably be facing dozens if not hundreds of manslaughter charges if not worse. At least the President had remained on board because of the military's assurances and was willing to take the political risk of jeopardizing American lives. Because this was Washington, his decision to risk lives would definitely be front-page news at some point in the future. Any juicy piece of information with this many people involved ALWAYS made it out to the press eventually.

The viewing stands were nearing completion as nearby roads were closed overnight to bring in the jamming hardware and install them in hidden compartments under the stands. Generators would draw attention, so large Tesla power packs and inverters were used at each location to silently power the jammers.

Five TV towers and crane-mounted TV platforms were just about complete disguising the triangulation system that would instantly locate anyone transmitting on a 72 MHz channel; not an easy task with enormous jammers on the same frequency in play at the same time. The triangulation hardware was also equipped with invisible laser designators which would paint the culprit or culprits until innocent-looking bystanders from the Secret Service wearing special laser-illuminating glasses could apprehend them.

Mogadishu

Norm Lulham and Rick Sawyer, still under cover in Mogadishu, had drawn a complete blank on any of their tasks of locating Mustafa Habib or any intel on a possible link to the BSB. Rick's taxi driver had indeed ID'd the guy he had taken to meet Mustafa. While that added some credence to the idea that Al Qaeda and the BSB had met, the suspected BSB agent in question in London had been assassinated so for the moment that lead went nowhere.

The Mogadishu CIA team was under just as much pressure as Langley to come up with something that would help in intercepting the Independence Day attack.

Norm usually considered six PM as closing time when he could turn his mind off and head back to the tiny flat he had down the hall from Rick. He tried to keep to a schedule that would seem reasonable for the courier that was his cover identity.

Suddenly, as he was about to leave to head back to his apartment his specialized iPhone sounded a worrisome beep indicating a priority message:

'Amazon part number for your phone is M-RSNLH-GTP-23'.

He stared at it as shivers ran down his spine. The memorized code was easy to translate; MAYDAY – Rick Sawyer – Norm Lulham – Hide - Go To Port – twenty-three hundred pickup.

He reached under the broken air conditioner in the window and withdrew his service weapon hiding it easily under his loose-fitting macawiis garment and left the building immediately heading in a direction different from his normal routine.

He walked a few blocks wondering where Rick was and whether he'd gotten the message. Rick had been trying to recruit yet another taxi driver recently and there was always the chance he'd picked the wrong one, asked some wrong question, or seemed too curious and alerted one of the many bad guys to his presence. As a general rule, they tried never to be seen together so that if one was ID'd the other might escape.

Lulham hadn't been involved in anything threatening recently so he wasn't expecting any urgent messages. His immediate thoughts went to whether Rick had finally walked into a trap. As his partner, he wanted more than anything else to rescue him if, in fact, he was in danger, but he had no idea where to start. Phoning him was out of the question as it could put both of them in jeopardy.

Often, they tried to let each other know where they were and what they were doing but beyond Rick trying to recruit a source, Norm had no idea where he was. They had trained for this and there was nothing he could think to do beyond sticking to the escape plan.

After traveling a few blocks and checking for any surveillance he took a beat-up old taxi to a point near the port and made his way to a restaurant that he'd only visited once before but knew enough about it that it was open late and there was a secluded spot near the back.

After drinking entirely too much local tea, and waiting endlessly for Rick, he left just before closing and made it to the dark spot on the harbor that had been preplanned, still with no Rick.

It was a cloudy and very dark night, and they were feet away from him before he even realized the Marines in full Navy camo and blackened faces were on him and he was whisked away to the waiting US navy ship off the coast.

As soon as they were out of earshot of the shore he said, "Did you get Rick?"

The young commando who seemed to be in charge answered, "We were told to get whoever was there at twenty-three hundred and get out of there fast. I don't know about anyone named Rick."

To his distress, Rick wasn't on board the ship and no one knew anything about his situation.

Langley

With only about forty-eight hours left, everyone remained on edge and concerned that no progress was being made on tracking the two smaller IEDs.

Bill Carter, ashen-faced and red-eyed burst into the war room, "I have some good news and some terrible news." He waited for them all to sit down and pay attention.

"Firstly, we just received information that a hobby store filled an order for six high-end RC planes and controllers about two weeks ago. A Middle Eastern man who paid cash so no tracing there and we're too late to get any security camera footage as it loops about every ten days. The one thing we do have is the type of system and an exact frequency that will help the jamming and triangulation teams. Again, they were planes, not drones. It's obviously not a sure thing but we're going with it. And yes, it was a store in a suburb of Pittsburgh."

"I have some very bad news but you had to know that detail about the controllers."

He moved over to the large TV screen and plugged in a USB device and hit play, "There's no way to soften the blow of this."

Instantly the room exploded in expletives. Twenty seconds into it, David was the first to react as he gasped, "Is that who I think it is?"

The video was of some poor bleeding soul in a cage that was probably built for a large animal. Gasoline was sprayed on him as those around him spat threats and insults or cheered something praising Allah, and the victim was lit on fire.

The screaming was something none of them had heard in their lives as the flames spread all over his body. The poor man was experiencing everyone's worst nightmare as he tore at the cage trying to escape but finding no respite, screaming and writhing wildly in torture.

For Cristal, the flames engulfing his face and shooting a foot above his head was the worst. Some couldn't watch and turned away. The torture seemed to continue forever until the man slumped unconscious into an inferno on the floor of the cage and continued to burn, any skin and clothing that was left continued to peel from the body.

All that was left was the charred and twisted stick of a blackened corpse and the cheering of his tormentors who were in ecstasy and screaming Arabic phrases over each other. As the video ended with a narrator screaming something in Arabic, the charcoal remains of the corpse was still being consumed by fire.

Every kind of reaction swept the room, some screamed curses, many cried, pounded the table, or sat down hard in a total stupor. Bob Boutet vomited in a wastepaper basket just in time to pass it to one of the women.

As the screen went blank, Carter waited until the room quietened down just a bit before he answered David's question in a very unsteady voice, "Yes ... that was our own Rick Sawyer, one of our two undercover operatives in Mogadishu. Apparently, this happened last night as we were sleeping and they already have the video up on some of the Jihadi websites where they're claiming he was an infidel and a CIA spy.

"We picked up SIGINT yesterday that at least one of our agents had been ID'd by the bad guys but we were only able to connect with Norm and get him out.

They either had Rick already or they got to him before he could escape after we sent an emergency coded message.

"It's even more brutal. A closer look at the video shows he was tortured … there appear to be several fingers missing and other signs of torture … so we don't know what they got out of him before this. They were trained not to hold out in torture but to give plausible but misleading information. I think Norm and Rick had worked out their own parcel of lies mainly to protect from giving up their partner.

"I must tell you, I knew Rick quite well and I too lost my lunch when I saw this moments ago. I sent them in there and we knew there were dangers, but this?"

Tears appeared again as he continued, "Some of you knew him too. This is a very nasty business we're in and some of you have had field experience and know this. But this … if there was ever any lingering doubt about what these butchers are capable of … in civilized society there's no reason for this atrocity. It advances none of their goals. It's fed by raw hatred and religious fundamentalist insanity. They are not civilized. They're under some misguided thinking that their god demands this and that acts like this will cower us and force us to do what they want. They represent the absolute antithesis of what they call a religion of peace. How could you ever square that circle?

"Rick was a tough guy and knew what risks he was taking but no one thinks they're going to go out this way. We can only reflect on the fact that he's at peace now. His torture has ended.

"I'd personally like to avenge this in every way possible, legal or illegal, but we have a bigger problem and I have to ask you all to man up and put this out of your minds for the next few days until we've resolved the threats we face here at home from these monsters. They essentially want to repeat this atrocity in some fashion right here in the next two days; killing as many of us as they can.

"They'll pay for this somehow but for now, let's not let Rick's sacrifice be for nothing. We need to avenge this first by finishing his work and intercepting these attacks.

"Now unfortunately I have to run this video again and I want you to focus on the three assholes in the background." He recycled the video this time with the sound muted. "The one on the right we believe is a grainy image of Mustafa Habib. The others may be the first images we have of potential lieutenants."

He froze the video once they had seen the organizers in the background. "So, while we don't know how they found Rick, there's no doubt who ended up with him and who is responsible."

His voice started to falter again as he continued, "These are the same animals that have a target on us now. We'll get the ringleader and I sincerely hope it won't be pretty but for now, we need to remain focused.

"Our other agent, Norm Lulham made it to our extraction point and he's now safely aboard a US ship off the coast of Somalia. Now take a moment to process this BUT you all need to get back to work and find these bombs." At that, he marched out of the room taking the USB key with him.

All of the women, including Carole Glass and Cristal, were either sobbing or wiping their eyes as were most of the men. There was no doubt the boss was right, the only tool they had right now to avenge Rick's torture and death was to redouble their efforts to stop the coming attacks.

In the Director's absence, a silence descended over the room for the longest time interrupted only by whimpering and the occasional slap on the table or punch to a wall. There were no words. No one could think of anything to say. The image of their colleague's last moments would stay with them forever.

Still crying, Carole finally said, "That couple of minutes were the worst of my entire life. I hate this job and this world of monsters we have to deal with. I'm so sorry we all had to witness that. Rick will now be remembered as a hero for what he did to intercept that Christmas attack and his long dedication to that extremely dangerous job in Somalia, but no one signs up for that."

After a long pause, she said, "Everyone take ten and go get some air or a coffee."

Cristal, still sobbing, headed for the door and then said in a very loud voice, "When we get back, let's get this done for Rick!"

David, tears running down his face, put his hand on her back as she left the room, and it was clear she was still sobbing and shaking. As they got into the hallway he whispered, "I loved that guy. He came to my rescue when I was kidnapped by Al-Shabaab in Mogadishu last year.

"You told me Mustafa had a rep as more of a brainiac than a brute. Well, that's gone out the window now. He's another Khalil in my books and we're going to get him if I have to walk all the way there and strangle him with my bare hands."

She sobbed, "That won't be enough."

Baltimore

As Number Three of the Syndicate pulled behind yet another empty warehouse between Baltimore and Washington, he wondered how Number One found these places. Maybe he was in real estate, but part of their alliance depended on them knowing as little as possible about each other. He had gotten the secret message of where and when to meet only an hour ago, so this had to be important.

It wasn't long until all three were seated at the same old card table far enough away from their security people that they couldn't be overheard. Their relationship was an unusual one, designed to be strictly a secretive business and very lucrative. Number Two was the money man and provided seemingly endless funds to pursue their various agendas as well as personal payments to their own hidden accounts.

None of the very few others, lower in the alliance, knew how this part of the scheme worked, who they were, or even how many they were except that they were very appreciative of how they and some of their subordinates were getting rich as part of the Syndicate. Compartmentalization was taken to an insane level, with really only Number Three knowing the downstream actors, who were few and diminishing, and their occasional contractors who often had no idea who they were working for.

As they settled, Number One, the Intel and political linkage for the group opened with, "We have very bad news. Somehow the authorities have discovered the attack set for the National Mall Parade on Independence Day. I don't know yet how it was discovered but the authorities are busy putting countermeasures in place. They have jamming devices in play already to kill the signal to the bombs for the parade. Those big ones are buried and even if there was a way to change the triggering somehow, they're all under surveillance now."

Number Two, the more tentative of the group said excitedly, "Then we have to call it off! If they know about the bombs, they may be closing in on us."

Number One spoke immediately, "No, we need to let it go ahead. They'll catch the Al Qaeda guys and that will act as a buffer against us and evidence it was terrorists. Even if they dig up those bombs, there's no way they can trace their origin, so nothing leads back to us."

Two wasn't convinced and turned to Three, "What about our guy? You've got a guy there monitoring the parade and telling them when to initiate the attack. What if they catch him and find a way to track us down?"

Three was impatient, "Relax, will you? That guy was paid well and has no idea where the money is coming from. Besides, now that we know the attack will fail, he can sit anywhere in front of a TV and make the call to the triggerman. We've got every angle covered."

One took over, "I have good intel that they haven't discovered the other attacks. That's still a go, but if the individual attacks fail too, and they're our prime targets, we'd need a backup plan to take them out. I think we're in agreement that we don't want to lose them too. The whole rationale behind the alliance with these terrorists was because we were desperate to get the key targets and make it look like a terrorist attack, so they must be taken out, especially the CIA guy. If we don't get them then the fear of them closing in on us could become reality. Remember Bill Carter is no dummy and he's getting closer to putting the pieces together every day. Senator Fox Trot and her gang know that too, so again they'll eliminate us as a vulnerability before Carter figures out who we are. The only way to get Fox Trot off our backs is to get rid of Bill Carter.

"I have very reliable information that he's on to something. That search of everyone in the Intel community checking who was in the know, correlated to leaks they can confirm could be the thing that gives him what he needs to triangulate on me!

"It's a process of elimination. He has no reason to suspect me for the moment but that data mining will certainly get him to a very short list of suspects and I'm certain to be on it.

"And don't get any ideas of looking at me as the weak link here. I have an insurance policy like I'm sure you do … or should have. Anything happening to me won't turn out well for you two.

"I'm smart enough not to piss off our sponsors and be seen as a threat. It's not like I'm going to spill the beans so don't go running to Fox Trot. I have friends who can work out who you two are and will avenge anything that happens to me if either of you turns on me."

By the body language, he realized he had pushed a bit too hard and needed to walk it back, "No offense but let's get serious here. We have to stay united on this and get that Carter creep."

Number Three was shocked and concerned as One continued, "That's why we need a backup plan especially for him, but it can't lead back to us."

Three, in charge of field ops, agreed, "Let's not start any infighting. We need to stay united and get this thing done. I'm not ready to retire just yet and we don't need any of your fucking threats, okay?"

After a long pause until he had One's attention he said, "The best way to get a backup plan going is to use one of our own assets we can trust, but one from overseas to keep prying eyes away from us. The one I have in mind is reliable and disposable after the deed is done. I see no other way to keep it clean. I'll arrange it."

Two had been quiet, "I must say I took all that stuff before as a direct threat. This Syndicate has made us all rich men and I don't like threats or ultimatums. I have no such plan to retaliate because I thought there was a level of trust between us and that we're all in this together."

One interjected, "Okay don't get your panties in a knot. I'm just saying we have to take care of Carter quick. Once he's out of the way we'll have some breathing room and there are lots of things we can do to shore up our security, but he has to go first."

He waited for a second until he thought they'd bought his weak apology, "There's another problem. I want to take Habib out. You must have seen the video I sent you. He burned that kid alive after he cut off his fingers to try to get info out of him. I met that kid about two years ago at headquarters and he was your regular American go-getter type of kid.

"I knew dealing with these savages was going to be a mess. I'm still pissed he killed our Mr. Tom guy in London. Even though Habib knows only a little about us, in my books it's too much. He could be a threat to us in the short term. He may want payback when the parade plan fails in just a couple of days. He's too much of a liability so I say let's take him out."

Three nodded, "I'm with you on that. That barbarian stuff on that CIA kid turned my stomach but we must do it in a way that doesn't set his organization on a hunt for us. We have a few assets in Mogadishu who are playing both sides of the street as I've told you. They're keeping tabs on Mustafa. That's how I found him to make the deal. We could use one of those guys who may or may not be reliable to get him, but I prefer the CIA themselves to take Mustafa out.

"There's an NGO manager there, an OXFAM guy if I remember, who we think has fingers in several pies. I think if we get our local guy to slip him some current location intel on Mustafa, he'll get it to the people that want Habib even more than we do. If the CIA takes him out themselves, our hands would be clean."

Number Two growing fearful of repercussions spoke, "I'd still like to know how the Intelligence Community found out about the Mall attack just in case we have a leak somewhere. This is serious. Our first plan involving a target in the US and they uncovered it seemingly in no time. We need to investigate how they're getting information because we could be next. As to a plan to get at least the Director of the CIA and that Neanderthal in Somalia, I think your plans are prudent and I'm in. But no more threats, please!"

Number One nodded approval, "Just remember our lives depend on staying invisible. If there was even a hint of anyone closing in on us, Senator Fox Trot wouldn't hesitate to take all three of us out and you know she could and would do it."

He addressed Two directly, "You're the funding guy and you know she's well connected to our sponsors and a simple word from her to them would spell the end of us. Apart from the money we get, I like my neck the way it is.

"If we can find assassins then they can too. Remember those agri boys found us in the first place and who knows what other contacts they have. We have to continue to produce reliably or else. If they don't already know, they will soon know that the parade attack is a bust, so we need at the very least to get Bill Carter. If we get him, the heat will be off for a while.

"We've lost key assets in the UK and even though Three here likes his secrecy, I think Germany has been pretty much wiped out, so as you say, if you bring in someone from across the pond, they have to be disposable to ensure they don't get a lead on you or the rest of us."

He addressed Three directly, "You've been pretty quiet on this subject lately. How is our portfolio of field assets?"

Number Three hesitated just a little too long, "Not that it's any of your business. Each of us independently manages our own areas so I don't ask you how your Intel connections or political connections are going but to set your nerves at peace, I'm doing fine, thank you very much. We have adequate resources to achieve our goals and we'll backfill where needed. A large direct organization has its drawbacks as you know, so whenever possible we prefer to use contractors who don't know who they're working for. So rest easy, we're in good shape on my end.

"The backup plan I have in mind is of no threat to us and the agent will disappear permanently after the job is done."

The other two seemed less than convinced but saw no way to pursue the question any further.

They shook hands and headed back to their day jobs.

Number Three

On the way back to DC, Number Three enabled his encrypted phone app and called a familiar number. As his lone remaining European asset lifted the phone he said, "There's a major operation in play over here that needs some professional backup. I need you here yesterday. Find a way to dump the job for a few days and get over here pronto. Text me your flight and I'll pick you up at the airport."

Without giving his agent a chance to say anything he hung up.

***

Kathy had been just about ready to turn in for the night when the shocking call came in. She knew from her MI6 work that the US were investigating a potential terrorist attack in less than forty-eight hours and that they speculated that her Syndicate had teamed up with Al Qaeda for the attack. Speculation that she put no stock in. There was no way these people would team up with savages like Al Qaeda. Now her direct connection to the Syndicate was demanding her attendance at the same time as a 'backup'.

None of this made sense to her. She had become convinced, even in the face of their denials, it was her own Syndicate that had taken out her friend Jim Harden just after he returned from Africa. Jim had only hinted at why he was in Africa, but she was hoping it wasn't to meet with any terrorists. On top of that, she knew only parts of the story about the entire loss of the German team and the attempt on David's life only weeks ago outside his flat in London. It was no secret David thought her own BSB was behind that attack. David was smart. He had killed Jack Hammond and she feared she'd be next if he ever ID'd her as BSB which left her feelings for him entirely conflicted.

He was definitely a hunk and a serious catch, but she had passed the point of no return with respect to him with her BSB affiliation long ago.

From shortly after David's supposed death, she had taken steps by joining Hammond's team which precluded anything ever working between her and David when he resurfaced. The night at Les Misérables had been unexpected, magical, and risky but she felt it had served to take her off his 'suspects' list for a mole in the Branch.

Of real concern was the recent veiled threat that the Syndicate was aware of her night with David and they weren't happy about it. This trip was starting to look threatening. Could the Syndicate, or the BSB as they were known, be closing up shop and cleaning house, or were they flushing older members of the team for newer members who knew less about the actual workings of the network? And why did they need her as backup? Backup for what? Based in the US, surely they had their own local assets or contractors. Maybe they needed a patsy or fall guy. Either way they were definitely capable of any scenario.

She knew that the key BSB leadership in the US was about three strong and she had pieced together that one of them was the connection to the US political and Intel sectors. One had responsibilities she wasn't clear on and finally, her boss who she'd discovered was called Number Three, was in charge of the field people and operations around the globe. She knew this because Hammond had dropped a few hints of his understanding when he recruited her.

The money in her hidden accounts was great but a sense of foreboding was washing over her that this all might be coming to an end. At the very least, if there was a major operation going down in the US, in the backyard of the Syndicate, they'd definitely need a fall guy to take the heat. Lee Harvey Oswald came to mind and the widespread conspiracy theory that he'd only been a patsy for a larger, more powerful, and secretive organization ... just like the Syndicate.

It also worried her that she knew nothing about the rest of the operation. Clearly, there had been Jack Hammond and Jim Harden whom she knew. According to her MI6 colleagues, David had killed more than one Syndicate operative in Germany, so who was left? Beyond herself, she knew of no current agents of the BSB in Europe which brought her back to the thought that the time had come to shut it all down. Maybe it had run its course, or the big guys were closing in on the leaders so one last Hail Mary attack in the US itself and a fall guy to take all the heat and be disappeared.

No, there was nothing good about this last-minute unusual trip 'ordered' by her boss with no opportunity to ask questions. She was either being called in to be eliminated because of her liability tied to sleeping with David or to be used as a fall guy for a big operation in two days, or both.

She figured she had two choices. Run and hide with the money she had or go to DC and confront the whole thing head-on.

Suddenly running seemed like a really bad idea. Even though they compartmentalized, they couldn't know what info she had that could hurt them and the Syndicate would make it their mission to track her down and eliminate her if she attempted to disappear.

She had no idea the reach of their mercenaries around the globe and looking over her shoulder for the rest of her life was a non-starter.

There was no scenario that wasn't bad news for a trip to the US with this set of circumstances.

She concluded it wasn't a case of taking a few days off, zip over to the US, and then back to her MI6 duties. However this trip unfolded, it was the end of her MI6 career and she wouldn't be coming back to the UK. Time to execute her well-planned escape from the BSB and her London job and hope there was a fine early retirement after she confronted head-on whatever awaited her in Washington.

Somewhere off the Coast of Somalia

It had been about eighteen hours since the alarm went out but now Norm Lulham needed to wait no longer to find out what had happened to Rick.

At Bill Carter's order, he'd been taken aside and left to view the classified video that was on the dark web of Jihadi sites. He couldn't believe his eyes and nearly broke his hand when he punched a steel bulkhead on the lower level of the frigate. He cried openly for the next ten minutes, furious that his own CIA had failed to protect them and to warn Rick and incensed at the butchers who had done this to his friend and partner.

He and Rick had risked their lives for over a year now and felt they had been instrumental along with Cristal and David in intercepting the big Christmas attack on New York. He didn't yet know how Rick had been trapped but he was furious with HQ not being able to save him. Hell, they had drones and Signals Intelligence equipment all over the region to watch out for an ambush, yet his buddy had just been tortured to death by these rejects from a caveman's cult.

There was a nearby head, and he just made it as his stomach emptied.

He could not have imagined anything this cruel, terrifying, and inhumane could be on the horizon for their tiny team working in Mogadishu. He raced back to the head again.

Yes, such things had been filmed before, but you just never expected it would hit this close to home. They knew they were in danger at all times, but this? For a moment he considered what if it had been him and the terror he'd have felt.

His heart broke for his partner and his torturous end. Both of them had given up so much to work in this hellhole. Every emotion swept through him and he started dry heaving again.

Twenty minutes later as he was nursing his injured hand and trying to compose himself, the head of the Marine contingent, on a training mission on the ship, entered the small briefing room and closed the door, "I haven't seen the classified video, but rumors are rampant on what it contains. My sincere condolences for the loss of your partner. I'm sure everyone on board, if they knew what had happened, would want a piece of those animals."

Norm had nothing to offer and just sat forward in his chair, staring at the steel floor and trying not to cry in front of the Marine. His fists were clenched so hard his fingernails had cut into his hands.

"The one benefit, according to your HQ is that the monster who is the leader of the gang, Mustafa something, is apparently on the video and we now have a current photo of him and some of his buddies," as he handed a grainy cropped screenshot to Lulham.

"Your headquarters now knows for sure that it was this Mustafa guy's gang who ended up with your partner, so they know who these animals are."

Norm hadn't wanted to replay the video and hadn't noticed the men in the background. The big Marine wasn't cleared for the video and averted his gaze as Norm once more ran the muted video on the laptop they had provided.

He immediately recognized the face which wasn't much different from the previous photo in the CIA's confidential files. He hadn't noticed him standing in the background while he was focused on Rick's torturous death but indeed it was the same man with his guards in the Toyota Land Cruiser they'd intercepted at the football match last fall. 'Why didn't we kill him then?' he thought.

When Norm seemed finished the Marine continued, "But the screenshot isn't why I'm here. We've been tasked with cleaning up your apartment and agent Sawyer's, so we leave nothing for the bad guys to exploit. Bombing the building isn't an option as it's a densely occupied building with innocent families in harm's way.

"I've put together a crack team and frankly we need you to put yourself back in harm's way to guide us covertly to your two flats and collect anything we need to clean the sites. Hard drives, USBs, any paperwork, etc."

Lulham nodded as the Lieutenant Colonel continued, "We've had a high-altitude drone over the building since the alert went out to you and there has been no unusual activity so for the moment it would seem the bad guys don't know where you and Sawyer parked yourselves."

This hit Norm hard as he realized Rick had toughed it out to the end; held to the plan of misdirection during torture so he could save them from zeroing in on Norm, the apartment, and probably anything else they had tried to get out of him. He wasn't surprised Rick had stuck with the training and their rehearsals on misdirection, not dreaming of the insane level of torture he'd end up in.

That was just how Rick was; tough to the end and not deserving of any of what he got. A man of true integrity and most of the world would never know enough about his bravery. But Norm knew.

The Marine officer was still talking, "The plan is for you and five of my best guys to go in about two three zero by swift, quiet zodiac. Feet dry near the port by three hundred. Work your way under cover of darkness to your building and clean the place, back at the zodiac still under dark by five hundred and out of there. Do you think we can make it the one klick from the docks to your building without being discovered?"

Norm wasn't about to shirk his responsibility and he felt it was something he owed Rick, "Yeah, I know a path that should be really dark and quick and quiet going in. Coming out might be another thing as some of Mogadishu wakes up around five, but I don't see us taking two hours. Once at the building thirty minutes should be all we need. We'll be out of there well before five."

The Marine smiled, "Should be a cakewalk. You need to get weaponized, camo, face paint, comm, body armor, night vision goggles, etc. so I'll be back soon."

He spent the next few hours briefing the Marine landing party and going over detailed maps of the LZ, routes, alternates, meeting places if all hell broke loose, and the layout of the building including a list of what they had to retrieve. Code words for radio comms were exchanged as well.

Exhausted, he caught a few Z's before it was time to go feet wet. The ride in total darkness with almost silent electric motors was longer than he expected as the US warship was still orbiting over the horizon. It was another cloudy night and Lulham had trouble seeing even the camouflaged Marines at the front of their big powerful zodiac. He found trying the night goggles just made the seasickness much worse. He reasoned the guy on the helm either didn't get seasick or had to be using GPS to find his way to the landing spot because he could see nothing except unidentifiable lights in the distance.

All went as planned and they were at the building in under twenty minutes after making landfall. One member remained floating silently just offshore with the zodiac, one guarding each of the two entrances of the building leaving two with Norm to ransack the flats in the dimly lit building.

Silently mounting the stairway to his own flat which faced the stairway, Norm could see a note that had been slipped under his door. The regular signal he had set by placing a toothpick in the door jamb was still in place indicating it was likely no one had entered the premises. He turned to the two with him and whispered, "Change of plans. You guys start on Rick's apartment and I'll join you when I'm finished. I'll start on mine alone. I know where everything is."

They nodded and headed quietly down the hallway to Rick's flat.

Norm quickly entered his own flat, gun in hand, checked that he was alone and that the apartment seemed untouched, and opened what at first glance was a French travel brochure for Paris. Scribbled on the back in French was:

Voyage speciale pour vous ... BN

Boris Nugent was the head of the local NGO, OXFAM in Mogadishu and had acted as a cover from time to time for the two CIA covert agents. He had even hosted Cristal and David when they'd been in Mogadishu and he knew Norm spoke French. 'Special travel for you' was a pretty obvious hint but one that wouldn't raise eyebrows if the wrong person found the brochure.

Boris was smart as a fox, knew more than he admitted, and was better connected than most knew, yet he tried to stay out of the day-to-day. Officially he was just an NGO manager and he played that role well. Still, Norm and Rick had always felt he had deep and broad contacts in the city which until now he'd been reluctant to exploit.

Norm called him immediately, waking him from a deep sleep, "So you got my note. The hidden network in the city is all abuzz with the torturing and horrible death of Rick and that's even if he was a western agent. Of course, it sickens and infuriates me personally. My condolences, he was a great young man and a gentleman.

"Apart from the brutality of Al Qaeda, they all fear the US using the assassination as an excuse to once again invade the city as they did in the early nineties which would restart all kinds of mayhem. No one wants that.

"A guy I know and trust, claims he knows where Habib is this very night and that he's lightly guarded. If you decide to go after him it has to be alone, or my contact will bolt. I'm sorry but there can be no backup on this deal and it's only open now. I hope it's not too late. I'll text you an address in the next ten minutes when I contact him. You'll meet him and he'll drop you off near the place. If you decide to go, Good Luck!" and he hung up.

Leaving the Marines behind and sneaking out through his planned escape path, a ground floor window in an abandoned flat, he met with the unnamed and masked source at an agreed safe location provided by Boris.

Knowing this could be a trap to ensnare the other CIA agent he kept his hand on his gun at all times. If there was to be an ambush, then he'd make sure he took out a few of them and use his last bullet to ensure he wasn't captured and treated to Al Qaeda's torture.

Given his bond with Rick and his renewed hatred for Mustafa, it had been an instant decision to go all in, risking it all. Now that he'd seen the video, there was no way he was going to pass up a chance at some revenge.

The informant whispered instructions in Arabic and stopped ever so briefly to drop him off a few blocks from his destination and pointed silently to the target building. Thankfully, it was in one of the poorer neighborhoods and an area Norm was familiar with. The informant was quickly gone, and Norm found himself on a very dark night all on his own, totally exposed if it was a trap. Once the car sped off there wasn't a sound to be heard. He waited quietly hidden in an alcove in a building near the corner. No noise and no attackers.

So far so good. If this was a trap at least he hadn't been jumped in the car and his confidence was growing.

Langley

Director of the CIA Bill Carter had requested the team onboard the frigate to tackle the mission of cleaning up the Mogadishu flats. Eight hours earlier than Mogadishu, he and some of Carole's team sat in his office with a link to the ship as the mission commenced. Everything was going to plan until the leader of the team reported they had completed their task, but Norm was nowhere to be found.

Carter was incensed after getting the full report from the ship. Putting the phone on mute, he said to the small group around his conference table, "What the hell's going on? There's no way he was kidnapped right under their noses. Somehow, he got out of that building with sentries at the only entry points. Our guys cleaned up the two CIA sites and are evacuating as planned but they have no idea what happened to Norm. The Marines don't know the town so they can't go wandering around looking for him. What the hell is he doing?"

Almost simultaneously both Cristal and David said, "Habib."

After staring at each other Cristal continued, "He's gone after Mustafa Habib. I have no idea how he thinks he's going to find him because we've been searching for him forever but knowing Norm, that's what he's done. He's gone after Mustafa Habib to avenge Rick's death. Norm could be in a heap of trouble. Without backup, that's pretty much a suicide mission."

David took over, "There have to be reasons he didn't take the Marines with him. Number one, they don't take orders from Norm and they're in unfamiliar territory with a well-planned mission that doesn't include a major departure like going after Mustafa.

"Secondly, I'll bet somehow he has info from somewhere and it has to be a one-man job because of the logistics or something. He may even have launched this plan onboard the ship out of desperation if he had some idea of how to get info on Habib. He's not thinking clearly, and this is right after you gave the clearance for him to see the video.

"Normally Norm wouldn't put a gun to someone's head to get information, but this isn't a normal situation, at least in his mind. He may have gone berserk after that video and against his principles to get revenge, but I agree with Cristal, no doubt he's gone after Mustafa Habib by himself and it's certainly a suicide mission. In his mind, it is all about the rage and he's going to take irrational chances in his quest to hit back.

"Knowing Mogadishu, it could easily be a trap. Any person getting him info could be playing both sides. He's risking it all going in alone. I can only say I'd be tempted to do the same for Rick. I bet we'll know in the next couple of hours what's happened but honestly, I can't take another video like that one we saw earlier. So even if you don't pray, pray for Norm to get out of this alive."

***

Norm waited until the car left. It had stopped so briefly before the corner that any late-night observer might not have known someone had bailed.

The lighting around here was terrible which would work to his advantage. He checked his armaments, a nine-millimeter automatic pistol with a very effective silencer and a round in the chamber, extra ammo in a pouch on his armored vest, night vision goggles, military radio headset, and an eight-inch combat knife. Not much to go up against Al Qaeda's top guy and his bodyguards who all carried AK's.

From his stealthy position, a short block and a half from the target he flipped down his night vision goggles to get a good look at the area. Almost as if it was daylight, he picked out a sentry in the doorway of the target building. He was just returning to a seat, partly out of sight in the recessed doorway after apparently looking for anything odd when a car had sped away two streets over.

The goggles were good, but he didn't want them on if he got into any hand-to-hand stuff. Flipping them up he waited for about three minutes for his eyes to adjust which seemed much longer. The whole area was dead quiet. It was now almost four and this being a poorer working neighborhood, everyone seemed to be asleep, even the ever-present street dogs.

He crossed the street in a crouch to the same side as the target building and made his way along the buildings. Occasionally he saw some movement in the feet that stuck out of the entryway as the guard seemed to be trying to get comfortable and catch a few Z's on such a quiet unassuming night.

He kept scanning the two and three-story buildings and the rooftops lining the other side of the dirt road on the chance there were lookouts or snipers. When he finally crept up to the building, he simply stuck his head around the corner and put a silenced bullet into the sleeping guard's head from two feet away, catching the big sentry and his folding chair as they almost clattered to the ground.

Silence. No alarms or running feet. Now that he was in the entrance, he recognized the style of building.

A narrow single home affair with a shop of sorts on the ground floor and sleeping quarters on the second floor. Just beside the entrance was an ancient dirt bike, key in the ignition for a quick exit or chase he suspected, and a two-gallon gas can up against the wall which looked to be about half full. A plan was taking shape.

Opening the outside door carefully and extremely slowly he crept quietly with the night vision goggles on throughout the first floor finding no other personnel. In the darkness, it seemed like it was some kind of a tailor's business.

Silently climbing the stairs, he found only one room with an occupant. One with an AK-47 sitting by his bed. Gun pointed at the head, he got just close enough holding his breath to make out Mustafa Habib.

Deciding not to shoot him, he crept back downstairs, strategy, tactics, and years of training filling his brain. Moments later, goggles off, he had his hand over Mustafa's mouth and his gun in his face as the man at first shocked, instantly understood his predicament and laid still. It was clear the assailant was an American commando in full face paint and camo so kidnapping and Guantanamo immediately came to mind.

In perfect Arabic, Norm said, "What you're probably feeling right now is the gasoline soaking your mattress. In case you're wondering, I'm Rick Sawyer's partner and I have a message from him. This doesn't qualify as martyrdom. You're a fucking butcher and this is payback."

At that he quickly shot off the man's two kneecaps, something he'd been told was extremely painful. The next two shots were into the shoulders of the flailing and screaming man, effectively immobilizing him in the bed and two more rounds into the mattress lighting it in such a way that he had to jump back as the flames caught his eyebrows.

He was surprised at how slowly the fire seemed to spread but that didn't seem to help the screaming Mustafa. He dumped the remaining gasoline directly on him.

The screaming was intense as the man couldn't move with his damaged legs and shoulders as the flames engulfed him. Try as he might, he couldn't roll over or crawl out of bed. He was now totally engulfed in flames.

Norm took one last smiling look at the scene, turned his headset to broadcast, swiped at the man with his combat knife taking off two flailing fingers, and didn't wait for any nearby friends to come to the screaming man's aid. Habib was officially toast as he leaped down the stairs and onto the waiting motorcycle. Mustafa's screaming was waking the whole town. Only seconds had passed as he headed down the street in the growing cacophony of screams, lights coming on and a few bullets bouncing off the roadway nearby.

A few quick turns and minutes later he was about a mile away at the port, dumping the dirt bike off the pier and into the ocean. Thankfully, his radio worked and the Marines who had been part way back to their ship were on their way back to pick him up at the designated spot. Waiting the fifteen minutes for them to appear was excruciating as more and more sounds from the crime scene seemed to be approaching him with various teams of supporters and police out to find the assassin. A peek around the corner convinced him the entire building about ten city blocks away was still on fire. His heart finally returned to a normal beat on the stealthy run back to the ship.

The lead Marine finally said, "You're blocking the frequency. You can turn the broadcast off now. Was that what I think it was?"

Norm just nodded.

***

Word arrived back at Langley that they had Norm while Carter was still in his office with the team. Soon Lulham was back on the ship and Habib's demise was shared with a few of those on the ship and a smiling team in Langley. They took a moment of silence for Rick Sawyer, soon to be remembered with yet another nameless star on the CIA's wall of honor in the building's entrance. Carter made a mental note for a commendation and medal for Lulham. He immediately classified everything to do with the evening and passed the word on to the ship where Norm was. Clearly, rules of engagement and probably laws had been broken in Norm's actions, but Carter resolved to try to cover for it all somehow.

He'd have to have a private conversation with Norm to get a plausible story given there were no witnesses still alive, but he was willing to risk everything with the understanding that this was an asymmetric war and sometimes the rules had to be bent. Being a liberal-minded leader, it went against his principles that atrocities could be returned in kind but the vision of Rick in that cage was just too much. After all, all they had was Norm's own wild story of what had happened, and he couldn't be expected to incriminate himself in any investigation. It was also unlikely that Al Qaeda would ever have standing at the World Court in Den Hagg to present their complaint.

The captain of the aircraft carrier saw to it that someone 'accidentally erased' the recording that had come from Norm's mic after Carter had heard it and had requested some form of accommodation.

***

Back in the war room the next morning, Director Carter filled in the rest of the team with some of the classified information about Norm's adventures, sidestepping anything that could come back on Norm.

Chip Attwood was first to speak, "What do you think this means for the fourth?"

Cristal didn't wait for the boss to answer, "Nothing! Or at least nothing good. Word will get to the attackers fast that we burned up their boss in his own bed which will undoubtedly infuriate them. Burning infidels is allowed but not fellow Muslims, especially warrior Muslims. Remember Mustafa is also looked on by some as a religious leader. So no, they're not a happy bunch and probably more committed than ever to getting even with us. These monsters won't be cowed by this, but they'll certainly be motivated.

"We know they have the bigger bombs planted and they have the triggers, so everything is ready to go. We just don't know where the triggermen are or even how many of them are involved in the attack. We absolutely need something of a lead on where the smaller bombs are going. If this IS some kind of joint effort of Al Qaeda and the BSB then the BSB won't care about Habib unless this somehow affects their alliance but even that's another blind spot for us.

"I know we haven't discussed it but my thinking is these devices were built and supplied by the BSB as they probably have the money and global network to pull off all the logistics needed like hiring that road crew and disguising the contracting company. Al Qaeda is almost certainly the grunt work and triggermen especially given two of those devices were shipped to Pennsylvania. So BSB's work is likely done, and we only have the Jihadis still on the job."

Cristal was on a roll and while Carter realized he should have been orchestrating the meeting where all were his subordinates, this was when she was at her best, analysis and synthesis. So, he let her take the lead and nodded to Carole who got the message.

Cristal was just getting started, "Here's the part that confuses me. The National Mall attack is almost certainly after lawmakers. That sounds like BSB's targets with a bit of an advantage to Al Qaeda as they can claim they hit big names on a national holiday. But as we saw last fall and at Christmas, they want to terrify the general public rather than go after individual politicians. They're not usually into assassinations. Planes in buildings, blowing up shopping malls, and dumping raw nuclear material into water systems are more their style. Or at least it was Khalil's style.

"If our assumptions are right and there's a deal in play, why did Al Qaeda agree to abandon the mass terror agenda? We decided to build those stands as cover for jamming, otherwise, they may have killed only a few people with those massive, buried bombs. That's political assassination, not terrorism per se."

Carter finally spoke, "I think I see where you're going with this. Habib agreed to the parade attack which benefits mostly the BSB and potentially they get the two smaller devices for a more traditional terror attack. But what does that tell us? What would they attack with the smaller but still immensely powerful IEDs?"

There was total silence in the room until Carter spoke again, "Okay, the parade is in less than two days and we need to find these other two IEDs. Cristal and David are already calling this building home for the moment but we're going to have to switch to full-time, so Chip, see what you can do about cots and I'll authorize anything needed so the entire team can camp here until we've resolved these threats."

To the room he said, "So call your loved ones and tell them you won't be home. Tell them you're on a national security drill, no details, and you're tied up for the next two days around the clock. No leaks on what we're really doing. Any serious compassionate issues, see me directly.

"On top of what you're already doing, I want you to do the following:

"Call once more to all the local police departments and surrounding precincts of DC looking for anything unusual, even abandoned vehicles, especially around parades or large gatherings of people. Same thing for Pittsburgh and New York as those seem to be their preferred targets. Throw in Boston too with their Pops in the Park thing.

"Work with the FBI on any progress on that cell in Pittsburgh. One day we'll get to the bottom of what's going on there and today would be a good day for that.

"I heard this morning that Homeland has executed a mechanism to gather ALL recent police reports from around the nation and they've given them to the FBI to look for anything unusual. They cull them automatically using search algorithms. There's got to be close to a million reports, but they must have thousands to go through manually after that. Carole, find out if we can help by reviewing some of those. Take any staff you need from downstairs to help.

"Recheck all the major parades especially ones in locations of interest like ground zero in New York.

"Look through the high-priority targets once more and don't forget shopping centers.

"Double check all the fireworks displays one more time for anyone phoning in sick or trucks parked where they shouldn't be.

"You know the routine. Run through everything you've done already because things change as time marches on. Those buried IEDs were on no one's radar the day before they were buried so maybe there's something out there now that has changed and needs a second look.

"Also, any new things you can think of but sadly we're all here until we can declare an All Clear and that won't be until we find those other two bombs."

***

But try as they might, it didn't work.

Early morning and the parade was only a few hours away. Even though the team was still at it, Director Carter called his driver so he could race home and have a shower. It was a given that when the commotion of arresting terrorists on the National Mall during an Independence Day Parade appeared on TV there would be questions and he'd likely be on camera. He desperately needed a shave, shower, and a change of clothes.

As they turned the corner into his cul de sac Carter only had time to notice the old excavator by the side of the road as the bomb went off.

An hour later it was Bill Carter's wife Gillian who was patched through to the war room and requested to be put on speaker. In a shaky yet clear voice, she said, "They got him!

"The police said it was a buried bomb not two hundred feet from our home. I noticed them digging there late yesterday. Jim Foster, his driver was killed instantly. He had become a family friend and he had young kids."

After a sobbing pause, she said, "Bill is in a coma fighting for his life. They're giving him a fifty-fifty chance. He should have been killed outright but the paramedics think he must have been crouched down on the back seat. Half of his bulletproof Suburban flipped over several times and landed on a neighbor's lawn. Blew out most of the windows in our street and there were some injuries. Bill always wears his seatbelt, and all the special airbags went off so in a way he was lucky. We can only pray now.

"Bill had told me you were looking for two smaller bombs. This one wasn't small. There's a massive crater where our street used to be. Find the other one," and she hung up.

There was silence and horror in the room until Carole Glass said incredulously, "It was always a hit job, not a terrorist attack. They went after individuals. That's what the BSB wanted. Assassinate congressmen and senators in the parade and now this. It was never meant to be a terrorist attack and they went after the boss. They're assassinating people who threaten them."

The room was quiet as it all settled in. Bill Carter, their popular boss was fighting for his life nearby in some hospital.

Carole continued, "Who else could be a target and is not in the parade? I think we can eliminate the President as he's not planning any travel today. We checked that earlier.

"Make a list of every cabinet member and senior official. We'll start calling them; 'No travel and watch for IEDs'. Give them the size and shape of the bomb but it could be disguised. Watch for any recent digging or larger than normal parked vehicles."

Within an hour they had it. The Director of the FBI had been working from home given it was a holiday. He reported construction work across from his driveway. A backup team from the Mall descended within thirty minutes on the quiet street, jammed the right signals, and captured the triggerman sitting in a car down the street.

It was a giant relief to the team at Langley that the jamming had worked, and the triggerman had been caught with the exact RC controller they'd been chasing. So to some degree, the pressure was off on the much bigger bombs as the Independence Day Parade made its way down the National Mall. They were all much more confident now that the jamming would do the trick.

So it was, that when DC's Independence Day Parade was passing the World War II Memorial, a few of the TV cameras picked up some commotion in the crowd as undercover agents closed in on the target that had just activated the trigger mechanism for one of the bombs. He had been hiding about four hundred feet away near the Memorial itself. The jamming had worked flawlessly as had the laser painting and scanners which identified the triggerman. When surrounded by law enforcement he hadn't given much of a chase or fight. However, they had to take the controller off him with force as he was rapidly pressing every button and switch on the machine.

It was all over within minutes and the All Clear came back from the field commander. Fully redundant localized jamming would be continued until the huge bombs could be dug up and sent to Naval Bomb Disposal to be neutralized.

The press weren't happy with the wall of 'no comment' responses they got on the commotion near the parade and the Mid-Eastern man, tote bag over his shoulder, being led away.

The FBI, the DC, and the Capitol police could do all of the cleanup and follow-up including trying to track down whoever seemed to be talking to the bomber when he tried to trigger the device. They also had the job of trying to figure out who triggered the bomb that got Bill Carter.

Carole Glass, now in charge as the Director was incapacitated, led the cheering and high fives. One or two in the war room were teary-eyed either from the release of stress, exhaustion, pride in the job they'd done, fear for their very popular boss, flashbacks of their colleague in Mogadishu, or all of the above. They were all physically and emotionally exhausted and elated at the same time and totally spent after the intensity of the last forty-eight hours in lockdown. The sudden release of all that tension was too much for some and they became very emotional.

While the bad guys had gotten the boss, the CIA team had done most of the work intercepting the major attack on the Mall and killing Al Qaeda's most recent leader who had planned it all. They pretty much all agreed that had to be put in the WIN column.

After the congratulations subsided, Carole started sending her very tired team home in waves as the few loose ends were tied up. She assigned someone to handle the official cover stories and an agent to follow up with law enforcement on their investigation of the triggermen. The FBI, DC Police, Capitol Police, ATF, and the Secret Service were all on the job of investigating the attacks.

David and Cristal were still squatters at headquarters, so they were the last to be released.

Carole spoke as the last two left the room, "Cristal, I feel I need to remain here until my deputy takes over, and even though you must be exhausted like the rest of us, I'd really like an on-the-scene report on Bill. I know you're close to him. Even though you remain a target, could I ask you to head over to the hospital with your security detail and report back on his condition? I doubt anyone is sitting outside this building waiting for you. His wife could probably use some support from headquarters as well. Make sure she understands we're all praying for him and we'll do whatever she needs."

Cristal, totally exhausted, nevertheless spent a good part of the rest of the day at the hospital where all she could do was hold the hand of Gillian Carter, the Director's wife who, under the stress and fear wasn't very talkative.

Director Carter had narrowly escaped death, but he wasn't out of the woods yet with serious head trauma and several other injuries. The doctors had no forecast as to how long he'd need to be kept in an induced coma as they feared further brain swelling. Crystal knew a little bit about that having been in the same shape only a few months earlier, so she was of some comfort to the grieving woman.

David spared no time in getting back to their makeshift apartment at CIA HQ. He couldn't remember when he last had a full night's sleep and was unconscious in no time even though it was midafternoon.

Even Carole Glass was finally relieved and headed home for some much-needed rest.

So, it was a skeleton team on duty just after nightfall when the first alarm came in from Homeland Security about a radiation leak at a nuclear power plant.

Within minutes the alarm was escalated to a nuclear emergency and half of the Washington security establishment was being called back into work on Independence Day.

Dulles International

As agreed, Number Three picked Kathy up alone at the airport midday on America's Independence Day. Surprising to Kathy was his demeanor which seemed charming but tense.

As she put her bag in the back of his car, she retrieved her service weapon from her checked luggage.

On the alert, as they left the airport grounds, she took the weapon out of her pocket and made sure Number Three saw it. Immediately he panicked, "What's this?"

As she patted him down for weapons, she said, "Well let's just say that this little visit isn't going to go the way you planned. Today you're going to do some introductions. I'm proceeding no further with orders from this Syndicate until we get some clear indications from your partners that I'm a respected and long-term member of this team. Frankly, with all the deaths in our European squad, and warnings from you about my thing with David Crowe, I need some assurances and I'm going to get them. So, pull over at the next McDonald's, buy me a Big Mac and call an emergency meeting with your cronies."

Number Three could see she was serious, "Okay, I'll do exactly as you ask and refrain from setting off any alarms if you just promise me you'll give me a chance to talk before you do anything stupid like shooting me. You and I have some unfinished business and you need to hear me out for your own sake. Killing me would only sign your own death warrant."

Kathy thought about this. So far he had seemed to be honest with her in their personal dealings. Trust wasn't something she gave out freely, but he seemed serious about something she needed to know. She had no such trust intentions with the others, "You'll get your chance to explain a few things, now get moving."

An hour later they waited, parked, and hidden behind some hedges two blocks away from the prescribed warehouse until the other two SUVs had parked and two men from each car entered the building. Then she and Number Three proceeded to the meeting.

As they walked to the back door he said, "Their bodyguards won't hesitate to stop you."

"Just worry about yourself."

As they walked through the door the two bodyguards picked up that something was off and went for their guns. Kathy took them out easily with quick shots to the head. The noise in the empty warehouse was deafening as the other two members jumped from their chairs.

"SIT BACK DOWN!" she yelled, grabbing the wrist of Number Three and dragging him swiftly to the card table.

Number One, always the most assertive of the group yelled, "What is this? Aren't you one of us? From MI6 I believe."

As she pushed Number Three into his chair she said. "You got that part right. And you look familiar too. Aren't you on Bill Carter's staff at the CIA? I think we met on a video call some time back. Yeah, you're his EA, right? So that's where all BSB's intel comes from. Take that!" and she shot him from close range through the forehead.

Number Two dove to the floor cowering as she said, "Now you don't look familiar so you must be the finance guy," and she shot him in the face.

Number Three sat peacefully looking at his two dead co-conspirators as she turned the gun on him.

He turned to look directly up at her and said, "So are we going to have our wee chat now?"

She smiled and said, "Now that you're the last one and of no threat to me, sure. I can't imagine what you have to say to me."

Number Three finally smiled as she sat in Number Two's chair and he started, "Why do you think I asked, or let's say, ordered you here today?"

She smiled back at him, "I wasn't sure at first, but I'd say it was to clean up loose ends. One way or another every other Syndicate member I know of in Europe has been eliminated by you three or in setups by you; killed directly or information leaked in one way or another to set them up. Jim Harden and his friend after he returned from your mission to Africa was the worst. He was totally loyal, but I now suspect he was on a mission to meet with and make a deal with Al Qaeda. To keep links to those barbarians invisible, you had him killed. Now when I asked you, you denied it but you were not very convincing. You see the night before he was assassinated, he hinted at his little mission to Mogadishu.

"So, for some reason, top brass, that being your little club here, were cleaning house and getting rid of anything that could point back to them, especially you who I gather was the link to all the field agents.

"Your warning about my private night with David Crowe got me thinking. People like you don't give warnings.

"And then this story about needing a backup on some mission here in the US. That smelled like a setup to me. Needed a fall guy, did we?"

He smiled as he started, "It's amazing how much of this you got right and how much you got wrong. Let's start with assassinations. Your boyfriend Crowe and his girlfriend killed most of the European team all by themselves, not me. Do you think they're part of the Syndicate?"

She simply smiled at him as he continued, "No, I didn't think so. Jim Harden was assassinated by Al Qaeda sending us a message that they didn't like the fact that we had tracked down their boss. I can show you the email from them to that effect. The man who had Harden killed, the Al Qaeda boss Mustafa Habib, is also dead by the way. That was me. I leaked his whereabouts to the CIA in Mogadishu in payback for Jim and a CIA kid they tortured and burned alive just the other day. Obviously, I have no emails on that so you'll just have to take my word for it. Word should be out soon about the Al Qaeda leader's horrific death in Mogadishu.

"Going way back to last fall, I was the one who spotted David Crowe at JFK and alerted your old boyfriend Hammond. As you know, Jack wanted him dead in The Sudan and local press head shots of the supposed assassinated Englishman in Khartoum were sent to me as proof. So imagine my surprise when I spot him marching through JFK.

"Up to that point, Crowe was thought to be dead and not a threat. But he was about to blow open our whole network and, in some ways, it was a blessing he took out your buddy Hammond before he spilled the beans; AND Jack would have caved if caught. He was the weakest link in the whole scheme. It wouldn't have taken much for him to finger not only me but you too, as well as Willems in Germany. At his core, he was a weak man and I always regretted recruiting him. All the others in Europe are contractors and know nothing about us. You are the last.

"Now let's talk about today. We three," nodding towards the floor, "are the Syndicate. You were right, Number One there was the connection to the politicians and Intel. I knew he was part of the Intel Community, but I didn't realize he had graduated to Carter's Executive Assistant.

"Number Two was our connection to our bosses and provided all our funding. He was our weakest link. Number One as we now know, was actually on the CIA's senior staff and saw pretty much everything going across Director William Carter's desk. Carter was searching for the mole in the CIA and Number One, his Executive Assistant was right there under his nose."

Kathy waved her gun as if to say, get to the point.

"Anyway, Carter was closing in on us, and let me tell you, if he ever gets to find out about those two dead guys on the floor, he'll have the last pieces to the puzzle and we're both finished. That's why we made the deal to do an attack on US soil which has never been part of our domain. So why not hide it behind a terrorist attack and hide the biggest target, Carter, in a whole bunch of assassinations, all of which had some merit on their own?

"The 'terrorist' attacks were to have happened this morning. They messed up on the main attack on the Independence Day Parade and they missed the FBI guy but we 'almost' got Carter, the main target. The terrorists actually hit him in his armored car this morning. It was a very large bomb, but somehow he survived. He's in hospital in critical condition as we speak. He cannot be allowed to recover or we're dead. He'll quickly piece all of this together.

"Now to you and me.

"I could see the end coming. The fact that most of our network had been destroyed and we've become ineffective meant that someone above us would likely decide a wrap-up and cleanup was in order. My guess is that Number One here would have been given orders to take us all out. He even started threatening us very recently. He may in fact have come here today prepared to do just that but his guy with the gun lying over there won't be confirming any of that for us.

"If Carter was dead then Number One here was the one key member worth saving for those above us. So, close down the Syndicate and restart it when and if needed with him at the center.

"When Hammond recruited you, I told you to build a failsafe escape plan. I left enough hints like the warning about David that I was pretty sure you'd trigger that plan, heed my order and come over here. By jumping ship so quickly and killing four people I've no doubt you triggered your escape plan already because there's no way you're going back to MI6.

"I had a plan that was somewhat different from this but," he laughed, "your plan was a lot quicker and more effective than mine could have been. So bravo, you now have us almost exactly where we need to be. I mean really, if I had told you this story before you killed these four people would you have believed me?

"Now here is where we stand. I've been more than well compensated for my role in the Syndicate, and I have my own escape plan. I sold all my business interests a few days ago and for the moment, I have access to a Syndicate slush fund of about five million US dollars that I don't need.

"There's only one obstacle to both of us walking away and executing our escape plans to out-of-the-way places with no extradition treaties and that is Bill Carter. If he recovers, he will quickly put the pieces together and come after both of us. According to Number One there, no one else is close to knowing what Carter knows already. So, his theory of the Syndicate and its players will go with him to the grave. Yeah, Number One being found dead in a warehouse will be puzzling to others but that's all it will be. And they may even link your disappearance in London to Number One but if you're lucky they'll probably conclude that whoever did him, did you first. But none of that conjecture matters if you did a good job of escape planning.

"So, I think the deal is clear. You go to Carter's hospital and finish him off saving both of us and then execute your escape plan with an extra five million dollars and we say goodbye here and never think of each other again.

"Here are the details on how to find him given they secretly moved him to George Washington according to Number One there."

As he handed her the note he said, "I don't want to be looking over my shoulder for the rest of my life and I don't need the money so when I hear the deal is done, I'll transfer the money into your Swiss account we've used in the past and you have no need to seek me out.

"You and I can then separately toast the end of the Syndicate.

"How does that sound?"

Nasir

Could anything more go wrong? The big boss Mustafa Habib, butchered in the most horrible way by an unknown assassin and now the DC attack had mostly failed somehow, meaning the Syndicate would assuredly renege on telling them where the two CIA agents were hiding.

Nasir Abboud, now head man at Al Qaeda for the moment, was near his wit's end. The success of their main mission fell on his head. Thankfully, Mustafa had finally included him in the planning for the master assault but Abboud had thought from the start that it was too complicated and techie to work.

His mind returned to Mustafa and how he'd been found and targeted. Now Nasir was the target himself. It had only been the day before that they'd caught the CIA spy and filmed him being executed. Now someone, possibly another spy in town, had reciprocated but not with a religious justification, which made all the difference. Some infidel had taken it upon himself to brutally murder their leader and he could do it again unless they caught him.

There was no telling who it had been but given the viciousness of the attack the thinking was it was someone who had a serious objection to the way the CIA agent had been killed.

Ironically Habib hadn't been in favor of the torture and torching of the American spy but Nasir had talked him into it, explaining once more the rationale behind terror and the absolute need for it to be as unimaginably brutal as possible and the more public the better. He had also been the one to convince a reluctant

Mustafa to be in the frame of the video so the troops would associate him with continuing Khalil's penchant for dramatic assassinations and hitting the infidels hard.

The agent's capture had been less than informing. He had held out until he could no longer and answered some of their questions but clearly some if not all of the answers were lies. With the Independence Day attack so close they wanted a crescendo, so they decided to torture him and kill him before the big attacks in the US. That being so, they had little time to get any information out of him or indeed check out his answers.

It now appeared he had made up a name for his partner and where they both lived as well as names for anyone they worked with. The theory that torture doesn't work was familiar to Al Qaeda but this guy had been pretty good at misdirection with plausible answers when tortured. Nasir suspected he'd been trained for this and had key misdirecting answers memorized.

The overall driving force in this conflict was that Allah demanded retribution for infidels invading Muslim lands with their disgusting customs and poisonous 'democracy' where God's will was ignored and the rabid, populist rule of the godless masses won the day.

Someone, not following Allah, had treated Habib to the same unthinkable torture which had the effect on Nasir of a blood-boiling need for revenge. Allah demanded revenge too and being Al Qaeda's new leader, he had the means to deliver.

One common rumor on Habib's assassination was that the CIA had gotten to him, but there were two problems with that scenario. First the Americans usually executed these things with a missile or with an overpowering commando team like they'd used on Osama Bin Laden. But this was apparently executed by a loner.

Secondly, how could they have found him in the middle of town at a new safe house? They had been after Mustafa since he took over and missed him once before with a missile. How had they found him now? It had to be someone internal that had turned on them. Maybe someone who knew the agent they'd killed or didn't approve of the torture. Either way, the CIA or some other menace was responsible which made Nasir think he might be next. In response, he had doubled the security and planning that Habib had used. Still, he'd have to learn to constantly look over his shoulder and trust no one. This wasn't a job or a role he'd seen for himself. Two leaders taken out in the last few months and now he'd likely be the prized target. The honor of being the leader surely had its downsides.

He wondered what the US's response to the killing of their CIA agent would be. There was no telling if they'd seen the video yet and even if they had, it was unlikely they'd had enough time to put together a strike on Mustafa.

There was always the possibility of an overreaction and an invasion which would be more likely after their dual attack today on their Independence Day. Even though one of their attacks had already failed, the US would want to respond to the threat. Hopefully, the main attack would succeed but either way, they'd have to be ready for a reappearance of US forces in the Horn of Africa.

Al Qaeda's network was only now finding out that Habib had been martyred and his lieutenant had taken over at the helm. Given that reality, it was uncertain as to what kind of loyalty he could expect. He'd have to do something soon to win their respect and what he was watching now replaying on TV had set that quest way back.

CNN International hadn't carried the Independence Day Parade in Washington but they'd broken into regular programming to play a tape of some kind of police action at the parade. There was no information on what had happened beyond an arrest, but Nasir was under no illusions. Somehow the Americans had detected the plan to bomb the parade and had captured Al Qaeda's triggerman. He seriously wondered if the Syndicate had somehow screwed them. Either way, soon all Al Qaeda would know of the failure unless he found a way to divorce themselves from the Syndicate. Word had leaked out about an attack on this day, but the day wasn't over yet. If they were successful in the second attack, then all would be forgiven even if some knew of the earlier failure. The second attack had to work.

He had been assured by his contacts that the triggerman had only been instructed on the parade bombing and had no knowledge to cough up on any other plans.

Later on TV, there was a report of the CIA Director being admitted to the hospital in critical condition after some kind of vehicle accident. CNN later reported that it had been a targeted bombing that had injured the CIA Director but there was no update on his condition.

There was also no mention of the FBI Director so while they hadn't killed anyone, one of the IEDs had apparently done some damage to a key target. Whatever this meant to the alliance with the Syndicate would have to wait but if they hadn't reneged on the alliance and were serious about the attack then they wouldn't only be unhappy about the outcome but possibly blaming Al Qaeda for the failure. One more reason for a quick divorce but Nasir wondered how that could be achieved.

Now the BIG question; had the Americans also intercepted Habib's bigger plan which should be taking shape right about now?

He headed down to the basement of the safe house where his top tech guy was working feverishly on three screens on an old table.

"Tell me again how this will work."

The young tech looked up and saw the concern on the new boss's face, "Okay, as I've told you we've tested everything we can. Mohammed, our man near Pittsburgh, is at his computer. As you know, he has an intimate understanding of the control room at that type of plant. He once worked at a similar site.

"Our North Korean friend has given him the control panel simulator on his computer which he says is rudimentary but good enough … if it all works as advertised. There was no way to test that aspect without alerting the wrong people.

"When the attack comes, the North Korean will break into their system, locking them out and pass the internet access to me. Mohammed can then connect through me here. We did it that way so the North Korean cannot trace our people in the US and blackmail us. Then it's all under our control. We only need the team in the plant to do as Mohammed says they've been trained and abandon their posts, locking the place down on the way out. Mohammed is certain that he can do real damage to the facility in any number of ways, so we should be successful. He is very excited and confident."

Nasir was still worried, "Are there any signs the operation has been compromised, and can we trust this Korean?"

"Relax. Everything seems to be going to plan and the Korean gets almost nothing if it doesn't work. We've only paid him a small sum until now. It should all work but we won't know for certain until we try the hookup, and the Korean gets to see what their firewall looks like but he's confident that he can break in. Between Mohammed's knowledge of the plant's systems and security and the Korean's expertise in hacking, they have a plan that should work. It's getting late over there so you can stay and watch if you wish.

"As I said don't worry, brother Habib was a master strategist. He planned all of this out and double-checked everything. I'm confident we'll be successful, and we'll avenge his slaughter."

Nasir was still unconvinced. The day hadn't gone well so far. This was Habib's grand plan and Nasir had warned him that it was too complicated and high tech to work. All he could do now was wait for it all to play out, thousands of miles away and he had no way to even talk to the attackers without running the risk of the Americans being alerted.

Attack #2

They had timed it perfectly. The sun was just setting as Amal and Pierre, having driven the three hundred odd miles from their home near Pittsburgh were getting anxious. Following their GPS, they pulled off Fricks Lock Road about a half-mile from the plant. They parked the car behind a warehouse that seemed closed and soon had the gear in their backpacks. They walked quickly to get as close as they could to the old Schuylkill Canal.

The few nineteenth-century buildings in the historic village of Fricks Lock were posted as officially off-limits and had all been abandoned shortly after the power plant was built so there was no fear of running into anyone. That meant however that there was the risk of a patrol car checking out their vehicle parked behind the warehouse nearby, so they'd have to be quick.

Across the river, below the big cooling towers of the Limerick nuclear power plant, they could see the dimly lit control building only a few hundred yards away.

Even though they were confident no one could hear them, Pierre spoke in a whisper, "Why do you think we've not heard from your cousin Hamsa?"

Amal looked around to see how far they were from the closest buildings. Apart from the big plant across the water, he could see none of the abandoned houses or any other buildings; just trees between them and the car.

"I've no idea. All I know is he had his orders too and we were told very specifically not to share anything in case one of us was compromised. They call it compartmentation or something like that. All I know is he left last night. In fact, it may be a good thing he doesn't try to call us. He knows only that we have a secret mission too and he probably doesn't want to risk exposing us in any way. They could be tracking his calls and maybe ours too.

"When you were driving, I got a news flash on my phone that something happened at a parade in Washington earlier but there were no details. Let's hope that was them, but it could've been something completely unrelated. Either way, I'm not calling him until we get home. He'll probably be back before us anyway.

"I suspect there will be some breaking news soon because the one thing I do know is that we both had only today, US Independence Day, to execute our part of multiple attacks. Who knows how many there are? We have our instructions, the sun has now set so no one will see the drone, so let's just do it and get out of here before we're discovered."

They had the powder out of the special lead box and loaded on the drone and on its way within minutes carrying its special payload. Without running lights, they lost track of the drone soon after it took off. They navigated it towards the target using its onboard night vision TV camera.

Having memorized the building's drawings, it wasn't hard to find the fresh air intake on top of the main control building to dump their surprise.

***

It was just before ten PM as Sam Hillman, just completing his hourly monitoring checklist of the reactor, sat up so he could see over his console, "Frank, there's a new pot of coffee ready. I'm getting some; need anything?"

Frank Garrison, in command on this shift, had just about dozed off and was jerked awake by Hillman's question. He shook the sleep out of his head, saw there was nothing of note on his console, and said, "Yeah, you'd better get me something. I can't stay awake. I hate this shift."

There were only three of them on duty in the control room at Limerick this Independence Day, but Sam had seen a couple of cleaners in the main office earlier. Dave had just headed to the men's room, so he'd tell him about the coffee when he returned.

As he rose from his chair to shake off the cobwebs, suddenly a very bizarre and loud claxon started sounding about once per second; loud enough to wake anyone.

Hillman was first, jumped, and ran across the room to the security panel yelling as he went, "What the hell is this?"

The screen was showing a flashing yellow block.

Frank yelled out across the room, "There's nothing on my console. Isn't that a radiation alarm?"

"Yeah!" Sam yelled back. Studying the legend, he screamed, "It's in the loading dock and it's a yellow alarm so it's relatively low level but hell that claxon scared the shit out of me. Man, it's loud."

Sam continued to yell over the alarm, "That loading area is at the far end of this building, and thank God it's not part of the containment building. What the hell could be leaking radiation in the loading dock? Do we have any spent fuel rods on their way out? Maybe something fell over and started leaking. I'll tell you one thing. I'm not the one going in there to check it out. Where's the emergency response handbook?"

As Dave rushed back into the room Frank reached the console where Sam was and said loud enough to be heard, "I've never heard a radiation alarm and I don't like it."

"What radiation?" Dave asked almost in a panic, still struggling with his belt.

As Sam turned to Dave, he saw two cleaners at the locked glass control room door and gave them a sign indicating 'all's okay' even though he had no way of knowing that.

Now a phone was ringing on Frank's desk, and he was pretty sure he knew what that was. The backup control facility at headquarters had seen the alarm too.

Frank picked up a nearby phone and clicked on his line just as the claxon doubled in speed and the warning block for the loading area turned red. Sam shouted, "Holy Shit. This is serious."

Frank could only hear enough on the phone to know there was someone there, "Frank Garrison here," he yelled, "I can't hear you but I'm the lead operator at Limerick and yes we know we have an alarm. It's in the loading dock area and it just went red. It's not in the containment building and we've no idea what's causing it."

Before the person on the line could say anything a second different sounding claxon started and a yellow block indicating 'Main Office' started flashing on the screen. Sam whipped around and spotted the two cleaners in the main office pasted up against the locked glass door wondering what was going on. It was clear to them from Sam's face that all was definitely NOT 'okay'.

Frank now had no hope of hearing the person on the other end of the phone as a third claxon started and a yellow alarm for the 'Control Room' they were standing in showed up on the console.

Over the noise, Frank yelled into the phone, "Hell, we've got three alarms now. One is red and we're yellow here in the control room."

Just then the two yellow alarms went red and a fourth yellow started alarming. If the person on the phone was speaking, Frank still couldn't hear a thing over the claxons but when he saw the red in the control room his mind was made up, "EVACUATE!" he yelled as he dropped the phone.

The cleaners were already running for the emergency exit as the three operators crashed through the control room door. Frank being in charge, and the last one out, hit the big red Emergency button at the exit. He glanced at his personal radiation monitor on his company badge and thankfully it was still green.

At Consolidated Energy's backup control center more than six hundred miles away near Chicago, the security officer on duty had just hung up the phone with someone named Frank who said something about several alarms which were popping up on his board too. This had never happened before but after fishing out the Emergency Operations Manual he did as instructed and activated the right emergency protocol button on his security panel indicating serious alarms at Limerick.

He read the instructions again to ensure he had hit the right 'panic' button, but the instructions said nothing about what to do next. He assumed the protocol he had activated had alarmed somewhere or notified someone who knew what to do.

Minutes dragged by slowly as he waited alone just staring at the alarms as they increased on his screen. Just after nine PM in Chicago the phone finally rang. The voice on the phone said, "This is Gus. I got a text alarm, what's happening?"

Assuming he must be talking to some backup tech type who had been aroused by the protocol he decided not to test for credentials and just blurted out, "The board started lighting up with alarms at some place named Limerick. As per protocol I initiated the proper response and called the control room, but they couldn't hear me with all the noise from their alarms. Now the board shows five red alarms in parts of the loading area, office, and control room. Some guy named Frank seemed to be the one in control, but he couldn't hear me asking questions. The last thing I heard him yell was 'Evacuate' before the line went dead and now the screen is blinking AUTOMATIC across the top."

"HOLY SHIT!" was all he heard, and the line went dead.

Now alone again with an alarming console, he wondered if he'd done all he was supposed to do. He turned down the volume on the alarms and looked up his own security manual under emergency procedures. It had the same instructions, but it had one more step; 'Wait for backup'.

While waiting, he Googled Limerick Power Station and was shocked to find out it was a NUCLEAR REACTOR ... and with multiple alarms ... and the control room evacuated ... 'HOLY SHIT!'

**

Gus Molson, Consolidated's level two support was quickly in his car and racing towards their emergency control room. Minutes ago, he'd been contemplating taking the kids to the Independence Day fireworks by the lake just as the sun was getting low near Chicago but now some security shift guy had hit the panic button on a nuclear power plant that was reporting radiation leaks, had been evacuated and was now ostensibly abandoned and on autopilot. With red alarms, the protocol had skipped first-level support because this wasn't likely going to be something that could be handled by coaching the onsite operations team.

Suddenly it all came into focus as he realized, 'Hell, if that report was right, there is no onsite operations team!'

By the sounds of the panicked phone call and with a red radiation alarm they wouldn't have had time to execute an orderly shutdown or maybe even a SCRAM if that old reactor still had the infamous 'Single Control Rod Axe Man' system.

He wondered if a fully operating reactor had ever been abandoned. Chernobyl of course came to mind but even that had been a severely mismanaged shutdown for some tests, and it all happened over several hours where they had time to try and save the thing.

But this was a reactor that had just been vacated while it was ostensibly operating normally, except of course for a radiation leak. The guy on the phone had listed alarms outside of the containment building so that could be a plus if it was accurate.

How the hell did this happen? There was no doubt the local guys had to get out of there with red alarms in their building, but an ABANDONED reactor. Still, he wondered how he'd react to fast-moving 'high level' radiation alarms going off indicating an unsafe control room. He remembered that the alarms in the occupied parts of the campus were sensitive to give occupants time to scramble out before they received dangerous doses of radiation. There was no question that this particular operating procedure, which he hadn't reviewed in years, would have demanded them to get out immediately.

This was big! Really Big! The biggest thing that had ever happened in his career because by starting that protocol to bring him in, he was sure alarms had also gone out to a host of other major organizations, chief of which would be Homeland Security and the Nuclear Regulatory Commission. Homeland would likely alert the FBI, the CIA and God knows who else. Probably even the White House and probably NORAD. There'd been drills for this but not to the extent of getting everyone on the line at the same time. He wondered what he was about to face.

He reasoned, somewhere in all those headquarters, a late-night skeleton staff due to the holiday, was doing the exact same thing, pissing their pants and calling in the big guys. Any minute his phone would be ringing with questions he couldn't answer. In minutes he'd likely be the point man at a console at the backup control room and responsible for getting control of whatever was going on. Being the senior guy in control of the plant from the backup location, he'd be the one everyone would be looking to for answers. He vowed to himself to be cool and conservative and not to speculate too much. It would be too easy to freak out a bunch of bureaucrats and politicians, every one of whom would have their own agenda he feared.

He clicked on hands-free calling, "Call Consolidated central dispatch."

In moments he had a female at the answering service on the phone, "This is Gus Molson, technical backup support, badge 021562 and this is an emergency. Look up Limerick Generating Station's posted schedule and get me a cell number for the lead operator on duty and connect me. I don't want the landline for the facility. It has to be his cell number. Limerick, lead operator."

It took about a minute, but finally he had Frank Garrison on the line. After a short introduction, he said, "Okay tell me what happened."

"Well, everything was quiet and normal until alarms started going off. It all happened so fast … seconds actually. First alarms in the loading dock area and then spreading through the building to the main office and then the control room. We went red in the control room within a minute or two max, and I called abandon ship, if you know what I mean. That's the protocol, right?"

"Yeah, but before that, what were you guys doing?"

Gus wasn't happy with the way that came out.

Frank's voice said it all. Almost screaming into his phone, he yelled, "Absolutely nothing! We were a tiny staff just monitoring operations. There were only three of us. Nothing was scheduled to be done tonight. We were just sitting there when all hell broke loose."

Gus knew he had instantly pissed off the operator, whom he'd never met, but this wasn't a time for tip-toeing or worrying about hurting people's feelings. It was on him now to do something about this mess.

"Okay, I get it. Don't get all excited. But something must have happened. Were there any software alarms, explosions, power failures, strange sounds, load imbalances, circuits thrown, anything at all?"

Exasperated, Frank responded, "Listen, I told you man, not a thing, it all came out of the blue. Everything was quiet and I was just about to walk across the room to get a coffee when suddenly all hell broke loose. Seconds before I had looked at the load on the network and it was completely flat across the phases at about eighty-five percent which is a normal level for this time of night on a holiday. There was absolutely nothing going on and no reason for the whole place to go haywire. We thought maybe it was spent fuel rods that had fallen over in the loading dock but we changed that protocol years ago. We ship them as they're removed now. And besides that, these alarms shot through the building in seconds."

Molson's first thought went to a false alarm but then how could you get multiple alarms in different parts of the building. It couldn't be a hack because none of Consolidated's systems were connected to the internet. It couldn't be a computer fault because alarms were on the central computing node and just like an aircraft it had multiple redundant voting computers that would have alarmed first if any of the three central processing units was faltering and didn't agree with the others. It had to be something real for several different, independent radiation alarms to go off. His attention turned back to the operator on the phone, "So when you left, there was nothing going on in the containment building in terms of anomalies or alarms?"

"Not a thing. The board was clean."

Something just didn't make sense, "Where are you now?"

"I just pulled over about a half-mile upwind of the plant. I can see it but I'm not going back there until we know what's going on. I think the other guys all took off home. And let me warn you, I'm out of here if my personal radiation badge alarms."

"Listen. You DID hit the emergency button on the way out of the room, right?"

"Sure did. Why? Is central reporting I didn't?"

"Nothing like that. Just confirming. I'm in my car on the way to central control but the night shift guy confirms your plant is on Auto."

"Thank God. Can you imagine no one babysitting that thing? I mean it should run without issues as long as nothing goes wrong, right? But man, you need to get to that backup site fast so someone has their hands on the wheel. Has anything like this ever happened before?"

"Not on this side of the planet."

Garrison shivered thinking of Chernobyl or even Fukushima.

Gus couldn't see where he was going to get anything else out of this, so he told Garrison to stay put in case he was needed and signed off.

After a few seconds to assess the situation, he called back to dispatch, "This is Gus Molson again. We have an emergency at one of our plants, again it's Limerick. Check your protocol on who must be notified inside Consolidated management and send out the messages. In particular, I want you to look up the details for third-level technical support and tell them to be on standby."

It took him a further eight minutes to reach the tiny backup control room in the basement of one of Consolidated's office buildings on the periphery of Chicago. He had seen this bare-bones setup a couple of times during drills but this wasn't a drill. As far as he knew, this emergency backup control facility had never been needed but was mandated by the NRC for something just like this. He kept telling himself, this is not a drill. This is the real thing.

The security officer looked relieved to see him, "Thank God you're here. Is it true that the alarm is from a nuclear power plant?"

Gus stopped in his tracks, "Have you spoken to anyone tonight about this, other than me?"

"No. Why?"

"You have a non-disclosure clause, and this is highly confidential company information at this time. In fact, Homeland Security is now aware of this. We have legal protocols we must follow and priority one is NOT panicking the public so ALL information on this must follow the protocol for announcing anything and Homeland Security is in charge of that. You and I are legally muzzled on this under the law. We need all levels of government and law enforcement to know first, and they'll decide if and when there's anything to announce. That screen says we're on full automatic operation. I'm a certified operator so everything's under control," he hoped. "Your job of monitoring alarms is over for now so just sit back and watch for the rest of your shift and see me before you leave. Don't call anybody and don't tell your wife when you go home; if you have one."

The evening security guy wasn't impressed with the tone but after all, that WAS a nuclear plant with no one locally at the controls and he didn't want to mess with Homeland Security.

At the back of the room was a wall of manuals covering emergency procedures for each plant controlled from this tiny backup room, which no one had ever thought would get used. But now he figured the nation would be happy that the NRC had mandated its readiness.

Gus found the binder for Limerick and started thumbing through the emergency Quick Reference while in "AUTOMATIC" mode.

If dispatch had done their job, then the senior 'Incident Manager' on-call would already be on his way. The 'Backup Controller's' immediate instructions were to use the remote-control terminal to cycle through all the normal checks on the instrumentation at the plant. Each step and the expected nominal range for readings were all listed in order.

After about fifteen minutes, hands starting to shake, he was confident everything was nominal, and the plant wasn't in any immediate danger but for some reason, he felt the pressure building. Still, leaks throughout the control building of radiation were both alarming and puzzling and as more monitoring organizations started to wake up he realized he'd become very busy and the center of attention.

Thankfully, there were still no alarms in the actual reactor or containment building but they had multiple alarms in areas that should be safe. The immediate fear was that some calamity had knocked out radiation sensors in the containment building and radiation had already reached the control building. Yet so far there were no signs of any critical control problems in the reactor itself that might explain the alarms; it seemed to be chugging along just fine. A false alarm seemed possible but in several different areas at the same time? That still made no sense unless the source was moving like a liquid or a gas. Clearly, it wasn't something like a burst fuel rod left unattended in the loading dock because not only was that now against regulations, but it also didn't explain how the leak could be moving. After all, nuclear fuel was in pellet form which might roll a few feet but not between rooms throughout a building.

'Now where the hell is that Incident Manager?' he wondered.

At that very moment, a hefty guy in a t-shirt and sweatpants entered the tiny room looking pretty sweaty like he'd run all the way there. He announced himself as Jack Clarke, the on-call Incident Manager, "Fill me in!" he blurted out.

Clarke showed himself to be a no-nonsense character but well informed as to the type of reactor at Limerick. Gus did what he could to bring him up to date, but Clarke had all the same questions he had, and he didn't like any of the available answers either.

Jack Clarke then spent about ten minutes on the phone with Frank Morrison asking pretty much the same questions and getting nowhere.

Clarke and Gus Molson agreed that something didn't sound right. There seemed to be nothing going on in the containment building. Nothing that could explain alarms going off in a building a few hundred feet away. Whatever it was it had to be some freak occurrence that only affected the control building, but that conclusion didn't help them to figure out what it was or what to do about it. The site seemed to be completely normal except for the alarms coming from a building that had no radiation sources. They kept going back to the computerized alarm system. Could it somehow be malfunctioning?

Even if someone had broken stiff regulations, it would be hard to see how spent fuel rods or new fuel rods in the loading area could set off alarms in the office and control room. Unless possibly radiation had somehow gotten into the ventilation system and spread throughout the building.

So far, all the alarms were limited to one building on the site. If in fact, they had red alarms throughout only that building then the reactor was in no danger because they had full control from here in Chicago. Still, the cleanup of any spill would be long and expensive. One thing they agreed had to be done was to order in some mobile air monitoring equipment for the entire area around the plant so the public could be assured that none of the radiation was leaking from the building into the atmosphere or into the nearby canal.

The red line on the phone finally rang … NRC headquarters were finally awake.

Langley

As part of the Homeland Security team, the CIA's senior team was on the list for the alert to the problem at the nuclear power plant. Carole had gotten home around two PM, quickly showered after more than forty-eight hours on duty, and had fallen asleep even though it was much too early to get into bed for the night. She slept longer than she wanted so it was just after ten when she was suddenly awakened by an unusual sound as her phone signaled a special text alarm.

Alert: Nuclear Plant alarming in Pennsylvania

Maybe it was the fact that it was Pennsylvania again, but something told her that even though this was primarily a domestic concern, there was always the chance, especially today, that it could have an international connection and the CIA needed to be on this. She shook off the sleep, rose quickly, splashed some water on her face, adjusted her minimal makeup, and put on some fresh clothes.

On her short rush to the office, hazard lights flashing, she got the latest from Homeland Security dispatch that things had escalated, and they now knew the onsite operations team had abandoned the plant's control room and Homeland and the NRC had a concall established.

Now with her siren and strobes front and rear, she didn't expect any problems from local police. As acting CIA Director, she had a full security detail who were doing their best to keep up with her. This was the first time she'd had to respond to an emergency and the high-speed driving had her focus on overdrive.

On both sides of the highway, the various towns around Langley were in full swing with their fireworks displays. With her barreling down the highway with flashing strobes, it made it all look like the climax in some disaster movie, but this might actually be a real disaster. Finally, her security seemed to get the message, caught up, and took the lead with sirens and lights flashing.

She decided there and then to call in the war room team even though she had just sent them home after a grueling two days. Most of them had been home less than ten hours. She called her lieutenant and had him track down the team and get them in, pronto.

She knew this would be tough on them. All of them had been on duty for two days straight trying to find the secondary IEDs. They had just been working with very little sleep and now were being asked to leave their families again. If there was a nuclear plant in trouble somewhere in Pennsylvania she wondered if DC and the homes of her staff were in harm's way. That would be another load to bear for the staff, so she prayed the wind direction was favorable.

On reaching the office, Cristal, David, and her overnight lieutenant were already there and helping. She reviewed the emergency notice that had gone out from the Nuclear Regulatory Commission and she joined the secure concall in progress. NRC's Incident Response center in DC was taking the lead.

The NRC's Incident Commander was wrapping up, "So, that's it. NRC has a Field Operations Center less than twenty miles away from that plant in King of Prussia and they're standing up a Go Team. They should be assembled and operational in about eighteen hours if this thing turns out to be serious. FEMA is on the line, but we have no guidance for you at this time. Right now,

Consolidated and the staff onsite seem confused as to whether we have a real emergency or not as the alarms seem to have nothing to do with the reactor itself. Starting any kind of evacuation around the plant would alert the press and social media and we'd have widespread panic on our hands.

"Consolidated requested mobile environmental monitoring vehicles which is prudent. They've been activated and should be there sometime tomorrow. For the moment we see no reason to panic or start any extraordinary procedures but Consolidated, we need you to keep us updated minute to minute so we're counting on you to call in everyone you need so we can get to the bottom of this. Is it an emergency or not?"

Jack Clarke answered for Consolidated, "Let me assure everyone we have on the line that we have our A-Team on this as we speak," he exaggerated, "and we don't see anything FEMA could be doing right now. As you just said, we think starting any kind of evacuation around the plant would unnecessarily cause panic. We have a top-rated operator right here who is in control of the plant and it seems to be operating nominally right now."

Carole wasn't getting much out of the DC briefing, so she waited until most of the team had arrived and then briefed them with the little info she had.

She wrapped up with, "While they've no idea why they have alarms going off at the reactor near Philly, which is concerning on its own, the plant seems to be under control remotely and doing just fine. But given the fun we had earlier, and the fact that this is Pennsylvania again, there's a chance this could be something. After all, they're saying this is totally unexpected, and worse, they can't explain the alarms and their Incident Commander didn't seem too convincing that they knew what was happening and had a handle on everything. After all, it's an operating nuclear power plant and it's been abandoned. I don't think that has ever happened before. They're running it remotely from Chicago and I don't think that has ever been done before either. At a minimum, we have a very risky situation here.

"Something about this just doesn't feel right and this is still Independence Day. So, with the Director in a coma, I decided to call you all back in. Does anyone see reason to believe this could be related to the attacks in Washington?"

There was silence in the room as each one looked to others to come up with an answer. All heads eventually ended up looking at Cristal who seemed to excel at moments like this.

Finally, Cristal who had just spent much of the afternoon visiting the Director in hospital and had less sleep than the others, spoke, "I too suddenly have a really bad feeling about this.

"At Christmas Khalil had two attacks and the first one was the small one. The JFK contamination was more of a nuisance in the end. No one was going to be killed. It was all about scaring people, shutting the place down for months, and the economic loss. It was also about the threat to travelers who wouldn't trust us to clean it up and wouldn't want to use JFK. But mostly it was to distract us, get us all focused on JFK, and stop looking for the rest of the nuclear material and potential perpetrators.

"The whole thing today could be looked at as a similar decoy. What if the IEDs were just a distraction? Sure, people would've been killed but not many. Heads of departments would have been assassinated but the average Joe wouldn't fear for his life because of an attack on some politicians. Just hours ago, we were lamenting how unusual it was that Al Qaeda had switched from terrorism to an assassination model. Generalized 'terror' is usually their goal. For that, they need to scare the hell out of average Americans."

Her voice was getting a little more urgent, "Remember, we never figured out if they'd used all the nuclear materials … AND we know they were looking for someone with drone experience. What if they dropped something on the building to force them to evacuate the plant?"

One of the team said, "But it's being controlled remotely, why would they want the plant abandoned. It still has all of its security systems active?"

Shock ran through the room as it seemed they all had the same idea. Carole suddenly saw the threat and grabbed the phone interrupting the concall with a large cast including Homeland, NRC, FEMA, and the Consolidated Incident Manager, "Jack, CIA here. We have an idea. Take me through what you guys did in terms of abandoning the site and what security measures are in place."

Jack Clarke, at Consolidated's backup control room near Chicago, knew he was talking to what was probably several rooms filled with government security types and chose his words carefully, "Well, as they abandoned the site, they hit the Emergency button, which we've confirmed because we now have control from here. That button sent out several alerts and put the plant essentially on autopilot consistent with our Emergency Plan on file with the NRC. We're following that plan to the word. All security is in place with all doors automatically locked, all proximity alarms and cameras active, and control of the plant transferred to our panel here. With the hardening we've put in place in the last few years, an Army platoon would have difficulty breaking into that place now.

"As I reported twenty minutes ago, everything seems quiet, and the plant is running normally but we're now discussing an orderly shutdown. Why do you ask?"

Carole nodded to Cristal who seemed just about ready to jump out of her skin. She broke in, "After analyzing threat profiles on nuclear plants for months, we're somewhat familiar with your security setup. That plant is never connected to the internet for security reasons but how are you able to control it remotely?"

The hair stood up on Jack's neck and he paused before he started, "Good point. We used to have dedicated underground comm lines to every plant's control room but that in itself presented reliability and security problems so yes, when firewalls, and encrypted tunnels reached a certain point we switched over to a secure internet connection but ONLY in the case of a total emergency and only with a plant abandonment with an active reactor like this one. The plant is completely isolated from the internet under normal circumstances meaning an internet hack couldn't have started this emergency.

"But yes, that Emergency button put us on a secure link and the direct answer to your question is, now we're on a highly secure, encrypted line on the internet. The good news is we have a firewall and sophisticated access controls, BUT all that security is a few years old by now so I can't certify we're bulletproof on that.

"I don't know offhand when NRC most recently certified that setup and it's certainly not common knowledge that we go on the internet in one very specific emergency situation. Only someone on the inside like one of our senior operators would know how and when we'd be on the internet. They'd also have to know how to hack a very sophisticated system and they'd have to know we were on an 'abandoned plant' emergency footing. Anyway, we have direct control over that line right now and the reactor is humming along with no signs of trouble."

NRC was conspicuously silent on the matter. More and more the security community on the line were forming a picture of a potential threat.

Chip being the most techie in the room spoke next, "So your doors are locked and no bad guys on camera trying to get into the plant but can you confirm you have affirmative control on that plant?"

"Another great question. The direct answer is no. So far we've only been monitoring the plant. Remember we're on autopilot right now. Think of flying a jumbo jet by remote control from the ground. We want to be very careful before we stick our nose in there and start throwing switches. Given we have no physical access, we must be careful in what we do. Any mistake we might make cannot be fixed by running down the hallway and throwing a physical switch. Nuclear reactors are very finely tuned and finicky, so you don't want to mess with them if they're stable. But I see your point. We need to confirm we actually have positive control of the plant. Let me get the operator to do some trivial thing to ensure our definitive control."

Gus Molson sitting nearby in Consolidated's tiny backup control room had been listening in, nodded, and turned to the screen. In a loud voice to be heard on the concall, he said, "I'll reset one of the alarms in the Limerick control room which is alarming red right now. It should go off for three seconds and if it's still alarming it should go red again."

He hit Enter and nothing happened. Jack Clarke standing behind him whispered, "How long before we see a result?"

"That's it!" he almost yelled, "It was supposed to go off instantaneously and come back on in three seconds. The alarm didn't shut off. I have no control over that alarm. We might not be in control of that reactor. In fact, if we've been hacked, I'm not even sure we're seeing what is actually happening there! All the readings are stable and nominal. Maybe too stable."

As this began to sink in he said, "Let me check the encrypted tunnel. That operates like a VPN or like the little lock on your browser when you're connected to your online banking.

"SHIT! The CA, the certificate of authentication is wrong. We have no authenticated communication with that control room at all. Anything could be happening there! I don't know what the hell I'm reading or trying to control on this screen but it sure ain't coming from a secure connection to that control room!"

Carole, forgetting for the moment that even the White House could be on the line yelled to her team in the room, "HOLY SHIT, this is a terrorist attack!"

Within thirty seconds they'd piped in Frank Garrison, the Limerick operator who was still parked about a half-mile from the plant awaiting instructions. The Incident Manager took charge, "Frank, this is Jack Clarke, Incident Manager at Consolidated. You're on the line with lots of security heavyweights. We cannot confirm we have actual control over your plant. You're sure you hit the emergency on the way out?"

"Yeah, certain, I hit it hard enough to break it. Well, you know what I mean."

"When was the last time that button was certified to be working?"

"Last month. We test it monthly. But that can't be the problem. The Consolidated guys told me they see Automatic on their screens, the only way for that to happen is if the handshake happened and control was transferred."

Gus Molson nodded and said loudly for everyone on the line, "He's right. At least the first step worked but it looks like we have no control now. Either something has broken in the control hookup or we've been hijacked."

"HIJACKED?" Frank screamed into his cell phone. "You mean some bozo is running my reactor?"

Jack Clarke realized he had to get control over the situation, "Frank, let me remind you this is an open line with many participants including the White House. From where you are can you see anything unusual at the plant?"

Frank hesitated, now thinking he had to be more careful. If someone else was monkeying with his plant it could blow, "Listen guys, give me a few minutes, I'm going to get closer but not real close."

While Frank was relocating, Carole brought everyone on the secure concall up to date on the theory the CIA had that terrorists might have leftover nuclear material from Christmas and had used a drone to dump it on the plant to force the emergency evacuation just so they'd be forced to connect to the internet allowing a hijacking. But that it was only a theory.

Everyone on the line waited impatiently until Frank spoke again, "I'm two hundred yards from the plant and I see nothing. No cars, no people, no movement, no sign that anything is wrong ... HOLY

SHIT! … the cooling towers … there's no steam coming out of the cooling towers!"

Washington DC

Earlier, given the circumstances and just to close the loop, Carole had dispatched one of her agents to work with the various law enforcement teams handling the aftermath of the IED attempts. There was always the chance that this wasn't over and coordinated attacks, an Al Qaeda specialty, could be in the works.

Wilson Damns, one of the few local and capable agents not exhausted from a forty-eight-hour shift trying to intercept the Independence Day attack, was now anxious to get everything they'd discovered in the last dozen hours to Carole Glass. He had just picked up that a reactor might be under attack. He was put through to the war room and Carole asked David to handle it.

"Listen, I've been working all day with the team interrogating the two guys we picked up on these bombings; one at the Mall and one outside the FBI Director's home. We still don't know who did the job on the DD.

"Anyway, they're not giving us much yet but from fingerprints turns out these two are Yemeni refugees from about a year ago and they live together. The FBI and Penn BCI raided their home, went through their computers which ties them to the Jihadi networks, but we haven't had time to try to crack the encryption to read all the messages.

"BUT, one of them came in with a brother and a cousin and it looks like they're all part of a cell. They were all living together. We also found a drone in one of their rooms and as you know we've been looking for Jihadis with drones since we decoded that text.

"Problem is the other two aren't home. We got the names they're using and some info on a vehicle from a neighbor. I also got from the BCI a cell phone number registered to one of them. They just ran a check, and the phone isn't showing up on the local network. My fear is if you find that cell phone or the car it might be near that power plant and they might have a drone too."

David gave him a number to text everything to, thanked him, and signed off. Thinking how often these leads went dead because Al Qaeda compartmentalized all the time, he realized that even if they found these guys, they probably knew nothing helpful in securing the plant. Still, they had to be apprehended ASAP and interrogated, so he passed on the info to another of Carole's direct reports for follow-up. In the case of Limerick, the damage had been done and they were probably long gone. For now, the big issue was, what had they done exactly, and was there an atomic bomb in the form of a meltdown in Pennsylvania about to go off?

Still, there was a long-shot chance that the ones who attacked the plant would know how the internet connection had been hijacked which could be causing ongoing harm now. So, he impressed on Carole's guy the urgency of finding them.

The Hacker

Just as everyone thought all control had been lost at Limerick, an anonymous call with 'critical information about a nuclear plant' was switched through to the war room from Homeland Security, given the CIA had the lead on the investigation and seemed to have the best theory on what was happening.

Carole took the call on speakerphone, "This is Carole Glass, Acting Director of the CIA. This had better be worth my time. If this is a prank call, hang up now or face National Security consequences."

There was a very long pause until a squeaky voice, obviously altered by the use of some type of technology, spoke "Listen, I just thought you'd want to know that your Limerick nuclear reactor is under attack."

"Who is this?"

"You think I'm crazy?" continued the squeaky voice, "And don't try to trace this call, that won't work."

Carole thought for a second. This could be one of the attackers, "What makes you think we have a hijacked reactor?" She realized right away she'd used the wrong word and given away too much.

"So you do know! Good. Okay, let's not be coy. Let's just say I'm a patriotic American living downwind from that reactor and anxious to keep myself alive. Right after this call I'm getting out of here because I don't like what I see.

"I happen to have a certain set of computer skills and tools. Some people think of me as a White Hat Hacker if that means anything to you. One of my nobler pastimes is watching for intrusions on government sites.

You guys are hopeless at protecting your networks. Frankly, I have robots pinging them all the time to check to see if their firewalls are working properly.

"One of my scanners alarmed a while ago that the Limerick firewall which is normally invisible, appeared on the internet. You really need to do something about how you assign IP addresses.

"As you probably know, that site is never on the internet. It was completely open just enough time for me to realize that multiple ports were wide open to the world for about ten minutes. It would take some serious hacking to crack your encryption and your firewall. A state actor comes to mind but unless you've regained control of that firewall, someone else is running your plant.

"Anyway, for about ten minutes, any competent hacker with the right tools might have entered your systems during that window. I have said tools and I was able to access all your control system computers but not being a power generation expert, I could only tell that playing with any of the controls would likely be very dangerous.

"That only lasted about ten minutes and now it's locked down again. If it was me trying to hijack a site, my first action would be to delete the credentials file and set only one failsafe username and password to provide admin access, spoofing all other log-in attempts."

Chip Attwood being the most techie in the room spoke up, "So if no one can get in, how do you as a patriotic American hope to help us?"

"I know who did it."

There was a long pause until the strange voice spoke again, "Well to be clear, I have his IP address which I gather you don't."

Carole spoke, "And what do you want for this information?"

"Nothing! Just don't start any investigations to find out who I am and get control of that damned reactor, please. The IP address is 41.78.72.147. That's the host IP and of course, they use Network Address Translation, so you'll need help to get the actual GPS location of the user. With your muscle, I'm sure you can get the ISP to cooperate.

"I checked it out. It's in Mogadishu Somalia so you'll have to call Hormuud which is the ISP there and find out who connected to your IP address at Limerick at 21:56-ish New York time. You can bet there will be only one and he's your hacker."

Chip broke in, "Do you think that's a real IP address? They could be spoofing it?"

The squeaky voice continued, "Do you really think these guys are that smart? Remember we're talking about Somalia and I don't have your intel but it's probably Al Qaeda going after a mass-casualty attack and I just don't think they're smart enough technically to mask themselves. As for the hijack, there are a few people out there who might be able to initiate it including me. Still, I'd be looking for either a hostile state actor or more likely given that Somalia is involved, a mercenary and ex-high-level Black Hat guy from Russia, China, or North Korea who sold them the access because living on the net as I do, there's no way Al Qaeda has those skills. This was a state actor or someone who used to work for them and stole some sophisticated software tools and has a pretty fast PC in his basement.

"Of course, a really effective hijack would be for a state actor to spoof the Somali IP to make it look like Al Qaeda but that would be a mystery inside an enigma, so

I'd bet on the terrorists who seem to care less about retaliation for something that is clearly an act of war.

"But I've solved enough of this for you. TTFN," and he hung up.

Chip responded to the puzzled faces, "Ta Ta For Now."

Carole frowned as David asked, "Can we just cut the line going into the plant? Cut them off the internet?"

"No!" It was Chip Attwood. "We don't know for sure what they're up to and if we can break into their connection, we'll need it to fix anything they've done. If we cut anything it has to be closer to their end so we can still attempt to take over the control room. Remember that's a hardened facility and in a lockdown like this, we just heard that it would take a platoon and too much time to physically break into the building without blowing up the control room. A control room that may be radioactive. We need that line, or we'll have no control.

"There are a lot of automatic processes I'm sure and I'd imagine unless they have an operator with experience on this type of reactor, they will have problems doing anything serious. Remember, we just got their IP address, so this looks pretty amateurish."

Clarke from Consolidated had been conferenced into the hacker call and broke in, "He's right. The automatic safeguard controls won't let you easily damage the reactor but someone on your end at the CIA or FBI should look into any individuals on the terror watch list that might have operator knowledge and have worked at this or a similar plant."

Frank Garrison from his car near the plant was apoplectic, "Are you people crazy? Did you not hear me? There's NO steam coming out of the cooling towers and I see no scenario where that's a good thing. That's steam going to the generators and circulating cooling water for the reactor and it isn't happening. Somebody knew how to bypass safeguards and shut down at least one critical system. They've got someone who knows this plant. For God's sake stop second-guessing. Don't hesitate, this is real and it's bad. Safety systems have definitely been bypassed.

"I don't know all the math, but I know you can't cool down the nuclear reaction that fast to the point of killing the steam in the towers even if you drop all the control rods and we have no access to the SCRAM system. Look up Chernobyl. A mishandled shutdown can be catastrophic, so right now all we know is someone is monkeying with my reactor and they know what they're doing. Without cooling water or steam going to the generators we have a hot reactor and containment unit and it's likely getting a lot hotter. We were at eighty-five percent output at the time, so it was chugging along pretty good when this all started. No steam means it's hot and getting hotter!

"One problem for sure is the steam itself. Where is all that superheated steam going if not to the cooling towers? If it's cut off in the containment building, we're screwed and it's going to blow. You need to get someone who can run scenarios quick because we could be looking at the 'China Syndrome' ... a complete meltdown and a containment explosion before that. I'm thinking we're looking at hours and not many of them. These reactors are a bit of black magic. They still don't know what the sequence was for the explosions at Fukushima. That kind of heat triggers runaway chemical reactions like hydrogen production. We only know that when you screw with them, bad things happen, either hydrogen explosions or superheated steam would be my first guess. You can't mess with these things. They're way too powerful and when they get out of the envelope everything accelerates. Any one of probably ten different things could spell disaster. That's why we have so many safety systems but not if someone is turning them off."

Clarke responded, "Everything you say is true. Okay, I'm on it. We have some people on the way in who can grab the drawings and run the scenarios to see what damage we can assume and what kind of time frame we're on. We should have everything we need in terms of the heating capacity of the reactor and the volume of the containment building. I agree, pressure from the superheated steam isn't our only problem but it's likely our first and at least the biggest known problem for now."

Carole started handing out assignments, "Cristal and David, you take the IP address and run with it.

"Chip, you find me a way into that control room over the internet because it looks like a forced physical entry might be too late. If they're on the internet then there's likely no terrorists in the plant, yet someone started those alarms. David has people chasing down what we think is the drone team that was likely involved in emptying out that control room. As you said, that site is hardened against attack and we probably don't have time to bring in a tank to force our way in. See what you can do and be ready if we can break that link.

"Sally, you work with Homeland. Get on that concall and brief them on what we know now. They need to take the lead on any warnings or evacuations, but I want to know what's going on. I also need you to work with the NRC, FEMA, and the FBI as they'll be implementing their disaster plans. Remind them all that we have the investigative lead as this is an international attack likely coming out of Somalia and we may need military assets in the region."

Just as they were breaking up to set off on their separate assignments, Gus Molson in the control room at Consolidated headquarters had an idea, "There may be a back door. I mean a software back door. As that guy who phoned in said, the terrorists may have deleted the access files killing all approved credentials meaning even if we do get the internet line back, we may be locked out, but software engineers often leave a back door. An access path that isn't in the access control tables so they can get in even if the system denies all logins. It's used when testing the software and often left in either intentionally or by accident."

Chip was on it, "I hope you're right. How do we find it?"

Gus continued, "Find the software engineer who wrote it. The control software was a government acquisition so we must have the actual software source code around here somewhere. Maybe we can find a name in the code. If I remember, government software contracts require all modules to provide sources and they must list the code author. Even if that wasn't true when this stuff was written, these guys typically have big egos and tend to leave their names in the comments. I'll get on it right away."

Gus put the phone on mute and turned to Clarke, the Incident Manager, "Where the hell is third-level support? They should've been here by now. They should have thought of searching the code right away."

Clarke sneered, "That job's been open for more than a year. Hell, you're second-level responsible for diagnosing complex issues and how often do you get called in on something like this. Third level is an NRC requirement, and their job is to take your analysis and build software fixes but we've never needed it and we don't need to get into that now. This is on you so get working."

Mercifully, the software code sources were exactly where they should've been, in the files for the Limerick-type reactors at the Chicago backup site. It appeared that at least four reactors were using the same control room software which gave credence to the idea that an ex-operator at one of the plants could be the one in control. Gus passed the information on to Chip Attwood so the FBI or CIA could focus on a short list of potential terrorist operators who had worked at one of the four plants.

The first name Gus came up with from the ancient printouts in the right part of the software source code was an Anatole Pushinski. The company that had won the contract to furnish the software was in Palo Alto and there was only one Anatole Pushinski in the phone book. They got lucky in that he was the one and still living in the Palo Alto area. But it turned out he was the team leader and not the actual designer or coder but he had an idea of where to find who might have worked on the access control piece of the software. It took him twenty minutes to find the name from more than thirty years earlier and now the CIA team using the FBI was trying to track down someone who could be retired or even dead by now.

Everyone was on edge as a search went out for a James Connelly, a software engineer who at one time, lived in Palo Alto, California.

Sally was already back on the joint call and filled in all parties on the breakthrough they'd made with the anonymous caller. CIA had the lead on trying to break into the internet line to the plant, but she confirmed their assessment that no steam coming out of the cooling towers meant only one thing; a potential meltdown and broad radiation release into the atmosphere.

When Carole had screamed 'terrorist attack' on the line Homeland had gone immediately to a Red Alert and authorize FEMA and law enforcement to start evacuation plans starting with the communities nearby the plant, and based on the wind direction, communities to the direct northeast of the plant and extending north and east as quickly as possible. Calls went out immediately to first responders in the area who immediately called in all off-duty officers.

If there had ever been a plan for such an event, no one could remember it and the immediate question was, where do we send all those people? Someone pulled out a 'Hurricane Evacuation Plan' and they started with that, minus the local sheltering plans.

Mogadishu

Cristal and David decided to work alone and grabbed a nearby conference room with a couple of phones.

Cristal opened with, "We have to bomb them. If they're in Mogadishu they're probably in a safe house with the top guys monitoring this attack. We have no time to mount a team and send them in. We need a Tomahawk cruise missile from a ship or a Hellfire from a drone. You check the CIA's own assets' locations and availability and get DOD onside and ready in case we need them. My Arabic is better than yours, I'll handle the ISP."

David nodded and grabbed a phone to call the one contact he knew at DOD.

Cristal took out her phone and looked up ISPs in Mogadishu. According to the squeaky voice, it was Hormuud, and she guessed he was right. They seemed to be the big guy on the block and after a little research the host IP address checked out too.

She suddenly realized she was about to call in a missile strike on a target she couldn't verify. The only intel she had, came from a no-name caller with unknown motives. Still, if his information checked out, only a bad guy would have connected to the Limerick plant ... if Hormuud could and would help.

Her call got picked up by their support desk and she was quickly up to the overnight supervisor in charge. She knew time was of the essence and realized she was going to have to be hard on this guy.

Using the proper Arabic greeting, she moved quickly to the point, "What I'm about to tell you is Top Secret and your life is in immediate danger so don't hang up on this call and do whatever you need to do to verify what I'll tell you. I'm very serious, if you hang up you will die."

The frightened man on the other end decided to see where this was going.

"I'm a senior agent at the CIA in Langley Virginia in the USA. There's a hack in progress against a nuclear power plant in America. The hacker is in Mogadishu and is using your facilities to damage the nuclear reactor. Possibly millions of lives are at stake. I have a drone circling over Mogadishu at this moment," she lied. "It has several Hellfire missiles ready to fire. One of them is now aimed at Hormuud Tower, Howlwadaag Street, Bakara Market, Mogadishu," she lied as she read the address directly from the internet home page for the utility. "That's your address, right? No need to confirm. But I don't want to use that missile to cut the internet lines in your building that the hacker is using. I want to hit only the hacker.

"At 21:56 our time, that would be 5:56 your time, the hacker from IP 41.78.72.147 hacked into a nuclear power plant site at IP 198.162.100.10. I know that IP address is one of your local hosts for your internet services, so I need you to go to your logs RIGHT NOW and give me the street address of the modem that made that connection. Write this down, 5:56 your time, the hacker from your host, IP 41.78.72.147 hacked into our site at IP 198.162.100.10. You need to find that log entry VERY FAST!

"As I've already said. We want the hacker but if we can't get to him to stop his attacking our nuclear power plant RIGHT NOW, we'll take out your building cutting the lines and eliminating all witnesses to this call. Do I make myself crystal clear and what is your answer?"

Cristal was mindful that there was the possibility that Hormuud's IP address could have been spoofed by a hostile state actor BUT if Hormuud came up with a connection internal to their server at 5:56 then it wasn't a spoof, and they had the culprit.

It was almost seven AM in Mogadishu and the shift supervisor hadn't expected to live through anything like this in his life. He had never had a woman talk to him with this authoritative tone before and that in itself was maddening. Western women acted like men he thought.

His immediate thinking was that this was probably a hoax BUT the call was in fact coming in from a +1 country code making part of her story believable. The calculation was simple. The amount of trouble he'd get into for giving out a customer's address without the proper authorizations was minimal compared to what would happen if this woman was telling the truth. If she was telling the truth, then only Jihadis would be affected and that was okay with him.

Still, he thought to himself, 'I'll be shocked if I find a log entry with those exact IP addresses at exactly 5:56'.

It took him about ten minutes on a terminal but stunningly he found the exact connection. He checked quickly and indeed the target address came up as registered to a US power utility so back on the phone he gave her the address of the modem in Mogadishu. He hung up and decided to take a walk and a cigarette break a few blocks away.

It took David almost twenty minutes of intense negotiation with Carole's help to get DOD to move on the target. The CIA had its own drones, but none were anywhere near where they were needed. In the end, DOD didn't want to move without getting approvals all the way up the ladder because they'd be 'starting a war' with a sovereign nation and they were even talking about trying to get State Department approval, now at around eleven PM on a holiday, before they went to the President. Their rules of engagement just didn't allow such action without the President.

The deal that was struck was that, at the request of the Acting Director of the CIA, the captain of the Carl Vinson aircraft carrier off the coast of Somalia transferred control of one of his weapons to the CIA rep who had recently been ferried over from one of the task force's frigates, a Mr. Norm Lulham. Acting on behalf of the CIA, Norm wasted no time and pressed the button to launch the Tomahawk cruise missile.

Four minutes later a house exploded in southwest Mogadishu and the connection to the Limerick power station dissolved. A house that Nasir Abboud had, on a hunch, departed only thirty minutes earlier.

The night supervisor at Hormuud had returned to his office and saw the explosion across town from his third-floor window in the Hormuud Tower. The big flash came from approximately where he assumed the address he had given out was located. It was such a large bang that he felt assured they wouldn't have to trouble themselves with his building. But just to be safe, he logged into a terminal and shut down the line that serviced that part of town. By the time anyone noticed he was certain any residual threat would be gone. He also made sure there'd be no trace of his earlier incoming phone call.

At the time he'd wondered why the caller hadn't simply asked him to cut the line but given the circumstances, they probably wanted to ensure they killed the bad guys in case they had a backup plan to get on the internet.

His first thought was that he alone in Mogadishu knew the whole story and it was going to remain that way.

PA Turnpike

The FBI and the Pennsylvania State Police worked quickly and tracked the car carrying two terrorist drone pilots by pinging the cell phone they'd been alerted to. They took their time, seeing as the perpetrators were likely headed to their home base just outside Pittsburgh and they set up the intercept on a special stretch of road on the Pennsylvania Turnpike.

Multiple unmarked cars had culled the late-night traffic behind the target in such a subtle fashion that the two, driving in the dark and congratulating themselves, hadn't noticed that there were only a few cars behind them and keeping well back.

So as they entered the Tuscarora tunnel they were clueless about the orchestrated action around them. The roadblock at the opposite end of the tunnel came as a shock as did all the flashing lights closing in fast behind them. There was nowhere to go.

They gave up without a fight and denied everything.

Being careful, they'd retrieved the drone but both it and the car itself set off the radiation alarms of the FBI team. They themselves had traces of radiation so they had to be transported in a van with protection for the law enforcement team.

One important find was the cell phone that had been used to track them. The phone wasn't locked, and a quick search of the call history showed they'd made several calls earlier to a landline outside of Pittsburgh which started an additional urgent action against a potential new target. The timing of the calls put it right in line with the attack.

The person on the other end was either part of the mission on the power plant or an accessory. These guys had no computer or internet gear with them so in discussions with CIA headquarters there was a good chance the new target was the operator who might still be trying to damage the plant.

But the two they'd just picked up stayed silent. They claimed profusely that they had rights as refugees in the US.

Given they were headed in the direction of their apartment and with the lack of any additional weapons in the car, it was concluded that their mayhem was over and at least this team had no additional targets tonight. A full interrogation of the pair would have to wait.

Focus shifted to the new phone number which quickly turned up an interesting address. Indeed, the occupant according to LinkedIn had been a nuclear power plant operator at a sister reactor. CIA headquarters wanted that man quickly as it was highly likely he was the one actually in control of the Limerick control room, or had been until his link to the reactor control room suddenly went dead.

They were dashed to find the apartment unoccupied. The thinking was that when his line went dead he assumed they were on to him and fled the scene with his computer but he'd used his own apartment so they had a name and description for a BOLO.

The problem was they still had no idea what he had done to the plant and what kind of threat they were looking at.

James Connolly

James Connolly turned out to be a pretty common name and after more than thirty years he could live anywhere; if he was still alive.

There were no James Connollys in the recent Palo Alto directories.

Finally, one of the team suggested using LinkedIn again where professionals often listed their occupation and work history. After some research and a few late-night calls, they finally felt they had the right Jim Connolly.

He had moved at some point to downtown LA so a local FBI team was dispatched to the address on file after the phone registered to that address continually went to voicemail.

The doorman of the condo building confirmed his being a resident of the complex and that he'd stepped out only an hour before. As the doorman was answering questions, James Connolly returned to the shocking realization that all the guys in the FBI jackets in the lobby were looking for him.

It took some coaxing and assurances that he wasn't under investigation to get him to understand the situation and start answering some questions.

At first he had a hard time remembering whether he'd left a back door in the access control system and was a little surprised that his generalized access coding had been in a nuclear reactor's control center and that it might still be operating after all these years. He knew the trick he'd often used to break in but he needed the one set of credentials he'd used.

After some thought he remembered that at one point he'd used the unusual name of a girl he had run into in his younger years. He had used her first name, Honeysuckle as the username, and her last name, Lipschitz was the password. Control Shift ALT F was the trick to break into the back end of the credentials system. This was quickly passed on to FBI headquarters and relayed to the ongoing concall.

Limerick

Frank Garrison was getting pretty sleepy by this time after his twelve-hour shift and sitting watching his ailing plant from his car, now about two hundred yards away. People he understood to be spread all over the US were working to stop or reverse the attack. Thankfully, his personal radiation badge continued to show green. His phone was running down but shuffling through his glove box he found a charger for the car. How lucky was that, he thought? What would he have done if the line had suddenly dropped? His only alternative at this time of night around here would have been to head home and he'd be out of touch for thirty minutes until he could get to his phone charger. He smiled thinking of the panic of an untold number of security organizations all over the country if that had happened.

"Frank, are you still on the line?" It was Clarke from Consolidated HQ.

"Where else would I be? Have you guys made any progress? This situation cannot be getting better."

"Listen, don't ask me how, I think it's classified anyway but somehow our international folks have knocked the bad guys off the line and we've just received backdoor access to the remote system control so we're back in. That's the good news. The bad news is they've done something to screw up the controls and Gus here can't get full control. We need you to get back in there and do some stuff.

"We now know the radiation in the control room was a decoy and current readings in there are very low. Looks like they dumped something into the air conditioning system, and it's been mostly cycled out by now. Radiation levels in the control room are approaching ambient so it's safe to go back in there.

"We can't say the same for the containment building because we only have a couple of non-critical sensors in there right now. You need to get back in there fast and keep talking to us on this phone or if your battery is low, call us on a land line."

Garrison was a bit tentative having been shown in training what radiation poisoning could do, "Are you sure it's safe in there right now?"

"Yeah, the readings indicate low rads so you should be fine … for at least a few hours and we'll keep an eye on the readings from this end."

"Okay, I'm trusting you guys. My battery is almost dead so I'll phone you back on this number when I'm in there. Make sure the doors are unlocked so my access card will work."

Langley

Carole figured it would take a little while for Garrison to get in so she muted the call, turned down the speaker phone, and took one earphone out so she could monitor what was happening as she turned to the rest of the team who had been drifting in, "Well we know we shut down their line to the plant and found a back door, so we have partial control again. Status, please. Homeland first."

Sally had been keeping up on a separate line with Homeland Security and had a handful of notes, "They activated their emergency protocols and man are they taking this seriously. They've assumed we're looking at a full and imminent meltdown which means they're evacuating as many as they can in the immediate area and some towns and farms downwind of the reactor. They've called in all first responders for miles around to help. The prevailing winds are from the southwest at this time of year which isn't good because there are large populations to the northeast.

"Given a potential meltdown, they've ordered water bombers and other assets to the closest airports. Believe it or not, normal water is a primary moderator of neutrons which is what keeps the reaction going and part of the plan would be a continuous stream of water bombers over the site but that has big issues. It creates lots of radioactive steam and possibly hydrogen releases, so water bombing is an emergency and short-term solution to slow down any threatened meltdown.

"Apparently there's hope though. The right solution is a new discovery by Sandia Labs using something called 'granular carbonate materials.' Don't ask me what that means but it's only been done in the lab with good results. The problem is no one has mountains of that stuff sitting around. In the lab they work with tiny quantities and the feds haven't funded any kind of a stockpile so far. It's completely new and it might take days or even weeks to manufacture enough of the powder and then find a way to drop it on the molten mess in the reactor if we need it. So, for the short term, water bombing is the only tool they have.

"There's a river, or actually a canal next to the plant. It could be used but it's a meandering body of water. There's only one straight stretch of about a mile and a half and it's only about three hundred feet wide so only the smaller, slower water bombers can pick up their load there. I'm pretty sure they cannot even attempt it at night so tomorrow morning would be the earliest if they're needed, meaning if we can't get the reactor SAFED as they call it.

"Fireboats won't work because they'd have to get too close. One team has gone off to see if there are any robot fireboats or could one be rigged up quickly.

"The closest open water is the Atlantic, full of salt water but that's okay. The water bombers can only use that if it's almost dead flat which we can't count on but there are lots of bays within a reasonable distance from the plant that could be used once they control the water and air traffic in the area.

"The Delaware River is the closest, southwest of Philly and it's about thirty miles from the plant, not ideal but if they have enough bombers, and they're fairly sure they can get their hands on lots of them, then a constant stream of them might do the job.

"Also, helicopters won't work because they're too slow and would be over the hot zone too long. And of course, after Chernobyl, there isn't a fireman alive who doesn't know that going near a meltdown is a suicide mission.

"Lastly robots might work for a while until the radiation zaps them, but they have limited control ranges so they're looking into what they can do and how to get them working on the site but all of that takes time which according to FEMA, we may not have.

"Besides that, any water will go into airborne steam immediately from the heat even if the core is doused and weakened. Some radioactive spillover will make it into the river. So they have to douse it first before they try to bury it in that special carbon stuff and then entomb it like Chernobyl which will take months. They'd need to build specialized, shielded robots to do the job because again no self-respecting American is going to want to approach a meltdown in progress.

"As for fallout, the jet stream right now takes everything northeast directly over New York City and all the big towns southwest and northeast of the Big Apple. The good news is that the jet stream is high, fast, and dry at the moment and there's a low-pressure zone well off the coast of Nova Scotia so if this thing blows, most of the really dangerous stuff may fall as rain over the North Atlantic but timing is everything. A few changes in the weather and New York City is almost in the bullseye with Newark, Hartford, and Boston right behind it. They can't effectively evacuate any of those cities in under a week even if they knew what to do with about thirty million people. Where can you house and feed that many people?

"One positive thing though, this is not Chernobyl or even Fukushima with its four reactors. Chernobyl was built at the time to be one of the biggest nuclear plants in the world. Limerick is a lot smaller and a different design, still you don't want it melting down. As we heard earlier, no steam coming out of the cooling towers could mean several things but according to the NRC, none of them are good and some of them are terrifying.

"Bottom line is, this thing better not melt down or we're drowning in shit."

Carole broke in, "So what about New York City's administration? Aren't they likely to demand a total evacuation? You know what clout and political power they have, never mind people on their own just panicking and heading south."

Sally continued, "According to their emergency plan, that would kill a lot of people with car accidents, medical emergencies, and the like so no. That could be the real disaster with people trapped in cars in the summer heat with radioactive stuff falling on them. Imagine TOTAL gridlock. Every road being blocked for weeks with abandoned cars, people trying to escape, running out of gas, food, and medicine. Forget about fire trucks and ambulances getting through to say nothing of the looting and other crimes that always accompany unrest and hobbled law enforcement.

"But that doesn't mean that as soon as word breaks out there won't be a mad dash to get out no matter what the guidance is. Some think gridlock could be the big surprise issue with SUVs trying to go cross country to get out and people stranded on foot in the open everywhere. Basically, everyone who hits the roads will run out of gas in the gridlock and be on foot in the open which is the worst situation.

"Their plan is to use the Emergency Notification System to tell people to stay put, not to chance travel which they're warning would likely be deadly, but if they decide against the best advice and travel, head northwest or south on back roads to break up the congestion. People who are stuck in the cities will be directed to seal windows and doors or better yet, get underground. There are still some old radiation shelters, and the subway systems will be put to full use. But again, how do you feed a couple of million people for days or weeks initially in a hot zone even if they've escaped the immediate impact?

"All ferries in NYC could be used to transfer people down the New Jersey coast to God knows where. They're still trying to figure that one out. We REALLY need the weather to cooperate, and it almost never does.

"The main message is that with some help from the jet stream and civic order only minor radiation to moderate symptoms may occur in the short term and the feds are sending in tremendous amounts of medicine, which I'm quite sure is a lie. No one has millions of doses of potassium iodide or the other ones I didn't write down.

"Homeland knows this could be bad but frankly they have no plan for anything like this. There will be arguments about whether they should have had a plan but that's for much later.

"Panic might be even worse than the radiation, but they won't know the full impact until the NRC can give them estimates of the quantity and type of any leaks from the plant. They're just starting now to plan for the worst. They're completely ill-prepared for a full meltdown but they're busy doing what they can.

"Oh yeah, and they sent out an emergency message to all nuclear plants to be prepared for a decoy attack on control rooms. We've asked law enforcement to station cars at each plant and watch for drones. Even if they do try again, apparently the terrorists in Somalia have no internet connection available. Anyway, if

Independence Day was the target, they're running out of time.

Sally wrapped up with, "Again, the bottom line is, that thing better not blow."

There was silence in the room until Carole nodded to David and Cristal. Cristal started first, "USS Carl Vinson, in the absence of full military approvals, turned over control of one of their Tomahawk missiles to our CIA rep on board who happened to be Norm Lulham. He promptly dropped it on the bad guys in downtown Mogadishu which we tracked from that anonymous caller."

Several in the room smiled and clapped until Carole nodded to Cristal to continue.

"As we can see, it was successful and we probably took out a few bad guys as well. It will be a while before we know if any of the top guys were at the target or if there was any significant collateral damage. You're going to want to backdate the authorization for Norm, so HQ is on the hook for the action and not our local hero. And the State Department will need to justify the military attack on a sovereign nation. I'm going to kiss and hug that man when he gets back stateside."

A few in the room continued to give moderate applause in support of the now-famous Norm Lulham.

David took the cue and took over, "We got fingerprints from the DC attackers so that pointed us to a home near Pittsburgh once more. Our Wilson Damns following up on the IED attempts and law enforcement in Pennsylvania came up with a good idea of who the people were on the attack on the nuclear reactor. Two relatives were missing from the premises and evidence they had drone capabilities. We tracked their cell phone and about half an hour ago apprehended them on the

Pennsylvania Turnpike. They had a drone and other stuff that was all radioactive, so we know it was them. They aren't talking but the contents of the car and their direction indicates their work was done and they were headed home. The thinking right now is that with the two in DC and these two, we just shut down a cell or at least part of a cell. We so far missed the guy that got the DD but teams are highly motivated to track him down.

"Investigating the phone of the drone team we got a lead on someone with nuclear power plant operations experience. They were talking to him around the time of the attack so we're closing in on him as we speak."

At that, Carole heard voices on the call again and turned up the speaker phone mouthing to her direct reports in the room that they were back into the plant.

Frank Garrison had made his way back into the control room at the Limerick Nuclear Power Plant and was apparently still nervous about the yellow alert blaring in the room. After checking the room's radioactive counter, he put the phone on speaker and said, "Looks like I'm okay in here for a while, where do you want me to start? I've just logged in to my console and canceled that damned claxon so we should both be able to see everything now."

Jack Clarke, Incident Manager in Chicago nodded to Gus Molson, "I still have very few readings from the containment area, so we have no control there right now to fix that steam issue."

Garrison sat down at his terminal, "Yeah, they're all dead here too. The hacker must have switched off the containment monitoring and control computer systems and that takes a few minutes to get back online which I'm just rebooting now. That system has all containment instrumentation, alarms, and controls on it. All I can see right now are door alarms which are on a different system. You're right, we need those systems to get control of whatever is happening in there."

Molson broke in, "I don't remember how old that plant is. Do you still have a bank of the old analog strip charts you can check?"

"Yeah, we have that along the back wall; while we're waiting, I can check them." He turned up the speaker volume as he left his station.

Seconds later he said, "Hell they're not working ...OH SHIT ... I thought they were all dead, but the needles are buried off the top of the charts. Temperature, pressure, radioactivity, all unreadable off the top of the charts."

As the containment monitoring systems came online alarms started blaring again and showed up on the consoles in the Limerick control room and in Chicago. As Gus Molson was sitting at his console, he was the first to see the numbers and the alarms, "GET OUT OF THERE! IT'S GONNA BLOW!"

Frank Garrison didn't bother going back to his console as he raced for the door just as all hell broke loose.

The shockwave knocked him off his feet as all lighting disappeared and all the ceiling tiles and fluorescent lights came crashing down around him. All the glass between the control room and the main office was flying everywhere. The blast had knocked the breath out of him, and he could feel glass falling down his neck as he picked himself up.

Suddenly there was incredible banging on the roof as massive pieces of three-foot-thick concrete with rebar from the containment building rained down on the control building, some of it smashing holes here and there right through the roof.

Apparently, without major injury, Garrison stumbled through what was left of the control room and the office, now under battery-powered emergency lights. As he was slipping on broken glass he had only one thought in mind … lethal dose. A quick glance at his personal monitor confirmed the horrifying truth … bright red.

Failure

Carole Glass gasped as the entire team in Langley, and everyone spread across the US on the call realized what had just happened and felt the immediate sense of total failure. They all immediately tried to position themselves on a map of the US to see if they or people they knew were downwind of the meltdown.

Jack Clarke confirmed it on the phone, "We've lost all readings again. In the seconds that we had data, we saw them spike off the charts. There can be no doubt that the damn thing blew, and the core of nuclear material must be now going supercritical with nothing left to slow it down. That explosion would have eliminated all the moderators and it's melting down as we speak and burning everything around it. Everything around that plant is now a hot zone. Pray for that guy we sent in there."

This was the second time in less than a year that all of Homeland Security and the CIA had failed to stop a terrorist attack. Yes, they had foiled attacks on a shopping mall, the NYC water system, and the parade at the Mall, but JFK had been a rude awakening and this one was the mother of all failures.

Cristal thought about the people who'd die tonight and over the next few weeks, months, and years because of radiation poisoning. She wasn't sure but she feared many times more would likely die today and over the ensuing years from radiation exposure than died on 9/11. After all, NYC was only about eighty miles downwind of that plant. Add in all the big towns and cities like Newark, Stamford, Hartford, and Boston and even if the weather cooperated you were probably looking at more than fifty million people directly affected. Radioactive ash from the core fire and steam would rain down on northeastern cities until they could get control of it which would be weeks if not months.

The death toll could be anywhere from hundreds to many thousands over time. And who knew how long it would take to encapsulate the site. After Chernobyl what firefighter would offer to commit suicide to work on the plant? The whole idea of water bombers was suspect too. What pilot would want to continuously fly over a smoldering radioactive puddle belching out radioactive steam, even if they were traveling at high speed? On top of that, high altitude drops would do no good as the water would disperse and evaporate in the rising heat from the molten pool before it hit the target. There was a canal nearby which meant the water table was only a few feet below the plant. That meant that when the molten core burned its way down to the water table they'd have explosive, radioactive steam belching out even faster.

Her thoughts went to the other losses. In addition to lives and health, this would cost billions, maybe trillions for mitigation, cleanup, and the prospect of permanently unusable farmland, towns, and even cities. Who'd want to live downwind from any nuclear plant after this? This would certainly spell the end of nuclear power in the US and probably around the world. Sometime tomorrow house prices across the country would plummet if they were within a hundred miles of a nuclear power station.

The costs in lives lost and the fear of attacks would likely force every plant to be decommissioned which in itself she knew would cost billions to shut them down and clean them up.

Suddenly she thought of all the families who had their life savings in a home that even if they did escape the radiation, could never go back and had lost everything. She wondered if FEMA insurance had ever thought of such a thing and even if they did, did the US have enough money to compensate possibly tens or hundreds of thousands who'd likely lose everything? The same was true for any businesses in the radiation zone.

The conference call was so busy it was difficult to hear who was speaking. Clearly, the whole Intelligence Community had failed and now the focus turned to FEMA, the Red Cross, local law enforcement, and all the other organizations that would be tasked with responding to the biggest catastrophe in US history.

Carole looked around the room and saw the same desperation she was feeling. She didn't have to paint the picture she had in her head for them. They all had their own idea of what this meant. Some would be primarily concerned for Frank Garrison who, if he'd survived the containment building blowing, would certainly have gotten a fatal dose of radiation along with anyone living near the plant. Some would be terrified if they had relatives or friends downwind of the plant.

The CIA's job had nothing to do with mitigation. Their job was over, and they'd failed. Homeland was in cleanup mode now; bolster FEMA's efforts, find everyone responsible, and help the FBI bring them to justice.

After what seemed an endless silence, she finally spoke to the small group in the room, "Can anyone think of anything we need to do?"

Total silence.

DC

David and Cristal awoke later than normal in their tiny apartment at CIA headquarters. Langley was far enough south that unless the wind changed, it was outside the envelope of danger from the power plant. Brave men were already doing their best to cool down and slow the meltdown by bombing the site with water.

She made the mistake of turning on the news before her coffee, and of course the news was crazy and full of horrendous stories of gridlock, estimated death tolls, and the like. Several TV stations were offline as their sites had no doubt been abandoned. It seemed like everyone had a different take on the weather and whether it was good or bad for the big northeastern cities. But the radiation was already setting off alarms all around NYC and hospitals everywhere in the northeast were overrun by people with real and imagined effects of radiation poisoning already.

The big centers of DC and Philadelphia were far enough south that unless the wind changed, they were in the clear for now but even their local news showed masses of people clogging the highways south.

I-95 just south of DC was a mess on a good day but escaping locals and many from the tristate area had turned it into a total parking lot with reports that cars hadn't moved for hours; some were already running out of gas and being abandoned. Police were warning people a hundred miles north that it could be a week or more before enough cars could be towed or pushed out of the way to open one lane for emergency vehicles only. Abandoned cars would be treated as scrap and bulldozed out of the way if required.

Homeland and FEMA were doing what they could, but certain areas were now off-limits to even first responders, so it was impossible to estimate an initial death toll, and anyone injured was on their own. Some evacuations had occurred before the blast but there was no going home for those people. No mention was made of any employees, so they were left in the dark as to what had happened with Frank Garrison.

After a quick and awkward breakfast in the building cafeteria, Cristal seeming to have nothing to do, announced that she wanted to check in on the DD. Bill Carter would surely still be in a medically induced coma and given he was at Walter Reed, she suspected getting to see him might be problematic.

She called his wife at their home. "Mrs. Carter it's Cristal Serpe?"

"Hello, please call me Gill."

"Okay, well as you know we blew it and the terrorists were successful and the primary focus has turned to others for mitigation. There's little to do here beyond some cleanup, so I was hoping to pay a visit to the Director. I think you know what he means to me but I'm guessing that due to medical privacy concerns, security, and military rules, they probably won't let me in. Is there any update on his condition or can you assist me in a short visit?"

There was a long pause on the line and then she spoke, "There's no change. I do know how close the two of you are. Bill often spoke of you. I'll approve a short visit, but you won't be very satisfied. As you might expect, he's still in a coma. But the bigger issue is that he's no longer at Walter Reed. You see the press announced a bit too much about his situation and given you all think there may be some inside connection to the attack, Carole authorized some security precautions.

Now he's under guard at George Washington University hospital on the third floor, room three fourteen under the alias of Jesus Garcia. I picked the name. I'll inform the guards that you should be expected in the next few hours. Only a few close staff and the Secret Service know of his name and location so I'm sure you'll be discreet."

David decided to accompany her along with their security detail, one of whom joined them on the third floor at the hospital. The Director's guard by the hospital door and Cristal's protection knew each other so the new arrival replaced him as he had to stay with Cristal, giving the man a much-needed coffee break. Guests were limited so David decided to join the DD's protection to get a coffee.

***

As per protocol, Cristal closed the hospital room door leaving her guard outside. Director William Carter looked at once peaceful but also sick and helpless with a heavily bandaged head. Knowing little about the monitors hooked up to him, she tried to get a reading on his current situation.

She had only been there a few minutes admiring the man who meant so much to her when she heard the door open behind her. As she turned a familiar face was holding a silenced gun aimed at her chest.

"Well, what do you know? This is an unexpected surprise. Cristal Serpe as well as the Director of the CIA. I must say, this is more of a pleasure than you can imagine. Where is our David? Is he close by?"

Cristal's first thought was to her weapon, but any move right now would be deadly.

"No, you're not going to answer that for me, are you?

"There's a rumor though that the two of you have patched up your differences; sad. He's quite a catch actually."

Cristal's brain was working overtime. So, Kathy Sloane had to be MI6's BSB mole after all but here she was on the wrong side of the pond. Clearly, the guard outside the door was dead; she could see one of his feet just outside the room.

Sloane kept her distance to ensure no surprises from her catch.

To Cristal's shock and horror and before she could react, Kathy turned her weapon and put two silenced slugs into the chest of William Carter and quickly returned the gun back to Cristal's torso.

She was too far away to lunge at her so Cristal was frozen as Kathy just smiled. In the background, the instrumentation was starting to go wild which she realized meant her dear Bill Carter was on his way out and there was nothing she could do. She wondered where all the nurses and doctors were.

***

David was carrying two coffees as the elevator door opened and a nurse ran by crying. Immediately he spotted the dead guard outside the DD's room. Coffees down, shoes kicked off, gun drawn, he sprinted the twenty yards and silently rounded the corner to the horror show in front of him as Kathy said, "I'm sorry but I'm a bit pressed for time today as you can imagine, but before I go let me tell you about Les Misérables."

The nine-millimeter slug took off a good portion of Kathy's face as she fell dead before she hit the floor.

The noise was deafening, and blood splattered across Cristal's face which she rapidly wiped using a sheet from the DD's bed. There was no question now that both Kathy and Bill Carter were beyond resuscitation.

After gathering her senses and moving out of the way as nurses and security arrived, Cristal took what she assumed would be one last look at her boss.

With a large hole in her face, Kathy was beyond help and the medical staff turned to see if they could do anything for Bill Carter but even Cristal could tell it was too late.

She stood there stunned for a few moments until David took her by the arm and encouraged her out into the hospital hallway stepping over the dead guard, "Are you ok?" he asked.

She finally looked him in the eyes and said, "Yeah ... I'll be okay ... That was close. The roles are reversed and now you've saved me from certain death, but why did you shoot? Why not put your gun to her head and demand she drop hers? I'm sure she's BSB and would have lots of intel for us. Once again we have nothing."

David was shaken himself and staring back into the room at his old girlfriend on the floor. The highs and lows of their relationship raced through his mind, primarily that amazing night in London.

As he started to come back to reality he said, "The Secret Service agent I just went downstairs with told me that they'd just this morning received an anonymous tip from a female caller about four dead bodies near Baltimore claiming they were the last of the BSB, they'd closed up shop and were out of business. Apparently, these murders happened yesterday so with all the other stuff, we hadn't heard about it.

"One of the dead guys turns out to be Carter's Executive Assistant. If the tip was true, then he was the mole getting all of the CIA's intel to the BSB.

"When I came around that corner she was the last person on earth I expected to see. But suddenly it all made sense. It had to be her that killed the four of them and called in the tip. Why else was she here in the US and in Carter's room with a gun drawn? The BSB wanted him dead but they didn't finish the job yesterday.

"She had to have had an escape plan and it certainly didn't involve leaving you or Bill Carter to chase her. I have no idea why she came here to kill Carter, but I'd bet it had something to do with the BSB hit on him yesterday. They must have thought Carter was closing in on them. We'll never know.

"Still with her wrapping up the BSB, there was no way you were getting out of this room alive. Looks like she had already killed four we know of. Best I can figure is that she felt threatened after so many BSB agents were taken out, figured she was in a dead-end job, and decided to shut them down herself before they got her first.

"She had just killed at least six people including the guard and Carter here and all to engineer her escape. There's no question she had it all worked out and you unfortunately were standing in the way of her freedom. You were dead meat. There was no scenario where you were going to be left alive. She left me no choice, it would have been a shootout if I had hesitated, and you'd have been the first to go. Thank God you didn't look at me as I came through the door or again, she'd have killed you first thinking she might have time to turn on whoever was behind her, not knowing I was armed. I had a split-second decision to make and the more I think about it the more I'm sure you were a finger twitch away from a well-placed kill shot."

Cristal was still shaken but she could see the logic in his surprising reaction to seeing Kathy holding a gun on her. She wanted to clean up properly before all the interrogations started with the arriving law enforcement, but as they started down the hallway she said, "What was this reference of hers to Les Misérables?"

David looked straight ahead and said, "That ... I have no idea."

***

None of the BSB's ending made the news including four dead near Baltimore and three dead at the hospital as the airways were totally monopolized by the recovery and evacuation news tied to the power plant explosion and meltdown the previous night. Even the Director of the CIA's death in the hospital was almost an afterthought.

Al Qaeda had already claimed victory for the Independence Day attack and was making the most of their ability to hit America hard in retaliation for decades of their imperialistic interference in Muslim lands.

After two days of mandatory downtime and a visit to the agency's psychiatrist, David and Cristal were back at work looking for some way to help out in the aftermath of this most recent attack on the homeland.

Carole Glass was acting Director of the CIA for the moment. It was a sure bet that pretty much all of the top people at the CIA and maybe the FBI and Homeland Security would be replaced after such a complete failure to protect the country. No weight of explanations would appease the politicians who were already piling on the CIA as their first target.

Senator Francine Taylor, darling of her right-wing QAnon followers and nicknamed Fox Trot from her days as a former Navy pilot, was as always, first in line with the press leading the charge of blaming Homeland and the CIA in particular, for their intolerable incompetence.

Specifically, she took it upon herself to release what was classified information identifying the BSB and its key member the Executive Assistant to the CIA Director as evidence of the total incompetence of the Intelligence Community. How could they not have noticed these traitors in their very midst? She claimed it was the scandal of the century and promised a full Senate investigation by her Intelligence Oversight Committee.

Front and center on all the news programs, she was already putting forward her choice to run the CIA even before Director William Carter's body was cold.

International Waters
near Caracas

Number Three woke late on his new superyacht a few miles off the coast of Venezuela. Money from the Syndicate had paid for a good portion of his new toy.

His chef had just been in and replaced the coffee and danish that must have been delivered earlier and was now cold. After a sip of the coffee, he went straight to the news on his built-in screen.

The news was of course dominated by the nuclear meltdown in Pennsylvania. Those sneaky terrorists had been planning something much bigger than their deal from the start and it gave him pause that he may have helped them in some way, even if it was only as a cover. Still, that was not his primary interest. A quick search of news clippings for 'Director of the CIA' confirmed Kathy Sloane had been successful but the story also claimed the attacker had been killed by an unidentified law-enforcement type.

He smiled as he realized he had no worries coming from Kathy Sloane getting any bright ideas to come after him and now he had an extra five million dollars to top up one of his investment accounts. A few of his stocks had taken a beating with the meltdown's influence on the market. Still, his broker assured him that in any catastrophe there were always winners and good investment opportunities. The losses on his diversified portfolio were not serious and Kathy's additional present would more than cover them.

He glanced over at his night table where his new birth certificate for Jorge Hamilton lay, taking eight years off his age, 'why not' he thought. It had cost him surprisingly little to get his name, citizenship, and boat registration all changed by the right contacts in Venezuela. 'Ah Venezuela, no extradition and everything for the right price.'

His mind shifted to the party on his yacht set for tonight. He was flying in a few friends to celebrate his retirement and this new amazing toy. That and some hired entertainment and a few girls from an agency in Caracas would make it a great final evening in the harbor. Then he'd be off tomorrow for a self-imposed exile in international waters until he was sure no one was looking for him.

This new superyacht was a pretty ritzy home for hopefully only a few months and the crew were okay with weekly personnel swaps and replenishment of consumables from the mainland.

Now all he had to worry about was whether Senator Fox Trot knew of his existence. She knew Number One and was in frequent contact with him and it was a good bet she knew Number Two because of mutual friends and conspirators in the funding circles. If the other two had kept their promises, his name had never been divulged. Still, she was a worry. According to One, she had at least hinted at threats to the Syndicate so there was always the chance she could find his old identity making the new one even more important.

The other worry was anyone on Bill Carter's team putting the pieces together and getting a lead on a retired and missing Syndicate member.

But that was all for later; tonight was Party Time!

Langley

Part of Carole's job was a memorial for Bill Carter which in the big scheme of things would mostly be overlooked as again, everyone was focused on the meltdown of a nuclear reactor.

All hell was breaking loose north and east of what remained of the plant. There was no question it would be weeks before the real assessment of the human and material damage could be calculated. Homeland hadn't announced an immediate fatalities total which was increasingly infuriating the press.

The weather was cooperating and radiation levels in the big population areas like NYC were high but not critical for the moment. Still, hospitals were full, and patients were being transferred all over the northern US due to capacity issues.

Water bombers from as far away as California and parts of Canada were dumping water like never before on the steaming pile of molten radioactive fuel but a permanent solution wasn't yet on the table. The fifty miles or so northeast of the plant were a no-man's-land and probably would remain that way for at least decades.

David was just leaving the cafeteria after getting a coffee when Carole pulled him into an empty corridor. "Listen, this isn't for public consumption, but something told me I should bring you in on this. We just got the autopsy back on Kathy Sloane. She was pregnant."

David stood there staring at her as the blood drained from his face.

The End

Appendix

Selected Characters in the two Cristal novels

Caution – some spoilers

Cristal Wiggins (born Serpe)
- Daughter is 2 yr. old Tiffany Wiggins
- AKA Virginia Cummings in Mogadishu – other aliases in Germany
- Initially lives in Cincinnati with husband Bob Wiggins and baby Tiffany 2+ years old.
- 5'6" dark hair (initially, now blonde) blends in well with Arabs – Parents are Italian (Mary) and Portuguese (Frank) Serpe.
- 33, born in Dayton and went to school of journalism and was cheerleader at Northwestern Medill School of journalism – studied Arabic and did a year with Peace Corps in Jordan – gave up after 1 year due to cultural norms – woman's role.
- Won several titles in university in mixed martial arts
- Recruited by William (Bill) Carter into CIA out of school - they helped her get a job with CNN overseas as an intern-producer because she spoke Arabic.
- Works for 8 years throughout Africa/Middle east as CIA unbeknownst to her employer CNN
- Tells CNN (and CIA) she's finished and comes back to the US, pregnant, and gets a job producing a local news show in Cincinnati

Commander David Crowe aka Daniel Boone aka Abu Nistal
- Cristal's love interest and Tiffany's biological father
- Senior field agent at MI-6 – framed by Jack Hammond – captured by Cristal - hid in Guantanamo
- AKA Victor Brookes in Somalia
- 6 ft. handsome – speaks French and some Arabic
- 2 yrs. on an exchange program at CIA earlier in his career
- British – 34 – educated at U of Lancaster Engineering in northwestern England

- Recruited by MI6 out of college and worked the Middle East, Balkans, and Africa on Intel missions– attached to British consulates as commercial attaché.

Khalil al-Adel
- Worldwide Al Qaeda Leader out of Somalia
- The "American Jihadi" -.Mr. Berkant in NY attack
- Disguise expert

- Speaks several languages

- Grew up in Detroit

- Has cousins in Pittsburgh

- Immigrated to Detroit when he was 4

- Dad and older brother killed in road rage incident in Detroit – shooter went free

- Left Engineering before graduation

- Born in Yemen – now Somalia

- Brutal – films beheadings and stonings

William (Bill)Carter aka DD
- 55 – like a father figure to Cristal
- Now Director but kept nickname of DD – Deputy Director
- Hired Cristal - Thinks of her as a daughter

Carole Glass
- Bill Carter's deputy
- Becomes acting Director of the CIA

BSB – Bean Stock Boys/ The Syndicate
- Cabal started by Agri – muscle and political manipulation mostly in Africa
  - Number One – Intel and politics – bossy lead – Exec Assistant of DD
  - Number Two – funding and Agri contact ... tentative and afraid
  - Number Three – field team and operations

Greg Wiggins – aka Bob Watson
- Illegitimate Husband of Cristal – from Wichita – truck driver – abandoned wife and two small kids because of gambling debt to loan sharks – faked his own death and changed his ID – now arrested and jailed and being divorced by Cristal

Tiffany Winslow
- BBC/MI6 in Sudan – recruited and worked for David Crowe
- Close friend to Cristal, stoned to death by Khalil

Jabir Habib.
- Younger brother to Mustafa Habib
- Leader of FLN - Front de Liberation Nationale (Freedom Fighters and Al Qaeda linked) in Burundi until Abu Nistal (David Crowe) takes over thinking they are not Al Qaeda related but true Freedom Fighters
- Launched campaign into the US to kidnap Cristal and trade for Abu Nistal/Daniel Boone/David Crowe – killed by David and Cristal at kidnapping site

Frank Garagus
- CIA London manager

Hakim Ghani
- Driver at JFK airport for Khalid – killed at Kensico dam/reservoir
- A new employee at the water company

Bob Boutet
- CIA expert on Khalil

Aaban Abboud
- Young Arab who will try to blow up shopping center
- Cousin to Nasir Abboud

Sir Richard (Dick) Brighton
- head of MI6 – Crowe's boss

Jack Hammond
- BSB and mole in London at MI6

James Owens
- young video tech outside Hammond later Crowe's office

Franz Becker
- David's old friend/contact in Frankfurt
- Daughter is Nicola Becker in Paris
- Killed by Kurt Willems

Kurt Willems
- BSB head in Frankfurt
- Killed Franz Becker
- Killed by David during interrogation

Rick Sawyer
- Under cover CIA in Mogadishu

Norm Lulham
- Under cover CIA in Mogadishu

Boris Nugent
- OXFAM boss in Mogadishu

Jason Fletcher
- CIA guy in Nairobi

Kathy Sloane
- an old girlfriend of David and Jack Hammond – eventually BSB in London MI6

Herr Merkel
- German BND head

Samir Abadi.
- Videographer for Khalil in McDonald's

Nasir Abboud
- Lieutenant to Mustafa Habib – eventually 3rd head of Al Qaeda
- Cousin to Aaban Abboud

James Harden aka Mr. Tom
- American BSB living in London sent to meet Habib
- Killed by Al Qaeda in London bombing

Mohamed Latifi aka Paul Petrillo
- ex-Jihadi from call in Colorado to Cristal

Freja
- Dutch nanny to Tiffany in London

Jim Saxon
- Threat analyst at Homeland Security

Sam Hillman
- Tech at Limerick Nuclear Power Plant

Frank Garrison
- Lead operator at Limerick Nuclear Power Plant

Gus Molson
- Consolidated Energy backup operator in Chicago

Jack Clarke
- Incident Manager at Consolidated Energy

Wilson Damns
- CIA guy assigned to DC investigation after IED discovered

Gillian Carter
- Bill Carter's wife

Sally 1
- Works for Carole at CIA.

Sally 2
- Shipping clerk in California

www.ingramcontent.com/pod-product-compliance
Lightning Source LLC
Chambersburg PA
CBHW071151250626
47159CB00001B/64